HUMANS CLAIMED

Zandian Masters, Books 5-8

RENEE ROSE

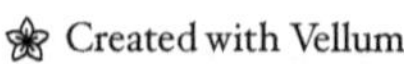 Created with Vellum

WANT FREE BOOKS?

Go to http://subscribepage.com/alphastemp to sign up for Renee Rose's newsletter and receive a free books. In addition to the free stories, you will also get special pricing, exclusive previews and news of new releases.

HIS HUMAN VESSEL

CHAPTER ONE

The restraints around Bayla's wrists kept her from rubbing her nose.

In dim awareness, she tried to move her hand again to relieve the itch, but it caught, yanked against an unyielding strap.

With a sharp inhale, she jerked fully awake as the memory of the huge horned alien with an injector gun rushed back. He'd shown up at the fertility farm where she and sixty other human females had been enslaved and bought her following a brief inspection. Then, without a word to her, he'd pressed the device to her neck, and everything had gone black.

She blinked at the light and took in her situation. She was naked, strapped down to an examination table by leather cuffs. The alien, who was not an Ocretion, the species who'd taken over Earth and enslaved all humans, wore a white lab coat and stood near a window with his back to her. This being was taller than humans or Ocretions, and he had purple-hued skin and eyes. He spared a glance over his shoulder at her sudden movement then turned back to what he was doing.

His silent treatment irritated the hell out of her. Did he not speak Ocretion? No, he must. She'd heard him speaking to the fertility farm slave masters when he'd bought her.

She licked her dry lips. "What are you doing with me?" Her voice cracked from lack of use.

The alien turned and walked to her side, a needle in his hand.

She flinched when he approached, but, with the restraints, couldn't move. "Did you hear me? Can you tell me what's going on?"

He ignored her and pinched the skin at the crease of her elbow, inserting the needle then drawing a vial of blood.

She looked away, her stomach queasy. Although she'd been bred and raised for nothing more than this purpose—to have her body poked and prodded, inseminated and vacated over and over again, she still hadn't grown used to it.

She attempted to distract her mind as he fit a second vial to the tube. The lab room was small but bright. The window was unusual—she wasn't sure she'd ever seen one like it. It didn't let in much light, but a skylight in the ceiling somehow magnified sunlight through a crystalline structure, casting beams throughout the room. In fact, there didn't appear to be any artificial light in use at all.

Having spent most of her life in a metal box with no natural light, she found it a profound improvement. It would be almost cheerful if she weren't naked and strapped to a table. With no clue what was going to happen to her.

"Where are we? How long was I out?" she tried again, but still the alien ignored her.

He walked away, and she allowed herself to look at her arm, now neatly bandaged.

"Hello? Can you hear me?"

He turned. Despite the alien features, she found him exceptionally handsome, but that was probably the fertility drugs talking. He was tall and broad-shouldered. His skin was purple-ish peach and smooth, his hairless jaw square. The horns on the top of his head gave him a rugged appearance.

"Is it customary where you came from for a slave to speak before she is spoken to?" He sounded more curious than angry.

A flush of something foreign rippled through her at his rebuke. She couldn't be embarrassed, could she? Did she really care what this horned alien thought?

She kicked up her chin. "Normally, I am informed immediately what is expected of me," she said primly, as if she lived to serve her masters.

"Ah. I see. Very well. I shall inform you. I am Daneth, master physician for the Prince of Zandia. You will call me *Master.* You will maintain silence unless I speak directly to you, especially if others are in our midst."

She feigned remorse and lowered her eyes. "Yes, Master. What will Master use me for?"

"Our species lacks females of breeding age. I purchased you as a vessel to implant and grow a Zandian young."

The familiar wave of nausea and dread filled her. *Not another pregnancy.* She couldn't bear to have another baby taken from her arms. Of course, this one would be an alien, so maybe it wouldn't hurt so much. She hoped conception would be a long and difficult process. She needed time to steel herself for another loss.

"In addition to your silence, I expect your complete obedience and respect. Any defiance will be immediately punished."

It wasn't anything new. Every slave master demanded the same, and yet, from him, it sounded halfway exciting. Perhaps that was only because she was naked and immobilized when he gave the pronouncement. What orders would she have to obey?

"Will I be sexually serving you?"

The doctor's brows flew up, and he dropped the test tube he'd been shaking. It rolled under her bed.

Had she flustered him?

He bent to pick it up, and, when he stood, he'd composed his face. "That won't be nec—" His eyes fell on her mouth and stayed there. She swore his horns stiffened and tilted in her direction. He cleared his throat. "No." His voice sounded thick.

Her gaze dropped to his crotch, where the bulge of his cock seemed to grow for her.

When he noticed her focus, annoyance flashed over his face and his shoulders stiffened. He turned back to the counter, where he appeared to be running tests on her blood samples.

So. Her hot alien master found her attractive. To her surprise, that pleased her. Was it because he didn't seem to welcome the attraction? For the first time, she had a bit of leverage on a master. He may not want to act on his attraction, but, as a breeder, she'd been trained to satisfy, and she had no doubt she'd get him to cave.

Based on the way her nipples stood up as she contemplated her seduction, she doubted pleasing him would be much of a hardship.

He muttered to himself in what sounded like a voice log of her test results. "Estrodial, 25 to 75 picograms per milliliter, progesterone..."

"Will I sleep in your bed?" She began her cock-tease.

He whirled, his skin turning a darker purple. When his gaze fell on her erect nipples, he blinked rapidly. He referenced the cuff he wore on his arm, which had some kind of readout. "That idea arouses you?"

What did that cuff tell him? She hated having her game turned back on her. She shrugged, affecting cool indifference. "Not particularly."

He tilted his head, studying her. She didn't love his attention, this time, though, because it was definitely more curious scientist than interested male. "I understand humans have a different sense of truth than my species, but this is your first and only warning. I will punish every lie."

Something tightened in her belly and loosened between her legs. Heat uncoiled there, swirling and pulsing.

~.~

Beautiful as she was, Daneth hadn't expected to be turned on by his new slave. She was his test subject, nothing more. He'd examined both the prince's human mate and her mother without having any physical reaction to their nudity or inherent femininity, but this one...this one was different.

Just the sight of her sprawled out on his table, her dark brown hair fanned out around her head in glossy waves, sapphire blue eyes mesmerized, made his pulse quicken. She had a full, wide mouth, designed to suck a male's cock. Her lush body was soft in all the right places. Ample breasts to feed a baby. Wide hips would carry the larger Zandian young easily.

Unlike Lamira and her mother, who had been half-starved on the agrifarm where they'd worked, Bayla had been kept inactive and given decent nutrition —everything necessary to make her an excellent breeder. He'd chosen her exactly for this reason. He'd run a search on the genes of every being in the galaxy, and she came up as the best suited for his project.

But those full ripe breasts taunted him now. He longed to weigh them in his hands, squeeze her nipples and test whether he could bring her to orgasm through breast stimulation alone. Though he hadn't had practical experience in over twenty solar cycles, and even then, very little, he'd studied up on the arousal and sexual satisfaction of human females. He'd shown Zander how to pleasure his female.

It didn't help that she actually seemed to *desire* his sexual interest. He could only attribute it to the fertility drugs she'd been on for the past six solar cycles, since she'd been placed on a human breeding farm.

Still, he needed to maintain a distance from her. She was his subject for the most important experiment of his life. He would *not* complicate things by seeking pleasure from her. While he was sure it wouldn't happen to him, he'd seen the way his stoic ruler, Prince Zander, had been utterly changed when placed in contact with his human mate, Lamira. Normally calm and rational, Zander had become as emotional as his human female, easily angered and jealous. So had Seke, the Zandian Master at Arms, when he'd mated Lamira's mother Leora. Even Lundric, their chief of security, had killed a human over his new mate, Cambry. It would be important for him to maintain his rational sensibility with Bayla.

But now, as his cuff reported her arousal levels growing by the second, he had to force back the foreign sensation of lust. Why did she lie about her arousal? It didn't make sense to him. "Bayla, you need not fear me if you tell the truth. I am a fair master and you are safe here."

She struggled with her restraints.

He touched her shoulder, steeling himself against the softness of her skin, the scent of her arousal. "Be at ease. I don't wish you to hurt yourself. Your examination is not yet done." He snapped on a set of protective gloves, the best money could buy. The fit was so tight and the protection so thin, he should be able to sense everything as if his hands were bare. He rubbed two fingers over her slit, seeking the entrance.

They tucked easily inside her.

"Natural lubrication present and plentiful," he reported to the data recorder on his cuff.

Her breath quickened, and she squirmed beneath him.

He frowned and gave a quick shake of his head.

She went still.

Good. He didn't want to have to punish her, though he'd already threatened it. But, already, she seemed better trained and more obedient than the prince's mate had been. Of course, Bayla had been house trained to service males.

For some reason, that idea made him grit his teeth.

Odd. It wasn't like him to experience emotions of any kind. Would he become as possessive and jealous as Prince Zander had? Perhaps something in the human genome activated some emotional center in the Zandians. It might make an interesting study in the future.

He palpated along the front wall of her cavity, using the hand outside her to press down on her belly. "No irregularities. Wall thickness normal."

His cuff blinked her climbing arousal rate. She'd gone from 30 percent to 70. Her breath had quickened, making those exquisite breasts move up and down.

His cock swelled in his pants.

Perhaps he should test her sexual response rate. He would need to know if she couldn't orgasm, as it could affect the implantation.

He withdrew his fingers and reinserted them.

Bayla's eyes widened, and her pretty red lips parted in surprise.

His thumb found her clit, and he rubbed it as he scooped his digits in and out of her.

Her tiny cry turned his cock rock hard. Her breath rate sped up even more, her soft belly fluttering up and down while her thighs tightened in the restraints.

He pumped quick and fast, making short thrusts inside her, sliding his thumb over her clit every time.

Ninety percent aroused.

When she moaned, he switched up the rhythm, reaching deep inside her to find the nerve bundle on her inner wall that connected with the clitoris. She cried out, sounding almost agonized, but his cuff blinked *100 percent aroused.*

Her walls contracted around his fingers, squeezing and pulsing so hard it almost pained him not to have his cock inside her instead.

"Healthy orgasmic function." His voice sounded lower to his ears as he spoke the report.

He waited until her shudders subsided then eased out and disposed of the glove. Without thinking, he brushed a lock of hair from her eyes. The gesture seemed easy and natural, though he'd never had a female of his own. Bayla was not his mate, but he supposed a desire to care for her made sense, as she was his responsibility. He required her health and well-being for his project.

Bayla licked her lips. They were dry.

Veck. He should have noticed that earlier.

"You wanted to use your cock inside me, instead, didn't you?"

Her words sent an unpleasant jolt of shame through him, as if he'd been caught masturbating by a teacher or some other such scenario. Anger followed close behind.

"You will remain silent unless you're spoken to," he snapped.

"Your cock is hard for me," she murmured, wriggling against her bonds and somehow managing to look like the most exotic creature in the galaxy. Already, the scent of her arousal had filled the room, affecting him like a drug.

"Enough." Control slipped from him, like *she* had somehow become *his* master, though she was the one naked and bound. If she pushed any more, he would snap. He would *veck* that inviting pussy into oblivion and back.

And that was absolutely wrong. Being out of control with his slave would cloud his judgment. The survival of his species depended on him having a clear head with Bayla.

"What are you afraid of, Master?"

He gritted his teeth and fetched a leather paddle from the box of implements he'd ordered in preparation of owning a slave. "Release ankle cuffs," he commanded, and the rings that held her ankle cuffs to the bed sprang free. He picked up her feet and pulled them high into the air, exposing her backside and the swollen lips of her sex.

Smack. He brought the leather paddle down crisply across her buttocks. "I told you not to speak out of turn." He slapped her again. The leather was pliable and thin enough to leave a surface sting without causing much damage. He considered it to be the lightest implement of punishment in his arsenal, apart from his hand.

Even so, she jerked with each slap, her lovely ass bobbing. He hadn't expected the sharp satisfaction he experienced disciplining her. He'd expected her training and punishment to be a nuisance he'd have to endure in order to have her body at his disposal for his experiment.

He brought the paddle down with quick, sharp strokes, over and over again. By fourteen, she caught her breath enough to plead.

"Please," she gasped, still bending her knees to pull against his hold on her ankles. He could have attached them to a cord on the ceiling, but he'd been too irritated to take the time.

Which, again, wasn't like him at all.

This human might be more than he bargained for.

"Master, please. Ouch! I'm sorry!"

Twenty strokes. Thirty. He stopped and examined her punished bottom. "Thirty strokes with the leather paddle produces pink coloring on buttocks," he reported to his cuff.

*Forty percent aroused, i*t blinked back at him.

Oh yes. He remembered that from Zander's mate. Punishment produces arousal in a certain percentage of human females. An odd quirk in human sexuality.

He stared at the nectar glistening along her swollen sex. *Vecking* beautiful. "Subject aroused by punishment."

Bayla's head jerked up in surprise.

He arranged her knees open, the soles of her feet together. She held the position for him, head still lifted from the bed, watching him with an intensity that made his heart expand in his chest.

He positioned the leather paddle between her legs. It was narrow enough to fit against her sex. He tapped her pussy with it—more of a warning slap than anything fierce.

She mewled but held the position. An obedient slave.

"Bayla, you are not here to breed. I forbid you to breed with any male in the pod, including myself." He slapped her pussy again, a little harder.

She squeaked again.

"I understand the hormones make you needy, and I promise, if you're a good girl, I will always take care of those needs. Understand?"

He wished those incredible breasts weren't still heaving with her breath.

She nodded. "Yes, Master."

"I don't want to have to spank you, but you will not, under any circumstances, offer yourself to me that way again." He delivered another slap to her pussy. "Are we clear?"

She bit her lip and bobbed her head. "Yes, Master." Her voice broke a little, and he looked at her sharply but saw no sign of tears. Her readouts showed elevated pulse and some stress, but nothing at a worrisome level.

He nodded curtly. "Good girl. Time for your rectal exam." He didn't really need to do a rectal exam, but there was no harm in being thorough. "Can you hold still, or do I need to cuff your ankles again?"

It pleased him beyond comprehension when she said in a small voice, "I will hold still, Master."

Stars, he wanted to bring her to orgasm again right then. But she didn't deserve it. She'd been naughty and goaded him on purpose. Besides, he wasn't sure he had regained control of his own lust yet.

⁓.⁓

Bayla's ass stung, but her swollen clit pulsed insistently, despite, or perhaps because of the pussy spanking he'd given her. Shame prickled hot, too, although she couldn't decide if it was because she genuinely regretted irritating Daneth or if the spanking itself had been so humiliating. She would've thought, after all the objectification she'd suffered as a breeder, nothing would bother her. But, apparently, not so. The spanking hadn't been overly painful, but it had been degrading to the extreme, and something about it being administered by an annoyed, sexy alien doctor amplified the intensity.

Her entire body still trembled, and now she had to suffer through a rectal exam. *Dearest Mother Earth.*

Daneth snapped on another glove, and, thankfully, squeezed some kind of lubricant onto his index finger. He had the assured touch of a doctor, not a lover, as he screwed that—*oh stars, ack!*—*thick* finger inside her ass.

She'd been probed there before. Not in a state of arousal, though. As his thick digit filled her, her pussy turned molten again, moisture seeping.

He swished it around, checking for deity knew what, then pumped a few times.

Her breath caught in her throat and she made a strangled sound, somewhere between a moan and a cough.

Daneth checked his cuff again and glanced at her face curiously but withdrew his finger.

Both relief and disappointment flooded her. Her pussy clenched on air.

"Release cuffs."

The loops holding her wrist cuffs in place sprang open. She pulled her arms down, relieved to have the pressure off them.

"Your examination is complete." He placed a large hand on her upper arm to help her to sit. "Can you stand?"

She swung her legs over the side of the examination table and stood. Daneth steadied her with the hand at her elbow. "Yes, Master," she reported once she was sure her legs weren't asleep.

"Good. Come with me."

He led her to a door at the rear of the laboratory or examination room—it seemed to double as both—and pressed his palm to a screen.

The door slid soundlessly open.

She gaped at the room beyond. It, too, was lit by a bright skylight, and defined opulence. The large chamber featured a floating oval bed in the center of the room. An intricately woven rug in shades of turquoise, beige, and white decorated the floor. Two walls were painted the same pale turquoise, two in cream. No, when she looked closer, she realized the wall was not painted turquoise but a turquoise-dyed plaster, which gave it the rich depth of varying shades of color.

The room spoke of extreme wealth. She had been farmed out to a wealthy Ocretion family to breed with the master there, and their rooms paled in comparison.

In the far corner was a washroom, and just inside the door floated a large cage.

That must be for her.

"Is this...your chamber?" she asked with awe.

"Yes. You will sleep in the cage. That way I can monitor you at all times. I installed a comfortable pad."

She walked over and peered in the cage, depressing the cushy mattress and fingering the blanket. It was made of the finest material she'd ever touched, impossibly soft. Whoa. Her cage was luxurious.

"I can add more pillows to support your body when it grows."

Oh. Right. Her lip curled at the thought of being pregnant, stomach clenched at the memory of those infants taken from her body, from her. She didn't want to go through that again.

But she had to say, she'd take this opulent cage and the quirky but not unkind Zandian master over her past assignments any planet rotation. She needed to figure out how to avoid or stall the pregnancy part.

Daneth indicated a tiny table with one chair. "Sit. I've sent for food and drink. I can see you're thirsty."

He could see that? How? His solicitousness gave her a tingle of excitement. But he was her physician—he needed her to stay healthy. The male didn't actually *care* about her feelings.

She settled on the indicated hover chair, her naked bottom still tingling from the spanking. "Do I get clothing?"

"Clothing is not necessary at the moment."

She'd been kept naked before. Many times. But, usually, to make her attractive to the male who would breed her. Daneth didn't want to breed her, he wanted to implant her.

"Wouldn't it be easier—you know—for me not to be bred here, if I was covered?"

A muscle ticked in Daneth's jaw, but, more interestingly, the bulge at his crotch grew when she mentioned breeding. Foolish though it was, she loved the sense of power it gave her, knowing she could get a rise—literally—out him.

"*I* will not breed you," he said stiffly. "You will be given something to cover with before I take you out into the pod."

She squeezed her own breasts with a feigned nonchalance, as if fondling herself happened naturally at any time. "What is the pod?"

Daneth's horns stiffened and leaned forward, the irises of his eyes darkened to a beautiful violet. He glared at her breasts. "You are speaking out of turn again."

"Am I, Master?" she answered innocently. "I thought you were speaking to me."

He folded his arms across his massive chest. "I understand humans incorporate lies as a means of speaking," he said with crisp recitation, as if remembering some report he'd studied on humans. "Sarcasm, you call it."

"That wasn't sarcasm, Master." *It was playing dumb.* But she wasn't going to explain that human way of speaking, either. She kneaded her breasts. Her fondling had the unintended effect of turning her on—not that she hadn't already been aroused from the rectal exam. She squirmed in her chair.

Daneth looked at the readout on his cuff and scowled. "I will find you some clothes," he growled, stalking to a shelf unit against the wall and opening it. He yanked out a tunic and brought it to her. "Put this on," he snapped.

She slipped the tunic on and tied the belt around her waist. "No panties?" She made her question as innocent as she could manage, and tipped her pelvis forward, running a finger along her slit.

Daneth's eyes narrowed. "You're teasing me."

Okay, so the doctor wasn't as out of touch with humans as she thought.

She made her eyes wide and childlike. "No, Master."

"And that's a lie." He pulled her out of her chair by the elbow and flipped her to face the table, clipping her wrists together behind her.

Though she'd been bold a moment before, fear washed through her. Punishments on the fertility farm had been dreadful—electric shocks or confinement in a small, dark space. What would the Zandian doctor do when truly provoked, as he appeared to be now?

He pushed her torso over the table until her belly lay flat, her cheek pressed against the smooth, polished surface. "You will not lie to your master." He must have tucked the leather paddle into his lab coat to carry with him because it magically appeared, searing her ass with quick, decisive slaps.

Relief that he'd chosen the same implement as before poured through her. This paddling was nothing compared to what she'd endured in the past. Still, he spanked so rapidly, she couldn't relax and breathe into the pain, either. Her pulse galloped and bottom clenched under the onslaught.

"You will not tempt or tease your master."

"No, Master," she gasped. Or should she have said, *Yes, Master*? She couldn't think with the endless spanking, which seemed to only increase in intensity. "I'm sorry!" she tried.

To no avail. He kept on paddling. She hadn't been counting, but he'd certainly gone well beyond what he'd delivered the last time, and the strokes were much harder.

"I'm sorry!" She twisted her cuffed wrists against the restraints, not because she expected to get free but because her body couldn't help but seek some way out of the pain the doctor delivered. "Please!" She wasn't above begging. "Please, I'm sorry!"

He kept going. It seemed nothing would make the doctor stop now. The pain became more manageable as her ass turned numb, but nothing diminished the overwhelming *stress* of being on the receiving end of her master's displeasure in such a personal and intimate way. It was so different from Ocretion punishment where she'd been a number on the farm.

Her legs trembled, breath came in quick gasps, and all the shock and strain of managing her new environment welled up, choking her. A sob escaped her before she could swallow it down, and then, to her horror, she broke into a full crying jag, the stress of adapting to the new environment pouring out in big, ugly tears.

~.~

Daneth froze. He'd intended to spank his little slave to tears, and yet the moment he realized he'd achieved his goal, he wanted to take it back. Everything in him screamed to comfort her. To stop the tears, which stung his senses with their salty scent.

He slid the paddle beside her on the table and stroked her burning bottom. He didn't have the will to report the data on the color of her as—hot red—or how many strokes it had taken to achieve tears—134.

He cleared his throat, trying to think what to say to the tender human, so easily broken with a simple leather paddle. It hurt his chest to hear her sobs. "It's over now," he murmured. He rubbed her bottom and down her legs. "Release wrist cuffs," he commanded softly. The magnet holding the two wrists together released, and her hands dropped to the table.

He made circles on her back with his palm, marveling at how light her skin was. Almost white, which contrasted beautiful with her dark hair. So different from his skin color.

"Bayla—it's over. You're forgiven." What made him say that? He doubted she cared about his forgiveness. But her sobs did slow.

He slipped an arm under her and lifted her to standing. She kept her back to him, the quiet in the room punctuated by her sniffles.

Must calm the female.

In that moment, it hit him harder than ever before how little he understood females. He hadn't mastered relations with females of his own species. How in the stars did he expect to navigate them with an emotional human?

"Bayla," he coaxed, turning her around.

She dropped her chin to her chest, hiding her face from him in a curtain of dark waves. *Veck*, she was beautiful.

Though his usual sense of interpersonal relations would dictate he simply leave her alone—give her some privacy until she'd recovered—he couldn't bear the thought.

My female requires calming.

Odd that he considered her *his*. But she was. He'd paid for her. She was his slave, and he was her master.

"It's over now, Bayla," he repeated. He checked his cuff for her vitals. Her elevated pulse showed stress, and the arousal meter read 60 percent. He was surprised she could be aroused and crying at the same time. Another oddity of human females.

Her legs wobbled, and she swayed. He moved without thought, sweeping her up into a cradle carry before he realized he meant to.

She lifted her tucked chin and gazed up with surprise, her arms slowly moving to circle his neck.

Something in his physiology turned haywire then—his head swam, and the room seemed to swoop, even as his chest filled with something gooey and warm.

To his shock, Bayla tucked her face against his neck.

He inhaled sharply at the pleasure the gesture produced in him. Not lust this time, something different, something deeper. It stemmed from that need to comfort her—satisfaction that he'd seemingly succeeded in some small measure because she'd turned *to* him rather than away. Which seemed wrong, since he was the one who'd made her cry in the first place.

His scientist brain short-circuited. He'd spent a lifetime living in his head, guided only by logic. This foreign flood of emotions literally dampened his ability to think.

What power did human females possess that caused Zandian males to lose their minds? He needed to find some way to distance himself from this beautiful girl before he jeopardized his project.

But his emotions had full control of his body, now. His mouth murmured, "You need rest," and his feet carried her across the room to her cage. "Open cage." The door sprang open but he made no move to put her inside. It didn't feel right.

Since when did he make decisions by feel?

He carried her to his sleepdisk instead, laying her on the soft mattress and sitting beside her. Her dark tresses fell in a wave, hiding her face from him. He stroked them back, telling himself it was only to see her, to evaluate her emotional state as her doctor, but his fingers never stopped stroking. He petted her, soothing away her sniffles and hiccups.

Sweet human.

A knock sounded at the door, and he saw from the screen inside that a servant stood outside with his human's food. He flicked the coverlet over her naked, paddled bottom and called for him to come in.

"I'll take it." He accepted the tray right there on the bed, arranging it on his lap.

Bayla lifted her dark head and sat up, eyes fixed on the tray, and he kicked himself again for not having provided her with alimentation sooner.

He placed the tube from the liquid bag into her mouth.

Her nose crinkled adorably, but she sucked the tube. The moment the liquid reached her mouth, her long black lashes flew wide. She sucked in earnest, draining the bag in a matter of moments.

"Sixty milliliters of kai juice," he reported to his cuff.

"Kai juice," she echoed with awe.

"You liked it?"

She licked her full lips. "Oh yes. Is that for me?" she asked, pointing to the food.

"Yes."

Before he finished speaking the word, she'd pulled the tray to her lap, snatched up a spoon, and tucked into the savory grain dish Chef Barr had prepared.

He observed with fascination as she stuffed the food in her mouth, rolling her eyes and moaning with pleasure. Watching a being eat had never been such an arousing experience. Her full, lush lips closed around the utensil; that little pink tongue flicked food from the corners of her mouth. Her obvious pleasure with every bite made his cock go as hard as it had been when he'd brought her to orgasm earlier.

She finished the entire tray of food in record time then dabbed her lips with a napkin and smiled shyly at him.

"You were hungry," he observed.

She shook her head. "I've never tasted food so good in my life. I'm stuffed, but I couldn't stop eating." She rubbed her little paunch.

Adorable.

She tilted her head at him. "Do Zandians eat?"

"Only once a week. Every ten planet rotations on Ocretia. We gain most of our energy from sunlight."

"Wow." She licked her lips again. "You're missing out."

He laughed—actually *laughed*. When had he laughed before? He couldn't remember a time. Another sign he needed distance from this enchanting creature. Except he couldn't bring himself to take it.

They were sitting close—so close her side pressed against his, and her sweet human scent under the citrusy oil from her initial washing filled his nostrils.

She leaned her head toward him and tucked her face against his neck, like she had when he carried her. "I'm sorry I was naughty, Master."

Oh stars.

His cock surged in his pants, the demand she show him how sorry she was leaping to his lips. He bit it back just in time, but she seemed to sense the change in him, or perhaps she saw the growing tent in his lap. She licked a line up his neck.

After the lesson he'd taught her, the action should have infuriated him. Hadn't he just told her not to tease? But nothing in the galaxy would make him tell her to stop.

She reached his ear and nipped at his earlobe.

His horns thickened, mimicking his throbbing malehood.

"I know I'm not for breeding," she said, her voice husky, "but I have been trained to pleasure a male."

Vecking stars!

Lust seared through his entire body, nearly making him pant for breath.

Her small hand cupped his balls, then wrapped around the base of his cock through his clothing.

He yanked his tunic up as the beautiful seductress slipped past him, off the bed and onto her knees on the floor. Like a compass drawn to the magnetic pole of Zandia, he whirled to point his cock toward her generous mouth and shoved down his pants.

Her berry lips parted, tongue extended as she leaned forward and gave a single, lap. She sat back on her heels and lifted her beautiful blue eyes, the spark of laughter making them merry.

Teasing. She was doing it again, but this time he *vecking* loved her for it.

He had to bite back the command that sprang to his lips: *On your hands and knees.*

Yes. He wanted to claim her. Long and hard, without mercy. *Veck* her until her cunt squeezed tight and milked his cock of its rainbow-hued seed. *Veck* her until her throat became hoarse from screaming and she learned the hard lesson of teasing her master. And then he'd *veck* her again. And again.

He wanted to strap her to his table and perform endless hours of intimate examinations that made her squirm and drip with arousal. To take her over his lap and make her next spanking long and personal—his hand, her ass. Slow, and deliberate until she fully absorbed who owned her lush little body, who made the commands and who obeyed.

"Suck it," he rasped, but the harsh command did not have the effect of cowing his torturous female. No, he saw the thrill of victory in the curve of her lips before she opened that intoxicating mouth wide and took in his full length.

His shudder was close to earthquake proportions, traveling from thigh to groin. He was like a youth, still learning the glory of stroking off to images of naked females. But they'd never looked half as good as this fetching human.

He surged forward and tore her tunic open and down her shoulders. "Take it off," he barked.

Again, victory painted her shameless shucking of the clothing.

Another shudder rocked through him from seeing her naked again, even before her lips closed around the head of his cock.

"Suck it hard," he growled.

She took her mouth off with a popping sound. "Yes, Master," she purred and returned to her task, taking him deep. He didn't fit—her mouth was far too small, but the clever female had learned some way of swallowing his cock, taking it past her uvula and into her throat.

He didn't recognize the beast-like grunt that came from his mouth, nor did he know the male who gripped Bayla's hair and forced her over his cock, faster, deeper.

"*Veck, veck, veck yes,*" he hissed. But he didn't want to come yet. Not until he'd tasted the female like she sampled him.

He used her hair to pull her off his cock, biting back a groan when the cool air hit his wet skin. "Up, up, up." He was too rough with her, lifting her by the hair. Some urgent need had taken over his body, overruling all reason, all care. He scooped an arm behind her knees and lifted her into the air, turned her and plopped her on the bed with her legs facing away from him, her head hanging off the edge. *"Suck."* He fitted his cock into her mouth once more.

She obediently closed her lips around it, resuming her skillful sucking as he leaned forward and pulled her knees apart. When her thighs parted to reveal her glistening core, he groaned, *"This pussy."*

How could he not honor it with all the *vecking* reverence it deserved?

He slapped her inner thighs open and delved his tongue between her labia, parting them to trace a circle around her inner lips.

She made a sound in her throat, which reverberated around his cock, and he plunged in and out of her mouth, *vecking* it too fast, making her choke and gag. Though he heard her sputtering, he couldn't stop himself. He sucked and nipped her lips, tongued her clit until the hood retracted. He wished he had the vibrator handy to shove inside her while he sucked the stiff little nubbin, but he had to settle for his thumb. He slid it inside her and worked his middle finger between the cheeks of her ass while he suctioned his mouth over her clit.

She screamed around his cock, which only made him more violent with his thrusts and sucks. His middle finger landed on her anus, and he tapped, making it contract tight. Pistoning his thumb in and out of her hot channel, he continued with the frantic sucking, the anal stimulation until he could no longer contain his own excitement. With a roar, he thumb-*vecked* her fast and hard and pulled his cock out of her mouth. Gripping the erupting organ, he decorated her full breasts with his cum. Bayla bowed up from the bed, her pussy squeezing and releasing his thumb while her legs danced frantically across his coverlet, slipping on the silky fabric as she sought purchase to lift her pelvis higher.

"Beautiful, beautiful girl," he croaked when she'd finished. He smeared his rainbow-colored cum all over her tits.

She lifted her head and pushed her breasts together in some kind of offering.

Though he'd never seen the position before, he somehow intuited her invitation and fit his cock between them, gliding back and forth in several glorious strokes of heaven.

Though already wrung out, another mini orgasm rippled through him, and he ejaculated more, coating her belly.

When he straightened, surveying the sight she made, he barely mustered any guilt for his actions. Sprawled out in naked glory, coated in his spunk, she appeared fully claimed. By him. He hadn't bred her—hadn't broken his most important rule. But she *did* belong to him. And as her physician, it was his responsibility to keep her fertile young body in peak sexual condition. Since she had hormones pumping through her, part of his job would be seeing to her satisfaction. There was no harm to it, other than his own loss of control. But it was coming back, now that he'd spent. He'd have to be careful it didn't draw him away from the importance of his project.

And establishing both dominance and trust with his slave was important. Perhaps this was the form of bonding their Master at Arms Seke had employed when he'd given Lamira's mother, Leora, obedience training.

"Come." He picked her up. "You need cleaning again."

Her limp body trembled as Daneth carried her to the washroom, but an inner strength surged through her very soul. The sound of his victory shout still echoed in her ears. To see him lose control for her, to have her mouth give him such satisfaction, her body tempt him, made her blood sing.

Never in the solar cycles she'd been a breeder had she cared for or connected with the male who'd used her body. What was it about Daneth that made it so incredibly different? It was like she'd been born for this purpose alone. Not the reason he purchased her—not to be a vessel for a Zandian baby, but for Daneth. She belonged with him. She belonged here. She just needed to avoid the pregnancy part so she wouldn't get her heart broken again.

Daneth stepped into an enclosed cylinder and set her on her feet before stripping off his clothing.

She bit her lip, stifling a fresh moan at the sight of his body. Though he was older, his form was anything but worn out or decrepit. The male still appeared to be in his prime, his body a mass of lean muscle. He had no body hair, save for the very closely cut brown hair on his head.

When his gaze fell on her body the two horns on the top of his head shot forward, leaning toward her, the same way his huge cock lifted in salute. Did the male ever have trouble recharging? From the size of his erection, he appeared ready to go again already.

She shrieked when the enclosed area filled with water and Daneth laughed, slipping an arm around her waist to pull her close.

"That's right. You were asleep the last time I brought you in here."

She flushed. The idea of Daneth having her naked in the washtube while she was unconscious brought up a flutter of thrilling images.

He traced a finger down her breastbone. "No. I didn't take advantage of you. I prefer my females to be awake when I use their bodies."

"I prefer to be awake, as well," she murmured and stood on her tiptoes as the water level reached her neck.

"It will cover your head briefly. Hold your breath."

"How did I not drown last time?" she demanded before gulping a breath and suspending it in her lungs. The water flooded over her head then drained as quickly as it had risen. She blinked at the tall male wedged in the tiny space with her, water dripping from her lashes.

"I covered your mouth and nose."

Somewhere in the back of her mind, it occurred to her that she should be offended or scared about the things done to her while she'd been unconscious. Yet, all she felt was warmth, knowing Daneth had taken care with her, as if some part of her knew he always would.

Soap sprayed her body from all directions. She squealed.

Daneth pushed her back against the shower wall and rubbed the soap over her breasts, kneading them until they grew heavy and full, her nipples pulling taut into stiff peaks.

"Did you do this last time?" she panted.

"No."

She reached for his cock and closed her hand around the base. "Did you have this?"

"Yes." The word came out rough and deep.

She tugged on his cock, the soap lubricating his skin and making her palm slip along his length. He buried his face in her wet hair, breathing roughly as his hand slid down her wet body to the apex of her thighs.

A spray of warm water came out of the jets, rinsing off the soap, but she hardly noticed because Daneth screwed a finger inside her.

She squeezed and yanked his cock with ferocious urgency, and he responded with his own intensity, plunging a second finger inside her and thrusting up. He found the secret place inside her inner wall that made her come apart. Her third orgasm of the planet rotation ripped through her. She choked on her scream, pumping her fist over his cock as if her life depended on it.

Daneth shouted, coming against her belly as he sank his teeth into her shoulder. Heat enveloped them, the warm drying breeze from the machine too stifling. Daneth hit a button and the door swished open. They both fell out with a gasp of cool air.

Her legs were made of rubber, but it didn't matter because Daneth picked her up and carried her to her cage.

She curled up naked on the soft mattress, eyes already drifting closed as the doctor arranged an unimaginably soft blanket over her. In the back of her mind, a voice warned her not to get so comfortable. Good things didn't happen to slaves, especially not ones who hoped to avoid doing the duty they'd been purchased for.

But she'd worry about that tomorrow.

CHAPTER TWO

Bayla moaned and slid her hand between her legs, her fingers finding her damp core.

"No."

The sharp word jerked her awake, and she opened her eyes. She lay on her belly in her cage, hand between her legs.

Fertility drugs gave Bayla erotic dreams on a regular basis, but nothing compared to the one she'd been having. Doctor Daneth had been pounding into her from behind, his pure animalistic lust a heady drug.

She'd never had satisfactory sexual relations, despite the fertility drugs that made most males far more appealing than they might otherwise be. But after her incredibly erotic first planet rotation with Daneth, she'd been steeped in lusty thoughts and sensations.

She'd fallen asleep immediately after he put her to bed the night before, but when she'd woken in the night, she'd found the cage positioned right beside Daneth's bed. He'd opened his eyes and shushed her to sleep like a baby. She remembered waking in the early morning to find him standing beside the cage, staring down at her with hunger, but when she'd stirred, he'd merely turned the cage away and told her to go back to sleep.

Now, though, he appeared beside her cage, his brows locked together in obvious displeasure.

She pushed herself onto her elbows, too groggy to understand what she'd done wrong.

"You do *not* have permission to pleasure yourself."

Oh. She rubbed her forefinger and thumb together, wiping away the traces of her body's natural lubricant.

"You are the subject of a very important medical procedure. I cannot have you taking your sexual satisfaction into your own hands. I forbid you to touch yourself without my permission. Understand?"

Not really, but she nodded anyway. "Yes, Master."

His eyes narrowed as if he knew she was blowing stars up his ass. "If I find you've been masturbating—and I will know"—he indicated the cuff on his forearm—"I will whip you until you cry. Are we clear?"

Her bottom clenched, cheeks flushed with heat as she remembered how he'd paddled her to tears the planet rotation before. "Yes, Master," she muttered.

"I mean it. Your orgasms are mine to control. Every one of them. Your body belongs to me. You're my vessel, and I'm going to keep you in perfect condition for the duty for which I chose you."

She wanted to scowl, but she schooled her features to something more agreeable.

His vessel, my ass. Well, not literally.

He wasn't a bad master, and, so far, her surroundings—the cage, the food, Daneth's room—were so preferable to the fertility farm, she never wanted to go back. But she also didn't want to be implanted with an alien. She didn't want to grow a baby inside her, only to have it taken from her a third time.

"Open cage door," he commanded, and it sprang open. "Out."

She climbed to her hands and knees and backed out. Daneth molded his hands around her waist and lifted her down, though he could have easily lowered the cage. *He wants to touch me.* A thrill of power flicked through her.

He placed her feet on the floor. "Come. A small punishment to help you remember this rule."

"I didn't know the rule, Master," she wheedled, but his frown stopped her from going on. He sat on the edge of his bed and beckoned her to him.

She approached and started to drop to her knees between his legs, prepared to suck him off again, but he stopped her with a hand on her forearm and dragged her across his lap instead.

His hand cracked down on her bare ass, but it didn't fall hard. *A small punishment*, he'd said. Maybe he just wanted to have her over his lap. He peppered her ass with light smacks that only succeeded in making her more horny.

Oh.

Was that his intention? Torturing her through arousal because he'd claimed ownership of her orgasms?

Heat pooled between her legs—playing this strange new game with the sexy doctor excited her. Especially when he stopped and rubbed her tingling buttocks. "You like having your ass spanked, don't you, little human?" The rough quality of his voice told her he liked it as much as she.

When he pulled her cheeks apart, though, she squeezed her ass together and squirmed on his lap.

He delivered a much harder smack to her ass. "You will hold still, or I will strap you down."

"Ouch! Yes, Master." She spoke the words expected of her, but stopping the squirming and relaxing her bottom was another matter.

Daneth tapped one cheek. She bit her lip, her buns instantly tightening again until she forced her muscles to soften. Once more, the doctor prized her cheeks apart, and a cold blob of liquid dropped on her anus.

She flinched, trying to squeeze again, but Daneth's finger rubbed it in a circle then something cold and hard pressed against her back entrance. She lifted her head, craning to see over her shoulder. "W-what is that?"

"A plug. To remind you who controls your body. I will take it out when I feel the lesson is complete."

His words angered her, even as fresh heat rushed to her core.

She tried to resist the object, but he pressed insistently until her tight sphincter had to open or incur pain. The muscles yawned, and the plug stretched her wide.

She mewled, not so much from discomfort, although there was some, but more from the sensation of intrusion. Invasion. Humiliation at having him claim this part of her body in addition to her uterus. This hadn't been a punishment on the fertility farm. But an attractive alien doctor hadn't been part of the equation, either. Was she embarrassed because she cared what he thought of her? Did she want more respect? That was stupid. Slaves don't get respect.

The plug seated in her, and the discomfort eased, but the sensation of fullness remained.

"Put on a tunic." He tipped her back up to her feet. "I will take you to the kitchen to eat."

She wasn't sure how to stand, much less walk, with the plug inside her. She tried, making a stiff-legged trip across the room to fetch her tunic, which he'd hung on a hook the night before. It turned out the plug didn't inhibit her movement, but the jostling of walking certainly provided a cascade of sensation to her anus, making her pussy drip.

She slipped on the tunic. "May I use the washroom, Master?" she asked.

He looked up from his study of his cuff readouts with impatience. "Of course. Don't interrupt me for foolish questions."

Grr. How was she to know whether she was allowed to use his washroom or not? For all she knew, slaves had their own separate facilities. She kept her annoyance to herself, though, and took care of her business.

When she returned to the chamber, Master Daneth clipped her handcuffs behind her back and attached a collar and chain around her neck. Apparently, he thought she'd try to escape once they left his room.

Please.

Where would a human slave go? And why would she leave the incredibly luxurious comforts of her current situation? Her life had suddenly improved in almost every aspect—from food to surroundings to her new master. She wasn't going to make a run for it and risk the Ocretion death penalty for runaway slaves.

Nope, she wasn't stupid. She'd lucked into a decent situation for the first time in her life and she intended to work it to her advantage as long as she could. She just needed to figure out how to stay here but avoid the pregnancy part.

~.~

Daneth held the chain attached to Bayla's collar and escorted her down the corridor. Her full lips parted as she took in her surroundings. "Where are we?" she breathed.

Since he hadn't spoken to her first, he didn't answer. He didn't want to establish a situation in which she could interrupt his thoughts with every foolish question that popped into her head.

To his satisfaction, she lowered her eyes and muttered, "Forgive me, Master."

Excellent. A quick learner.

They passed the great room, and she slowed, drawing in an extended breath. He was about to jerk the chain to hurry her up when he caught the childlike wonder in her eyes. Against his better judgment, he slowed his steps. "This is the great room, where Prince Zander receives his species once a week."

"It's...incredible." She craned her neck to take in the vaulted ceiling and crystal-amplified skylights.

He never paid attention to his surroundings, but, seeing it through her eyes, he supposed Zander's palatial pod was quite opulent.

He and several other palace officials had managed to get the young prince out of Zandia alive, along with enough Zandian crystal to purchase this pod. When Zander became a young man, he'd dedicated himself to strategic trade, increasing his wealth exponentially. Enough to fund the war to take back their planet.

It was Daneth's life's work to ensure there were Zandians left to inhabit it when that finally happened. Encouraging the young prince to mate had been his first project. Now that the next being in the royal line had been conceived, he'd returned his focus to the project involving Bayla, his intended vessel.

"Master, please tell me—what is this place?"

He could hardly issue a rebuke when she asked so sweetly. *Veck,* the way she stared up at him with those pleading blue eyes made his resolve crumble to pieces. But he was smart enough to know that it was an act on her part.

She'd learned to play the part of obedient slave and eager sex kitten. It was probably what kept her from beatings or ill-treatment.

"You're in the Zandian palatial pod, temporary home to Prince Zander, until we retake our planet."

He saw the flicker of intelligence as she digested that information. Yes, she may play the part of a simpleton, a childlike female who'd learned to be docile and subservient, but he'd be wise not to underestimate his beautiful human.

"Where is the pod? There is sunlight here."

"We are stationed in Ocretion airspace, above their planet. They granted Prince Zander asylum when we lost Zandia."

"How did you lose your planet, Master?"

"The Finn overtook it and killed most of our species. That is why my work is so important."

She paled. "H-how many of you are there left?"

"Probably less than two hundred. And most are my age or older. There are no females of breeding age whatsoever."

She peered up into his face in a way that made his pulse jump. "How old are you, Master?"

Was it wrong that his dick hardened every time she called him *master?* Stars, he hadn't expected to get a power trip over owning a slave. It had been a necessity for his experiment, nothing more.

"I'm fifty-two." *Too old for you.* Why then, had the urge to breed her overcome him seventeen times since he'd purchased her?

His hand drifted down to mold over one cheek of her ass, bare beneath the tunic. It was a proprietary gesture. He'd given in to the urge to touch that soft flesh simply because he could. She belonged to him and her body was his to train, touch, and use as he required.

Out of the corner of his eye, he saw flashing on his cuff. *Thirty percent aroused.*

His cock thickened. His fingers twitched toward her core, wondering if he'd find her slippery and wet between her legs again. But this behavior was foolish. He had things to do, and the girl hadn't been fed yet.

He gave her ass a light slap. "Let's go, slave."

"Yes, Master." So *vecking* agreeable. He didn't know what to do with a being who pretended to like him. It had never happened before.

He took her to the kitchen, slapping her ass every time she slowed to ogle a piece of art or finery. He told himself this was part of her discipline. It certainly wasn't because he couldn't keep his hands off her firm, rounded ass.

He introduced her to the palatial pod's chef. "Master Barr, this is our newest human acquisition, Bayla. If all goes well, she will also be pregnant within the week and will have the same dietary needs as Lamira." He released the magnet clip on her cuffs to free her hands.

Bayla lifted her gaze to him. "Who's—"

He arched a brow, and her mouth clamped shut. *Good girl.*

Barr bowed. "It will be my pleasure to feed another human female." He indicated a seat at his counter and heaped a serving of grain cakes on a plate. "Lady Lamira grows heirloom fruits and vegetables originally found on Earth. Doctor Daneth believes those foods are best suited for the human body." He brought a smaller plate with a pile of tiny red fruit to her. "These are called strawberries."

Bayla's full lips stretched into a wide smile which did something strange to Daneth's insides. They squeezed and turned in the most uncomfortable way, and something akin to anger flushed through him.

Anger? At what?

His hands clenched into fists at his sides. He wanted to shove the little red berries up Chef Barr's nose... *oh*. Could this be jealousy? Surely not. Why would he envy old Barr feeding the slave.

His slave.

Yes. *His. Slave.*

Was this some primordial instinct to provide for a female rearing its head? Or the need to demolish all competition for said female?

Bayla finished chewing the strawberry she'd popped into her mouth and moaned. "Master Barr, I've never had a strawberry before, but it's the best thing I've ever tasted in my life."

Barr's skin darkened in a blush, and he bowed.

Yes, Daneth wanted to shove Barr's head in the oven. He didn't like Bayla talking to the chef. Didn't like her smiling. He definitely didn't like her moaning like that.

He checked his cuff. *Twenty percent aroused.*

Good. If he'd found her arousal had increased over eating strawberries, Barr would've lost several teeth. Considering she'd been 30 percent aroused when he'd touched her backside, the 20 percent probably related to her sitting on a bare, freshly spanked ass with a plug in it.

He tapped his fingers on the counter, grateful that she ate so quickly this time. She cleaned both plates in mere minutes.

"Would you care for more, Bayla?"

"She's finished," he snapped. Not that he'd ever deny his slave food, but if she wanted more, she could eat it in her cage. "She will take her meals in my chamber," he said, "unless I escort her out."

Barr bowed again.

He picked up Bayla's leash and wrapped it around one hand, tugging her off her chair. "Hands behind your back."

Her immediate obedience gave him a small thrill. "Attach cuffs," his voice commanded, and her wrists locked together.

Veck. The bound position only pushed out her breasts out farther. Her nipples poked out of the thin fabric of her garment, as if begging for his touch. Add to that her downcast eyes and submissively bowed head, and his cock was suddenly too large for his pants.

Gritting his teeth, he jerked the leash. He had to stay focused. She was a vessel for his project. Nothing more.

"Come." He led her back down the corridor.

Two guards approached and stopped at the sight of Bayla. One of them cleared his throat. "Doctor Daneth."

The same impatience he'd experienced in the kitchen intensified. He wanted to drag Bayla away from these males and lock her up in his room, perhaps never let her out. It would be for her own protection. An unbred female might prove too much of a temptation around the pod. He recalled what happened when Prince Zander's mate, Lamira, had been left alone with a guard. The guard had attempted to force himself on the female.

"Warriors, this is Bayla. She's part of an important protocol to repopulate our species."

Both males took on a look of hunger, their gazes traveling up and down her small body.

"She will not be bred," he snapped too sharply, but neither lifted his eyes, which seemed to be locked on—*veck.*

The belt wrapping around her tunic had tugged free, and it gapped open, giving the males a clear shot of her incredible breasts.

He snatched up the edges and yanked it closed, which only succeeded in freeing the belt completely, so it dropped to the floor.

Bayla dropped to her knees to pick it up, twisting and arching to show her breasts off more as she used the hands pinned behind her back. When she rose, she faltered crotch-level because—*vecking hell!*—both males sported enormous erections.

Fifty percent aroused. Fifty-five percent aroused.

Even if he hadn't seen the flashing indicator on his cuff, he would have known. He recognized the scent of her arousal.

To make matters worse, Bayla made a show of herself, letting the tunic hang open while she struggled against her bonds to cover herself. Her lush naked body made the guards' eyes nearly pop from their skulls.

Rage overtook him, even as his rational side analyzed the situation. *Zandian male exhibits need to show dominance in the group and claim the lone female.* He made mental notes to study his reaction later. Like Prince Zander, when Lamira was placed into his keeping, aggression and anger overtook Daneth's logic.

He yanked the chain, nearly jerking her off her feet, and marched back toward his lab.

"Master Daneth," she gasped, running to keep up with his long strides. "I dropped the belt."

He didn't *vecking* care. Some being would return the belt later. Right now, he needed to get her into his lab and away from every male in the pod.

He pressed his palm to the door to open it and yanked her into his office.

Breathless, cheeks flushed, she looked more beautiful than ever. He had to resist the urge to punish her mouth with his lips first. But no. Over his knee.

He dragged her to the examination bed and put one knee up on the footrest, bending her over his thigh with her torso resting on the bed.

"Bad. Girl." He gripped her bound wrists and pushed them, with the tunic, up to the small of her back.

Bad girl. The words made her belly flip. She'd known she irritated Daneth. She'd been trying for jealousy and had obviously succeeded. But the moment his hand started paddling her bare ass, she realized, as she had the previous planet rotation, she'd bitten off more than she could chew.

"Oh, ow," she whimpered.

He paddled fast and hard. If it wasn't his full strength, she shuddered to think what that would be, because his hand struck like wood. It was so much worse than the leather paddle had been. Each crack made her jump and flinch, but he held her tight, and other than prance in place and twist her head from side to side, there was nothing she could do to resist the terrible spanking.

She tried to breathe, to calm her body's fight or flight reflex and resist the pain with each inhale and exhale, but it became increasingly harder.

His spanking *hurt.*

And even through the agony, her pussy wept with arousal. The butt plug jostled in her anus with each smack and something about the bare bottom position, the humility of the chastisement made it intimate, embarrassing, and deeply thrilling. She hated it and loved it all at the same time.

"Stop! Please, Master, I'm sorry!" she cried, certain she couldn't take any more.

"I will not stop," he snapped, spanking harder still, which she hadn't believed possible. "I have punished you twice already for this behavior and I will. Not. Tolerate it."

Stars danced before her eyes as she struggled for breath. "Please! It's too hard! You're spanking too hard."

Unbelievably, that stopped him.

He stretched her cheeks up and out, like he was examining them for color and texture. "I am only spanking with my hand." The anger had drained from his voice, which held a scientist's curiosity now.

The moisture that she hadn't had time to weep during the spanking stung her eyes. "Well, your hand is awful." The tears in her voice made her sound pouty, and damn the doctor, he actually chuckled.

"Worse than the leather paddle?"

"Yes, Master." Still sulky.

"Dark red color after eighty-three strokes," he reported, presumably to his data recorder, not her.

"Climb up on the table." He patted the examination bed.

With shaking legs, she mounted the bed and curled up on her side, not wanting her throbbing flesh to touch the fabric of the table cover, though it was silky soft, not paper.

"Release wrist cuffs."

Her wrists fell apart, and she sighed in relief. The position had shown off her curvy assets—maybe too well—but strained her shoulders.

Her relief didn't last long. Daneth gripped her by the waist and arranged her on her back, drawing her knees up high to her shoulders and pinning her cuffed ankles in place there, so her pussy and bottom were spread wide, open for his examination.

Her anus pinched closed around the plug, squeezing and contracting in a shivery pulse.

He pulled her hands wide over her head, attaching them to the wall behind her. The effect was to lift and spread her breasts.

Her shaking increased, and so did her tears. Never in her life had she felt so vulnerable, so utterly exposed.

Daneth had transformed from angry, jealous lover back to the cool, clinical doctor and she wasn't sure she preferred this side of him. The calm, indifferent way he handled her now frightened her much more than the hard spanking.

He walked to a cabinet and retrieved several instruments.

"Wh-what are you going to do to me?" She hated the quaver in her voice.

Daneth neither looked at her nor spoke. He was back to ignoring her, as he had the previous planet rotation, when she'd woken to find herself bound to his table. It made her want to kick him in the nuts.

"I'm sorry, Master. Please have mercy. I didn't mean to make you angry."

He unwrapped and sprayed an instrument then approached. "Oh, I think you did." He still didn't look at her, directing his attention, instead, to her lady parts, spread and displayed for him.

He inserted the large phallus into her vagina, not checking for lubrication, although—dammit—it was already there. The probe filled her and she groaned, pleasure shivering down her inner thighs and making her toes scrunch up.

She panted, trying to get used to it, but he flicked it on, and the device whirred to life, vibrating so hard it shook her entire pelvis—hell, it shook the entire bed—and the plug in her anus seemed to spring to life right with it.

Daneth cocked his head, studying her pussy and the contraption inside. He fiddled with it. Suddenly, a small clamp attached to her clit.

She screamed, jerking uselessly against her bonds. "Oh stars, what are you doing?" she screeched. "Take it off. Please, Master, take it off. I'll be good, I promise."

He tilted his head. "Does it hurt?" Only mild curiosity, not concern.

"No. Yes. No, but I don't want it. Please take it off. Please? I'll be so good. I'll be a good girl for you. I'll never show my tits again. I'll never try to make you jealous. I'm sorry. I'm so sorry."

Daneth flicked off the vibrator and, for the first time since he'd spanked her, met her eyes. "You were trying to make me jealous?" His brows drew together as if the concept confused him.

Even though he'd turned off the vibrator, the shaking in her body hadn't stopped, Her thighs quaked, ass shivered. One stroke of her pussy, and she'd go off. "I'm sorry, Master." Tears leaked from the corners of her eyes, but she didn't know what they were about. Need, perhaps. Yet, she'd begged him to stop the vibration. Her mind tied itself up in a knot and then lay down and quit.

"Why?"

She struggled at her bonds. The strangest desire to be held in his arms arrived in her brain and once it landed there, wouldn't leave. She leaned her chest toward him, wanting him closer, needing his reassurance. "It excites me," she whispered. "I'm so sorry. I don't know what's come over me. I've never acted this way before."

Daneth's eyes, normally a purplish shade of brown, turned bright amethyst. His horns lengthened. He stepped closer and traced his thumb down her cheek.

She pushed into his hand, nuzzled it, craving it and so much more. "Please forgive me, Master. I was a bad girl, I know. Have mercy on me."

He leaned toward her.

She held her breath.

Would he kiss her? Release her bonds? Breed with her?

She stretched her neck trying to reach him. And then screamed because he'd flicked on the terrible, wonderful vibration again. "Master!"

His mouth covered hers, swallowing her next scream. He pumped the vibrator in and out of her stretched pussy while his tongue mimicked the movement in her mouth, taking her, claiming her, punishing her with each sweep, each thrust.

White-hot pressure built to the bursting point, and she exploded, orgasm rocking through her, lifting her hips from the table, though the action tightened and twisted her fully flexed knees. Her eyes squeezed tight, she screamed unintelligible words, and Daneth drew back and slapped one of her breasts, hard.

The orgasm went on and on.

He slapped her other breast, and she wept and moaned. The squeeze and release of her climax passed, but Daneth didn't remove the vibrating phallus, didn't stop looking at her with that cruel smirk.

"Master," she moaned. "Master, please. No more. I'm a sorry girl. I'm such a sorry girl. I'll be your good girl, I promise. I'll never show my breasts again."

"No. You won't." His voice sounded flinty, matching the hardened lines of his face. Was the strain due to desire? The enormous bulge of his cock tented his pants and lab coat. "You will never, ever try to make me jealous again. Nor will you show your breasts. You will not be permitted out of my lab or chamber without full covering on your body."

She wanted to remind him that she had requested panties the previous planet rotation and he'd been the one to refuse, but she didn't dare.

"You will not cocktease me. And if you ever cocktease other males on this pod again, you will never be allowed out of this lab or my chamber again. Understood?"

She bobbed her head. "Yes, Master. Please stop."

He kept her under his cool consideration, not moving.

"Please? Please, Master."

"I like hearing you beg so much more than I ever imagined I would." He slapped her breast. "What I don't like?" Another slap. "Seeing you aroused by other males."

Her face flushed with heat, and the urge to cry returned as the reason for his anger suddenly became clear. "I wasn't aroused by other males," she pleaded. "I wasn't."

He pinched each of her nipples between a thumb and forefinger and twisted until she screamed.

"Please, Master!"

"Don't lie to me. I embedded sensors in your inner walls to measure your level of excitement. I will always know."

Tears spilled, only because she knew it was true but didn't want it to be. She didn't want him to be hurt by her arousal by other males. She'd been teasing for *him*, not them. She shook her head, the back of her hair rubbing on the table covering. "No, no, no, no," she moaned. "It-it wasn't my fault. My body responded—it's the drugs. Not my fault."

Daneth released her nipples abruptly. "Perhaps it wasn't your fault," he conceded. "That much you can't control, can you, little slave?"

She shook her head. "No, Master."

He brought the backs of his fingers to her cheek and stroked, showing signs of mercy, though he still hadn't stopped the incessant vibration.

"Please?" she begged.

"Please, what?"

"Please, Master?"

He waited—apparently that wasn't the add-on he desired.

"Please take it out," she croaked. "Please don't be angry anymore. Please...hold me." She bit her lip, wishing those words hadn't tumbled out. She averted her gaze to the window as another tear tracked along the side of her nose.

The vibrator stopped. Daneth removed it and the anal plug, leaving her feeling empty and wrung out. "What does *hold me* mean?"

"Nothing," she answered quickly. "Never mind, Master."

"Release ankle cuffs." He pinched her chin and turned her face. "No lies, pretty human."

She blinked, surprised to see...was it *warmth* In his eyes now?

"Release wrist cuffs."

She moaned as her arms dropped and the blood rushed back into them with billions of pinpricks.

Daneth scooped her up. "Is this *hold me?*"

She tucked her face into his neck and nodded.

"You like this?"

Another nod. She looped one arm around his shoulder.

He carried her through the door to his chamber and toward the cage. "Why?"

She tightened her grip on his shoulder, not wanting to be put away yet. She didn't answer.

"*Bayla.*" His voice cracked like a whip.

Her bottom clenched. "It feels nice."

"Humans require physical contact." He didn't say it like a question, but he didn't sound certain, either. More like he was testing out a theory.

"Don't Zandians?"

~.~

Did Zandians require physical contact? If he'd been asked two planet rotations ago, he would've scoffed with an instantaneous, definitive *no*. But, feeling the soft weight of Bayla in his arms, the scent of her skin, the musk of her arousal filling his nostrils, he wasn't so sure.

"Not physiologically," he hedged.

What if Zandians did require physical touch? What if it brought them alive? Made them experience emotions they hadn't felt in thirty solar cycles?

No. That was foolish. He'd known having close contact with a human female might affect him. If he was going to complete his experiment successfully, he needed to pull back from her allure and focus. Concentrate. Stop allowing her to whip his emotions into a frenzy.

And yet, when those slender arms tightened around his neck, there was no way in the galaxy he could let her go. She *liked* this. She wanted him to *hold* her. How utterly ridiculous.

How precious.

Instead of attempting to place her in the cage, he detoured to his sleepdisk and made himself comfortable, scooting into a seated position with his back against the wall. Bayla's soft, heated bottom settled in his lap, teasing his stiffened cock. He'd loved torturing her with orgasms. Watching her face flush and eyes turn glassy. Hearing her plead for release. Oh *vecking* stars, the way she'd begged with him had made him rock hard!

Master, please. I'll be your good girl, I promise.

Those words made him want to flip her onto her knees and pound her pussy hard from behind. Pound her until she learned what it meant to be his good girl. To serve her master's every whim.

Veck, he was losing his mind.

Bayla must have drifted off to sleep in Daneth's arms. When she woke, she was alone in his chamber. She stretched, and her bottom protested, still sore from the spanking. She climbed off the sleepdisk and went into the bathroom, checking out her backside in the mirror. Still red. Looked like some of those marks would last a few days. She ran her hands over her cheeks, surprised at how little she resented her master for punishing her so mercilessly. Only warmth filled her chest as she thought of his jealousy and anger, of the way he'd held her afterward.

She wouldn't trade seeing those sides of him for anything.

She searched the shelving from which Daneth had produced her tunic and found panties and leggings, which she donned. She tried the door, but, as expected, it was locked. Still, he'd left her out of the cage, which she counted as a win. She strolled around the beautiful room, examining everything. Daneth had very few personal items and everything in the room bore the same order and precision she'd witnessed in his lab. Clothing was organized and neatly stacked, boots shined and lined up.

The door swished open, and she jumped then dropped into a low curtsy as Daneth entered.

"You're awake." His brusque, businesslike manner had returned.

She tried not to flinch, but all the warmth and softness she'd found when she woke fled, leaving her cracked and raw in Daneth's presence.

He reached for the ring on her collar and pulled her forward, clipping a leash to it once again. "Come. I wish to introduce you to the prince to receive his permission to begin my experiment."

His experiment. That was all she was to this male, and she'd do well to remember it. "Yes, Master," she muttered.

He pulled the chain and led her out of the chamber to the great hall. A young Zandian male stood near the windows, giving orders to several older Zandian males. His arm draped around the waist of a pregnant human.

She stiffened, the sight of a bred human bringing back the past several years with a sickening twist in her solar plexus. No matter how much better this environment may be, she was still only here for one reason—to produce a child she'd never know.

Heartache at the two babies she'd already lost washed over her, making her stumble.

Daneth reached for her elbow to steady her, and his solicitousness surprised her. She supposed she'd expected an impatient jerk of the chain.

The older Zandians left the prince and his human, who both turned to watch them approach.

"My lord, this is the slave I purchased for the implantation protocol," Daneth said. "Her name is Bayla."

She dipped into a low curtsy, her head bowed.

"Welcome, Bayla," the prince said.

"Zander, Prince of Zandia, and his mate, Lamira," Daneth said.

She remained in the curtsy.

"You may rise." The prince spoke with the easy assumption of power, clearly used to giving orders and having them obeyed.

She stood with her hands folded in front of her, head still bowed.

"I wish to begin the experiment tomorrow, with your permission."

Zander didn't speak for a moment. "Remove her chain," he ordered.

Daneth lifted his head in surprise but turned her to face him and unclipped the chain from her collar.

"Lamira, will you give Bayla a tour if she hasn't had one?"

"Of course, my lord. Come with me," the female said, smiling when Bayla lifted her eyes.

Lamira was beautiful, about the same age as Bayla, with green eyes and copper-colored hair. A smattering of freckles dusted her nose and cheeks. Like Bayla, she wore a collar, only hers was studded with beautiful crystals. A well-loved pet? A slave with benefits? Bayla wondered exactly what Lamira's status was on the pod. She'd been called Zander's *mate*. Did that mean his breeder? Or something more?

"Have you had a tour already?" Lamira asked as she led her out of the great room.

"I've been to the kitchen."

Lamira smiled. "My favorite place." She rubbed her full belly. "Would you like to see it again?"

"Of course. Are you in the *hungry every two hours* phase?"

"Try *hungry all planet rotation*." Lamira eyed her with curiosity. "You've been pregnant before?"

Pain drilled through her chest and she found it hard to breathe. "Yes," she managed.

Lamira's face clouded, as if she read Bayla's emotions. "I'm sorry. I was always grateful I hadn't been selected for sex or breeding. It must have been hard."

"It still is." She didn't know why Lamira used the past tense, but the female paled when Bayla corrected her.

They arrived outside the kitchen, but Lamira slowed to a stop before they entered, facing Bayla. "Are you unwilling to serve as Daneth's vessel?"

Her pulse fluttered, knots forming in every muscle of her body. Something about the female made her want to be honest, but she knew better than to trust a stranger. "I will do as is expected of me," she said stiffly and started to enter the open door to the kitchen.

"Wait." Lamira caught her arm and pulled her back. "If you're unwilling, I'll talk to Zander. You shouldn't have to do this if you don't want to."

But if she didn't, what then? Be sent back to the fertility farm for more of the same in a far less comfortable environment? No. At least, here, she'd have nine months of luxury. Even if it did end in another broken heart. "I'll do as I'm told." She shook off Lamira's hold and entered the kitchen.

Master Barr beamed when Lamira pulled out a chair at the counter and sat down. He waved at the empty one for Bayla. Before she'd settled, he swept a dish piled high with raw vegetables, cut into disks, and some kind of blue sauce for dipping in front of them. Fresh fruit and vegetables were a luxury she'd never enjoyed, even while pregnant and fed the best foods, so she leaped to partake.

"This vegetable comes from the planet Jesel, a planet with similar terrain to Earth that still retains some natural resources," Lamira said. "I'm growing several varieties here."

Bayla blinked, her brain slow to process this new information. "You're a...farmer?"

Lamira nodded. "Yes. Daneth purchased me from an agrifarm." She popped a vegetable into her mouth with as much alacrity as Bayla.

Bayla stiffened at hearing Daneth had purchased her. Had he examined Lamira as he'd examined her? Had he given her pleasure? She accidentally bit her cheek as she chewed the vegetable. "Daneth purchased you for farming?"

"No." She rubbed her tummy. "For breeding."

Hot and cold flushed over Bayla's skin.

"He has a program that runs the DNA of all registered beings in Ocretia. It can select for the best possible gene-match for breeding. I came up as the best match for Prince Zander."

For Prince Zander. Relief swept over her, and her stomach unknotted. She reached for another vegetable disk and dipped it into the exquisitely flavorful sauce—a creamy herbed concoction so delectable she would have picked up the bowl and drunk from it if Lamira hadn't been there.

"I thought you said you said you were grateful you hadn't been selected for breeding." She shouldn't have said anything, but Lamira seemed so open, she couldn't help herself.

Lamira nodded, licking a bit of dip from the corner of her mouth. "By the Ocretions, yes. I was devastated when I was first brought here. But it was the best thing that ever happened to me." She studied Bayla. "I hope it will be for you, too."

Something about the way Lamira looked at Bayla made her flush. It was as if the female gazed right into her head and saw her irrational attachment to the sexy doctor who wanted to implant her with another female's young.

"The Zandians on this pod aren't used to humans. They've remained quite isolated since they lost their planet. You may find it takes a while for Daneth to understand and develop empathy for human emotions, but Zander did, and so did Master Seke, my mother's mate."

Her face grew warmer. Was Lamira suggesting Daneth might become her mate? "I don't require the doctor's empathy," she said stiffly.

"Of course not," Lamira murmured, and Bayla kicked herself for being rude.

Bayla stuffed another vegetable into her mouth and chewed to keep herself from showing her hand and pumping Lamira for every bit of information she would share about Daneth.

~.~

Daneth waited for the prince to speak. Zander had obviously sent Bayla away so they might discuss her, and Daneth found his shoulders rising toward his ears with each passing breath.

When the women had disappeared down the hall, Zander said, "You cannot keep her as a slave."

The blood drained from Daneth's face. "I beg your pardon?" Somehow, he forced the words past his numb lips. Zander couldn't take Bayla from him now —not when he'd already authorized her purchase. Not when the protocol was planned for tomorrow.

Not when he'd discovered Bayla to be perfect in more ways than his gene-matching program had shown him. Perfect in every way imaginable.

"There was an incident on the training pod. Captain Lundric killed a human male who threatened his chosen female. Things came to a head. Master Seke believes it important that we not keep slaves on this pod or ever again. Zandians do not keep slaves. We never have. If we expect the humans on the training pod to fight with us for Zandia, we must offer them sovereignty. It is only right."

Daneth gulped air. "What do you wish me to do with her, my lord?"

Zander folded his arms across his chest. "You must give her a choice. She may stay or go. If she stays, she will still answer to you as her superior. She will participate in your experiment and give you her complete obedience. You may still discipline her as you would if she were your slave. Once she is pregnant, she will lose her freedom, as the young will belong to us, but after the birth, she may once again choose to leave, as she will be a free being on this pod."

"But if she chooses to leave, where will she go? Humans are not free anywhere on Ocretia."

"It greatly improves the chances of her staying, does it not?" Zander flicked his brows, and understanding swept over Daneth. This was largely a matter of semantics—no real change. Except that Bayla might choose a different slave master over him.

Veck—would she? He couldn't let it happen. He cursed himself for not establishing a closer bond with her.

He closed his eyes and worked to unclench his fists. "I see. I will speak with her now, my lord." With a bow, he left the great room in search of his slave. No—not his *slave*. His female.

He found her in the kitchen with Lamira. She jumped to her feet when he arrived. Was she relieved to see him? Or just exceptionally obedient? Either way, he liked it far too much.

Please let her stay.

He didn't put the leash back on but led her to his chamber with a hand at her waist. When the door had swished shut, he cleared his throat.

Bayla tensed. "What is it, Master?"

He drew his brows up, taken off guard by the question. "What do you mean?"

"You seem tense. Did the prince not give you permission to begin the experiment?" She tangled her fingers together, her eyes lowered, but he read concern in her tone.

His forehead wrinkled. He'd underestimated Bayla's powers of observation. Was she really so in tune with him she could sense his mood? The idea produced a riot of sensation in his chest. He couldn't remember any being caring to attempt to read him. He'd always been the observer, not the other way around. Not even his parents had paid attention to his mood as a child. And while he counted the beings in this pod as his friends, did they really know anything about him? The idea saddened him, as much as Bayla's noticing draped him with a sense of power and pleasure.

He cupped her chin, lifting it. "You're quite observant, little human. No, it's not that." He dropped his hand and paced away from her. As he struggled to find the right words, his tension mounted. What if she chose to leave?

What would happen to his experiment?

He refused to admit the disturbing feelings beneath that concern—what would happen to *him* without Bayla?

"Prince Zander has forbidden Zandians to own slaves." He let that hang in the air, reluctant to go on.

Bayla said nothing, which made it harder to guess what her answer would be. He forced himself to turn around and look at her.

The quiet intelligence in her regard rocked him. She was so much more than an incredibly fertile body. There were layers there he hadn't yet unpeeled. He may not have a chance now.

"You may choose to remain as my test subject. If you do, you will answer to me and remain subject to my discipline."

"And the alternative?"

Veck. She wanted the alternative. He paced the length of the room. "I can return you to the fertility farm. Or sell you elsewhere, to another slave owner if you wish." Hell. Why did he offer that? He didn't want her to choose to leave. And yet, the idea of sending her to a situation she hated put his teeth on edge.

"I see. So there's really no change, except I can choose to go back to my old situation if I like."

"You would no longer be my slave if you stayed," he said stiffly. "You would not wear my collar or sleep in a cage in my room. You would be given your own small chamber, though you still must obey my orders and perform any duties required by me."

She said nothing.

"So...what do you choose?" He turned to face her.

Her sapphire eyes studied him. "I would essentially still be a prisoner, though—on this pod? And I must do everything you say or be punished. But I won't wear your collar or sleep in your room. Is that correct?"

He nodded, the tension in him mounting. His fists clenched so tightly, his knuckles cracked.

"No." She lifted her chin and shook her head.

His heart stopped. "No?" The crack in his voice matched the fissure in his chest, growing wider and wider by the second. "You choose to leave?"

"If I stay, I wear your collar. Sleep in your room. I will not suffer the humiliation of your ownership without the reward."

Reward? The room swayed under his feet. He closed his eyes, drawing a long, slow breath in through his nostrils to clear his head.

She was staying. With him. She wanted him to be her master. *As her reward.*

It hardly made sense to him, and yet he'd never experienced such a sense of victory in his life.

"Come here," he said gruffly when he opened his eyes.

. . .

Bayla observed Daneth's tension, and his relief. She knew it was about his experiment, not her, but she still enjoyed the fierce satisfaction that lit his expression as she approached.

He caught her face in both his large hands and his lips crashed down on hers, tearing at her mouth. He nipped her lips, sucked them, dragged his mouth across them. He thrust his tongue between them, all the while holding her prisoner for the kiss.

Not that she wanted to escape. Her surprise at the passion she'd evoked in him pierced her with satisfaction. Her cool, reserved doctor had crumbled. She may belong to him, but he belonged to her, too. A victory she'd aimed to win from the start.

"Take your clothes off," he said roughly.

Was he going to claim her? To breed her? She found the idea far more appealing than his intended protocol. If she had his baby, perhaps it wouldn't be taken from her. Perhaps he'd keep her as his slave, and she'd tend to their child. The idea set off rockets of desire so strong, she could scarcely contain herself.

So she didn't. She stripped off her clothing and dropped to her knees, pressing her mouth against his crotch.

"*Vecking* stars, Bayla," he growled and shoved his pants down, allowing his full erection to spring free.

She licked around the head then took him deep, keeping her eyes lifted for his command. Her pussy clenched between her thighs, nipples hardened to stiff peaks.

He met her gaze, and his nostrils flared. He grasped the back of her head and shoved deep, causing her to choke and her eyes to water. Daneth didn't have mercy, though. He seemed to lose control, thrusting with the erratic force of a male about to climax.

She hollowed her cheeks and sucked until he came, burning the back of her throat with the salty tang of his essence. His thighs shook with the intensity of his release and the kick of power it gave her. Knowing she'd caused this loss of control in him, thrilled her.

He pulled out of her mouth and stared down at her, as if dazed at what they'd done.

"Master," she whispered.

"You chose me."

She thought she heard awe in his voice, but before she could dissect it, he had her up from the floor and on her back on his sleepdisk. He gripped her knees and drew her thighs apart, affixing his mouth to her core.

Five mind-blowing minutes later, she came all over his thrusting fingers, her clit suctioned tight in his mouth.

An hour later, after she'd come six more times from his talented fingers, she wept, certain she couldn't handle any more. "Please, Master. No more. I'm so tired."

He towered over her, smug satisfaction oozing from him. "Don't forget, you chose to be owned by me." He brushed the backs of his fingers over her cheek. "I decide when you rest and when you deserve pleasure."

She shook her head, her hair already rubbed into a tangle from the friction against the mattress. "No more pleasure," she whispered. "Please...rest."

He smiled indulgently. "Yes, rest now, slave. Tomorrow is your implantation."

A heaviness fell over her at the reminder.

He scooped her into his arms and carried her to her cage, placing her inside with care.

"What must I do tomorrow?"

He wrapped a large palm around her ankle and squeezed. "It's a simple and painless procedure. You must lie still and rest afterward to make sure it attaches. That is all."

"And then...grow a baby? Or young? What do Zandians call it?"

"Young. Yes."

"And who will care for the young?"

He patted her ankle. "Don't concern yourself with that. Your job is simply to carry the pregnancy."

Her vision dimmed, and cold rolled slowly over her. As she'd feared. One more baby she would never nurse. Never love.

She needed to make sure the pregnancy never took.

Daneth reviewed the protocol for artificial insemination again. He'd already followed every study and report out there on *in vitro* fertilization and implantation in humans and every other species remotely similar. Unfortunately, there was nothing on Zandians. His species had never used such methods for conception. They had a breeding season, which he'd nearly missed, but he didn't think it mattered so much in this case. He wasn't using any live Zandians for the protocol.

He had only a few viable Zandian eggs. They had come from Zander's mother, the queen, herself. He still thanked the stars he'd suggested harvesting them from her. She'd had a rough pregnancy with Zander and swore she didn't want a second child. He'd recommended she cryofreeze some while she was still young, in case she either changed her mind or wanted to find a surrogate for a future pregnancy. She had agreed.

When the palace was bombed by the Finn, he'd had the presence of mind to collect some of his medical supplies, and he'd taken the vial of eggs, along with several prize crystals so they might survive away from their planet. He'd instructed others who got out to take as many crystals as they could.

Zandian crystal—the reason the Finn took over their planet—was used in many technologies and therefore worth a fortune. Zandians prized it for far more than its open market value, however. They used it for light amplification to nourish their bodies. Without it, his species would be severely weakened, perhaps even die.

He snapped on a pair of gloves and picked up the slender instrument he would use to implant the tiny embryo he had cultured in the lab four planet rotations prior. He'd collected the semen of all the Zandians in the palatial pod under fifty solar cycles and run the donors in his gene-matching program for the queen. The program had chosen one of the guards, though he did not plan to tell the guard or any other being who the actual father was. He would only reveal that information to Prince Zander under orders. No need to complicate matters. Technically, the young would belong to him, as guardian of the Zandians species.

He glanced over at his human, who hadn't been nearly so agreeable as she had the previous planet rotation. She'd been peevish and quiet since she woke that morning. He suspected her delicate human emotions had her on edge over the procedure.

He should have found a way to calm her, but he'd been too wrapped up in his own desire to get everything perfect. He didn't have time for a slave's anxieties.

Except, now, as he looked at her pale face and pinched mouth, he wished he'd done more. Though the procedure would be painless, he wondered if he should sedate her.

She squirmed against her restraints and appeared uncomfortable, though he scented her arousal. He wondered which part of the scenario aroused her—her nudity or being restrained and at his mercy. Perhaps both.

He pulled her labia apart, indulging in the sight of her spread for him. "Open for your master." He probed her entrance with the instrument. She tightened her anus and vaginal opening against his intrusion, but, of course, could do nothing to resist. Even so, he scolded her. "I said *open*."

Her belly quivered as she drew in a breath. "I don't want to do this."

He stopped, surprised at what he suspected was total honesty. He'd expected her usual, "Yes, Master," which had been ingrained in her by her previous masters.

He paused in the further insertion of the probe. "Why not?"

She bit down on her plump lower lip and shook her head. "Never mind. I'm sorry, Master. I'm just nervous."

A lie.

He knew without looking at her readouts on his cuff. "What don't you like, Bayla?"

She leaned her head back against the table and stared up at the ceiling, her gaze fixed and unblinking. "It's fine, Master. I'm ready."

Later, he would wish he'd stopped and forced her to confess her concerns, but his mind was too full of his experiment. He flicked on the hologram that showed his progress inside her womb and found the ideal location to deposit the egg.

He left it there and withdrew the probe, watching the tiny embryo, magnified by his viewer, settle along the lining of her uterus.

He released her ankle cuffs and clipped them together, then to a chain that hung from the ceiling, to tilt her pelvis and hold everything in. "Comfortable?"

She shook her head. "No." Sullenness pervaded the monosyllable.

He arched a brow. "Try that again."

"No, *Master*." She sounded snide. "How long must I stay this way?"

He didn't want to spank her—not after things had shifted between them—but her petulance raised his hackles. The warmth he'd been feeling for her slipped away and he found himself returning to his old way of being. Impatient. Businesslike. Reserved. "Until I release you." He moved away, removing his gloves and disposing of them then cleaning up the supplies he'd used for the protocol.

Bayla was smart enough to stay quiet, though her discontent filled the room like a bad smell.

All the ideas he'd had about babying her that planet rotation—carrying her to his sleepdisk and feeding her from his own fingers—faded. Which was fine. She'd become a distraction. He needed to be focused on his work. She played a part in that work, but that was all. Somehow he'd allowed her human wiles to activate something in him—something that sparked and sputtered and exploded with life. But that tremendous energy was dangerous. It made males lose their focus, lose their control. Zandians, in general, were quite even-keeled, and he'd been the least emotional of all.

Science. Data. Medical studies. Those were the things that mattered to him.

Still, something wedged in the door of his heart as he attempted to slam it shut.

His female was unhappy. The itchy, achy need to fix the situation kept creeping back, no matter how many times he shoved it away.

With a sigh, he released the clip on her ankles. "Release wrist cuffs."

She didn't exactly glare at him, but there was a sullen set to her mouth as she regarded him warily. He scooped her up and carried her to his room. "Cage or my sleep disk?"

Why, in the name of the true Zandian star, am I offering her a choice? She was his slave. His test subject.

But his heart, his body, refused to acknowledge what his mind screamed.

Must care for her.

"Sleepdisk." Her arms didn't circle his neck. She didn't lean her head against his shoulder.

He set her on her back on the mattress and propped her ass up with a pillow. Then he flicked the loose end of the coverlet across her naked body. "Don't move from this position until I tell you. Understand?"

She nodded.

"Say it."

"Yes, Master."

"You're trying my patience this planet rotation, Bayla. I don't know what has you out of sorts, but you're this close to getting that pretty little bottom spanked." He held his forefinger and thumb a small width apart to illustrate.

Her jaw clenched, and she looked away from him. "Yes, Master," she mumbled.

Things still seemed unsettled, but he didn't know how else to straighten them. His eager-to-please slave had fled, and now he realized her docility, her obedience—had he even imagined...*affection?*—had nothing to do with him. He wasn't a better master than Zander had been. He remembered when the young prince had first taken Lamira and had called Daneth in exasperation and frustration with her disobedience. No, Daneth had simply been lucky that this particular female had been properly trained first. *Trained by some other being.* Why did that thought make his fingers clench into fists?

Punishment was what he had recommended to Zander. Striking human females on their buttocks and thighs caused pain but did no physical harm. This manner of chastisement, especially with required nudity or with the insertion of plugs in the anus, humiliated the female, and thus helped her find submission to her master. Or so the research had shown. He hadn't found punishing her unpleasant. In fact, he'd loved watching her rounded posterior turn pink and squirm under his hand. Knowing it aroused her had made it all the more pleasurable.

But, for some reason, he hesitated to punish her now. Perhaps he had enjoyed her voluntary submission so well that forcing it on her seemed wrong.

He shook his head to clear it. Zander's decree she wasn't actually a slave had him thinking too much. She as his to punish, regardless. She must show respect and obedience or suffer the consequences.

He returned to his lab and watched the hologram of the implantation once more. What if it didn't take?

He'd only created one embryo for this protocol and had used two eggs. The other egg hadn't proven viable. He only had one more left if this implantation didn't take. If that one wasn't healthy, the future of his species—at least for pure bred Zandians—would be hopeless.

He returned to his chamber with two needles and vials of hormone cocktails for Bayla and found her still in position, but with her arms folded across her chest in subtle rebellion.

~.~

She wanted to hate Daneth. Sometimes he made it easy, barking orders and acting like a typical high-handed master. Nothing she wasn't used to, but somehow more irritating coming from a male who had also brought her to orgasm on numerous occasions.

But, sometimes, he made it hard. Like when he'd brought her into his chamber to make her more comfortable. Obviously, he hadn't had to do that. And she hadn't been begging him. In fact, she'd been acting like a brat, and he still did it.

What did that say about him? Did he like her as much as she sometimes imagined?

He'd certainly seemed incredibly satisfied with her the previous planet rotation.

But she didn't want to soften toward him, especially because she was now hell-bent on ruining his implantation procedure. It would be easier to thwart his important endeavor if she thought of him as a heartless ass.

"What is that?" she asked, eyeing the needles in his gloved hand.

He sat on the sleep disk and hauled her body across his lap into spanking position. She heard the pop of a cap being removed.

"What is that?" she repeated. Alarm bells were going off. She didn't want to be shot up with medications, even though this, too, was nothing new for her. The intimacy of the position and his intended target were, however.

She yelped as he jabbed a needle into her ass. "Ow."

"Almost finished."

A burning sensation pinched at the needle site and, worse, liquid cold seeped in deeper. "What is it?" she snapped again.

Never in her life had she acted so inappropriately with a master—she certainly knew better, but something about Daneth's cool, collected resolve brought out the fire in her. She wanted to kick and scream until he stopped ignoring her and answered her damn question.

Apparently, it worked, because he fisted his hand in her hair and pulled her head up. "What have I told you about speaking without being spoken to?"

"You're jabbing a needle in my ass. I would say you're speaking to me, in a sense," she shot back, wisdom apparently fleeing her, along with her mind and her temper.

Another sharp jab bit her other cheek. Apparently he was perfectly capable of injecting her with only one hand. "Ow."

He tugged her head back more. "It's not your place to question me, Bayla." He said it so calmly, she wanted to knee him in the balls.

"Oh, really? Because it's *my* body you're injecting. Shouldn't I know what's going on?"

"It's not your body. You made a choice just one planet rotation ago, and you gave it to me, to science. This body belongs to me." He slapped the back of her thigh and shifted her off his lap and onto her feet on the floor. "Now, you will walk to the cabinet over there and bring me the box of implements."

She stared at him. Not in disbelief, because she'd fully expected punishment. If she was honest with herself, she'd admit she'd goaded him. No, she couldn't stand the lack of emotion, the lack of reaction from him. It drove her crazy.

She should seduce him. Getting him turned on had been her entry point to getting a reaction out of him. But she wasn't in the mood. If she were smart, she'd get moving before she earned herself more punishment. She trudged to the cabinet, retrieved the box in question, and watched him rooted through it.

Her traitorous pussy moistened at the entire scenario—standing naked before him, knowing what he planned to do to her, waiting while he made his selection. He drew out a thin wooden paddle—more like a flat spatula.

Just the sight of it made her contrite, already regretting her bad behavior. She dropped to her knees. "I'm sorry I was ill-behaved, Master."

He cupped her chin and lifted it, stroking her cheek with his thumb. The emptiness behind his eyes faded, and a trace of warmth returned. "That's a pretty sight." He studied her for another beat, and her body came alive under his appreciative gaze, nipples tightening, skin tingling. "You're sorry you're getting a spanking."

"Yes, Master," she admitted.

His lips twitched. "I have not instilled enough fear in you, have I?"

Her pussy and belly both clenched as one part fear, one part excitement zoomed through her.

He glanced at his cuff, probably noting her mounting arousal. "Over my lap," he commanded.

Tummy twisting, she stood and folded herself over his lap, which he'd angled to accommodate her torso on the sleepdisk.

The wooden paddle clapped down on one of her cheeks, and she sucked in air so fast she choked on it. Coughing her outrage, she squirmed, not managing to dodge the next smack that caught her other cheek.

"Hands behind your back." Daneth's deep command cut through her internal scream.

What would happen if she disobeyed? Not worth the risk. Not when each firm smack had her eyes watering. She put her wrists at the small of her back.

"Connect wrist cuffs," he barked, never pausing in delivering her punishment. "You have been naughty all planet rotation." He made the strokes harder.

She whimpered, rolling her hips on his lap as if it might help her dodge the blows.

"Now you will find out what it's like to have a spanking on cheeks already sore from fresh injections."

"I'm sorry! I'm sorry, Master."

"The injections contained hormones to support the implantation."

She lost her breath from the flurry of hard spanks. If she'd thought his hand was worse than the leather paddle, she now knew wood was the worst.

"What difference does it make to you?"

"None," she mumbled. He was right. It made no difference—not when she had zero choice about what he was doing. And she'd never been informed about her medications back at the fertility farm. "I was a brat! I'm sorry."

To her surprise, Daneth stopped spanking her and chuckled. He ran his large hand over her twitching buttocks, soothing away the throbbing sting. "It's hard to stay angry with you, pretty girl." His hand stroked down the outside of one of her thighs and came up on the inside. "When you're so *vecking* adorable."

She sucked in her breath when his fingers arrived at her core.

"When you're wet for your master."

She spread her legs.

"Do you want your master's cock?" He pinned her clit between his knuckles, capturing the little nubbin of pleasure and holding it prisoner.

"Y-yes, please." The words rasped from her throat.

"Where do you want it?" He squeezed it, making her writhe, sweat breaking out all over her body.

"There," she moaned. "My pussy."

"No." He gave her pussy a slap. "Your pussy doesn't deserve my cock." To her dismay, he abandoned her clit and coasted back, bypassing the entrance to her pussy and rubbing the pad of his finger over her anus.

"No," she groaned. "Not there." Despite her background as a breeder and her training for sex, she was an anal virgin. And the idea of taking Daneth's huge purple cock back there made her thighs go weak.

Daneth's hand disappeared and returned to her vaginal opening with some kind of probe. He inserted it without any kind of preparation. Not that she needed it. Her pussy dripped with moisture, pulsing with flashes of white-hot desire.

The probe whirred to life, setting up a vibration that stirred her entire pelvis.

She bit the coverlet and moaned, pussy clenching down on the device.

"Where do you want my cock, Bayla?"

Oh stars. Was he really still asking? He wanted to take her ass.

One part of her rejected that notion thoroughly. The other part moaned. Out loud.

Daneth rubbed something cool and liquid over her anus—a lubricant. Something pressed at her back entrance. Not his finger—another probe.

She squeezed her anus and her butt cheeks, but Daneth began pumping the vibrator inside her pussy, touching it to her G-spot on her inner wall.

She cried out, fingers splaying to take fistfuls of fabric, back arching to offer her ass up to him.

He pressed the hard, rounded tip of the plug against her anus, insisting.

Against her will, the ring of muscle relaxed, and he slid the plug inside.

This time, the moan that came from her mouth sounded more like a feral animal than human.

"Where do you take my cock when you've been naughty, Bayla?"

Her sphincter stretched and relaxed as he pumped the plug, and she found the sensation far more pleasurable than she could have imagined. "Oh stars, Master. Please."

"Please what, Bayla? Please *veck* your ass?"

"P—please" she panted, not sure what she begging for. "Please *veck* my ass, Master." She must be out of her mind.

Yes, definitely out of her mind.

Daneth lifted her off his lap and placed her fully on the sleepdisk. His hands were surprisingly gentle, and she found her body more than willing to submit to his touch. It was as if her body knew he was born to command it, all resistance leaving with the surety of his handling. He lifted her hips and shoved a pillow under them.

"Don't worry, sweet girl. I'm a doctor. Do you think I'd ever allow damage to your glorious body?"

His words intoxicated her. Her eyelids drooped closed as she settled her face into the mattress and spread her legs wide.

Take me, Master.

More lubricant. The rustle of clothing then the dip of the mattress as Daneth climbed up behind her.

She held her breath, tensing, but all he did was pump the two probes in and out of her holes, first together, then alternating.

She gave a high-pitched cry—half whining for completion, half moaning her satisfaction.

He removed the anal plug and replaced it with the head of his cock. Though she'd feared it for its size, the prod of stiff flesh was so much more satisfying than the hard plug.

"Yes," she moaned.

"When you're naughty, Master has to *veck* your ass."

Her pussy tightened around the vibrator. Daneth eased into her back hole. It was far too much, yet the pleasure outweighed the discomfort.

"Say it."

Huh? As she clawed at the bedcovers, she scrambled to understand his command. *Oh.* "When I'm naughty," she panted, sobbing as he drove deep into her ass, "Master has to *veck* my ass."

Oh stars. It was too much. Too incredibly hot. She wished her hands weren't clipped behind her back because she desperately wanted to work the vibrator in her pussy. "Please, Master. Oh please. Please please please."

As if he read her mind, he shoved his hand under her hips and went for her clit.

It was too much. Sensation exploded into a zillion particles, dancing lights all around her. Her entire body convulsed as her pussy clenched and released on the vibrator and Daneth rocked in and out of her punished ass.

"Master," she wailed, not sure why she felt like both laughing and sobbing, dying and being reborn all at once.

"Yes, your Master knows what you need." Daneth's deep voice seemed to surround her, wrapping her up in a blanket of his presence.

He certainly did.

When the most mind-blowing orgasm of her life had finished, she vaguely realized that before Daneth, her orgasms had been paltry imitations of the real thing. Nothing—*nothing*—came close to what she experienced with him.

"Lie still and take it," he growled, bracing himself beside her and pumping smoothly in and out of her ass while she lay collapsed and compliant beneath him. He came a moment later, roaring his satisfaction into her ear before he bit it, filling her ass with hot streams of his essence.

She wept then. Not for any reason other than satisfaction and release.

"Precious girl," Daneth murmured, kissing the back of her neck as he slowly eased out. "How do you always manage to make me lose control?"

She smiled into the covers, irrationally pleased at that statement.

CHAPTER FIVE

Bayla found her way to the kitchen the next morning after Daneth had completed his checkup and released her. He'd been happy with whatever he'd seen on his holographic projection of her uterus. Which only made her more conflicted about what she planned to do.

"Welcome, Bayla," Chef Barr said with a bow when she entered.

Was he bowing *for her*? No one had bowed for her in her life. She rewarded him with her widest smile.

"Good morning, Master Barr."

"I made dorkling eggs for you."

She had no idea what dorkling eggs were, but the food he placed in front of her smelled heavenly. "Thank you so much." She took a bite and chewed, moaning with pleasure at the explosion of flavor in her mouth.

Chef Barr beamed.

She swallowed the food and pasted on her brightest smile. "Chef Barr, you have access to Earth-based herbs, do you not?"

"Yes," he said. "What would you like?"

"Do you have parsley? Or cinnamon bark?" She kept her expression innocent and cheerful, hoping he had no idea how the herbs were used medicinally.

"I have fresh parsley. Lady Lamira grows it here. I do not have fresh cinnamon, but I have it in powder form. Would you like some parsley in your eggs?"

"Actually, I was wondering if you could make me a big batch of tea with it? Or I can make it," she added, realizing she might be out of line asking him for any favors. "It's really good for a human female's reproductive organs," she lied, letting her hand slip down to cover her belly. "I'd love to sip it all planet rotation today. I want to be the perfect vessel for Doctor Daneth's experiment." She took another bite to hide her guilt at the deception, but the eggs no longer tasted delicious. In fact, her breakfast sat in her stomach like a stone.

She choked down the rest while Chef Barr put a huge pot of water on to boil and left the kitchen.

Not sure of the appropriate protocol for handling dishes, she washed hers in the sink, dried it, and hunted through the cabinets until she found where to put it away.

Chef Barr returned as the water began to boil, a huge bunch of freshly cut parsley in his hand. He rinsed it and tossed it into the pot. "How long should I steep it?"

She nibbled her lip, guilt twisting in her gut. "I'm not sure. Until it turns bright green, if I remember right." She'd learned this trick from Sara, one of the midwives who tended to their births. Parsley could discourage implantation and possibly bring on a female's menstrual cycle, especially when used with other herbs. Of course, they hadn't had access to parsley on the fertility farm, but Sara had suggested it for times when they would be rented out to wealthy Ocretions for breeding. It was not a sure-fire way to end a pregnancy, but when used early and often enough, might encourage miscarriage. Sara had learned it from the midwife before her, and she'd passed on the information to all of them, since most would become midwives to the younger slaves when they were no longer of breeding age.

Bayla had loved midwifery, wishing she could somehow make herself barren and skip straight to that part of her designated life. She'd assisted Sara any time she could, learning about the herbs, about babies, how positioning during childbirth could ease labor pains.

She stood and watched the simmering tea, hoping Daneth wouldn't come in and grow jealous at finding her shoulder to shoulder with the elderly chef. Not that she didn't love his jealousy. She replayed the memory of his fury when she'd flashed her bare breasts at the guards. The pleasure at being coveted matched the satisfaction of having this power over a male. She'd never had power over any being before. It made her feel alive, and sexy. Vital and youthful. It was almost as if her life had begun the day she came to the Zandian palatial pod. Everything that had come before was a bad dream. A rehearsal for what real living would be like.

"That looks good," she said when the water turned a beautiful shade of green.

Chef Barr ladled some into a mug for her, and she blew on the top. "May I take the whole pot to Doctor Daneth's chamber?"

"I'll send it to you. Do you prefer it hot or cold?"

She took a cautious sip of the hot liquid. Not delicious. "Maybe cold would be better."

Chef Barr bowed. "Very well. I will chill it for you."

She curtsied back at him. "Thank you, Master Barr. You're so unbelievably kind to me." She leaned up and gave him a peck on the cheek, which made his face darken in purple.

He gave an embarrassed throat-clear and waved her away.

She walked slowly back to Daneth's chamber, stopping to sip the hot liquid every few steps.

She hoped Daneth wouldn't know about parsley. She doubted he would. The herb was an old human midwives' secret.

Why, then, was her heart jumping out of her chest, her nerves scraped raw over what she was attempting?

She hoped if something should go wrong with the implantation, Daneth would never know the cause, and she'd be free to stay here with him as his slave, learning to serve him, to satisfy him. Learning to use her body to command his.

~.~

In an hour, Chef Barr himself delivered a pitcher of chilled parsley tea to Daneth's chamber. Daneth opened the door for him, but he'd been wrapped up in his research all morning, and he simply mumbled a brief thanks to Chef Barr before turning back to it.

"Thank you so much, Master Barr," she said, dipping into a curtsy but watching that she didn't gush too much in front of the doctor for fear her still-sore bottom would become a target for his hand again.

He poured the green tea into a glass and handed it to her. "It is my pleasure to assist in this way." Oh sweet mother Earth. Please don't let him say what the tea is for. "I brought some to Lamira as well."

Bombs of terror went off in her face and chest. "Oh, that was kind of you." Had her voice wobbled?

Dearest Mother Earth, if she caused the prince's young to miscarry, she would probably be put to death.

"P-perhaps I'll go and see how she likes it," she improvised. "Master Daneth?"

He turned his body in her direction but didn't tear his eyes away from the hologram he was studying.

"With your permission, I'm going to visit Lady Lamira."

Now he looked. "Oh. Well...yes, I suppose that's all right. Don't be long."

She curtsied. "I won't be." She beat Master Barr to the door. "Which way to her chamber?" She forced her voice to sound casual.

"Down the corridor, take a right. That corridor dead ends into it."

"Thank you." She walked as quickly as she dared without arousing suspicion. The moment she Barr disappeared from her view, she raced the rest of the way down the corridor and knocked on the door.

It slid open. She looked wildly around the room and—thank the stars—saw the full glass of tea sitting on the table. Lady Lamira sat at the table across from a woman who looked like her, only older.

"Bayla," Lamira said. "Come in. This is my mother, Leora."

The older woman stood and offered her hand in the ancient Earth greeting.

Bayla shook it, but she was barely able to keep her eyes off the parsley tea. "Have you tried that yet? It's terrible." She picked it up.

Lamira's brows drew together, and her focus went to Bayla's hand holding the glass.

She couldn't think of a good excuse for holding it, but her mouth opened anyway. "I, uh, love it, though. You don't mind if I drink this do you? Good." Without waiting for an answer, she brought the drink to her lips, keeping it there until she'd downed the entire contents. "Oops. I'm sorry—I drank it all. I hope you don't mind."

Lamira's eyes narrowed and then went unfocused. When her focus returned, Bayla would swear she looked disappointed, as if she'd seen into Bayla's soul and found her lacking.

A shiver ran down her spine.

"Would you care to sit with us?" Leora asked.

She really wanted to run back to Daneth's room and hide, but she mustered her courage. "Thank you. I'd love that."

Lamira produced a spare hoverseat and drew it to the table so the three of them sat together. A plate of fruit sat in the middle, and Lamira picked up a berry and popped it into her mouth. "Chef Barr brought me a snack. I'm always hungry."

"Yes, I remember those days. My last pregnancy, I always wanted more meat. Sometimes I thought I'd eat my own hand off if I could." She stamped down the wash of pain that rose up at the memory of her last pregnancy. Where was that baby girl she'd birthed? She'd be nearly two solar cycles now. Were her slave masters kind to her? How was she being raised? And for what purpose?

The separation of slave families was the cruelest of all Ocretion policies. But here she sat with a mother and daughter who seemed to know each other. She turned to Leora. "Did you"—she cleared her throat, knowing her question was way too personal, but unable to stop herself— "did you get to raise Lamira?"

Only sympathy radiated from Leora—no sign of offense. "I did. But my first daughter was taken from me for sexual slavery. Lamira and I were lucky, I suppose. I was a factory worker when I got pregnant with Lamira. A human revolt originated there at the time." The woman's eyes clouded with pain, but then she blinked, and it was gone. "After the revolution was stamped out, they got rid of all of us to change the mix. I was sent to an agrifarm. It was hard work, but we were mostly left alone."

"And how did you end up here?"

"Prince Zander purchased her as a gift to me," Lamira said, the corners of her mouth turning up into a wry smile. "He helped us find my older sister, Lily, as well. She, too, is mated to a Zandian."

"Humans and Zandians are a good mix, then?"

Lamira rubbed her swollen belly. "It seems so. There are differences to work through, certainly. The innate dominance of their species is tempered by a code of honor. They are as capable of loving and bonded relationships as humans are. We haven't seen any of the cruelty of the Ocretions in them, despite their insistence on superiority."

A desperate and utterly foreign longing rose up in Bayla. At first, she didn't know what it was for. Family? Her lost babies? It resembled that loss. But then she realized—she wanted to be mated like these women. To have the loving and bonded relationship Lamira described. Having a partner or mate had never entered her mind as a possibility before. Unless some Ocretion master chose to purchase and keep her as his permanent sex slave, she would never be bound to a male. Nor had she ever wished for such a fate. She'd only ever trusted the other female slaves.

But to have an *honorable* male, such as Lamira described—a loving mate, one who purchased her mother as a gift to her—it was a dream she'd never indulged until now. And despite her better judgment, that dream took root in the center of her chest, spreading until it consumed her. Thoughts of what it would be like to have Daneth impregnate her, bring her a gift, hold her.

He already had. Held her, that is. He'd carried her to his sleepdisk and covered her with blankets. He'd held her in his lap, in his strong arms.

What if a male like him came to *love* her? Was such a thing even possible? She'd only ever thought about their relationship in terms of sex. In terms of *master* and *slave*. Now that she'd heard about Lamira's mate, she wanted more.

And that was a dangerous way to think.

Especially considering her enormous betrayal of her master and his beloved experiment.

Daneth carried Bayla from his chamber to his lab and settled her gently on the examination table. She carried the future of the Zandian species inside that incredibly precious body of hers. He wanted to drop to *his* knees and worship at the temple of feminine vessel.

Bayla seemed nervous, though, and a desire to comfort her took precedence, even over starting the examination he was so eager to perform.

"This won't hurt, little girl. No shots today. I won't strap you down if you promise to hold the position for me."

Pale-faced, her eyes seeming wider and bluer than usual, she nodded rapidly. "I'll do whatever you want, Master," she promised.

He stroked her cheek. So *vecking* agreeable. How did he get so lucky? He didn't always understand the complexity of his human's emotions, but, thus far, she'd been remarkably easy to train. It was his own emotions he needed to keep in check.

He lifted her knees and placed her feet in the stirrups to hold her legs apart. "Scoot your bottom down toward me," he instructed, perching on a stool at the foot of the table. She slid down, bringing him eye to slit with the ripe flesh of her pussy. An approving hum rose in his throat before he could check it.

He'd found those sorts of sounds more frequent. That morning, he'd actually been humming a song from his childhood as he entered his lab. After a lifetime of feeling impotent in his inability to help his species, he finally stood to achieve his greatest ambition.

But it wasn't only that. It was also the soft, feminine morsel of a human who chose—yes *chose*—to share his chamber, who wished to serve him and this project. The prospect of seeing her through this pregnancy, of keeping her afterward, perhaps even using her for future projects, filled him with a buoyancy he'd never before experienced.

He snapped on a pair of gloves and dragged one fingertip down the pink heart of her core. Her responding shiver made him smile. The scent of her arousal made him shift on the stool, his cock suddenly heavy between his legs.

He spread her labia open and simply stared at the glistening flesh beneath.

Bayla's inner thighs contracted. "What, Master?"

"Hush, little girl. Your master wants to examine the sweetest pussy he's ever seen."

Another contraction of her inner thighs, this one accompanied by a clenching of her entire pelvic floor. Her anus and pussy both tightened and lifted.

He stroked a feather-light circle around her clit. "Don't be shy. No part of your body will ever be hidden from me. It's mine to study, to probe, to care for. Do you believe I will care for you, Bayla?"

"Yes," she whispered. For some reason, she sounded half broken by his words.

He touched the pad of his index finger to her clit and made a vibratory movement.

Another clenching. This time her entire pelvic lifted from the table.

"Do you need your master to give you relief before we start the examination?"

"Yes, Master."

"Do you deserve relief?" He was only teasing, but when she didn't answer, he lifted his head to meet her eyes.

Her lower lip was clenched between her teeth, and worry creased her brow.

He shook his finger over her clit again. "Are you going to beg for your master's cock again?" The image of *vecking* her ass while she was in the stirrups filled his mind and wouldn't leave. He should be more concerned with her examination, but somehow its importance receded.

He pushed his thumb into her pussy, dragging a choked moan from her. "Hmm?" He tapped her anus with his middle finger. "Do you want me here again?"

"If it pleases Master," she murmured. Her words sounded demure, but she'd spread her knees wider, lifting her pelvis and pushing her pussy onto his thumb, arching to grind over it.

"I think it would please your master." He yanked off his gloves and took two pumps of lubricant from the dispenser. His cock was out and in his hand a moment later, getting bathed in lubricant. He nudged the head against her back pucker. "Does your tight little ass remember who it belongs to?"

Her anus tensed and quivered against the sensitive flesh of his cockhead.

"Hmm? Or will I have to spank it first this time?"

"No, Master," she whimpered, and the ring of muscles relaxed.

He eased inside her, gripping her thighs to hold her steady as he slowly filled her.

"Ung...ung," she moaned. "So big," she panted. "Master is too big."

"Take it." Despite the command, he went slowly, his slave's well-being his highest concern. He would never want to tear the delicate tissue around her back entrance. He pushed her knees farther open and toward her shoulders, lifting her feet from the stirrups. "Lie still and take your master's cock. That little ass was made only for me." He didn't know why he would make such a ludicrous statement, except in that moment, it seemed true.

His cock. Her ass. He knew nothing but perfection, nothing but the glorious slide into the tightest hole, the knowledge that receiving him this way required her complete submission. To his authority. To his cock. If she tensed or resisted in any way, it would only cause her pain. Yet her surrender brought her pleasure.

He could see it in the way her eyes rolled back in her head, the slackness in her open mouth, the flutter of her belly as she drew in breath.

He thumbed her clit again, rubbing slowly and eliciting a mewl of pleasure. As he continued, her eyes flew open, knees cranked wider. He pumped into her ass with deep, smooth strokes, his thighs shaking with the effort of holding back. Because he wanted to pound into her so hard she saw stars into the following planet rotation.

"Please, Master," she pleaded, alarm registering on her beautiful face. The alarm that accompanied the blinking red readout on his arm cuff. *Ninety-five percent aroused. Orgasm imminent.*

He angled his hand down to shove his thumb in her pussy, the heel of his hand grinding down on her clit.

She screamed, body trembling, tears leaking from the corners of her eyes.

"That's it, beautiful. Come for your master." He *vecked* her harder, his cock pounding into her ass until he, too, wanted to beg and plead for release. "Hell, yes," he shouted, plunging in deep and staying there while he *vecked* her pussy with his thumb over and over again to her screams.

She wept through her climax, coming all over his thumb, her anus tightening so much it strangled his cock and probably hurt her.

He waited until she finished before he eased out, murmuring soothing endearments as he stroked a hand down her sweat-glistened belly. "Sweet girl. Beautiful girl. That's my good little slave. You took your master's cock so well, didn't you?"

Bayla's legs flopped open as if she'd lost the ability to hold them up. Her beautiful breasts bounced with her heaving breath. He stroked her clit tenderly. "Good girl." He dampened a washcloth and cleaned them both before he settled back onto the stool.

Even then, he wasn't in a hurry to begin his examination. He leaned forward and planted a tender kiss at the apex of Bayla's sex. He wanted to bottle the sighing sound she made and replay it through the day, reminding himself of how she made him feel like a *vecking* hero.

But he had work to do—important work that he loved. He slid the probe inside her vagina and flicked open the hologram projection of the interior of her uterus. There—the embryo. He leaned forward for a closer look, zooming the projection up. Had the embryo implanted in the wall of her uterus?

If it had, it was only barely. It didn't look the way he'd expected, the way the research had shown a human embryo would look after in vitro implantation.

All the sluggish pleasure from his orgasm evaporated as he stared at the hologram, consternation twisting in his solar plexus.

He needed to check her hormone level. Immediately. He stood abruptly, causing her head to jerk up, but he didn't meet her eyes. Instead, he paced to the counter and prepared a vial and needle to draw her blood.

~.~

Bayla tensed, holding her breath. What had Daneth seen? Had she succeeded in her attempt to thwart the pregnancy?

The tension radiating from Daneth ought to be a good sign to her, an indication she had succeeded. Why, then, did her belly churn like she was going to vomit?

"I thought you said no more shots," she said when he returned to her side with a needle, though she knew the difference between a blood draw and a shot.

"I need a blood sample." He spoke curtly, without looking at her. Totally preoccupied with his thoughts.

"What is it?" She didn't know why she tried to get information out of him now, when he'd never been inclined to share with her.

He punctured her arm, and she looked away, hating to see the blood leave her vein. "It's over," he clipped a moment later, surprising her. Despite his consternation, he still seemed to be in tune with her reactions.

"It's all right," she whispered, hating the heaviness tugging at her solar plexus, weighing down her chest.

Daneth moved with graceful precision as he performed some kind of test on her blood. His low curse at the results ratcheted her tension level higher. What did it show?

When he returned to her side, he held a syringe. "I misspoke earlier. You do require a shot today."

She nodded quickly because she deserved whatever pain he gave her. She deserved a lot worse than the prick of a needle.

He jabbed it into her flank and injected her with whatever he deemed necessary. She wasn't going to ask the contents this time. There was none of the intimacy of being held over his lap this time, only the quick, practiced movements of a physician with his patient.

Her chest ached.

Daneth removed the needle and lifted his gaze. "I'm sorry."

His apology stabbed her heart. She was sure which was worse—the heaviness in his voice or the irony that the one time her arrogant doctor lowered himself to ask *her* forgiveness, she didn't deserve it.

"Is everything all right?"

"The implantation does not appear secure, and hormone levels are not where I expected them. I'm going to monitor you closely over the next few days. Hopefully, I can encourage the correct environment to support the embryo."

She didn't know whether she was relieved or disappointed to hear the pregnancy attempt wasn't over yet, and the confusion, the not knowing only increased her nausea. "I don't feel well." She swung her legs over the edge of the bed.

Daneth caught her in his arms before she managed to hit the floor. "What do you mean you don't feel well?"

"I need to throw up."

He set her back down and handed her a receptacle, which she filled with her breakfast. "Baby," he said softly when she finished, sympathy dragging out his tones. "I'm sorry. It was probably the hormones. I'll get a washcloth." He returned with a warm, wet towel, which he used to wipe her mouth and face. "Come, sweetness. Let's get you into bed."

She couldn't bring herself to protest the tender treatment she certainly didn't deserve as Daneth scooped her into his arms and carried her to his sleepdisk.

She rolled onto her side and closed her eyes, pretending to sleep.

What had she done? Her very soul was ripping from her body.

She wondered if she'd made a mistake. A horrible mistake.

˜.˜

Daneth knew Bayla's scent was wrong the moment he woke the next morning. He'd noticed she didn't smell as sweet the planet rotation before but had convinced himself he was imagining things. But, now, as she lay sprawled out like a sleeping goddess on his sleepdisk, he couldn't deny the slightly metallic scent to her flesh. No being with that aroma could maintain a pregnancy. Gathering her to his chest, he crooned softly in her ear as he picked her up and carried her to his lab. "Sorry to wake you, beautiful girl. It's all right."

"What is it?" she croaked, rubbing her eyes. He eased her onto his table. Her cheeks were flushed a pretty pink from slumber, and her dark waves fell across her face in messy perfection.

"I need to check you again." He put on his gloves, lubricated the probe, and inserted it into Bayla's warm body. The hologram verified what he already knew in his heart. The embryo had failed to implant. No sign of it appeared on the projection.

A great weight descended upon his shoulders.

"What do you see, Master?" Bayla whispered, eyes wide.

"It didn't take." He dropped his head into his hands, the disappointment too huge to conceal.

"I'm sorry." Her voice wavered. When he lifted his gaze, he found her lower lip trembled and tears glistened in her eyes.

"Bayla," he choked, his throat closing. "It's not your fault, sweet girl. I don't know what went wrong." He stood and sighed. "I suppose I should check your hormone levels again. The cocktail I gave you must not have been the right formulation for your particular body." He rubbed his forehead. "I don't understand it."

Bayla lay still as he collected a fresh sample of her blood and tested it. Like the previous planet rotation, the sample did not show the rise in hormones he had expected with a pregnancy, even when he'd augmented them with synthetics.

Veck.

Well, at least he had one remaining egg. He could try to create another embryo. It would be his last hope.

~.~

Guilt crunched like broken vows in her belly. It scratched at her skin, rasped in her throat.

Daneth—her master who had shown her more patience and kindness than any master she'd had, the male who lost control every time she used sex as a weapon—suffered greatly because of what she'd done.

He'd said little all planet rotation, but he'd rubbed his face or buried his head in his hands more times than she could count. He'd worked in his lab for the entire morning then, the rest of the planet rotation, he'd paced and frowned and rubbed his face some more.

She gnawed her own lip raw watching him, experiencing his distress as if it were her own.

Had she made the wrong choice? She'd only been trying to protect herself. She hadn't wanted to be used as a vessel, to have another child taken from her. But now she felt profoundly selfish. Daneth was trying to do something big—much bigger than himself. His desire to create a Zandian child was not for his own gain, but to save his species. And she'd destroyed his best chance at it.

Worse still, she wasn't sure she wished him success with his last-ditch effort to create another embryo. Because she would be the receptacle. She would be losing another baby.

But maybe it would be worth it. A sacrifice for the species. Not her species, but not a bad species. No one wanted to see a species go extinct. Not when there was a chance to save it. Yes, it was her duty. If Daneth was able to create another embryo, she would offer her body up. No more parsley tea.

"This evening is our weekly meal," Daneth told Bayla when he returned to his chamber.

She sat up from where she'd been lounging in her open cage.

"Every ten planet rotations we eat. We all dine together in the great hall. You don't have to come, but I'll bring you if you like."

She crawled out of the cage. "I'd love to." She'd been bored as hell since she arrived on the pod, not that she was complaining. She'd been enjoying the lack of work and the luxurious surroundings. But getting out and observing the Zandians interacting together would be far better than staying cooped up alone.

"I bought you some clothes." He tossed a wrapped package on the sleep-disk. His face sagged, appearing haggard and tired, as if he'd just passed forty planet rotations without sleep.

No one had ever bought her anything before. Despite her guilt, she couldn't stop the pitter patter of excitement that rose up in her as she peeled back the paper of the neatly wrapped package. Inside lay a silky blue garment, the exact shade of her eyes. She picked it up and gasped. The fabric was so soft and fine, it slid through her fingers like a live being. "It's beautiful," she breathed.

Daneth didn't reply, only glancing absently in her direction before changing his clothing. The light had truly dimmed behind his eyes, leaving nothing but a shell of the male she'd come to...*love?* Surely not. Yet why else would she care more about his fate than her own? Care enough to sacrifice what was left of her mothering soul to give up another child?

`She slipped it on—a skin-hugging sheath that clung to her curves all the way to her knees. The halter top tied behind her neck and plunged into a sexy vee between her breasts.

Daneth turned and then stopped, his mouth falling open. "Oh *veck*. You can't wear that."

She tugged the hem of the dress down, ran her hands over her hips. Did she look too round? Too risque? "Why not?"

Daneth rubbed his jaw. "I'll have to fight the unmated males off you."

"I'll take it off." She wasn't about to be contrary with him that night, not after she'd caused his present state of misery.

"No," he said sharply. "No. I want to look at you in it. You're so beautiful. I need something as breathtaking as you to keep my mind off...things. But if any male touches you—"

"I won't let anyone touch me," she said quickly.

A muscle in his jaw jumped. "You'd better not. Take off your panties."

"Pardon me?"

"You heard me. Take off your panties. I want to know that hot pussy is bare and waiting for my touch during dinner." He stalked toward her with the intensity of a predator.

She sucked in a breath, the sharp thrill of seeing the life back in him too pleasurable to move.

"Too slow." He twirled her to face the sleepdisk and bent her over it, rucking the dress up to her waist.

She reached back to pull off her panties, but he beat her to it, yanking them down to her ankles in a rough movement. His hand came down in a flurry of spanks, peppering her bare ass and the backs of her thighs. He slapped her legs open and spanked her pussy. He didn't say a word as he spanked, and while he slapped hard and steady, she didn't get the impression that he was angry with her.

No, he was *marking* her. Leaving his prints on her flesh to remind her she belonged to him—only him.

And she loved it. The pain registered only as heat and sensation, as the beginning of pleasure.

He spanked her until her entire ass, pussy, and upper thighs radiated heat, and then he stopped, rubbing his palm over the stinging flesh. "Good girl," he murmured. "You take your spankings like a good girl."

"Yes, Master," she murmured.

Except she hadn't been a good girl. She'd been a very, very bad girl.

CHAPTER SEVEN

If it hadn't been for Bayla shining like the brightest star, he wouldn't have been able to contain his foul mood. His failure to successfully implant the embryo weighed on him, heavier than an airship. But no matter how many times he reviewed the protocol, he couldn't find his error. Somehow, for some reason, Bayla's body had rejected the embryo. But why? His program had chosen her as the best possible vessel.

Hell, she practically screamed fertility. Those wide hips and ample breasts mimicked her big eyes and lush mouth. She probably had birthed her previous young in her sleep. He'd had no worries for how she'd carry through the pregnancy or how her birth would go.

Lamira, on the other hand, had always worried him. She'd been too thin to begin with, and her belly had grown too large considering she still had thirty planet rotations to go, if the young went by human gestation. If it went by Zandian, she'd have forty-five.

They were late to the table. Prince Zander and his mate were already seated at the head of the long table, joined by visitors from the training pod—Lamira's sister, Lily, and her Zandian mate, Rok, as well as Chief of Security Lundric, and his human mate, Cambry. Leora sat with them, but her mate, Seke, the Master of Arms, was missing.

Thinking Bayla would enjoy sitting with other human females, he claimed seats near the head of the table and introduced his lovely slave to every being. She curtsied and kept her eyes lowered, saying little, but Lundric's red-haired female immediately drew her into conversation.

For his part, he could scarcely pay attention. All he could think about was the last remaining Zandian egg.

Chef Barr and his staff brought out plate after plate heaped with food, but he had no appetite. Nor, it seemed, did Bayla, which was unusual for her. Perhaps the strange company made her nervous. He reached under the table to squeeze her hand.

"We require full surveillance of Zandia as it stands now," Rok was saying to Prince Zander. "We cannot make plans for the invasion without an updated view of things."

Zander frowned. "You're suggesting I send ships into Zandian airspace?"

"Yes, my lord."

"The moment a ship is spotted, the Finn will know we're behind it. All these solar cycles, I've led them to believe I am the pitiable refugee here, happy simply to have survived. They've left me alone because they believe I'm no threat. If they discover we sent battleships into their airspace, we lose all element of surprise."

"We won't be seen," Rok promised. Lundric nodded in agreement.

"How many ships?"

"Just one. Lundric and Cambry will fly it."

Bayla had been listening without making her interest obvious, but the news a human female would fly a ship brought her lovely dark head up.

Cambry gave her a wink.

Zander looked to Lamira. His mate possessed extrasensory perception, the kind more common in the Venusian species. Zandian crystal had increased her ability to sense and read energy. Lamira murmured something only Zander could hear.

"Very well. Permission granted. When will you go?"

"We'll wait for the Finn's next scheduled trade shipment and fly in under the cover of those ships and activity. Two weeks from this planet rotation."

Zander nodded.

Bayla still stared with seeming wonder that the human female could fly a ship. "Do you fly, too?" she asked Lily, then flushed. "Forgive me if my question is inapprop—"

"Yes, I've learned as well. I'm not as good as Cambry or her brother, Tal, but I love it. We have an entire human army training to take back Zandia—had you not heard?"

Bayla shook her head.

Cambry considered her. "Would you like to join?"

Daneth stiffened. "Her work is here with me." He made his tone hard. No one was taking Bayla from him. He'd bought her. She belonged to him. Hell, she'd still chosen him when Zander set her free.

Still, a cold fist of fear gripped his trachea at the thought of her choosing to leave. If she wasn't pregnant, he'd have no reason to insist she remain.

. . .

Bayla sat up straighter. Hearing the human females had learned to pilot ships and were serving in an army to take back Zandia cracked the reality she'd been living and set it on its side. These women were willing to serve Zandia. They weren't just sacrificing their attachment to babies, they were willing to lay their lives on the line for the Zandian species.

It made what she'd done all the worse. She wished to Sacred Mother Earth she could take it back. Undo the wrong. Save the embryo she'd so callously discarded. All for what? To save her already broken heart? How stupid and small. How cowardly.

She hated herself for what she'd done.

"What is it?" Prince Zander's sharp voice cut across her self-loathing.

The princess—or his mate, whatever, clung to the table with an expression on her face Bayla knew all too well.

She stood up, heading toward the princess. "Are you having a contraction?"

Lamira nodded, seeming unable to speak. The intensity of her contraction seemed stronger than the practice waves that came weeks before a baby is born.

Lamira's mother also stood, as did Daneth, and the prince, who moved to pick her up.

"Wait until it's over," Bayla said sharply, forgetting she was speaking to the prince. She knew what it was like to be touched or moved when in the middle of a contraction, and it wasn't pleasant. "My lord," she added.

"Is this the first you've had?" Bayla asked with concern.

Lamira shook her head. "Every...ten minutes," she gasped, eyes squeezing shut."

"For how long?"

"An hour."

The prince had frozen, his eyes only on his mate, his fear and concern evident.

Bayla scooted up by Lamira's side, tracing her fingertips over the woman's back in a light figure eight pattern, the way the midwives had taught her.

"It's too early for the baby, isn't it, Doctor Daneth?" Leora asked.

Daneth's mouth tightened, brow drew down tight on his forehead. "It is. Four weeks early by human standard. More by Zandian. Let's get her into my lab."

"Give it a moment to pass," she said. It may not be her place to give orders, but if there was one thing she knew, it was pregnancy and childbirth.

Lamira's white-knuckled fingers slowly eased their grip on the table, and she panted. "All right," she gasped. "It's all right."

Zander surged into action, scooping his mate into his arms and carrying her from the table. Daneth led the way to his lab. She, Leora, and Lily trailed behind, Leora and Lily exchanging a worried glance.

In the lab, Daneth placed the probe on Lamira's belly and opened up the hologram. He studied it for a tense moment. "The young looks healthy. No sign of stress." He glanced at Zander. "Any...ah...wetness or bleeding from the vagina?"

Zander glowered at the doctor.

"No." Lamira shook her head.

Daneth returned his attention to the hologram and measured the length of the fetus, from head to toe, then the width of the skull. "Size is small for a Zandian, large for a human fetus at this stage." He sighed and turned to face Zander. "Either way, he's not fully grown."

Zander's horns stiffed, and he looked positively lethal, as if he wanted to draw the sword strapped to his waist and slay them all. "Will he survive if born early?"

Daneth hesitated. "Yes, it's possible."

Bayla drew a breath of courage to speak. "Give her a glass of wine."

All heads turned to her, everyone blinking in amazement. Daneth gave a dismissive shake of his head, frowning. "Alcohol is contraindicated during pregnancy."

"It can stop preterm labor."

"Enough," Daneth snapped. "I will not endanger the health of the young—"

"How many pregnancies have you attended?" Her chest and chin lifted in challenge.

Daneth drew back slightly. "Only this one," he admitted.

She pointed at her own chest. "One hundred and forty-three. I may not be a doctor, but I do know babies."

"Get her the wine," Zander snapped, and Leora immediately left the lab for it. "What else?" he asked Bayla.

"You need to get her out of that position," she said, indicating Lamira's dead beetle configuration. "Get the baby's head off her cervix. Can you bring her to your sleepdisk where she can get comfortable?"

Zander immediately scooped up his mate, causing Daneth to jerk his instruments away before they were knocked to the ground.

Bayla stood back to let them pass. She twisted her fingers, watching Daneth grimly pack his equipment into a bag. "Forgive me, Master."

He gave a quick shake of his head. "No. I appreciate your input. You are right. My experience is limited." He slid a hand around her waist to guide her out of the lab. "Let's hope your primitive methods work."

She breathed a sigh of relief that he wasn't angry with her. It was short-lived, though, because a new worry planted itself in her mind.

What if Lamira had drunk the parsley tea?

Her stomach flip flopped like a sea animal out of water. Fear seized her, making her muscles so tight she wondered how she managed to move. Her world tunneled into the smallest sphere. All she knew was that she had to stop this preterm labor. She had to stop it or she'd never be able to live with herself. Of course, living wouldn't be an option if the prince found out she'd caused this.

They entered the prince's chamber. "What position?" he snapped the moment she walked in.

"Knees and forearms, to tip the baby down toward your ribs." She spoke to Lamira, who nodded and climbed into the described position.

Leora entered, followed by a servant who carried a pouch of wine with a straw. "Here's the wine," Leora said, taking it from the servant and bringing it to her daughter. She placed the tube in Lamira's mouth, and Lamira sipped.

"What else?" Prince Zander was looking at her, not Daneth.

"There's an herb." Her heart thundered and she worked hard to draw slower breaths. "Nettle leaf? Do you have that here?"

"I'll find out," Lily said, and exited.

"It's a matter of plenty of fluids and relaxation." She climbed up beside Lamira and traced the pattern on her back again. When she found Zander glowering, she backed off. "You can do this—light figure eights on her back. Or a light stroking of her ears. It calms the system."

Zander nodded, moving in with the determination of a man who'd trained his entire life for the task.

What else? She fought down her terror to remember what she'd learned. "Imagine there's a dial that controls how strong the contractions are," she instructed Lamira. "You're going to use your mind to turn that dial down. Later, when it's time for the baby to come, you can use it to hurry labor along, if you need. Understand?"

Lamira panted through another contraction. "I...don't know how," she gasped.

"Yes you do. Your mind has so much more control that you know. Simply tell your body to slow the contractions until they stop."

Lamira grunted and panted, but her body relaxed sooner than it had the last time. She drank several swallows of the wine.

"How long must I stay like this?"

"It's enough if you're tired. Rest."

The princess dropped to her side. Zander curled his much larger body around hers, cradling her from behind.

Fear still threatened to burst her chest. She wanted to ask Lamira about the tea. If she'd had some, she needed to tell Daneth so he might prepare some kind of cure. If there were any. But how did she ask without revealing her terrible secret?

Lamira lifted weary eyes to her. "Thank you," she said. "I think it's working."

Bayla tried to swallow around the tight band closing her throat. "Good," she whispered. "I'm sorry to say you must stay in bed for the rest of the preg-nancy. Bed rest will reduce the chances of early labor continuing or returning."

Lamira rubbed her belly. "I didn't drink the tea."

Bayla's body jerked in shock. The blood drained from her face.

"What tea?" Zander asked.

"I knew it would harm the baby."

Icicles formed on all Bayla's limbs.

"What would harm the baby?" Zander thundered, sitting up.

Daneth, too, turned his full attention on her, advancing slowly.

She took a step backward, eyes filling with tears. "I'm sorry. I did a horrible thing and"—she choked on her own spit— "I can't take it back." Tears spilled down her cheeks. "I wish I could."

"What horrible thing?" Daneth's voice was barely more than a whisper. She turned her focus to Daneth. "I'm sorry. I drank a tea so the pregnancy wouldn't take. I didn't want to have another infant taken from my arms. It hurt too much."

Daneth turned a ghostly white.

Prince Zander climbed off the bed, but Daneth blocked him from coming toward her.

"She's mine," he bit out, though horror, fury, and disgust warred on his expression. "I'll deal with her."

"Did you offer the tea to Lamira?" The prince's voice was deadly.

She shook her head quickly. "Never. Of course not. Barr brought it to her, but I ran here as quickly as I could and drank it before she did."

Zander pursed his lips, dark musing in his violet eyes.

"Go to my chamber." Daneth's voice couldn't sound more cold.

She didn't wait to be told twice, practically running out the door and bumping into Lily on her way. She couldn't stop the tears skidding down her cheeks as she raced back to Daneth's chamber.

~.~

Daneth saw through room through a haze of red. Betrayal coated his insides, hot and thick. Sticky and grotesque. He wanted to empty the contents of his stomach.

"If you'll excuse me," he said stiffly to the prince and Lamira.

"Yes, I doubt you're much good to us now, anyway," Zander muttered.

"I'll be back." He wasn't sure how he was able to speak when his lips had frozen.

He didn't remember how he got back to his chamber.

Bayla sat on his sleepdisk, twisting her fingers in her lap.

"Clothing off."

She moved quickly to obey, jumping to her feet and pulling the dress over her head.

Somehow, the exquisite perfection of her body only taunted him now. His cock still responded, despite what she'd done, and it made him all the angrier. Such a beautiful, agreeable package. And yet so flawed. She'd ruined everything—*everything*. His life's work, down the drain. The continuation of the Zandian species—over. But somehow the worst of all was *her*. What she'd done to him. The way his insides felt pulled out, tied in a knot, and shoved down his throat. The way he didn't know whether to throw her out or lock her up or just shake her until her teeth rattled. The sticky confusion inside him that screamed for him to distance himself before it was too late—and it was already too late—and to simultaneously dig in deeper with Bayla. To punish her. To turn her as inside out as she'd turned him. He selected a heavy wooden paddle from the implement box.

"Bend over the side of the sleepdisk."

Bayla's eyes pleaded for mercy, but she didn't argue or attempt to explain herself. She leaned over the edge of the sleepdisk, presenting her shapely ass for his punishment. Already, his handprints from earlier had faded.

Capturing her wrists, he pulled them up above her head. "Keep these here. If you reach back, or change position, you'll earn an additional punishment. Understand?"

"Yes, Master."

He closed his eyes, a wave of crushing disappointment rolling through him, making him sway on his feet.

He'd punish her. Nothing else could be done until he'd settled the score. He opened his eyes and drew back his arm. He brought the paddle down smartly across the center of Bayla's ass. He'd delivered three quick and powerful strokes before she let out a high-pitched scream that shot straight through the center of his trunk and out the other side.

He stopped, horrified that he'd elicited such a sound from her. He checked his cuff and found her pulse too elevated, the signs of stress too high.

Veck.

She gasped for breath, her back heaving on the mattress.

"Too hard," he muttered, rubbing away the bright red bloom of color.

"Yes!" she agreed.

He rubbed her flesh vigorously to reduce any possibility of bruising. Despite his fury with Bayla, he would never cause her real harm, and the idea he'd gone too far sickened him.

Her buttocks and legs trembled beneath his palm, and her back still heaved with sobs, but they were slowing.

He picked up the heavy paddle and tossed it into his waste receptacle. With his superior strength, he never needed to wield such an implement. Hadn't he made her cry with his hand alone?

But what she'd done warranted far more than a hand spanking. He selected a thin, reedy cane. It would bite her flesh and cause significant pain without going as thuddy or deep as the paddle.

Bayla hadn't moved from her position, but she turned her face in his direction. He brought the cane down against his leg to measure its bite, and her slender shoulders hunched.

Standing at her side, he lined the cane up to cut across both her buttocks and let it swing. Bayla rose up on both her tiptoes, a choked gasp sounding in her throat. It left a neat white line across her reddened buttocks. He flicked the cane again and left a second stripe.

Bayla let out a sob.

He snapped the cane again and again. There was a satisfaction in leaving the stripes across her clenching bottom. As her distress mounted, his eased, and a sense of calm settled over him.

He struck again. Bayla cried out. He checked his cuff. *Forty percent aroused.* It had been zero when he used the paddle. There was something about the measured pain that excited her. He continued caning her, striping down her buttocks to her upper thighs.

"Reach back and pull open your ass cheeks," he commanded.

Her hands crawled back and parted her plump, punished cheeks for him.

He lowered his wrist and angled the cane on the vertical. With far less power, he struck her between her buttocks, along the line of the crack, punishing her tender, clenching bottom hole.

She shrieked, her body popping off the bed. "No, please, Master!" She threw herself at the floor by his feet, wrapping her arms around his ankles. Then, probably remembering his dictate to remain in position, she surged back up and laid over the sleepdisk, her beautiful body trembling.

Something about her subservience—the desperate throwing herself at his feet—brought a surge of satisfaction. Of dominance and power. His cock thickened, and punishing became more of a pleasure than the desperate need to rebalance the scales.

"One more round for leaving position."

She wept into the covers.

He gave her four more stripes crisscrossing across the neat, even row he'd left before. "Pull your cheeks apart."

Despite her obvious misery, she remained in complete submission, reaching back to pull open her buttocks. He delivered one last spank to her crack and pulled her floating cage over to them, lowering it to the level of the sleepdisk.

"In your cage, now."

She crawled right in and stayed on her knees, her chest pressed to the mat, her hands reaching back to cover her welted bottom.

It was an adorable sight, one that eased his remaining anger. He rather enjoyed seeing her as a punished and sorry girl.

She'd made a mistake. One with terrible repercussions for him and his species. But she'd been punished and was sorry. He'd made many mistakes, too. He should have realized a human might develop an attachment to the baby she grew in her body. He'd been an idiot not to consider it.

He leaned his face against the cage. "You should have told me you didn't want the young taken from you. I would have let you raise it, if that was your desire."

Bayla drew in a great shuddering breath, her eyes red, cheeks wet with tears. "I didn't know," she wailed. "I was s-so stupid!"

"No, not stupid," he said firmly. "Never that. You were afraid. I should have asked more questions."

"I w-won't do it again. I promise. Can you culture another embryo?"

The brick returned to his solar plexus. "I'm going to try right now." Heaviness descended into his whole being.

He reached a hand through the bars of her cage and brushed the tears from her face. "Go to sleep, Bayla."

CHAPTER EIGHT

Bayla received punishment in every dream that night. Daneth whipped her, spanked her, paddled her, flogged her naked body again and again and, while she wept and mourned his anger, she never wanted it to stop. She deserved his punishment.

She needed it.

Only from him. In one dream, Prince Zander had picked up a leather strap and stalked to where she hung, suspended naked from the ceiling by her wrists.

She'd been terrified, but then Daneth had come and taken the strap from him.

She's mine, he'd said.

Yes, she'd wept. Had opened her legs wide for him to whip her pussy.

She woke to an orgasm, though she hadn't been touching herself. Her ass still hurt, but she loved the pain. She reached back to squeeze her cheeks, reactivating it.

The chamber was quiet—no sign of Daneth. She'd heard him come in long after she fell asleep, and then leave again before dawn.

She tested the door of the cage. Open. Daneth never locked her in. She rather loved that about him. He kept a cage for her but didn't lock it. She couldn't begin to understand why she adored her cage so much. Probably because it was hers. She'd never had her own belongings before, especially not plush, luxurious things like the cage and its furnishings.

She crawled out and padded to the washroom. After using the facilities and cleaning in the washtube, she emerged and dressed.

She didn't want to leave the chamber for breakfast. Daneth hadn't forbidden her to leave, yet she felt she ought to be confined. Or maybe she didn't want to see what the Zandians in the pod thought of her now. Assuming they all knew.

The sound of something smashing made her jump. It had come from Daneth's lab. She hit the panel that opened door to his lab and stopped short when she saw Daneth—her beautiful scientist—destroying his lab. Shattered fragments of equipment lay scattered across the floor. Daneth picked up a heavy instrument and flung it against a wall. When it didn't completely shatter, he picked it up again and repeated the action until nothing but small shards remained.

"Daneth," she whispered.

His head jerked up, and the misery she saw in his eyes made her heart stop.

"It-it didn't work?" she forced the words out of her numb lips.

He shook his head. "No more eggs. The last viable one died in you."

A sob choked her throat, but she held it back. Daneth needed her to be strong now. Weeping for what she'd done wouldn't help anything. "I'm sorry," she croaked. "You'll have half-breeds. Lamira's baby. You could breed me for more."

He stared at her, his expression haunted. "You think I'd ever let another male near you for breeding?"

She drew back. "Not another male. With you."

His lips curled in disbelief. *Me?* My genes are not worth breeding. I'm not a warrior. I'm nothing. An old scientist who never accomplished anything for his species.

"That's not true."

She had to shake him out of this desperation. Punishing her last night had soothed him—she'd seen the change in him, had loved it. If only she could get him to do it again, now. Change his focus, remind him of his power and virility.

She pulled off her clothing and cupped her own breasts. "This body was made for breeding, Master."

A tic sprang in Daneth's temple.

"Was made for your cock."

His nostrils flared.

She slid one hand down her belly to curl her fingers between her legs. "This pussy needs you. Claiming it. Punishing. Buried deep inside."

"*Veck,*" he cursed, stalking toward her. "What did I tell you about touching yourself?" Anger flashed in his eyes.

It went far beyond her breaking the rule about touching herself, but she didn't mind having it directed at her. Better her than his precious equipment. She could handle her male. How she knew that, she wasn't sure, but she did.

"You said I'd be punished." She dared him with her words, invited his chastisement. They needed this now.

He closed the distance between them in a few short steps, tossed her over his shoulder, and clapped her on the ass with his open palm. He continued spanking her all the way to his room, but when he set her down, the burn of his focus had the flames of desire behind it.

She cupped her mons again, goading him, taunting him. In a flash, she was on her back on the sleepdisk. He climbed over her and stretched her arms taut overhead, fastening her wrists to a ring on his headboard.

She spread her legs, bending her knees to give him the full view of her soaked pussy.

"*Veck*," he swore angrily, shoving her knees wider, pressing them flat against the bed. "You think to tease me with that pussy? *Me?* Your master? I *own* this pussy." He freed his cock from his leggings and gave his thick length a stroke. "I own you, Bayla."

She arched her pelvis, thrusting her tits toward the ceiling, writhing for his touch, no matter how roughly it came.

And it came rough. It came with a force that knocked her breath away. Daneth shoved into her without preparation—not that she needed it. Her pussy ached for him. Dripped for him. She needed him inside to complete her very essence. And when he took her with such force, it only felt right.

After what she'd done. After she'd deprived him of his life's work. A Zandian child. Her pussy.

Well she hadn't denied him her pussy, but she'd certainly teased and tempted him with it. Now, it was finally his. He'd found home, as far as she was concerned.

He surged over her, riding her like a she was a wild beast that required taming.

"Bad girl," he chanted, slapping her breast before plunging in and out of her again. He repeated the pattern: *in-out-in-out-slap*. Her other breast got it.

Her guttural moan screamed sex. Shouted wanton desire. Lust. Need. "Punish me, Master."

He bared his teeth, driving into her with such force he would've slammed her into the headboard if he hadn't braced her shoulder with one arm. "You like to get *vecked* by me?" he growled. "*Hard?* Like this?"

It didn't seem right to say *yes* because it felt too much like punishment, so, instead, she said, "I need it, Master."

His eyes glinted with satisfaction. "You do, don't you?" He continued to slam into her so deep. So hard. So good.

She couldn't help the noises he knocked out of her with each brutal stroke. Lurid sexual cries. Wild beast sounds.

"Bad, bad girl." He slammed in and out. Slapped her breast then slapped her face. Not hard. Not nearly as hard as he'd slapped her breast. But in the most satisfying way possible.

Her pussy turned to liquid heat.

"Oh *veck*, Bayla," he rasped. The sound of her name on his lips nearly made her weep. It sounded so intimate, so personal after he'd been calling her *bad girl.* She knew deep in her soul that she and she alone had been responsible for this loss of control in him. This animalistic response his body had to hers. No —his *being* had to hers.

As broken as they were, as she'd made them, they belonged together, magnetized by more than fate. By their very essence.

"Bayla." His voice cracked as if he might be the one to weep this time. He pointed at her. "Don't you dare come. You do not have my permission to come. You're a bad girl."

"Yes," she agreed, though his dominance put her so close to the edge it was painful. He pounded deep, two, three more times, then buried his dick to the hilt and came.

Though she tried to lie still, to simply be a receptacle with no pleasure of her own, her body recognized his release and instantly climaxed, her internal muscles squeezing his cock, pulling his rainbow essence up into her womb.

Daneth groaned like his finish pained him. He pulled out, pulled back, out of breath. With one quick movement, he flipped her to her belly. The position of her arms pained her—they were pulled up too high.

"Master, please—my arms."

He must have recognized her dilemma because he instantly commanded her cuffs release. "Give me your hands."

She obeyed and he clipped her cuffs together at the small of her back. Then he shoved a bolster pillow under her hips, lifting her ass.

She thought he might spank her again, but he parted her cheeks and dropped a blob of slippery lubricant between her cheeks.

"Did you think if you offered me your pussy, your ass would be safe from me?"

Unsure if he wanted a real answer to that question, she kept her mouth shut.

"No, I'm going to *veck* this little ass until every part of you knows I've been there. That I own this ass." He slapped her thighs open. "And this naughty pussy." He delivered a series of quick spanks to her swollen, still-pulsing pussy.

She heard the smack of him lubricating his cock. How he managed to get it hard again so quickly, she couldn't imagine.

He pushed both her cheeks wide, and the head of his cock nudged her back entrance. A shiver of fear and excitement ran through her. "Afraid of me, Bayla?" His voice was low and wicked, as if he savored such a thing.

"A-a little." She was, but only in a make-believe way. Daneth would never truly harm her body. He would never damage her. Hadn't he unclipped her wrists when she whined?

"This is how you learn surrender," he growled, breaching her tight entrance.

She willed her muscles to relax, to accept his full malehood, his dominance.

He filled her too full with his cock, so thick and long. He stretched her and used her, pulling at the top of her pelvis to angle it up, exactly the way he wanted it. He gripped her bound wrists and used them for leverage.

She moaned and yowled like an animal in heat. "Take me, take my ass," she babbled, pleading for what, she didn't know. "I'm your bad girl. I've been such a bad girl."

"Yes," he snarled, but she noticed his movements were far more careful this time. He didn't take her roughly, the way he had when she'd been on her back. Though he filled her beyond what was comfortable, he kept his strokes even and straight, didn't shove or jerk erratically.

He lowered his body over hers, one hand wriggling under her pelvis to cup her mons. Two of his fingers plunged into her wet heat. "You wish I was here instead, don't you?" His gravelly voice was right at her ear.

"Y-yes. No. I-I don't know."

He continued to pound her ass. "You don't know?" The heel of his hand ground into her clit as he pushed a third finger inside her. "You know you *deserve* my cock in your ass, don't you?"

"Yes," she gasped, stars already exploding in her vision. Daneth owned her body completely. If he'd turned her inside out, he couldn't have owned her more. He owned her ass, her pussy, her clit, her ears. He owned her mind. Her heart.

Yes, Daneth had truly put her heart in chains the day he'd collared her.

"I already came once. Do you know what that means?"

"No," she gasped, her body vibrating—trembling with the oncoming climax.

"It means I can *veck* your ass all. Planet. Rotation." He thrust extra deep on the last words and undulated the hand cupping her mons.

She went off like a turbo blaster, pussy squeezing his fingers in waves, ass still stretched wide open. "I'm sorry," she sobbed, maybe not truthfully. Sorry she had disobeyed or disappointed, not sorry for the most intense orgasm of her life. Not sorry for the climax still rippling through her tender body.

Daneth bit her neck and continued working her pussy and pumping into her ass until his legs shook and he buried deep and stayed. When his cock stopped pulsing, he covered her body with his, draping her with his warmth. "Intoxicating human," he groaned. "How can you have such a hold on me? I can't be near you without losing all control."

Daneth managed to separate his body from Bayla's, which seemed a far more difficult task than it should be. It was as if their bodies had melded together, becoming not two separate beings, but a third unrecognizable beast.

He hadn't meant to *veck* her so brutally. Hadn't meant to *veck* her at all. In fact, he hadn't wanted to see her again. Not until he'd controlled his temper. Not until he'd forgiven her.

Yet she'd made it unavoidable. She'd begged for it. Tempting him with that body. Yielding to him with such grace. She only made him think he was in control. But in actuality, *she'd* been controlling *him* from the very beginning, hadn't she?

He may be the one holding the whip, but she chose to take her whippings. She bent so easily, she'd never break. And in the end...in the end, maybe he'd been broken.

He'd lost everything. The hopes and dreams of a Zandian restart. The project he'd nursed for so many solar cycles. The last viable Zandian egg.

Not just that. He'd lost his mind. Probably his very soul, because he didn't know who he became when he was with Bayla.

And he hadn't forgiven her. The sex took the edge off his anger, but the underlying resentment was still there. The simmering anger at what she'd done. The sense of betrayal.

He needed to get away from her. He needed some space to find his head again. To decide what to do with the slave who was no longer of use to him.

Except that lie made his chest implode. She may not be of scientific use, but he could certainly think of a great many uses for her. Most of them involved her on her back with her legs spread. His mouth sucking on one of those pouty nipples until she got wet. Or sucking on her core, tasting her tangy essence while she writhed and wriggled in his grasp.

But he wanted to be cruel to her, too. Wanted to take a leather strap to her ass every planet rotation, keep her sore and sorry, surrendered. And that wasn't fair. He might actually hurt her, like he almost had the night before.

And keeping her close to him wouldn't help him find control.

He stalked into the washroom and shucked his clothing, and stepped into the washtube. Better to wash Bayla's scent from his body. Erase her from his mind. He needed space. Quiet. Sanity.

When he stepped out, clean and damp, he'd firmed his resolve. He put on his clothes and returned to the chamber.

Bayla lay in the same position he'd left her—humped over the bolster, her ass on display, legs parted. She still wore marks from her caning the night before. Neat red intersecting lines decorated her pale skin. Her dark hair spread out on the coverlet in silky waves.

He realized she probably hadn't moved because he'd left her cuffed there. "Release cuffs," he commanded, and the wrist cuffs fell apart.

"Wash and dress and gather up your things. I'm moving you to your own room."

She hadn't moved from position, but now she jerked up to sit. "Why?"

"I wish you to remain out of my sight."

Her beautiful, bow-shaped lips parted, long-lashed doll eyes blinked. She scrambled to stand. "We had a bargain." She sounded stronger than he'd expected, proof her submission was a farce. "I agreed to stay as your slave."

His lips tightened. "If you wish, I will return you to the Ocretions."

The color drained from her face but she jerked her chin into the air, grabbing her clothing from the floor and marching to the washroom. "That won't be necessary. I'll stay out of your sight."

Odd. His mind ran in several directions. He wanted to laugh at how cute she was mad almost as much as he had to fight the overarching need to soothe her. But this was what he wanted. Bayla out of his hair. What did he care if she threw herself a fit over it?

Clearing his throat for no one in particular, he left the chamber. He needed to get the servants to clean up the mess he'd made in his lab and to arrange a chamber for Bayla. After that, she was on her own. Not forever. Until he knew his own mind again. Until he had control of his emotions and stopped thinking with his cock. Until he was sure he was the master and not her slave.

CHAPTER NINE

Bayla knocked on the prince's door to check on Lamira. Though she'd showered and dressed, she felt anything but refreshed. A crushing weight pushed on her chest. Her joints had turned brittle, like she'd aged forty solar cycles. Cold numbness started in her hands and feet and crept its way up to her trunk.

The door slid open. Lamira lay propped up on the sleep disk, Lily, Leora, and Cambry by her side.

Bayla hesitated. The princess probably didn't want her there, not when she had the women of her family to support her.

"Come in." Lamira's green eyes searched Bayla's face with sympathy. She held a hand out.

Bayla had no choice but to enter and take the princess's hand.

"Thank you for your help last night," Lamira said.

She lowered her gaze. "It was the least I could do," she mumbled.

An awkward silence followed, which Cambry, the bold redheaded female, finally ended. "I don't blame you for what you did," she said. "They think humans are animals to be used and bred. They forget we have hearts and minds, too."

"Who is they?" Lamira asked, and Cambry colored.

"Sorry. I meant slave masters in general—I know the Zandians are different."

"Yes." She looked at her hands. Zandians *were* different, but she hadn't considered that when she'd acted. She didn't want to tell the women she'd chosen to stay, had given her word to participate in the study and then had intentionally thwarted it. How could she blame Daneth for not wanting her near him anymore? "Well, Daneth has no use for me now. I suppose I'll be returned to the Ocretions."

Lamira and Lily shared a look. "I doubt that," Lily said.

"Why not?" she asked.

"You know too much," Cambry offered. "You sat at the table and listened to the discussion of war plans. I don't think they'll be sending you anywhere."

A shiver ran through her.

"You could come to the training pod to serve as a soldier with us. There are lots of humans there, and they're treated decently. You just have to train for war, but it could be in any capacity. You could help Lily with the medical unit."

She nodded. The thought of leaving Daneth made her sick, but even worse was staying, being near him but banished from his presence. "Could I? I'd like to help that way."

"You'll have to ask Prince Zander," Lily said. "If he gives you his permission, you can leave with us this planet rotation." She looked down at her sister. "That is, if you're sure you're going to be fine."

Lamira nodded. "I haven't had any more contractions."

"Good."

"Do you need anything from me?" Bayla asked.

"No," Lamira answered. "Zander is in the meeting room in the long wing. Go and ask him and let us know the result."

She curtsied. "Thank you—all of you." She bowed her head in an arc to make the curtsy encompass each of them before she backed out of the room.

Her body trembled with nerves as she sought the chamber Lamira had indicated. She found the door open and Zander scrolling through holograms.

"Forgive me, my lord. May I request an audience?"

His eyes narrowed, but he gave her a single nod.

She entered, clasping her hands in front of her. "My lord...I was wondering if I might serve you and the Zandians by joining those on the training pod? I betrayed Master Daneth—and you. I deeply regret my actions and accept my punishment. But I wish to make amends. I want to be of service to the Zandians. I'm not much of a soldier but I could be of use to Lily in the medical unit."

"Daneth will have other uses for you here," he said stonily.

She curtsied. "My lord, I do not mean to disagree, but Master Daneth has banished me from his sight. He said he has no further use for me."

"I see." He pursed his lips. "I should throw you back to the Ocretions for what you did. But...I also recognize that you were of service to Lamira last night." Prince Zander's brown-violet eyes studied her for a long moment. "I will speak with Daneth. The decision will be his."

She stiffened, not so much because she feared Daneth would say no—although she honestly wasn't sure what he would say—but knowing the prince would speak to Daneth about her made her stomach flip flop.

If she was honest, she'd admit she was running away from Daneth. Away from the pain of his rejection, the devastation of witnessing his disappointment and knowing she was responsible for it.

Not knowing where else to go, she found her way to the kitchen, though she had little appetite. Still, Chef Barr was always happy to see her. At least one being on the pod was.

~.~

"Your human requested a transfer."

Daneth gulped air, hoping Zander's words would rearrange themselves into an order that made sense. "Pardon?"

"She said you have no further use for her. Is that true?"

Heat flooded his face—whether it was from anger or shame, he wasn't sure. "The last egg wasn't viable. I was angry," he said stiffly.

Zander nodded, once. "You have my utmost sympathy."

He scowled and looked out the window into the smoggy Ocretion sky. "These humans...are infuriating."

"Yes."

He whirled, checking to see if Zander was laughing at him. "You probably find it amusing how much I've lost control of the situation."

Zander shook his head. "You haven't lost control. You only feel that way because she aroused your emotions."

Among other things.

"I never experienced such levels of anger, jealousy, or frustration before Lamira. Perhaps this is what it is to mate. Or do you think it's more pronounced with humans?"

"I don't know," Daneth muttered and pounded the window with his fist. "It's hard to remember without Zandian females around."

Zander considered him. "I, too, pushed Lamira away when I thought I couldn't trust her. But it was a mistake. She bent my trust to protect her life. As an enslaved species, they've learned to do whatever they must do to stay alive. You must bear that in mind when you measure Bayla's behavior."

"I do. I have. I see my mistakes. I should have considered her feelings. Or inquired about them. I suppose I'm not used to beings with such intense emotions."

"Do you wish her to go?"

He felt as though Zander had picked him up by the throat, an invisible fist squeezing his trachea. Of course he didn't *vecking* want her to go. She was his female. His beautiful, precious, soft, sexy human. But she'd petitioned Zander for permission. She wanted to leave him. And she deserved her freedom, especially after he'd been so hard on her. He hadn't meant to mistreat her, but he sure as hell had.

"Let her go," he choked out, though he thought the words would stop his very heart.

Zander raised a brow. "Are you certain?"

He forced his head into a stiff nod.

"All right. I'll give my permission for her to leave with Rok and Lundric. They will make sure she's safe on the pod," he assured him, as if Zander knew Daneth's mind had already flown to what would happen to her there.

He walked back to his lab, his body an empty shell as if every organ had been removed.

Bayla...*gone*.

Why did that seem even worse than his life's work being ruined? Than the end of the Zandian species?

Bayla belonged to him. With him.

But he had to let her go. He cared enough about his lovely female to give her freedom. Especially if she'd asked for it. He would never impose his will on her again. If she didn't want him to be her master anymore, it wasn't for him to insist.

He entered his lab and shut the door, leaning against it and closing his eyes.

He'd survive.

Somehow.

CHAPTER TEN

Bayla didn't know which was worse—choosing to leave Daneth or hearing that he'd given his permission for it. For some reason, she'd thought he might fight to keep her. She'd imagined that even though he was angry, he still had feelings for her. But maybe she'd equated lust with love. Simply because she'd once inspired desire didn't mean he cared.

She had no personal belongings but brought along the clothing that had been allotted to her since her arrival on the palatial pod. Rok pointed at an empty seat on his ship and told her to buckle up. She stuffed the small bundle of clothing under her seat and snapped her harness in place. The moment they left the dock, her eyes watered.

Which was stupid. Why would she cry over leaving a male who didn't give a shooting star about her?

Lily sat beside Rok in the copilot's chair, but, once they were flying, turned and gave her a sympathetic look. "I never conceived. I don't know if I can. They shot me full of hormones to prevent pregnancy."

Damn Lily and her sympathy. The tears brimming in Bayla's eyes spilled over. She hadn't been crying over her lost babies, but now that wound opened, too. "I have two out there somewhere." She shocked herself at sharing something so personal. "One half-breed son born to a wealthy Ocretion. I'll never see him again. And a human daughter, a slave somewhere."

"Maybe Lundric could find her," Cambry offered, shooting a glance at her handsome young mate.

The warrior buried his fingers in her long red mane and appeared to be massaging her scalp. Cambry leaned into his touch.

Bayla's stomach tightened watching them, loneliness engulfing her.

"We can search the Ocretion databases." There was a note of caution in

Lundric's voice. "But I don't have the funds to buy another slave. I spent my life's savings on your brother."

Cambry's face went soft, and she locked eyes with her lover, unspoken messages seeming to transmit between the two of them.

"Don't ask me, I've been broke since I traded our last smuggling shipment for Lily instead of currency," Rok spoke up.

Lily leaned over and said something in his ear that made him smile.

"Well, the first step is to locate the young. Then we can figure out how to retrieve her," Lundric said.

She blinked rapidly to hide her tears of gratitude. "You all will really help me find her?" She'd never considered finding her babies possible. Had never dared dream of it, except the occasional sad fantasy that her daughter might end up in the same fertility farm where she worked. Even if that did happen, though, she didn't know if she'd recognize her. The Ocretions would purposely keep any identifying information from them both.

For some reason, her hand drifted to her abdomen and she rubbed it, as if she still carried her child there.

Perhaps she would survive the heartache of leaving Daneth. She had new friends. They wanted to help her search for her baby. And she a purpose—helping a nearly extinct species. Not in the way they'd wanted her to, but she'd still try to be of use.

~.~

Daneth's chamber screamed empty. The entire palatial pod echoed with silence, in fact. Or maybe that was his heart. Since Bayla had left and taken his *vecking* soul with her, the simplest tasks seemed a chore.

At first he'd thought his mood was low because his life's work and dreams had been dashed, but the longer the hours without Bayla stretched, the more he realized it was her.

He missed her clean, citrusy scent, the pleasure of her plump flesh under his hands, the softness of her skin.

Never in his life had he liked being around other beings—preferring to bury his nose in science, in his studies, but he suddenly hated being alone. He found himself drifting out of his lab and around the pod, yet he met no other being he wished to share his time with.

Every cell in his body seemed to ache for Bayla. Simply living became an agony.

Several times, he considered going after her, but he resisted. She'd asked to leave. She deserved her freedom.

He probably deserved this pain. He hadn't been kind to her. Hadn't listened or asked questions. He didn't know nearly enough about his lovely human. Sure, he had her file. He knew how many pregnancies and live births she'd had. Knew her age and her blood type. Knew her hormone levels. But he hadn't found out what was in that beautiful mind of hers. That enormous heart.

She'd loved her babies. She must have, or she wouldn't have found it too painful to have another taken from her.

Why hadn't he guessed that? Why hadn't he known what she held in the space behind those beautiful tits of hers?

He'd been selfish. He hadn't cared, plain and simple. To him, she'd been a vessel. A particularly lovely vessel, but a body he'd purchased for one purpose.

Only now did he wish he'd seen the woman behind the body. And now it was too late.

He went to Zander's room to check on Lamira, though he already knew from the sensors he'd implanted in her that she'd had no more contractions. He knocked on her door and entered.

She was alone, flipping through holograms on farming. He'd bought her from an agrifarm, and she'd brought her expertise in gardening to the palatial pod, filling the great hall with potted fruits and vegetables. He'd advised Zander to encourage her hobby, as it may benefit their species when they took back Zandia.

"How are you feeling?"

"Fine." She closed the hologram. "Actually, bored. May I get up now?"

He shook his head regretfully. "No. Bayla was right about bed rest." It pained him to say her name, and Lamira didn't miss it.

"You haven't forgiven her."

He drew in a sharp breath through his nose. Had he? "Whether I have or not doesn't matter. She's gone, and my project is at a dead end."

"None of the eggs were viable. Not even the one you implanted."

He stopped breathing. He'd measured Lamira's brainwaves and seen for himself the extrasensory abilities she had. "Is that true?" he choked.

She nodded. "It would have miscarried by ten weeks. Bayla only hurried the process along."

He staggered back a step, his gut reeling as if she'd punched him.

Bayla had made a mistake, but the outcome would've been the same if she hadn't. He'd blamed her for the downfall of his project, but it had been doomed from the start.

"Why didn't you say so earlier?"

"I only saw it this morning. I'm sorry."

He rubbed his forehead, suddenly exhausted.

"One more thing. Your project isn't lost. There are two Zandian females of breeding age still alive."

He went still. "What? Where?"

"I don't know where. Master Seke's two daughters escaped the genocide of

Zandia with Rok. I believe they survived and are out there somewhere. Master Seke and his lieutenant, Tomis, are out searching right now."

One small piece of his decimated heart rebuilt. Hope remained for their species. An even better chance of survival than his project afforded—if they could locate the missing females. He could extract eggs from them to impregnate multiple humans, even while the females themselves were bred. If the females and Master Seke allowed it, of course. And that hope immediately brought Bayla back to his mind. His perfect vessel.

"You should bring her back." Lamira must have read his thoughts.

But he couldn't. It wouldn't be right. He shook his head. "No. This information doesn't change anything. She's better off where she is. She didn't wish to be a vessel."

"She didn't want to have a child taken from her," Lamira corrected, shoving a fresh blade of pain into his ribs. "Pregnancy itself could be a pleasure to her, under the right circumstances."

His fingers curled into fists. He wasn't going to breed her—though she'd be perfect for the job. The idea of allowing another male to rut in her made him want to commit murder. "You...see that?"

Lamira's focus had gone soft, the way it did when she reached for information beyond her normal means. "Yes. She will love being pregnant the next time. And it will be soon."

His nostrils flared. Not his Bayla. Not by another male. He wanted to jump on a spacecraft and follow her to the training pod immediately. Kill any male —Zandian or human—who even *thought* about breeding with her.

But that wasn't right. He'd failed to consider her feelings and chosen her fate for her once with disastrous results. This time, she deserved to choose her own path. And she'd chosen to leave him.

As much as it pained him, he must honor her wishes and let her go.

Even though it would probably kill him.

CHAPTER ELEVEN

"Is this too tight?" Bayla wrapped a gauze bandage around the wrist of Tal, Cambry's brother, a young human male who made up part of the human army Prince Zander was training to take back his planet. He'd cut himself sparring with another human in their daily fighting practice.

In the two weeks since she'd arrived on the training pod, she'd tended to at least thirty such surface wounds in the medical unit, which also doubled as her chamber.

"No, it's perfect." He flexed his wrist to make sure it still bent with the bandage. Handsome and built of lean muscle, Tal was about the same age as Bayla. From his seated position on the cot, he gazed up at her with seeming attraction.

Funny how she had absolutely zero interest.

For the first time in her life, she was free to choose a mate of her own. On a pod with more a hundred humans, the pickings weren't all bad, either. But, despite the fertility drugs still in her system, she found no excitement in being near human males. Nor even the larger, purple-skinned Zandians, as stunning as the warriors were.

None of them were Daneth, the capable doctor who had locked a riot of emotion beneath a cool, clinical surface. Whose lust for her was so great, he lost all control.

Only when she remembered the way he'd taken her—so roughly and yet so tenderly, with so much urgent intensity—did she experience arousal.

Stars, would she ever find another male like that? The idea sickened her. She didn't want another male. She wanted to be back at the palatial pod, helping Daneth. Serving him. She wanted to be his breeder. To bear his beautiful young. To suckle them, raise them, and help the Zandian species live on with interspecies mixing.

If she were honest, she'd admit she hated it on the training pod. It was clean and well-kept, but a metallic, functional environment. It had none of the luxury and opulence of the palatial pod. The food was horrible. She slept on a cot in the cramped medical unit, which was no worse than what she'd had on the fertility farm, but between Daneth's sleepdisk and her cage's pad, she'd been spoiled.

She missed the colors and the amplified light of the palatial pod. She missed Chef Barr and the food.

But, mostly, she missed the sense of belonging. With Daneth, she'd held a power. She knew how to arouse her male, how to satisfy him. She'd enjoyed his desire. His need.

Here, she didn't feel helpless—not the way she always had on the fertility farm. But she definitely wasn't needed or powerful, either. She'd been assigned chores and duties, mostly in the medical unit, but it all seemed rather meaningless.

She tucked the loose ends of the bandage into the wrap. "That should do it. Try not to break the wound open. Give it a few days to knit closed."

Tal stood and smiled down at her. "Why don't I see you in the sparring ring? Don't you want to learn to fight?"

She shuddered. "No. Fighting isn't for me. I'll leave that to the stronger females, like your sister."

"What is for you?" His voice had softened, and he reached for her.

She stepped quickly back, stumbling against a metal table. "I-I don't know. Nursing, I guess." The emptiness in her stomach twisted into a knot. Nursing was all she had now. But it wasn't where she belonged. Again, her hand drifted to her belly, as if in memory of the babies she'd grown there.

Was breeding truly her calling?

A wave of nausea passed through her. She'd been queasy off and on for the past week. The nutrition packs on the pod probably didn't agree with her stomach.

But another thought hit her, causing her to sway on her feet.

Tal caught her elbow. "Are you all right? You look pale."

She sat down on the cot. "Yes. Yes, I'm all right. Just ready for the next meal, that's all."

"Well, come on. I'll walk you to the mess hall."

She shook her head. "No, you go on ahead. I need to finish something here."

He studied her for a moment then nodded. "Want me to bring you a nutrition pack here?"

She stood to prove she was fine. "No, I'll be right behind you. See you in a bit!" The moment he left, she threw open the cabinets, searching through the supplies. She'd seen a blood test kit somewhere. Or was it a urine test? *Yes!* She pulled out the urine test. She didn't know how to read, but they'd used these at the fertility farm. All she had to do was pee on a pad and watch the colors. Pink indicated a female baby. Blue a male. If it remained gray, she wasn't pregnant.

Her heart tapped a sharp staccato as she shoved the test in her pocket and headed to the washroom. There weren't many on the pod, and they often had lines of people waiting to use them, but those waiting after her would have to be patient.

Unbelievably, the washroom was empty. Everyone must in the mess hall for dinner. She activated the door, which swished open. Fingers trembling, she unwrapped the test. Yes, it was the same as she'd been given on the fertility farm. She could do this.

She peed on the stick and waited, forcing all conjecture out of her mind. No need to think until she knew for sure.

A long minute passed.

Then another.

She squeezed her eyes closed and forced her mind to stop churning. Either she was, or she wasn't. She was or she wasn't.

She was. With a boy.

She disconnected the results from the pee stick, disposing of the stick, and charged out of the washroom, a sheen of tears moistening her eyes.

Daneth's baby. The thought nearly brought her to her knees with joy. But as she jogged down the corridor, reality sank in.

Where was she running? To call Daneth?

What did she think he would do? He thought his genes unsuitable for a young. Would he want her to abort? Surely not. He'd probably send for her, to keep her under his medical care.

But that thought didn't cheer her, either.

She didn't want to be back in Daneth's lab if he didn't want her. It would be too painful. No, better to not tell him, or anyone, yet. She returned to the medical unit—little more than a tiny room with two cots and two cabinets full of supplies—and tucked the test results under the pillow on her cot.

~.~

Lundric rechecked the strap on Cambry's helmet for the fourth time. They stood inside the hatch of the battleship, ready for their reconnaissance mission.

She stopped his hand, closing her smaller fingers over his large ones. "It's on," she murmured.

His lips tightened. "I don't want you along."

"We've talked about this five hundred times. You agreed. Rok approved it. Prince Zander approved it. I'm your partner. We go together."

A muscle in his jaw tightened visibly. She reached up to touch his handsome face, the incredible male who, for some unknown reason, had decided she belonged to him. "I'm a warrior. Like you. That's what you love about me. Now, let's go get what we need."

He stamped his lips over hers, giving her a hard kiss. She hoped it was a promise of what he'd do to her when they returned. Her mate was never gentle, but she adored his passion and rough lovemaking.

"Let's do it." He sat in the pilot's chair and fastened his harness.

She slid in beside him, buckling hers.

"Recon One clear for takeoff," Rok said over the comms unit.

"All surveillance equipment activated and ready. Cloaking activated. Taking off," Lundric spoke.

They flew in silence as he turboboost them straight toward Zandia. Long minutes ticked by, yet, when Lundric broke through to the atmosphere for Zandia, it seemed far sooner than she'd expected. He entered alongside several larger airships, using them as cover, though they had their cloaking up.

She drew in a breath at the sight. The planet had been decimated. Mining operations were apparent everywhere. Earth overturned into mountains of tailings, huge pits pockmarked the surface. Huge vehicles streamed like insects, moving dirt.

She saw no sign of a population. It seemed the Finn had not taken Zandia as a place to live— Clearly, it served as a resource to rape.

She glanced over at Lundric. His skin had turned pale, mouth tightened. "It's sickening, isn't it?"

"Horrible." His voice sounded hollow.

"Rok, are you getting this?"

"We're getting it." Rok sounded equally grim. "Where is the capital? Can you swing around?"

Lundric changed the course of the ship, zooming around the arc of the planet for a different view. There, Cambry saw only the rubble of a destroyed city.

"It looks the same as the day I left," Rok said. "They didn't rebuild or clean up a thing."

"Where do you think they live? I mean there have to be workers on the planet, right?"

"Look," Lundric said, pointing at movement near the rubble. He expanded the image they were looking at.

Beings were camped everywhere in the rubble. In the twenty solar cycles since they took over, the Finn hadn't rebuilt, they'd simply occupied the space like vagrants, setting up lean-tos, tents, and other temporary housing amongst the rubble.

Cambry enlarged the image more, wanting to see the Finn up close. "Ugh."

They were troll-like creatures with fat, round heads and mouths full of sharp, ugly teeth. They appeared to be the same size as humans, if not shorter, but stout and bulged with muscles.

"Turn on X-ray sensors," Rok instructed.

Lundric did, and they saw a network of hollow tunnels beneath the earth. No beings appeared to be in them.

"Those were ours. That's how I escaped," Rok said. "It looks like they aren't using them. That could be our way in."

"Let's check out the other end." Lundric maneuvered the ship around the opposite curve of the planet.

Some of the tightness in Cambry's chest released. The terrain had been untouched on this side. Trees, bushes, and other green foliage grew. The land jutted and arced into natural mountains and hills, and water stood in lakes.

"Thank the true Zandian star," Lundric breathed.

Rok chuckled, his own relief evident in the quick release of his breath. "It's still there. That's great news."

"Yeah, for a moment there, I was wondering if this planet was worth fighting to get back," Cambry said.

"It certainly is." Rok's voice vibrated with pride.

Cambry spotted movement from the top of their viewing area. "Lundric, we have company."

Lundric dropped sharply and circled around. "Cloaking still activated."

"You have enough data. Get out of there," Rok barked.

"Copy that. Exiting Zandian atmosphere."

He circled around to go back to the line of air traffic where they'd entered, but an explosion rocked their ship.

Cambry's body flung against her restraints as the ship flipped and dropped into a spin.

"Controlling spin," Lundric reported tersely.

Incredibly, he pulled them out of it and shot away from the planet, breaking through the atmosphere into space.

"Cloaking damaged. Turbospeed inactive. One engine down."

"Stay in the air. Backup is en route to assist."

More shots were fired. Their pursuer had followed them outside Zandia's atmosphere.

"We're still under fire. Repeat, we're under fire."

"Return fire. Assistance is not far."

Cambry unbuckled and ran for the weaponry at the top of the craft. The last time they were under attack, she hadn't known how to use the weaponry, but she'd had more training since then. She buckled in and gripped the trigger on the laser guns. "Ready to fire."

Lundric dropped and flipped the ship, bringing her directly in front of their assailant. The blood rushed to her head, but her harness held her in place as they hung upside down. She let loose with all the firepower she had, striking the ship repeatedly.

Lundric yelled something, but she couldn't hear over the laser discharge.

The Finn's ship blew up, dropping out of view.

Lundric flipped their airship right side up, and her stomach roiled.

"Two more incoming," Lundric shouted.

Again, her mate managed to swing around to line her up to shoot. She missed one, but shot down the other, but they took a major hit to one wing. The ship wobbled.

"Hang on, I've got you!" Her brother's voice shouted through their comms unit.

Thank the stars! Tal magnetized their ship and shot into turbospeed, sweeping them away from their enemies.

Smoke filled the ship. Oh stars.

"Lundric?" she screamed.

He coughed. "I'm...all right. Stay where you are."

"Are we on fire?"

"I'm...putting it out."

She heard the spray of the fire extinguisher, and white powder filled the air, along with the black smoke. She couldn't see a thing. Couldn't breathe.

"Lundric?"

Her vision began to fade. No. Hell no. She couldn't pass out now. Lundric needed her help.

She unbuckled from her harness, but they must be upside down, because she fell onto her head, and the haze of smoke and powder faded to black.

~.~

Daneth gripped his medical case and strode briskly onto the training pod. Zander, himself, had flown them there the moment they'd received word of serious injuries. Lundric and Cambry had been shot down while on their reconnaissance mission, but their burning ship had been extracted by another ship.

"Where are the injured?" he barked. He hadn't been on the pod before and didn't want to waste precious time wandering around.

"I'll take you to the medical unit, Master Daneth," a guard nearby offered, already starting down the corridor in front of him.

He followed, leaving Zander to a briefing with Rok. The "medical unit" was nothing more than a closet-sized room, jammed with two narrow cots and cabinet of supplies.

Bayla. Even though he'd known he'd see her, the sight of his beautiful human nearly brought him to his knees. Whatever resolve he'd had to let her go evaporated when he saw her. Every cell in his body screamed for him to claim her, mark her as his, mate her. Yes, breed her. He wanted her in the most basic, primal way. As a male needs a female. As a lover gives his heart.

She stood leaning over Cambry, who lay unconscious on one cot, soot covering her face and clothing. Lundric sat on the cot beside her, dodging Lily's attempts to clean the gashes on his head and face.

"Don't worry about me," he growled. "*She's* the one who needs help."

"Everyone clear out," he ordered.

Bayla and Lily moved toward the door but didn't leave, clearly wanting to be of help. "You, too, if you're refusing treatment," he said to Lundric.

"I'm not leaving her," Lundric thundered.

Cambry whimpered.

"Your shouting won't help her head wound. This area is too small for me to function adequately. Stand in the corridor unless I ask you for something."

This time, all three of them exited, giving him enough room to set his case down and pull out the necessary monitoring equipment. He scanned Cambry for injuries. Multiple contusions, abrasions, and burns. The only serious injury was a blow to the head. He shot her with an analgesic and anti-inflammatory agent. When he pulled her eyelids back and checked her pupils, she whimpered again, which he took as a good sign. She wasn't too deeply unconscious if sounds and touch bothered her.

"Captain Lundric," he summoned her mate.

"Yes?" Lundric charged back into the small space.

"I will scan your injuries now."

"What about Cambry?" Lundric demanded.

"I have administered a painkiller and something to bring down the swelling. I expect her to wake soon. Now, sit down."

Lundric scowled but sat, staring only at his mate as Daneth performed a quick scan. He also had multiple contusions, abrasions, and burns.

"Bayla." His tone altered when he spoke her name, and he was certain everyone in the room would stop and stare. He hadn't been able to touch her yet, or speak to her, but his voice caressed the sweet syllables of her name like a lover.

"Yes, Master?" Her voice was sweeter and more musical than he'd remembered.

My darling. Please come here so I can hold you. If only. "You and Lily may continue with the cleaning and dressing of the wounds. Prior to bandaging, please use this solution to cleanse and this one to prevent infection. I also have a topical pain-relief spray that should be effective on the burns. You'll need to take more care with Cambry's wounds, as humans do not heal at the same rate as Zandians."

His sweet human moved in swiftly, following his instructions with attention and care.

He wanted to stop her. To sweep her into his arms and apologize. To tell her what she meant to him. But the timing was all wrong. The patients required attention first.

Soon, though. Soon, he would attempt to win back the heart of the only being who'd ever seen beyond his walls.

"Let me hold her," Lundric demanded, trying to reach past Bayla to pick up his mate.

"Don't move her," Daneth snapped. "Cambry needs rest and quiet. You have given her neither. If you wish to be a comfort to your mate, sit beside her and hold her hand. Speak to her softly and ask her to wake up. All else is a detriment."

The huge warrior appeared appropriately cowed. He wedged himself into a squat beside Cambry's head and stroked her hair, murmuring softly as Bayla cleaned her wounds.

"Lundric, when you're ready to have your wounds tended, please let me know," Lily said. "In the meantime, I'll get the Zandian crystal to help you recharge."

Lundric nodded absently, never taking his eyes from the young red-haired beauty at his side.

Cambry's eyelids fluttered and opened. "Where's Lundric?" Her slurred words still managed to sound urgent.

"I'm right beside you, baby."

"Did we make it out?"

"Yes. Tal rescued us. We're on the training pod."

She attempted to lift her head and groaned.

"Here." Daneth handed the pillow from the other cot to Lundric to prop Cambry's head. In the place where the pillow had been, lay a rudimentary pregnancy test. He'd seen them before but had always preferred blood tests. He picked it up. It read positive for a male young.

"To whom does this belong?"

Bayla swung her sapphire blue eyes on him, dark lashes blinking as the color drained from her face. Her full lips parted, but no sound came out.

Something in her expression made his heart pound. "Bayla?"

Her knees buckled, and she dropped into a faint.

～．～

The world tilted and rushed by her. Her queasiness returned tenfold. She seemed to be moving swiftly down a corridor. Only she wasn't walking. She blinked as the universe came back into focus. Daneth held her cradled in his arms as he carried her somewhere.

"Master?"

"Hush, darling. I have you. Are you pregnant?"

She whimpered. She hadn't wanted to tell him. Didn't want him to feel obligated to take her back, when the sight of her still made him angry.

"Shh. You don't have to say anything. I can smell it on you. Your master's going to take care of you." He cursed and turned around. "Are there no empty chambers on this pod?" he grumbled.

His closeness and scent comforted her. She nuzzled her face into his neck.

He found the Zandian bunkroom and brought her inside, where he sat on a cot and rocked her back and forth like a baby.

A fresh wave of nausea kicked in. "A little less motion, please," she pleaded.

Daneth stopped abruptly. "I'm sorry. Are you going to be sick?"

"No...probably not." She gave a shaky laugh.

"I can't believe you're having my young," he said in awe. "Bayla—"

"No." She covered his mouth with her fingertips. "Whatever you're going to say—don't. I don't blame you for not wishing to see me after what I did. I hope, someday, you'll forgive me. But I want you to know that his pregnancy doesn't have to change anything. I can remain here with my kind."

"Enough." The sternness returned to Daneth's voice. "I made a mistake. I never should have sent you away from me. I didn't want to be apart from you then, and I certainly don't want it now. I won't leave here without you." He stroked her cheek. "You belong to me, Bayla. You're mine." His fingertips traced over her pulse and down to her collarbone. "And it turns out, there's nothing to forgive. Lamira's extrasensory perception told her the egg wasn't viable anyway." He ran his index finger down her breastbone, reminding her of the time he'd thrust his cock between her breasts. "And I researched this herbed water of yours. It's nearly impossible for parsley tea alone to cause a miscarriage. So let go of your guilt, sweet girl. You did no further harm to what was already damaged."

Her eyes burned with tears of relief. *Thank the stars.* Daneth's forgiveness alone would've made her heart sing, but knowing she had not been responsible for ruining the last chance and prolonging the Zandian species lifted a huge burden from her shoulders.

"Will you forgive me for not including your feelings in my plans to save my species?"

She ducked her head against his neck again. "Yes."

"Good." His palm circled her belly.

A shiver of pleasure ran through her. She'd never shared a pregnancy with a partner before, but somehow her body, her very essence knew how *right* this one would be. She'd have a mate to take care of her, to share her excitement, to make a family with her.

He bit her ear. "You're carrying my baby." His gravelly tone sounded all-male. All proprietary and proud.

"Yes, I am." She turned to look up at him. "You're happy?"

"Beyond happy. I'm ecstatic."

She had to ask. "You'd never take this baby from me?"

He leaned his forehead against hers. "Never in a million solar cycles. And I'll help you get your other babies back, too."

Her heart tumbled around in her chest. "Will you? Just one might be reachable. A full human girl. She'd be two solar cycles this spring."

"I'll find her. I promise you." He swore it like a solemn oath, and she believed him.

His wrist cuff blinked with an incoming message. He answered immediately. "Yes, my lord?"

A hologram of Prince Zander's face sprang out in front of them. "I need you on the ship, now. Lamira's having contractions again. She said the child will be born this planet rotation."

Bayla surged up off his lap.

"We'll be right there," Daneth said. He caught her hand, and they raced together down the corridor to the dock.

Prince Zander already had the engines on the ship running. His face had lost color, turning a pale shade of lavender.

She threw herself into a seat and buckled the harness, smiling when Daneth double-checked her work before he sat in his own. Daneth picked up her palm and squeezed it. "Why are you smiling?"

"Births are a miraculous event," she said, the joy of every birth she'd witnessed thrumming through her.

Daneth's face softened, the warmth behind his gaze nearly stopping her pulse. "I'm so glad you'll be beside me for my first."

CHAPTER TWELVE

Daneth marveled at the confidence and strength of his beautiful slave. No, not slave. His mate. And maybe still his slave. Because, if he guessed correctly, she *wanted* to be owned by him. Hadn't she chosen it freely already once? His female liked to serve on her knees, to boggle his mind with her incredible body, to plead and pretend that he was in charge, when she knew she had him wrapped so tightly around her little finger that he'd tie himself in a knot to make sure he stayed there.

"Make this sound—*uhhhhhhh*," Bayla coached Lamira. "If the mouth and lips are soft, the pelvic floor will relax, too."

"Uhhhhhhh," Lamira moaned.

Leora joined her, and the three women toned together, their primitive song reverberating off Zander's walls.

Zander sat on the edge of the sleepdisk, holding Lamira in a squat on the floor by her armpits.

Daneth had to suspend his medical mindset, which screamed for him to strap Lamira down to his examination table and pull the young out of her by whatever means necessary, putting an end this agonizing waiting. But he trusted Bayla, who insisted that birth was a natural event.

"I think it's working," Lamira gasped.

Bayla squatted beside her. "I see his head!"

Zander leaned forward and began murmuring in Lamira's ear, almost as if in prayer. "Lamira. You're doing so well, beautiful. Our son is almost here. Just relax and let him come. Make your music, little one."

"Uhhhhh," Lamira, Leora, and Bayla sang again. Lamira's tones shortened and then stopped as the infant slipped from her body into Bayla's waiting hands.

Daneth surged forward, ready to scan and provide emergency care, but Bayla held up a finger. "He's perfect," she murmured.

And he was. A pair of tiny horns twitched on top of his bald, wrinkled head, declaring his Zandian genes, despite his light skin.

"Let me see him," Lamira whispered.

Bayla quickly wrapped a spidersilk blanket around the child, still tethered to his mother by his umbilical cord. "Lift her up on the bed now." It was beyond strange to hear Bayla giving Zander orders, but their prince obeyed, scooping Lamira up and holding her in his arms on the bed.

Bayla placed the infant in Lamira's arms. "You're not quite finished, my lady. There's still the afterbirth." She tugged on the cord as she massaged Lamira's abdomen. The placenta emerged on the next contraction.

He moved in to clamp and cut the cord and perform the scan on the tiny half-breed.

"He's perfectly healthy," he declared when he finished.

Lamira burst into tears of joy, and even Zander's eyes watered as she put the babe to her breast to teach him to nurse.

Bayla, too, started to cry. He wrapped his arms around her from behind and pulled her against his much larger body. "It will be our turn next," he murmured in her ear.

She turned in his arms and gazed up, lashes wet with her tears. "I love you, Master."

Now his eyes stung. He claimed her mouth, kissing her until his clothing grew tight and constrictive against his heated flesh. He had to pull away or risk *vecking* her against the prince's wall. "I love you, too, Bayla. Tonight, we mate."

Judging by her look of happy confusion, she didn't know the Zandian mating custom of piercing their females and adorning them with crystals. Good. Then he'd surprise her. He already knew there'd be no question of her submitting to him in any way he asked her.

"Shall I make the announcement to our species?" he asked prince Zander.

Zander didn't take his eyes off the tiny infant, who'd already learned to suckle. "Yes. Thank you."

CHAPTER THIRTEEN

"We received a transmission from the palatial pod, Master Seke," Tomis said, checking their ship's data after another long planet rotation of following dead end leads in the pursuit of Master Seke's daughters.

"Open it."

The hologram sprang open, featuring the head and shoulders of Daneth, the prince's physician. "A new Zandian prince has arrived." The doctor beamed. "Lamira gave birth to Zander's son this evening. Both the infant and the mother are in excellent health." He bowed, and the transmission flickered off.

Seke gave a shout of joy and immediately sent a transmission to his mate, Lamira's mother.

An incoming transmission made Tomis' smile fade. "Master Seke," he called out sharply, interrupting his mentor's conversation. "We're receiving a transmission from Zandia."

"I'll return in a moment, my love," Seke promised, ending the transmission and swinging around to join him at the ship's controls. "Answer it."

In all the solar cycles since the Finn had overtaken Zandia, they'd made no contact, choosing to ignore the existence of the few remaining Zandians, just as the United Galaxies chose to ignore the petitions Zander had filed demanding the return of his planet and its resources.

A hologram sprang open, and it took all Tomis' training not to flinch at the grotesque figure hovering in midair before them. Short and grayish, with a round head and a mouthful of pointy teeth, the Finnian king appeared more beast than intelligent being.

"I am King Fluut of Zandia. Who are you?" the ugly being snapped.

"I am Seke, Master of Arms."

"An unauthorized ship containing one human and one former Zandian was found in our airspace this morning."

Seke showed nothing in his expression, though he already had received the full report on Lundric's ill-fated mission.

"I was willing to ignore the existence of the few remaining members of your species, including the being named Zander, since he posed no threat. However, all amnesty has been revoked. All remaining Zandians will be terminated, starting with your prince. Bring him to me now."

Seke folded his arms over his chest. "I think not."

King Fluut smiled, revealing a row of rotten fangs. "Then I'll begin with this one, instead." He yanked a—*holy star of Zandia!*—young Zandian female into view. Was she one of Seke's daughters?

Tomis drew his sword, though it was only a hologram. He couldn't take his eyes off the stunning brunette, who fought against the Finnian king's rough hold with controlled rage.

Seke went rigid, but he gave a stiff shrug. "What does the prince care about a peasant?"

The king's eyes narrowed, as if he recognized Seke's bluff. "So it isn't true that there are no Zandian females of childbearing age, then?"

A tic started near Seke's eye.

"We might be willing to compensate you for her safe return."

"Good." The king gave a greasy smile. "I'll exchange her for your prince. You have one week to deliver."

"A Zandian week? Or Ocretion?" Tomis asked, because they weren't the same.

"Ocretion." The hologram flicked off.

Seke gripped the back of his pilot's chair with white knuckles. "Talia," he croaked.

Tomis swung his sword where the king's head had hovered. "I'll get your daughter back," he swore. "Before the week is up. You have my word."

***

Thank you for reading *His Human Vessel!* As you might have guessed, the next book, *Her Mate and Master*, will be an alien-alien relationship. I'm hoping you find them just as hot.

CHAPTER ONE

Naked, she twisted and tugged against the chains holding her captive. King Fluut, the repugnant ruler of the Finn, had hung her on the wall across from his throne in the capital of the stolen planet Zandia. Yes, strapped her to the wall. *Naked.*

She didn't think it was sexual for him, though. He didn't look at her body with anything more than disgust. *Feeling's mutual, asshole.* The nudity was some kind of degradation game.

She'd been a royal idiot coming to Zandia, but her home planet had been like a living, breathing entity, calling to her. After a lifetime of hunger and weakness, of going to sleep at night bone-tired, the promise of strength from Zandia's crystals had sung to her.

That part had, at least been true. Even in her current, dire predicament, tiny bubbles of energy coursed through her body, enlivening parts she scarcely knew existed. The unfortunate side effect was an awakening at the notch between her legs. And the nudity did *not* help.

Her pussy warmed and moistened, clearly disconnected from her brain, which knew this situation was not the least bit sexy. Her clothes may be off, but it sure as hell wasn't playtime. Why then, did her damn nipples stiffen every time a new male walked into the room?

The males were *beastly.* Literally. The Finn were a horrid, ugly species. Short, gray-skinned, with grotesque flat noses and vicious-looking teeth. The king was the worst of all, his pointy teeth half-rotten, face wrinkled and sagging.

No, her body definitely wasn't interested in these males. But she did find herself imagining males of other species. Human. Zandian. Not that she'd ever seen a Zandian male. Hell, she hadn't even known she was Zandian until last solar cycle.

A traveler at the bar where she'd served as a slave her entire life had mentioned it in passing, asking how she survived away from the crystals.

His words ignited her, like she'd been zapped by the fiercest electrical storm space had ever known. The hair on her head had stood up, blood heated and spun in her veins. She'd run after him, knowing she'd get a beating from her master, Thurn, when she returned, but not caring.

"What do you mean?" she'd asked. "What crystals?"

The customer, a rough-looking trader, had looked at her like she was the biggest idiot he'd ever seen. "You don't know about the crystals?"

"*What. Crystals?* Please tell me what you're talking about."

"You've heard of Zandia, right?" His voice dripped with derision.

She'd flushed and shaken her head. "You said that's where I'm from?"

"Yes. You're a Zandian. Zandia is your home planet. The one your species came from? It's made up of crystal—the crystal used to power laser weaponry. That's why the Finn invaded and killed off most of your kind. Supposedly, the Zandians used the crystals for energy. They don't require food or drink, just crystal. Something like that, anyway. That's why the Finn killed them off."

She'd gaped, trembling with the new knowledge, a million beliefs about her existence crashing around in her head until Thurn arrived and yanked her away with a bruising grip on her upper arm.

Take me there, she'd almost begged the stranger, but her good sense prevailed. She couldn't show her hand to her master. Not until the right opportunity presented itself. And it had. She'd finally had the courage to steal from the till and escape, purchasing passage straight to Zandia.

Which she now saw had been as impulsive as it was stupid. Blame it on the crystals, which now had her body afire, lust pumping through her veins, feeding her like the oxygen. What would a Zandian male look like? Purplish skin like hers? How tall would he stand? What kind of cock?

Stars, was she thinking about cocks?

She shifted restlessly against the bonds that held her secure against the wall. The king usually ordered her taken down from the wall and sent to the dungeon for the night. She wasn't given clothing and was paraded through the entire dungeon for every male in every cell to gawk at, but, thankfully, had a private cell.

She couldn't wait to go there. Not just for the relief of being released from the dreadful position on the wall. But, for the first time in her life, she needed to touch herself. *Down there*. Desperately.

I'm coming for you, Talia.

Tomis slumped in his seat on the prison ship, attempting to look like nothing more than a two-bit smuggler. A ruffian, who'd made the mistake of attempting to buy Zandian crystal on the black market. His plan—a suicide mission at best—was to get into the Finnian prison below the capital of Zandia before getting himself killed.

If he made it that far, he planned to break out with the beautiful Talia, possibly the only female Zandian of breeding age in the galaxy, the daughter of Master Seke, his mentor.

The Stornigian sitting across from him stared openly. "You do know what they'll do with you when you get to Finnian Outland, don't you?"

Finnian Outland. That pissed him off. The planet's name was *Zandia*, rightful home to the *Zandians*, ruled by Prince *Zander*, son of the dead King *Zander*. Zandia was his homeland—a crystal encrusted planet of great natural beauty and wealth.

He lifted his upper lip in a scowl and played stupid. "What?"

"The Finn exterminated your entire species. Systematically. As in, hunted down and killed every single living Zandian they could find. You think they'll let you live three seconds on their planet?"

Their planet. *Vecking* assholes.

He grunted as if he could care less, but a familiar sickness gripped his solar plexus. One part hatred, one part despair. That any species would commit such an atrocious act of genocide made him ill. And he remembered every bit of it. The screaming. The falling buildings. Bloodied bodies. His mother shoving him in a packed airship just before it lifted off. Watching her wave goodbye, fist shoved in her mouth, weeping, just before another bomb obliterated the ground she'd been standing on. Her final act had been to save his life.

He'd spent his life to date training for revenge. To make her sacrifice count, take back the planet for his ruler, Prince Zander.

But, first, Talia.

Now that the Stornigian had called attention to him, the rest of the prison airship members stared, too, curiosity glinting in their eyes. Ten were Finn. One human—probably an escaped slave. Three Stornigians.

One of the Finn spoke up. They were short, ugly creatures—round heads, sharp pointy teeth, grayish skin. "You're Zandian? I didn't know there were any of you left," he jeered. "Where've you been hiding?"

Tomis affected a shrug. "Here and there."

"What are you in for?" another Finn asked.

"Illegal trade."

"How'd you live without the crystals?" the first Finn asked. "I thought they were necessary to your survival." That had been the reason for the Finn exterminating his species. They believed Zandians wouldn't simply vacate their planet and take refuge elsewhere. Not when their biology required the crystals for charging. When Master Seke had evacuated Prince Zander from the falling palace, he'd had the wisdom to load as many large crystals as they could carry, allowing the small community of refugees to survive these years away from Zandia.

He folded his arms across his chest, adopting a *veck off* posture to let them know he wouldn't be answering any more questions.

The small prison airship bumped to a landing, and heavily armed guards came in to escort them off. He prayed finding Talia wouldn't be too difficult.

By the one true Zandian star, if the Finn *motherveckers* hurt that female, he would kill every *vecking* last one of them.

But that aggression wouldn't serve him now. He shoved it down, stowed it for later. For the moment, he needed to play it cool. If Fluut, King of the Finn, believed he was on official Zandian business, he'd be executed immediately, and so would Talia.

Sweet Talia.

He'd never met the female, but he'd been willing to die for her from the moment he saw her terrified hologram in the transmission from Fluut.

I'll exchange her for your prince. You have one week to deliver.

That had been two planet rotations ago. Eight more to go then Talia would be killed.

One of the guards jabbed him in the ribs with the butt of his giant laser gun. Tomis drew the pain in, used it as fuel for his power.

Pain is merely sensation, Master Seke used to say during training. *Register it. Use the information. Do not give it more weight than it deserves.*

Talia was Master Seke's daughter, missing since the Finn invasion of Zandia. Seke had believed her dead until recently, when Rok revealed he'd escaped with two female children. Tomis had been helping Seke search for them ever since.

He made himself stumble and swerve, as if weak and off-balance, when the guards shoved him off the prison ship. His clothes were dirty and tattered, boots worn. He'd done everything he could to appear like a nobody.

A guard stood at the entryway, scanning their bodies for disease, their barcodes if they had them. He had none. He'd been a free being his entire life.

"Who's this?" the guard demanded when he took in Tomis.

"Smuggler. Trying to buy crystal. Thought King Fluut might want him for extra leverage."

The guard's face stretched into a greasy smile, showing a row of pointy teeth with food bits stuck between them. "Excellent. Take him to the prison for holding."

Yes.

Step two of his hare-brained plan had worked. Now he just had to find Talia and escape.

When the scan was complete, the guards dragged him roughly forward and down two sets of metal stairs to the dungeons. Exactly where the Zandian plans had shown it to be. He carried no weapons save his fists, but his body had been trained to kill from his first planet rotation after the Zandian geno-cide. His two aces in the hole were the massive solar flare Seke planned to trigger to take out the Finn's power tonight and the extensive underground tunnel system below the dungeons that the Finns didn't seem to know existed.

He just hoped Talia was in the dungeons, too.

He kept his head down as they trudged past cell after cell, filled with every miserable species of being he could name. Almost all male. No other Zandians.

The guard placed his hand on the panel outside a cell and it slid open. Three huge beings looked up as Tomis was thrust forward, into the cell, and the panel slid shut.

He flexed his muscles and cracked his neck. If they needed to get the proof of dominance thing over first, he was ready. Hopefully, they'd let him fight them one at a time, but that was probably too much to ask.

"No fighting," the largest one grunted, as if bored. "Or they take away your meals."

Huh. That was unexpected. He sat down on a bench beside the hulking being of a species he couldn't readily identify.

"Meals good, are they?" he asked drily. Zandians required little food so long as they had contact with their crystal, so such a thing didn't matter to him.

The guy snorted. "Not much else to look forward to around here."

Okay, so his cellmates were friendly. Or at least non-threatening. He'd passed his third test. It almost worried him how smoothly things had gone. He'd figured he had a 70-30 chance of dying before he reached this point.

"Have you seen any beings like me? A female?"

All three of his cellmates shifted. "Oh yeah. We've seen her. We've seen *all* of her."

His hands balled into fists and teeth clamped down tight. "What the *veck* do you mean by that?"

"You'll see her, too. Just wait until suppertime."

His patience snapped, and he lunged forward, wrapping his fist around the male's bulky throat. "What. In the *veck*. Are you talking about?"

"No fighting," the guy wheezed, not moving a muscle to stop Tomis. His self-restraint put Tomis to shame, and he released the male.

"Just wait. You'll see," he repeated.

Veck. Tomis sank back to the bench and rubbed his face. He didn't know what in the hell was going on and couldn't stand the implication that all the males had seen Talia.

He forced himself into stillness, quieted his mind to wait. There was nothing else for him to do until the power went off, anyway. Time passed—a few hours, perhaps.

The sound of catcalls and shouts down the corridor made him lift his head.

His giant cellmate jerked his chin. "Here she comes."

He flew to the panel of bars and leaned his head against the cool metal, grateful the bars weren't electrified like most modern prisons. He knew from Zandian history this dungeon had been in use for thousands of years. With his neck cranked, he could see down the corridor at—oh *vecking* stars—what had they done to her?

Two guards dragged a naked Talia past the cells.

His muscles flexed and bulged with the need to fight for her freedom. He shoved down the urge to call out to her in their language, to tell her he'd come for her and promise to get her free. *Tonight.*

Instead, he backed up a step, sinking into the shadows when she passed their cell. Even so, her gaze jerked to him, violet eyes widened. She stumbled, and the guards shoved her forward, hard.

Tomis suppressed the growl of rage rocketing up into his throat, kept his face perfectly blank. But the scent of Talia lingered. By the one true Zandian star—did he smell her... *arousal?*

He closed his eyes, reviewing the image of her burned on his retinas. She was slender—too thin. Small for a Zandian. At least, he didn't think females were normally so small. The elders he'd met were not. She was almost human-sized, yet still exquisite. Long legs, her bare sex dainty between them. Flat belly. Two pert breasts. *Were her nipples stiff?*

His cock hardened, remembering. He replayed the scene in his mind in slow motion. She'd looked right at him, tossed that thick, reddish-brown hair over her shoulder and, yes, the dusky purple peaks of her breasts had turned rigid when her eyes widened.

He adjusted his aching cock in his combat pants. Well, that was unexpected. Stars, he didn't need the extra distraction. This female's capture had already brought out more emotion than he'd felt in all the years since watching his mother's death. Zandians weren't normally hotheaded. They were logical, practical. Warriors were well-disciplined and dispassionate. All that had flown the moment he'd seen Talia's hologram.

Well, he'd have to treat the emotion the same way he did pain. Use it as information and power.

Power to free his female.

~.~

She crumpled to the floor of her cell and brought her fingers between her thighs.

Stars, yes. *Relief.* She explored her folds with novice fingers, found the most sensitive place—the one that sent spirals of pleasure out through her body when she touched it—and rubbed.

She'd seen another Zandian. A male.

At least, she thought she had. One of the prisoners had been watching her. She'd never seen him before, and he'd pulled back, like he didn't want her to see him. But his skin was the same color as hers. He also had horns on the top of his head. Did Zandian males have horns? She wished she knew more about her own species.

Thurn, her asshole master, had never even told her what species she was. He'd led her to believe she was *human*. She'd thought she just hadn't seen a human yet with her skin color. Of course, believing she was human kept her firmly enslaved, hadn't it? Humans weren't free anywhere in the galaxy these days, particularly not in any Ocretion territory. She'd always thought running away would mean her certain death.

Well, turns out it had. She had a death sentence hanging over her head now for a different reason. King Fluut would have her executed if the Zandians didn't trade their refugee prince for her by the end of the week. *Pah.* She wasn't holding her breath for that to happen.

Her thoughts drifted back to the prisoner as she rubbed frantically at her swollen flesh. He'd been at least a foot taller than her and massive in size. Bulging muscles, strong jaw, sharp, intelligent eyes. He watched like he'd been expecting to see her, but she knew she hadn't seen him before. She would've remembered.

What would it be like to be taken by a male like that? She had to believe his cock was in proportion to those spectacular muscles. Would it hurt? She stifled a groan. Nothing could hurt more than this ache between her legs right now. What in the hell was happening to her? It had to be the crystals.

Suddenly, the prison fell into complete darkness. For a moment, there was no sound—no whir, no hum of machinery, no buzz of lighting. Then shouts and clangs filled the air.

She scrambled to her feet just as the door to her cell scraped open. Not the automatic whoosh of the door, but the mechanical grind of a mechanism forced.

A hand closed on her forearm. "I got her! I found the female!" a gleeful male voice rang out.

"Shut up, asshole. Do you want to have to fight the rest of them for her?" Another male entered and tugged the cell door shut. "Where is she? I get her first."

No.

She wrenched her arm in the first male's grasp but only succeeded in twisting her own flesh. She kicked out with the heel of her foot and heard a grunt.

The noise around them grew louder. Guards shouted commands, prisoners whooped, laser shots lit up the corridor with temporary blasts.

One of the males backhanded her, and she fell to the floor but used the position to scamper between his legs, toward the cell door. It clanged open again and she heard the scrape of a boot but couldn't see who'd entered.

He shouted something in a language she didn't understand.

She grabbed his ankle and sent him sprawling into the other two men. The crack of fists against bone filled the cell, but she didn't stay to see who came out a winner. Instead, she slipped out the cell door and into the corridor.

Big mistake. Prisoners choked the artery, fighting each other and the guards. Shots lit up the passage like flashes of lightening; bodies fell below her.

A male grabbed her and dragged her into a cell, then shoved her to her knees.

She rolled away and kicked in his direction, hoping she'd connect with his groin. She couldn't see a damn thing in the darkness. It didn't seem to do much damage because, the moment she stood, he had her by the waist again.

The flash of more laser fire illuminated a huge horned male in the doorway. He shouted something at her in a foreign language. A shiver of recognition went through her. *The Zandian.* He'd been the male who'd entered her cell and fought the other two. He wanted her for himself.

He shoved her back into the darkness and the slam of flesh on flesh was followed by a heavy drop to the floor. She wasn't sure which male's fingers closed around her wrist until the urgent words came from his throat again with the repetition of the word *Talia.*

Maybe she should be glad that her first sexual experience would be with a male of her own species. She had been fantasizing about exactly this a few short moments ago. But being raped in a prison cell wasn't her idea of a good time, no matter how good-looking the male.

She whirled into him and brought her knee up. This time, judging by his grunt, she did connect with groin. It didn't stop him though. He snaked an arm around her waist and slapped her ass, still speaking his melodic language.

She fought for freedom, managing to get a punch in somewhere on his head.

He caught both her wrists, pinned them to the wall and slapped her ass again. Her body responded as if this were foreplay, not assault, nipples tightening, blood rushing to the juncture between her thighs. Her bare ass tingled, coming alive to his slaps. "Do you not understand me, Talia?" He switched into Ocretion.

"No. And who's Talia?" she panted. He stepped even closer to her, caging her against the wall with his larger frame, holding her prisoner. Would he take her like this? Up against the wall from behind?

Heat flushed through her body and damn if her muscles didn't go weak, as if they'd already decided surrender was inevitable. Her knees trembled, breath sawed in roughly.

"You don't remember how to speak Zandian?" He released her.

She took the opportunity to dart for the door, but the warrior—there was no doubt in her mind that's what he was—moved too quickly. He caught her elbow and hauled her back.

She swung for his face again, but her fist only caught air.

"Stop fighting me," he growled. Two more sharp slaps fell on her bare ass.

How did he see in the dark? When she continued to fight, he wrapped an arm tight around her waist and hauled her off her feet, her back against his front. She clawed at the massive forearm cinching her belly.

"I'm here to rescue you, female." His hot breath puffed over her ear. He strode forward, out of the cell and shoved his way down the corridor with her kicking the whole way. "Every minute you fight me is time we could use escaping." Lights flashed, and he ducked under a fist flying his way. "The generators will come on any moment. Now, will you do as I say and walk on your own feet?"

"Yes," she agreed, mainly because she couldn't breathe with him squeezing her diaphragm.

He dropped her to the ground, smacking her ass again, presumably to keep her moving. She shot a glare over her shoulder even as her pussy dripped from the attention he kept giving her nether regions.

Laser light lit up the opposite end of the corridor, illuminating the enormous warrior. The warrior's gaze burned with fierce intensity, swallowing her and the path in front of them. His nostrils flaring, he swung his fist in her direction. She screamed as it slammed into someone just behind her. She blinked, her retinas imprinted with the vision of the warrior's magnificent arm used as a lethal weapon. So strong and capable.

"Here." He pressed something soft into her hand. A piece of fabric. "Put this on."

Her fingers untangled it as they ran. His shirt. He must have taken it off for her to wear. She yanked it over her head, arms fighting for passage through the holes as his scent washed over her, masculine and clean. Like leather and wood and soap.

They reached a T in the corridor, and he shoved her to the left. She sure as hell hoped he knew where he was going.

"Every being face down on the floor!" a Finnian guard shouted just ahead of them, scattering laser fire everywhere.

The warrior shoved her down behind him and lunged at the guard. She heard the thud of a body hitting the floor and the clatter of a weapon. In the next flash of light, she saw the Zandian had the weapon. "Come on," he urged, helping her to her feet. He closed his large hand around hers and dragged her down the hall. At the end of it, they reached a set of stairs. Instead of going up, the warrior pulled her behind them. It sounded like his hands were running over the wall, as he whispered something in his language.

It was a beautiful language. She wished she understood it.

A click sounded, and the wall rolled away with a rumble. Behind it, damp air greeted her, along with more darkness.

The warrior gripped her hand again and pulled her down stone steps. "What's wrong with your eyes?" he demanded. The wall rolled closed behind them.

"What do you mean?"

"You can't see in the dark."

"You can?" That explained how he moved so fast in the pitch black. "*Ow!*" She stubbed her big toe on a rock.

The warrior emitted a low curse and scooped her up into his arms. His scent hit her like a blast of heat, warm and inviting. It was all she could do not to nuzzle her nose against his thick neck.

"What was the name you called me?"

"Talia. You're Talia, daughter of Seke, master of arms to the Prince of Zander."

Something slithery and cold twisted in her solar plexus. An unnamed discomfort. "No. No, I'm not."

⁓.⁓

The pleasure of carrying Talia exploded beyond all expectation. Feeling her small form tucked up against him, her bare legs smooth and soft against his forearm, invoked the fierce protector within him. The same piece of him that had roared to life the moment he saw her in captivity. But that was nothing compared to the hunger that simmered below all heroics. Forgetting the feel of her ass under his palm or that she was bare beneath his shirt was an impossibility.

He wanted to lower her to the floor and explore every inch of that soft flesh with his hands. With his tongue. His teeth. And *veck*, yes, with his cock. But that wouldn't be happening. Talia was Master Seke's daughter, not to mention the only Zandian female of breeding age alive. A common-born warrior like him wouldn't be worthy of mating her. And to claim her without intending to mate her would be dishonorable at best, and a violation of Prince Zander and Master Seke's trust at worst.

"You're not Talia?"

"No."

"Then who are you?"

She was quiet for a moment. "I don't know." Her voice cracked. "Maybe I am..." She squirmed in his arms. "Put me down," she said sharply. "Put me down now."

He knew nothing about females. Nothing about managing a being's emotions, yet he knew without a doubt she wanted out of his arms to retreat into herself. He didn't want to allow it, yet he couldn't stomach refusing her request, either. He settled for easing her to the ground but keeping his arms locked around her waist.

She lunged away from him, but he held her fast. "Where are you going, starshine? You can't see in the dark, and you don't know the way out."

"I don't know," she spat. The brokenness in her voice flayed him.

"Who do you think you are, starshine?"

She drew in a ragged breath. Her body trembled against his, her back to his front, the soft curves of her bare ass torturing his thighs.

His cock thickened against her back.

"They...called me Ray. Until ten weeks ago, I thought I was a human slave."

His arms involuntarily tightened, the insult against her making him ready to slay every slave master she'd had. "*Vecking* stars, Talia, I'm sorry."

She turned in his arms. "Don't call me that. What makes you think I'm Talia?"

He brushed a strand of hair back from her face, nearly groaning at how perfectly her cheek fit in his palm, cradled there a moment before she pulled away. "Your father recognized you in the transmission from Fluut. He and I have been looking for you for the past forty planet rotations. We just found out you and your sister might be still alive."

She struggled once more in his arms, and this time he allowed her to leave. She stumbled until she hit a wall and leaned her forehead against it. Her sniffle ripped his chest open.

He wanted to draw her back into his arms, soothe away her shock. "Do you remember anything from...before?" Before she was a slave. Before Zandia was overtaken by the Finn. Before the survivors were separated from their families and home.

"Not a thing," she whispered.

He couldn't resist going to her now. His fingers closed lightly on her shoulders. Standing there in the dark, it seemed he knew her completely, understood her, even though they were perfect strangers. "We understand your airship crashed on Stornig. A guard had taken you and your sister and a laborer named Rok from the castle. He was shot down over Stornig. Rok was rescued and fostered by a Stornigian family. He never knew what happened to the females or the guard aboard his ship."

"How old was I?" Her voice came out rusty, crackly.

"I'm not sure. I think you were six solar cycles. Maybe more."

"And my sister?"

"Hasn't yet been found. But we only started the search recently, after Rok told us about his escape." He slid his fingers down her arm and clasped her smaller hand in his palm. "Come on. Can you walk? I'll feel better when we're out of these tunnels and away from the capital."

She gripped his hand and followed his lead, walking gingerly along the rocky surface. "Who are you?"

"Forgive me." He stopped walking, faced her, and bowed, even though she couldn't see him. "I am Tomis, a member of Prince Zander's Royal Guard, apprentice to Master Seke, who is our master of arms and your father."

"What if I'm not who you think I am?"

He caught her hand and started walking again. "If you're not Master Seke's daughter? It doesn't matter. I'm here for you, whoever you are."

"Because they want me for breeding?"

Something cold slithered through his chest, and a prickle of foreboding touched the back of his neck. He didn't want to lie, so he went with a different truth. "Because the moment I saw your hologram in Fluut's transmission, I knew I had to be the one to rescue you."

She snorted. "Bit of a hero complex, then? What if I didn't want to be rescued?" She stumbled, and he swung her back into his arms without thinking. Where he'd wanted her from the beginning.

She kicked her lower legs as if annoyed, but her slender arms snaked around his neck for purchase, which he didn't mind at all.

"I'd say you don't have a choice." He sounded gruffer than he meant to, but it was the truth. He wasn't budging from Talia's side until he'd brought her somewhere safe. Actually, he'd prefer to never leave her side again, but quite a few other Zandian males might take issue with that. His teeth bared at the idea of challenging males. A wild beast clawed at his chest, ready to defend his turf, pierce his female and mark her forever as his.

Not. His.

She was the daughter of Seke, his mentor. The male who'd been like a father to him after his escape from Zandia. He had no right to *veck* with Seke over rights to his female offspring.

"We'll see about that," she muttered, and another twist of foreboding tickled his nape.

But he was Talia's protector, whether she liked it or not. He'd keep her safe. Even if he had to keep her prisoner to do it.

CHAPTER TWO

So it isn't true that there are no Zandian females of childbearing age?

King Fluut had taunted Master Seke with this question when he'd threatened to kill her.

The idea had made goose bumps stand up on her arms then, and her skin crawled even more now that Tomis had confirmed how badly they wanted her.

If he thought she was sticking around to become a breeder for the Zandian species, he was sorely mistaken. She hadn't escaped a lifetime of slavery to become sexually enslaved to a different master, even if this one did have the same color skin as her.

No thank you.

While she appreciated the rescue from King Fluut, she needed to cut ties with Tomis as soon as possible. There was no way she'd allow him to take her to his Prince Zander or the male he claimed was her father. That story could be a giant hoax to make her come along without a fight. He painted some kind of happy family reunion, when, really, Seke could be nobody to her. She had no memory of a father. Of a family. A sister. Nothing. The language wasn't familiar to her. Nothing had jogged any memories loose of Zandia or their species.

Talia. Ray turned the name over in her mind. It rang no bells. Was she the female Tomis believed her to be? Part of her didn't want to completely reject his story. Especially considering how appealing she found the male.

He carried her like she weighed nothing, weaving through the underground corridor for kilometer after kilometer. He was an incredible specimen of malehood. Broad-shoulders, iron-muscled, and, yet, so gentle. The worst he'd done was deliver a few slaps to her ass. Which, unfortunately, had thrilled her. She wished to hell she knew if his story was true.

But she couldn't risk following him blindly.

After several hours, Tomis reached what appeared to be a dead end. He placed her lightly on her feet.

"Did you take a wrong turn?"

"No. I memorized every map of our planet before I came. We should be outside the city walls now. This must be the exit."

Our planet.

That much was true. No matter what she believed about her species, this planet certainly was hers. Her body had responded the moment she arrived, strengthening. Ripening.

Tomis ran his hands along the stone wall.

She joined him. "What are we looking for?"

"A small lever or catch made of metal. That's what I found when we entered."

Her fingers brushed over a protrusion. "I found it." She lifted it, but nothing happened. Tomis' large hand closed over hers and, together, they pressed it down. She ignored the flutters of excitement that ran through her at his mere touch. It must be the crystals making her body more sensitive because sensation seemed to shoot up her arm, straight to her chest like tiny prickles of heat. Or awareness.

What if she tried this male before escaping him? What was the harm in that? She'd managed to keep her virginity all these years—it was the one thing she could say for Thurn as a master. He'd protected her sexually—never allowed the males they served in the tavern to touch her. Why, she couldn't fathom. He could've made a great deal more money selling her body than using her as a barmaid. Perhaps because he'd raised her from childhood, he'd kept some semblance of protectiveness for her.

But now that she was on Zandia, she had no interest in maintaining her maidenhead. Her body desperately craved the feel of a hot-blooded male between her legs. To satisfy the ache that grew worse every day.

She didn't have the slightest clue how to seduce this male, though. He hadn't shown any interest in claiming her. No—that wasn't true. She'd felt his cock pressing against her back earlier. She tilted her ass backward as a wall of stone rolled aside, but it was too late to catch his attention. Tomis was in warrior mode, pulling her behind him as he peered around the wall into the starlit night. The corridor had been hidden in the crevice of a giant boulder, blending into the natural surroundings. They appeared to be in an unsettled area of Zandia.

"Stay here," he breathed, pushing her back into the corridor as he crept out silently, arms bent at the ready to smash any foes. She wondered why he didn't use the laser gun at his hip.

There was no way she was staying in the tunnel, though. What if the entryway rolled shut and she got locked in there alone? She had no way of navigating that maze or finding another exit.

She followed, keeping her footsteps slow to avoid making sound. Could she outrun the male?

Doubtful.

She'd have to find a hiding place, then. She moved with unpracticed stealth in the opposite direction from the one Tomis had gone, skirting the giant boulder, searching for any kind of hiding place. Another crop of large stones lay beyond, and she made her way toward those, praying they weren't already inhabited by a being or beast.

She never found out because she stepped on some kind of trigger and giant metal cage dropped around her, its floor snapping up beneath her feet before it lifted back off the ground. Her heart shot up into her throat, choking her scream. Were the beings who set the trap around? Fists closing around the cool metal bars, she shook her prison but found it solid, not budging.

"Tomis!" she cried, cursing the fear in her voice. He was less threatening than the unknown trap-setter at the moment. She could always run away from him again later.

"Talia?" The note of alarm matched her own. Like a beautiful wild animal, Tomis appeared from around the boulder at top speed, his steps nearly silent despite his mass and velocity. He leaped a distance of nearly two lengths of her body onto the cage, causing it to swing on the tree branch where it hung.

He uttered a low curse and scaled the cage, shaking the structure when he landed on the roof. Another oath.

He vaulted to the ground, landed softly, and surveyed the cage. He slid beneath it and let out a low chuckle. "Don't worry, starshine. They left a key."

"Who left a key?"

"Probably the last Zandian inhabitants here. Before the genocide. It looks old. I looked around before you ran into your trouble. There's no beings about. Doesn't look like any have been here in a long time."

He emerged with a curved piece of metal on a chain, which he stretched to the hinge on the floor of the cage and fit into a small slot. The bottom fell open, and she tumbled to the ground. He smiled and reached for her hand to help her to her feet. "It must have been for trapping beasts. Come on."

She toddled forward on shaking legs. "Wh-what kind of beasts?"

His gaze swept the darkness around them. "Could be a number of animals." His smile faded and brows went down. "What in the hell were you doing over here?"

"Nothing," she answered quickly. "Simply checking this area for danger."

Tomis' eyes narrowed. "It is dishonorable for a Zandian to lie." He closed his fingers around her wrist and yanked her forward, against his body. "And I'm fairly certain that was an untruth, little female. I believe punishment is in order."

Her bottom tingled at the memory of his earlier slaps. But she feared punishment meant something far worse. Why then, did her nipples pucker as if he'd suggested something far more appealing? Something...sexual?

With a swift yank, he ripped his shirt from her head, leaving her stark naked, the way she'd been when he found her. Her body immediately responded, breasts growing heavy, pussy moistening.

Stars knew why she didn't run. Simply stood there, waiting to see what he would do next. Her body hummed with possibility, with desire. Bottom clenched with the possibility of feeling his palm again.

He gripped her hand, the same way he had in the tunnels, and tugged her to the boulder, where he pulled them both to the ground. In a flash, he had her upended over his extended thighs, her ass presented.

She should have run.

Except nothing would make her miss finding out what happened next. What the huge warrior would do with a naked female sprawled across his lap.

He brought his hand down on her ass, and her enchantment with the situation immediately vanished.

"Ouch!"

"I know, sweet female. I intend to make it smart." His large palm crashed down on the other cheek. He continued, picking up speed, spanking harder and faster with each passing moment.

She quickly deemed it enough and attempted to scramble away, but he held her tight with an arm clamped over her waist. No amount of wriggling or kicking could make him stop.

She kept her mouth shut at first, determined not to let him know how much it hurt, but he went on and on with no sign of stopping. Her bottom burned—she was certain her lavender skin had turned magenta.

"No more!" she cried, rolling her ass over his lap.

He responded by slapping the backs of her thighs, where the flesh was far more sensitive.

"Tomis, please! I'm sorry!" She hadn't meant to apologize, but it tumbled out and seemed to do the trick, because the warrior stopped and ran his palm over her burning ass.

~.~

"I like it when you beg." He hadn't meant to say that out loud. But it was true. He enjoyed it far too much. He'd liked punishing her far more than he should have, too. Her beautiful ass turning rosy under his hand, her squirming hips pressing against his erection, the little gasps she made.

She'd liked it, too, though he doubted she'd admit it. The scent of her arousal nearly made him dizzy with lust.

He stroked the curves of her ass, though he knew he should stop touching her, get her *vecking* gorgeous form off his lap before he lifted her to her hands and knees and pounded her hard from behind.

Oh stars. The things he wanted to do to that hot little body of hers.

His pulse stuttered when she slowly parted her thighs.

Holy Zandian star, did she want him to touch her there? Without contemplating the consequences, he slid his fingers between her thighs and rubbed roughly over her wet slit.

Her moan made him bite down hard on his lip, drawing blood.

He dragged his thumb down the crack of her ass, massaging it against her anus while his digits continued to explore her slick feminine folds.

She arched her ass up to his hand, giving him all the permission he needed.

He sought her clit and rubbed it with his middle finger before dipping it lower and exploring her tight entrance. He screwed one digit in, his heartrate kicking up another notch when she wriggled and moaned.

"Do you need me to satisfy that ache between your legs, starshine?"

"*Yes.*" Her immediate reply punched his cock into the stiffest erection he'd ever had. And then it hit him. *Zandian breeding season.* They both were responding to the natural urges of the planet, which drew their bodies to mate like some inexorable force. Well, who was he to argue if her body required satiating?

He wouldn't *veck* her. He couldn't. But he could certainly give her a little relief.

Massaging her anus with his thumb, he pumped his middle finger in and out of her. But the urge to taste her overcame him. Stroking wasn't enough. She needed his mouth, his tongue. He withdrew his finger and flipped her over on his lap, lifting and parting her thighs. He draped one over his shoulder and held the other knee wide, giving him access to the pink heart of her sex.

"I need to taste this sweet little pussy," he rumbled and licked a long line from her anus to her clit.

She let out a shaky sound, her pelvic floor contracting and lifting.

"Do you like that, starshine?"

"*Yes.*" Again, no hesitation.

It gave him all the encouragement he needed to go on. He traced her inner lips with the tip of his tongue then sought her clit, flicking his tongue over it. She tasted like...perfection. He wanted her feminine tang to be all he ever feasted on.

Her cry of satisfaction made his cock throb. He'd have to jerk off soon, or Talia would end up filled with Zandian cock, *vecked* without mercy until her head spun.

He buried his face between her legs, licking and sucking her labia, nipping them. He plunged his thumb inside her, *vecked* her quickly with short, hard strokes.

Her fingers tore at his hair. "Tomis."

"That's right, starshine. Who knows how to take care of your greedy little pussy?"

"Y-you do." She pulled him tighter and the leg hooked over his shoulder. He suctioned his lips over the little nub of her clit, sucking hard.

She clamped a hand over her mouth, stifling her scream.

He pumped his thumb and sucked, his middle finger finding her anus. "Who, Talia? Say my name again."

She arched into him, rubbed her juicy pussy against his mouth, her anus clenching and trembling beneath his touch. "Tomis!"

A surge of satisfaction whipped through him, despite the throb in his cock. Fulfilling his female was all he cared about. He tap-tap-tapped her back hole, and she shattered, her thighs clenching, feet dancing, bottom lifting and clenching. Her pussy squeezed his thumb in quick pulses.

She stuffed her knuckles into her mouth, howling around them as her bottom bucked against his face.

He waited until every last tremor released before he eased his thumb out and kissed every part of her pink center. He pressed his lips against her inner thigh and disentangled her legs from his shoulders, lifting her ankles high in the air.

Her pert little ass lifted high in the air, her protruding sex taunted him. He started spanking her again, enjoying the new position, the way she bucked and jerked under his palm. After a dozen smacks, he stopped and kissed each reddened cheek. "That's for being an unbelievable temptation to me." He lowered her hips to his lap, tucked her knees against his chest, and stroked her tantalizing curves.

"What's holding you back?" Her husky voice nearly made him come in his combat pants. Her head lay on the mossy ground, chestnut hair fanned out around her heart-shaped face.

He delivered a light slap to her flank. "You're not mine to take. *Veck,* I wish you were. The planet—" He tightened his grip on her thigh.

She leaned up on her elbows, causing her breasts to shift and slide with gravity.

His mouth watered to take each of those dusky nipples in his mouth and suck until she clawed at his shoulders for more.

"What is it about the planet?" She sounded breathless. "It's doing something to us, isn't it?"

He nodded. "The crystals—they fuel our bodies. Plus, it's breeding season. Once a solar cycle, Zandian females come into season. It lasts forty-five to fifty planet rotations. Have you felt it before?"

A furrow appeared between her brows, and she shook her head. "What makes you so sure I'm Zandian?"

He gave a short bark of laughter. "Starshine, you are everything that is sacred and beautiful about a Zandian female." He allowed his gaze to roam where it had wanted to be the entire time, absorbing the lusciousness of every curve, every valley. Nothing about her wasn't perfect, from the delicate slope of her collarbone to the twin globes of her breasts—just enough to hold in each of his hands—and her flat belly and long, muscular legs. And he'd never forget exploring the sweet flower hidden between those thighs.

"But why can't I see in the dark like you?"

He frowned. "Perhaps because you've been away from the crystals for so long. And you appear underfed, love." He hoped she wouldn't take it as an insult, but she certainly seemed too small to be the daughter of the enormous warrior, Seke.

She attempted to roll away from him, but he held her captive.

"Am I right?"

Her jaw firmed, but she nodded. "I was often hungry, yes."

He dropped a kiss on her knee. "I'm sorry. I'm sure you'll recover quickly now that you have access to the crystals."

She tilted her head. "What about you? Haven't you been away, too?"

"I was lucky enough to escape. My mother put me on an airship with the governor of my district. They took as many children from our province as they could. Later, I was fostered for arms training to your father on the palatial pod that became Prince Zander's home. Prince Zander escaped with several large specimens of crystal, and they created crystal baths on the pod for any of his species to use. If he'd known of your existence, you would have been invited to use them, and given refuge and training, if you desired."

She studied him warily, as if unsure whether to believe him.

He stroked his palm up her firm thigh, circling it around the curve of her hip. "I speak the truth, Talia. I would never trick you. Zandians have honor."

She wrinkled her nose. "Is it honorable to strip females and slap their bare asses?"

He grinned. "You're not hurt. Tell me that you're hurt, and I'll never do it again."

Even in the darkness, he saw her face flush darker purple. She reached for her ass and stroked it. "No, I'm not hurt."

"You liked it."

More violet stained her cheeks. "I did not."

Yet, the scent of her arousal bloomed once more.

Veck. He'd been attempting to alleviate the ache in his cock by not moving, but his erection punched out again.

"I'm hungry," she said, probably to distract him from the conversation.

He arched a brow. "Are you, starshine? The crystal core of the planet should provide enough."

Confusion flitted over her face. "You don't eat?"

"Once every ten planet rotations. We don't require it for energy, only to provide a few nutrients our bodies require." He shifted her off his lap, the need to satisfy this lovely female on every level too strong to remain still. "If you're hungry, though, I'll go hunt."

"No, I'll wait. I thought I required food." She sat up and reached for his balled up shirt.

He snatched it away from her. "Sorry, love. You're on clothing restriction for running off."

Her eyes widened and full lips parted and, judging by her scent, the edict left her more aroused than angry. "Wh-what do you mean?"

"I'll give you this shirt back when you've earned my trust. Until I get you to safety, starshine, you're in my keeping, which means I'm your master. When I give you an order, you obey or suffer the consequences."

~.~

Her pussy clenched, despite her anger. "And the consequence is my nudity?" Damn her voice for wobbling.

"Yes. It will help you remember I'm your master."

As much as she wanted to slap his face for saying it, her body reveled in the idea. Heat prickled all over, her bottom clenching and tingling as she remembered the spanking. It hadn't hurt. Not in retrospect. It had shocked her. Stung, a bit, but she understood his design had been to put her in her place, not to harm her. Same as stripping her of clothing.

It wasn't a new concept. King Fluut had employed the same one, hadn't he? Stripped her and hung her on his wall?

"Same as Fluut, then."

The smile fell away from his face, and she instantly regretted the comparison. They were not the same at all. Fluut had been cold, heartless, and disgusting. Tomis had said if the spanking truly hurt, he wouldn't do it again. He was kind and handsome. Extraordinarily handsome, now that she had time to study. Sturdy jaw and an easy, generous smile. Wide brown-violet eyes rimmed with long, dark lashes. His hair was closely shorn, making the horns stand out on the top of his head.

His brows furrowed and jaw clenched in a mulish angle, and he lifted her by the armpits and settled her straddling his lap. "Did you like being naked for King Fluut?"

She rocked her pelvis over the hard bulge of his cock. Scratch that—it was a conscious movement. Because for whatever reason, Tomis hadn't acted on his desire, and it gave her leverage. As inexperienced as she was, she knew exactly how to torture him.

Her stiff nipples pointed toward smooth, hairless chest, and she dragged them against his flesh, glorying in the choked gasp she elicited. "No. But, even then, I had this ache between my legs. This desire from being on this planet."

Tomis' scowl almost frightened her. Was it over her teasing?

"You didn't ache for him," he said stubbornly. *He's jealous.* The thought had accompanying victory bells.

She rocked over his lap again. "You're right," she murmured, taking mercy on him. She leaned forward and nipped his ear. "I wondered about being taken by a Zandian male. Wondered what he'd look like, how it would be."

Tomis' breath drew across his teeth like a hiss. "Am I...what you expected?"

Even better. She reached for one of his horns. "All except for these. What are they for?"

A shudder ran through his body the moment she touched the horn, and it thickened and stiffened against her fingers.

"They're erogenous," he choked.

A thrill of power ran through her. "Is that right?" she purred, gripping the horn hard and using it as a handle to stand up.

She ran her tongue over one while she squeezed the other.

"Talia," he gasped, hands flying out to grip her thighs. His fingers dug into them when she took the thickened horn into her mouth and sucked hard.

"Oh *veck*. You're going to make me come in my pants like a youth."

"Show me your cock." Yes, she was all sexual power now. It flowed through her, stronger than the energy from the crystals. "Is it the same width as these horns?" She traded horns, sucking the opposite one as she squeezed and massaged the first.

"Bigger."

She'd known it would be, but it still thrilled her to hear it.

"Take it out," she repeated.

Tomis drew one hand away from her thigh and brought it back with a slap. "Little female, you don't give orders around here." He proved it by ignoring her command and applying his fingers to her dripping pussy. He stroked along her folds, sending spirals of pleasure out in all directions from where he touched. He worked one thick digit inside.

She sucked harder, bringing her mouth up and down over his stubby, pulsing horn.

He removed his finger and slapped between her legs, but it seemed his control was limited. "By the Zandian star, Talia. You're killing me."

"You'd better stop spanking me, or I'll bite," she warned, skimming her teeth over his sensitive horn.

Her world flipped as Tomis threw her to the ground, somehow managing to cushion her fall with his arms.

"Not in charge, starshine," he growled, picking up her ankles and paddling her ass and pussy with his huge palm.

It felt *wonderful*. She wanted more of it. More spanking, more fingering. And stars, yes. She wanted that thick Zandian cock he still hadn't shown her.

He dropped her ankles, and she allowed her knees to fall open, exposing her throbbing pussy. Hands on his hips, he loomed over her on his knees, breath raking in and out of his mouth, eyes dark violet embers.

"Give me orders, then," she dared him.

He slapped one of her breasts, surprising her with the intensity of his glittering gaze. "How will I survive this?"

"Show me," she whispered again.

His huge chest lifted and fell, and it thrilled her to know she'd made him short of breath, when she doubted much of anything winded the massive warrior. Slowly, he pushed the front of his pants down and freed his huge cock.

"You wanted to see this, baby?" He gripped the base of his length, causing it to surge forward.

It was her turn to groan because the sight of his malehood fanned her flames of desire even hotter.

Zandian breeding season.

That was the only reason she wanted this cocky, beautiful warrior. Not because they had a special connection. Or because she trusted him to her rescue. She didn't. Couldn't. But there was no harm in getting a little pleasure for once in her life. And she'd escape from him on the next planet rotation.

Tomis fisted his long, thick dick, pumping up and down its length. "Get on your hands and knees, starshine. Give me your mouth." His harsh, guttural command produced no outrage, only desire. She crawled into the position he described, parting her lips for his malehood. He guided it into her lips with a thick curse.

The size stretched her jaw wide as she worked to take him deeper, gagging when it hit the back of her throat.

Tomis wrapped a fist in her hair controlling her movements.

She reached for his thighs, sat back on her heels and let him use her mouth as he saw fit.

"Holy *vecking* stars, holy *vecking*—" Tomis snapped his hips forward and back, shoving his cock in and out of her lips. She shifted to take him into the pocket of her cheek, looking up to judge how he liked it.

"You keep looking at me like that, little female, and I'm going to shove this cock so far down your throat, you'll choke. There's a limit to my control, Talia, and you are pushing it."

She couldn't speak because her mouth was stuffed with his throbbing malehood, but she hummed her agreement.

His fingers tightened in her hair and his movements grew jerky; hard muscled thighs tensed and trembled under her hands.

With a roar, he came, pulling out and pumping his cock as he decorated her breasts and belly with his rainbow-hued seed.

He surprised her again by falling over her, pushing her to the ground and stamping his lips over hers. His tongue delved in, twined with hers as his cock slid into the gap between her legs, along her wet slit.

"*Veck.*" He shuddered as he pulled away, all the way back to his knees, wiping his mouth with the back of his hand. "You'll be the death of me, starshine. I'm never going to survive being alone with you—not even for another planet rotation—without *vecking* you in every way invented. And a few other ways, too."

She grinned, satisfied with this new power she wielded over the huge warrior. Proud of herself for pleasing him as much as he'd satisfied her.

She made a show of rubbing his cum into her skin, watching the flare of stark hunger and animal pride in his gaze. "So, what's stopping you? Do Zandians believe it dishonorable to claim a female without mating her first?"

He tucked his cock back in his pants and settled beside her, rolling her to face away from him and nesting against her backside. "Something like that," he muttered.

"I thought Zandians didn't lie."

He leaned up on an elbow and traced the shell of her ear with his calloused fingertip. A shiver of deep pleasure went through her. Every tiny experience with this male was a first for her. First orgasm. First blow job. First kiss. First cuddle.

In that order.

"I will never lie to you, little female. That's a promise." He struck such a serious tone, she actually believed him. "You're important to our species. Before we found out about your existence, there were no females of breeding age left. Prince Zander had to breed with a human, and other warriors have taken human mates as well.

"So, you see, it's not for a peasant—a miner's son who only became a member of the royal guard because he's one of the few young males alive—to claim you. You are far too important to our entire species. Your body rightfully belongs to the prince, if he wishes to claim you. Or for him to choose how you should be bred. Not for me."

His words struck her like a javelin through the chest, coated her mouth with the bitter taste of betrayal. She shouldn't be surprised. She'd known this was the reason he'd been sent for her. But now that they'd become intimate, some piece of her must have hoped the situation was different. The stupid part was that she couldn't decide which hurt worse—that he believed she was nothing more than a body for breeding, or that he wasn't even willing to fight to claim her.

She bit her lips and forced herself to remain still, although the instinct to elbow him hard in the ribs and take off running nearly overpowered her. She wouldn't make it two steps, though. She'd have to wait for a better moment to escape Tomis.

Or somehow prevent him from giving chase.

CHAPTER THREE

Tomis slept little, keeping watch over the beautiful female.

He'd had sexual experiences before—mostly paid with human slaves—but nothing came close to the desire this female provoked. Even after she'd sucked him off, he'd been hard as a rock for her. Sleeping beside her was both an honor and an agony. Her scent had him in knots; her soft skin brought him to the brink of bliss.

She'd stiffened when he'd explained why he couldn't claim her but he couldn't puzzle out what had offended her. He'd assured her of her safety. Surely she understood how honored she would be back at the palatial pod.

Hell, he fully expected to have their roles reversed, with him groveling at her feet. For now, though, he thoroughly enjoyed mastering her.

Probably too much. His mind flitted to his mentor, Master Seke. Would the male have his ass over stripping his daughter naked as punishment?

Possibly.

But Seke had trained Tomis and his other pupils with discipline and consequences. Had won their undying allegiance and love as master through methods of humiliation and reward. Wasn't it from Seke he'd learned mastery?

As the Zandian star peeked over the horizon, lighting the day, he sat up quietly, careful not to disturb his charge. Zandia was still beautiful. He'd studied the planet his whole life, and had memorized every inch of the maps brought back from a recent expedition, but nothing compared to actually being on her again. The Finn had mined the areas heaviest with crystal and, by some stroke of mercy or luck, had left at least half the planet untouched. Though their king resided on Zandia at the moment, he hadn't claimed the planet to inhabit—they had their own territories. Since they'd hunted down and killed every last Zandian on the planet when they took over, the area now had an eerie feel, as if the planet's crust bore the memory of the genocide.

Despite that, it was exquisitely beautiful. Peaceful, even. Plant-based life-forms had thrived during the Zandian absence. Trees hung heavy with fruit; the ground was covered in soft, thick moss sprinkled with tiny white flowers. *Caralee* flowers, if he remembered right.

He leaned over Talia. She appeared to remain asleep, though not peacefully. A furrow marred her perfect brow. Despite his requirement that she remain naked, he'd draped his shirt over her during the night to keep her warm. He twitched it higher and stood to gather food, in case she did, indeed, require alimentation.

Keeping his tread silent, he explored the area, finding a *fue* tree with a few ripe *fue* fruits hanging from it. In the tree, two furry *shalpies* played together in an adorable mating dance. He stopped to watch. He hadn't seen animals in the wild since he was a child.

He heard Talia's footsteps behind him but didn't turn, pointing silently up to the branch so she, too, could see the sweet animal play.

It would bother him, later, that he didn't register any danger before the pain exploded in the back of his head and everything went black.

~.~

Please don't let him be dead.

She'd wanted to knock Tomis out, not kill him. The sound the huge warrior made when crumpling to the ground made her stomach torque almost as much as the crack of marble against his skull had. Considering how little experience she had with physical assault, it was possible she'd killed him.

She hesitated, peering down at his stunning body, cringing at the way his limbs had fallen at an odd angle.

He let out a low groan.

Not dead. Incapacitated. She took off running as fast her bare feet would carry her. She had no idea where to go, but, as far as she was concerned, she could stay on Zandia, live out in the wild on her own. The strength she felt on the planet made her loathe to ever leave it—dangerous enemies or not. And loneliness was nothing new. She may have interacted with a multitude of beings at Thurn's tavern, but she'd never had a friend. Thun had forbidden her extended contact with any being. Probably because he didn't want her finding out she wasn't human, the lout.

She crashed through the brush, not caring where she went, so long as it was far away from the male who wanted to bring her to his prince for breeding. Asshole.

Except he wasn't an asshole. And that made her all the more bitter at not being able to trust him. She'd *wanted* to trust him.

She ran until her legs gave out and a twist in her side made her stop and double over, wheezing. She'd run three times as far as she could have back on Stornig. *Thank you, Zandian crystals.*

She straightened and gasped. In the curve of the valley below stood the rubble of a bombed village. Metal and stone twisted together in an unnatural heap. Goose bumps prickled over her arms as if the ghosts of all those murdered by the Finn stood up to be counted.

It was horrible, what had happened on Zandia. How could the Finn kill every inhabitant? Females and young alike?

An animal skittered by her feet, making her lurch backward. She fell into giant leaves—a bush of some sort—except the leaves snapped closed.

Her scream punctured the air before she could stop herself. Tight bands of giant leaves cinched her, squeezing her very breath. She struggled to free herself but couldn't even wrench an arm free from the terrorizing flora.

Excrement, excrement, excrement! Zandia had carnivorous plants? This was not the death she foresaw for herself. Not even close. She screamed again, once more willing to signal her self-appointed rescuer, Tomis, the lesser evil in this situation.

Like before, he appeared at top speed, a mixture of fear and fury on his face. His eyes widened when he took in her predicament, and the alarm in his expression did nothing to relieve her.

"Get me out of here," she whimpered like a complete tool. She'd just bashed his head in with a rock, and now she begged him to save her? But he would. She knew it without a shadow of a doubt. Tomis was hero material, through and through. He identified as an honorable warrior. His duty was to rescue her.

He tore at the banded leaves, but it was as if they were made of steel. They didn't budge.

"Hurry, please! It's getting tighter."

"Stop struggling," he bit out as he picked up a large, sharp rock and hacked at the base of the giant greenery.

"Your gun! Use the gun. Please, Tomis—it hurts."

"If I use the gun, I risk detection by the Finn," he grated. But he wasn't getting anywhere with the rock.

The plant squeezed her ribs. "I can't breathe."

"*Veck.*" Tomis pulled the gun from his belt and knelt at the stem, pressing the nozzle right up against the plant's flesh. He shot into the aggressive vegetation.

She screamed as electrical surges charged through her limbs, making her teeth buzz and her hair stand on end.

It did the trick, though. The plant loosened its hold on her.

"It worked. It worked." She freed one arm and reached for him. "Pull me out. Please." She ought to add an "I'm so sorry I tried to concuss you," but he'd already clasped her hand in his mighty palm. The muscles in his chest and arms, even his neck, bulged as he leaned his weight back and pulled her.

She moved an inch. Then another. Then she came flying out, landing on top of Tomis and knocking him back to the ground.

"Thank you," she breathed. "I—"

He threw her off him and surged to his feet. Grabbing her hand, he pulled her up. "Come. We have to find water to wash that acid off your skin before it eats you alive."

Stars, what was the sound that came from her lips? It resembled no word in any language she'd heard in the galaxy. It was more like a pitiful, animalistic wail.

Acid off her skin?

Yes. Yellow-green slime covered her body from the neck down. And it was starting to burn. No, that was just the power of Tomis' suggestion. Hell, either way, she needed it off before she lost it. She took off running, trying to keep up with Tomis.

He seemed to know where he was going, his long strides sure. "Watch the hole," he barked, pointing to the danger as his feet flew along. She did her best to follow but she soon reached her limit again, a cramp twisting in her side like a knife.

"Wait! Sl-slow down...I can't go on," she panted.

Tomis turned, eyeing the slime on her body with disgust before he swung her up in his arms.

"No, you shouldn't—" she protested, but he already had. The massive warrior took off running once more, even faster than before. Unbelievably, he carried her straight to water. Somehow, he'd known where to find a river. He plunged in, lowering her body into the cold water. Reeds choked the banks, tiny colorful waterbeasts swimming in and out of them.

She gasped at the temperature but used her hands the way Tomis did, rubbing the goo off her skin with a brisk motion. She shucked his shirt and wrung it out in the water. Tomis continued scrubbing her skin, his large palms working her body. The goo washed off, but her skin tingled where it had been.

"How did you know where to find water?"

"I've studied the geography of our planet." His large palms coasted over her curves, slowing down, igniting a new sensation along her sensitized flesh. The slippery substance was gone. Tomis was just touching now for sport. One giant palm closed on her breast. He squeezed until she gasped, pain burning a twin flame with pleasure.

Hunger mingled with anger in his dark-amethyst gaze.

Oh right. She'd knocked him out with a rock and run away. There would be a reckoning now.

Their bodies tangled in the water, the stones beneath her feet slick and moving. She clung to him for footing.

Hooking her arms higher around his neck, she jumped up and wrapped her legs around his waist. Better to appeal to his hunger than anger. "I'm sorry, warrior," she murmured.

He gripped her hair in his fist and yanked her head back with one hand while his other palmed her ass, fingers digging into her soft flesh. "You will be." The promise in his tone wasn't angry, only dark and sensual.

She sucked in her breath, but her pussy clenched with excitement. She couldn't bring herself to fear this male. He'd saved her life three times over already. He wouldn't do anything that couldn't be undone.

He stalked out of the river. Water dripped from their twined bodies. His hulking form was warm and solid against her softer one. He deposited her under a tree, where he ripped a flowering vine down from a branch. He grabbed her wrists roughly and pulled them together, winding the vine around her them.

"What are you doing?"

"Making sure you don't run," he gritted.

She ought to worry, ought to be planning her next escape, but all she could do was watch in fascination. She liked him angry, dark purpose oozing from his swift, capable movements. This male could get them out of any situation. He'd come alone to an enemy planet with no weapon but his two hands and had busted her out of the dungeon. He'd navigated through underground tunnels and unmarked terrain with nothing more than his eyes. He'd known how to handle animal traps and carnivorous plants. Apparently, he knew how to handle her rebellion, too.

He looped one end of the vine over a branch and pulled it taut, lifting her arms over her head until she had to launch to her tiptoes to follow it.

"Ouch. You're hurting me," she whined, only because she knew he cared about such things.

His mouth remained firm. "You'll survive."

"I'm sorry about your head," she offered quickly. "Are you all right?"

One corner of his mouth quirked in a wry grin. "I'll survive."

Were they smiling at one another? Was he over being angry now that he had her bound and on display? She danced on her toes closer to him, her nipples tight, pussy throbbing, but he ignored her and stalked away.

"Wait! Where are you going? Don't leave me here like this! What if a beast attacks me? Or another being?"

He stopped long enough to turn and shake his head. "I won't let that happen, starshine."

I know you won't.

This male was capable of anything. She sighed and sank into her bonds, spinning around to entertain herself. She tiptoed out, as far as her toes could reach then let go and allowed her body to swing.

"Now you're the one hurting yourself," Tomis said drily, appearing once more. He carried a thin reed like the ones from the riverbed and a handful of small brown fruit.

She eyed the items doubtfully. "What are those for?"

He smacked the reed against his leg. "I think you can imagine."

Her bottom clenched. *Ouch.* The reed would hurt. No worse than any beating she'd received from Thurn, her former master, but somehow she knew this punishment would be far different.

Tomis's mouth quirked like he was enjoying himself, for one thing. For another, Thurn had never stripped her of clothing or tied her up. Or worn such a wolfish expression.

Her nipples beaded up again as the breeze blew over them. Her skin had dried, but the acid had sensitized it.

Tomis dropped the brown fruit on a stone and used a smaller stone to crush them. A thick oily substance oozed out. He gathered it in his palm and approached her with glittering eyes. Yes, he definitely was enjoying this.

"*Slu* honey will soothe your skin, in case any of it was burnt." He slathered it down her front, dragging his large palm between her breasts to her belly, then curving it around her hip. Both hands found her breasts, massaging the oil in a circle. He drew back one palm and slapped her breast. "Bad girl."

She closed her lips on a tiny *eep.*

Punish me, Tomis.

It must be the crystals, the planet talking. It must be breeding season taking control of her body because she arched into him, offering her breasts for his slaps. He slapped the other one. It hurt, but she wanted more.

He scooped some more oil and turned her around, coating her back and buttocks. He oiled the insides of her ass, rubbing along her crack. "You'll need extra honey here. Do you know why, Talia?"

"Why?" *Was that my husky voice?*

"Because after I apply the cane, I'm going to *veck* that little ass until you scream."

She tucked her tailbone, squeezing her buttocks together.

Tomis slapped one cheek, hard. He wrapped an arm around her waist and splayed his palm over her belly, bringing his lips close to her ear. "Because nothing helps a disobedient little female remember to mind her master like a long, hard *ass-vecking.* Isn't that right?"

A shiver ran through her, along with some dark longing she didn't recognize.

Tomis continued massaging oil into her anus. The hand on her belly drifted lower, cupping her mons. "Ah. See? You're already wet for me. You know you deserve this, don't you, naughty female?" When she didn't answer, he slapped her ass again. "Don't you?"

"Yes, Master," she whispered. She'd lost her mind completely.

Tomis groaned and rewarded her with a wriggle of his finger over her clit. "I like when you call me *Master.*"

I like when you touch me there.

She didn't say it. He already knew, didn't he? How the male could know his way around her body so well, she didn't understand, but it seemed he did.

He continued to oil her, positioning her legs wide apart, standing on the tips of her toes as he ran his hands down them, stopping to tease her pussy with a quick flick of his tongue.

He picked up the reed and slapped it into his palm.

Didn't it hurt him?

"Say it again. Who is your master?"

She eyed him, pulse ratcheting up higher as he approached. "You are. Tomis. Tomis is my master."

"That's right." He circled around behind her and sliced the cane through the air. It landed in the center of her buttocks, and she shrieked, surprised at the shock of pain and the line of fire that followed.

"Owwwww," she moaned, going limp against her bonds. She twisted to angle her ass away from him, but he caught her jaw, pulled her up to his face.

"You will hold your position and accept this caning like a good girl."

She wanted to challenge him and say, "Or what?" but he silenced her with a hard kiss to her lips.

"If you do, I'll consider your pleasure when I claim that ass."

Her pussy contracted; tremors ran down her inner thighs.

He leaned over and applied his cunning lips to her nipple, sucking it to a stiff peak, grazing it with his teeth then pulling away and slapping the side of her breast. "Now, push that ass out and hold perfectly still for your stripes, and I won't use the cane on these beautiful tits, too." Another slap to her breast.

"Y-yes, Master." What in the hell was wrong with her? She must have lost her mind. Was that actually her wanton voice calling this male *Master*?

Tomis strolled behind her again. "Ass out. Legs apart. Hold still."

Damn, if she didn't do exactly as she was told. Assuming the position had her pussy leaking, apparently thrilled at this form of brutal attention. This punishment with the promise of a reward at the end.

The cane struck again, right below the last wicked stripe.

She bit her lip to stifle the yelp. Holding the position was an impossibility, though. Her legs danced beneath her of their own accord, the smarting on her ass creating the need for movement.

Tomis laid a hand on her hip, holding her still. "Starshine, what did I say?"

"I'm trying Tomis—Master."

He swept her hair to one side, baring her shoulder, and sank his teeth into her flesh there.

A tremor of desire rippled through her. The line between reward and punishment had become so blurred, she wasn't sure whether she'd earned his approval or ire. All she knew was that she wanted all of it. Everything this beautiful warrior had to offer. And more.

Her body screamed for his attention. For his touch. The pain he inflicted.

With his hand at her hip, holding her still, he delivered another stripe, and another. Each one made her cry out, but Tomis' steadying grip kept her in place. He whipped the thin reed all the way down her ass to the backs of her thighs then back up again, until pain had her every sense on high alert and her pussy molten.

Tomis slid an arm around her waist from behind. "Good girl," he breathed in her ear as he reached up and untied the vine holding her wrists up. If he hadn't caught her, her legs would've given out, but, instead, she fell backward, against his hard body, to the safety she'd known would be there.

"On your knees, female." He nudged the backs of her knees with his, causing them to bend and drop to the ground.

She waited, listening to the sounds of his clothing rustling.

"Elbows down, starshine. Show me that pretty little pucker of yours."

This was insane. She should get up and run. Make another break for it. She should not allow herself to be *ass-vecked*, as he called it, as a punishment.

But her body disagreed. Her inner thighs trembled right up to the apex, where her pussy contracted and released on air, desperate for something.

He slapped her pussy and she slid her knees open even wider, desperate for more touch. "You want me here, don't you?" he crooned, his fingers mercifully rubbing a slow caress over her weeping slit. "Don't you?" he repeated sharply, applying another spank when she didn't answer.

"Yes, Master."

He palmed both cheeks of her ass and spread them wider, his glorious tongue slipping over her sensitive bits, dragging all the way up to her anus and circling there.

Her breath shuddered out of her, and she dropped her face onto her hands.

"You've been a *vecking* torture to me from the first moment I saw you, Talia." Tomis' voice grated deep and rough. He applied fresh oil to her anus, demanding entrance with one of his digits as he massaged it in.

She whimpered as he penetrated her, oiling the way for his far larger cock. How would she ever take it?

Why did she want to?

"You may not be mine to breed, but you sure as hell earned this ass-*vecking*." His finger retreated, replaced by the prod of his cock.

She tensed, the muscles in her back cording up as she attempted to squeeze her ass.

Tomis slapped one cheek, hard. "Open for it. Take your master's cock." He put his weight into it, pressing down until her sphincter muscles yielded.

She mewled as he filled her, stuffed her too full, beyond what she could take. And yet she did take it. Her body accommodated him, opened for this punishment, this humiliating pleasure that already pushed her to the brink of ecstasy. Her toes curled in, pussy leaked moisture down her inner thigh.

Tomis gripped her nape, holding her captive, forcing her face down into the cushion of her hands as he moved in and out of her.

Her mouth opened, yawning to mimic her anus, and she moaned low and steady. Her pussy suddenly seemed pitifully empty. She snaked a hand underneath herself, but Tomis followed, catching her wrist and bringing it back.

"Not until I decide you deserve it." He pinioned both wrists to the ground above her head with one hand while gripping her nape in the other.

"I was good," she protested, "you controlling bastard."

He let out a low chuckle. "This is a lesson, starshine. What am I helping you remember?"

She groaned. "You're my master."

"That's right, sweet female. I'm your master. I decide when and if you receive pleasure."

"Now," she insisted. "Now...please?"

He released her wrists and shifted his angle of penetration. And—bless him—he brought his fingers to her swollen clit.

She nearly exploded at the first touch, so needy for it. "More."

He slapped her clit, rubbed it. Stuffed his fingers into her empty channel. "*Veck*, Talia. You're so tight. So *vecking* beautiful."

"*Veck* me," she pleaded, using his term, even though he already was.

He shouted a curse and pounded harder into her, his strokes growing erratic. It hurt and satisfied her at the same time.

"Tomis, please," she screamed.

He spanked her pussy in a quick series slaps. Stars danced before her eyes. He flattened her to the ground, straddling her ass as his huge dick plowed into it, filling her, his fingers stuffed in her pussy.

She screamed herself hoarse as Tomis slammed to his finish and her orgasm ripped through her like a tidal wave of release and pleasure. Lights exploded behind her eyes, her legs tightened and shook, pussy squeezed and squeezed, and Tomis pumped her ass full of cock.

~.~

His body exploded, cells flying apart and rearranging in a new shape, leaving him utterly changed. That was the only explanation for the experience of claiming Talia.

And he *had* claimed her—thoroughly—even though it hadn't been her pussy.

Probably way too hard. *Veck*. He hoped he hadn't hurt her. He rolled her over, his weight balanced on his hands beside her head, holding his body above hers.

"Are you all right, little female? I know I was rough."

She blew out a sigh and reached between her legs, her fingers stroking lazily. "You are a beast." She tempered the complaint with a smile, and relief poured through him.

He'd satisfied his female. No, not *his*. Tragically not his.

He sank to the ground beside her and pulled her wrist away, pinning it to the ground and replacing her fingers with his. "*My* pussy. Mine to pleasure. Not yours."

She drew up the leg farther from him, and tilted her hips to give him better access. "Didn't you give me a long explanation last night of how it's not?" There was a bitter note to her voice that he didn't understand but resolved to dig into later. He kept his fingers moving slowly over her damp folds, his goal pleasure rather than completion.

She made a sweet purring sound.

"Why did you run away, Talia?"

She stiffened and tugged at her pinned wrist. When he didn't allow her freedom, she snapped her closer knee up to squeeze out his hand.

"*No.*" He launched over her, prizing her knees apart and pushing them up to her shoulders. Her sweet pussy spread and lifted. He dragged his tongue up her slit. *Ah, the taste of her.* He'd missed it. This was where he belonged, pleasuring his female through her breeding cycle, giving her relief, seeing to her every need.

Except, she was right, he'd told her he wouldn't breed her.

He flicked his tongue four times quickly over her clit. "Tell me."

She moaned and gripped his horns with both her hands, giving tit for tat.

He swallowed the groan in his throat as his cock punched out once again. *Control, Tomis.* If they waged a contest to determine who would break first, it wouldn't be him. He trained as a *vecking* warrior with the discipline instilled in him by Master Seke. Her *father.*

He flattened his tongue and dragged it over the length of her slit. "Tell me, beautiful, or I'll use the reed on you again."

She released his horns and glowered, pushing up on her forearms. "I'm not leaving here with you. And your inability to comprehend my reason seals my decision."

He released her thighs and sat back, a chill creeping through his midsection. He rubbed the lump on his head from where she'd bashed him with the rock, willing his brain to work faster, to understand. *Think, dumb-veck.* He'd said something that had made her stiffen the night before.

"You don't wish to save our species." A cold numbness slithered down his neck, coating his chest and arms.

Her expression closed, and she rolled away, putting on his shirt and tossing him his trousers. Both were still damp from the river, but the beautiful Zandian star shone high in the sky, warming them.

"I don't wish to become your *breeder,* no. Is that so hard to understand?" The steel in her voice gutted him.

He yanked on his pants. His sense of honor, of commitment to his prince and planet, warred with the tumult of emotion he felt for this slip of a female. Was it fair to ask her to lend the use of her body to save their entire species?

Maybe. Maybe not. But he hadn't *asked,* had he? He'd told her. He rubbed his jaw, watching as she stalked off. "Wait." He caught her in two long strides and swung her around to face him. "Let's talk this out. I *vecked* up. I didn't offer you a choice, and I'm sorry."

The stiffness around her mouth fell away, revealing a layer of vulnerability that kicked him in the balls.

"Forgive me, Talia."

Her big beautiful brown-violet eyes stared up into his, and he saw uncertainty wavering there.

He cupped her cheek, stroking her soft skin with his thumb. "Please?"

A flash of misery came and went, replaced by the stubborn lift of her chin. She put her hands on her hips. "Are you going to let me go?"

Veck.

Veckity veck veck veck.

"Talia—"

She yanked out of his grasp. "That's what I thought."

The sight of her retreating back clanged like an alarm through every molecule of his body. *Don't let her go. Never let her go.*

"No, starshine. Wait. *Please.*" He jogged to catch up but didn't touch her this time, simply matched her pace. Gave her the freedom she needed. "I won't bring you in against your will. I give you my vow. A Zandian warrior never breaks his word."

She stopped and faced him, and he lifted his arm in the traditional Zandian greeting, forearm bent, fist pointed to the sky. Her brows drew together in puzzlement, studying it as if it jogged some memory in her.

"Let me protect you. It's what I was born to do." He knew that now, without a shadow of a doubt. Fight for Zandia, yes. Win back the planet, of course. But his first priority would always be to keep this female safe. Provide for her. Keep her.

No, not keep her. She wasn't his to keep. She wasn't even Prince Zander's to keep, now that he'd given her his vow.

Guilt twisted in his solar plexus, but he shoved it back down. Giving his promise had been worth it. Winning Talia's trust was paramount. He could convince her to help her species later. *After* he secured her safety.

"You won't give me to your prince?"

He wanted to explain that Zander wasn't to be feared, that he'd protect and honor her, but that conversation could happen later. He shook his head. "Not unless you wish it. On my honor. Allow me to keep you safe. Please, Talia."

She gave a wobbly nod. "Yes."

Veck if he didn't want that hope-sprinkled *yes* to answer a different question. But it wasn't one he could ask. Even so, relief poured over him, warming his inner chill, and he grasped her hand. "Come. I believe we're close to a special place."

"How do you know your way, here? You can't remember from your childhood."

"No. Part of my training was memorizing maps and learning the terrain—the flora and fauna."

"So what was that—that terrible *thing* that grabbed me back there?"

"*Anacaya*. A carnivorous plant. It normally feeds on *sharkhounds* or small *fieldbeasts*."

"I don't know what *sharkhounds* or *fieldbeasts* are, either." She laughed, the most musical sound he'd ever heard.

"*Sharkhounds* are about this high"—he held a hand out at the level of his upper thigh— "and they hunt in packs. Together, they could take us down." He smiled down at her when she clutched his hand more tightly. "Don't worry, I'm watching for them. *Fieldbeasts* are larger but docile, unless you're a challenging male during mating season. They're herbivores with large tusks. Very tasty. Are you hungry, starshine?"

"No." She sounded surprised. "I guess the crystals are working." She licked her lips, and a shot of a different kind of hunger seeped into his groin. Did she feel it, too? She must, because her gaze flicked across his chest, trailing down to his crotch, where his cock bulged against his pants.

"What is your plan for our escape, exactly?"

"There's a ship junkyard several planet rotations' trek from here. I'm hoping we can make one work."

"*That's* your plan?" Incredulity spiked her words.

"What?"

"It's kind of weak, don't you think?"

He grinned. "So was my plan for getting you out of the dungeon, but I managed it. The backup is holing up out here in the wild until Prince Zander launches his attack. Then we—I mean, I—join the fight."

"You can't contact some being to pick us up?"

He shook his head. "Any form of communication off the planet would tip off the Finn to our location. We're safest staying silent. No laser gun. No comms unit."

She muttered something he didn't catch.

They walked for the first part of the day in a comfortable silence. He used the location of the Zandian star and the river to orient himself and led the way, holding branches and pointing out foot-traps.

"Why do you suppose we haven't seen any beings? It's so quiet. Too quiet."

"Prince Zander sent a ship over to image the planet, and it seems the Finn have centered their attention on mining the area near the capital, where the majority of the crystal is concentrated. After they wiped out the Zandian population, they must have removed their presence from the rest of the planet. We are fortunate. It seems they have not chosen to settle here, only to mine it."

Talia gazed around. "I can't imagine why they wouldn't want to live here. It's so beautiful."

It was foolish, but her appreciation pleased him, as if it meant she might be more willing to align herself with Zander and her species. Join the fight to win back and repopulate the planet.

He gripped her hand to help her over a large rock. When she winced, he kicked himself. He hadn't seen to his female's needs.

"Wait, starshine." He sat on the rock and pulled off his boots then his stockings. "I'd give you my boots, but they wouldn't fit. You can at least wear these to protect your feet." He handed her his socks, still damp from the river. "If they don't disgust you."

A genuine smile lit her face, striking him square in the chest with its brilliance. Veck, *let me earn that smile every planet rotation for the rest of my life.*

She accepted the stockings and pulled them on, knotting the fabric in the back at her calves to keep them from slipping down. A rumbling sound of approval made its way out of his throat. "I never knew stockings could be so *vecking* hot."

She laughed that musical laugh again, lifting his very being. "That must be the crystals talking, warrior."

"No," he swore. "All the holograms of naked Zandian females I jerked my cock to as a youth could not compare to you. Exactly as you are now."

She put her hand in the center of his chest and gave a gentle shove. "Definitely the crystals. But, keep up the compliments, and I might give you a show later." She sashayed down the path ahead of him.

He growled, shoving his boots over his bare feet, his gaze following her bare thighs, the hint of her delectable ass beneath his shirt. "You must have forgotten who is master here. I could revoke your clothing privileges again at any time."

She made a rude Ocretion hand gesture over her shoulder without looking back.

He jogged to catch up and smacked her ass, hard. She jumped forward with a squeal. The scent of her arousal went straight to his cock, which he had to adjust in his combat pants.

He smacked her a few more times as he passed her. "*I* lead, beautiful."

She popped him in the ass, and a sharp burst of laughter erupted from him.

He turned and snatched her wrists. "Some being wants another spanking." He made his voice low and suggestive.

Her body responded, nipples beading up. She licked her lips and angled her head back to look up at him. The heat of her skin through his shirt tingled against his bare torso, bringing every cell alive.

"Lovely little female. If you were mine to mate, I'd keep you naked at all times."

She gave his chest a shove, which didn't move him back a centimeter.

In fact, he stepped even closer, bringing one leg between hers and bending his knee to bring his thigh against her sex. His pulse stuttered when she rocked that perfect pussy down to meet it, lids going to half-mast.

"That's...ridiculous." She sounded breathless. The ridiculousness of his statement didn't make her stop grinding.

He looped an arm around her waist to hold her firmly against him and dropped his palm to squeeze her tight ass while she rocked slowly forward.

My female requires sating.

It was his job, after all. A female in season experienced discomfort if she didn't receive constant release. It would be cruel of him not to see to her needs.

"You'd keep me like a sex slave?" The breathy quality of her voice negated any pretense of offense.

He grinned. "*Veck,* yes. I'd hide you away from any other males. Keep you tied up, naked. Available for my pleasure at all times." He dragged his teeth down the curve of her neck, bit her shoulder.

She ground down harder, faster. "You're...sick."

He used both hands to pull her ass cheeks apart, wriggled a finger against her anus.

She gasped.

"Are you sore here from your *vecking,* baby? I'll go easy on your sweet little pucker."

He swallowed her moan with a hot, demanding kiss, tongue licking into her mouth, twining with hers.

"Tomis," she panted, when their lips broke apart.

He leaned his forehead against hers, helped her rock her delicious pelvis over his thigh with one hand on her ass, while a finger from the other hand continued to massage her back hole.

"I am sick, starshine. You make me so *vecking* feverish, I can't even see straight."

A needy, impatient cry came from her lips, and she fumbled frantically at his pants.

"Oh stars, no." His palm shot to cover hers, pressing her fingers around his cock through the material of his pants. "Don't let it out, or I'll throw you down and *veck* you so hard and long you won't walk for three planet rotations."

She closed her fingers around the outline of his cock and squeezed. "Promise?"

"No, no, no," he groaned, but urged her hand to stroke him, rubbing up and down, the fabric of his pants only enhancing the experience.

She gripped his cock and pulled it in the direction of her pussy, which had left a wet spot on his pants where she'd ground. "Pretend I'm your mate, Tomis. Show me what you'd do."

"*Veck*, Talia. Don't do this to me. I don't want to—" He gave his head a hard shake to clear it.

Master Seke's daughter. Not. Mine. To take.

"I want it," she chanted. "I need it." She slapped his shoulder. "Dammit, Tomis, stop being such an ass."

Discipline. He attempted to drag his brain back online. She required discipline. He was her master. He'd punish then please her. It would give them both relief.

He dropped to one knee and pulled her over the other, presenting her ass for chastisement.

Her fingertips reached for the ground, legs kicked. "Damn you, Tomis!"

The red welts from the cane that morning had already faded, just as the bruise on his head had shrunk. Thankfully, Zandians healed quickly, especially in the presence of the crystals. He clapped his hand down on her ass, fast and hard, pouring every ounce of his sexual desire for her into the punishment.

She yelped and cried out, cursed and condemned him, but he continued on, turning her perfect, heart-shaped ass red. He smarted the backs of her thighs, shoved them apart, and slapped her inner thighs.

Eventually, she stopped cussing and started to plead. "Please, Tomis. Please, please stop. I need you. I need your fingers, your cock. I need something. Please."

He wasted no time plunging his fingers into her welcoming channel. He made a cone of them and beat them in hard, his knuckles smacking against her clit.

His sweet little female came almost immediately, her scream of satisfaction echoing off the nearby rocks. *Veck,* he prayed there were no beings anywhere nearby. Her pussy squeezed his fingers in short bursts, and he continued pounding her with them until she'd finished.

He lifted her and dropped to his ass, pulling her onto his lap.

Breathless, face flushed, eyes glassy, her beauty socked him in the gut.

"Better?" He might be breathless, himself.

She nodded, awe shining from her lovely expression. "A little."

He shoved her shirt up and nibbled on one nipple then laved it with his tongue. Ah, *veck.* He had to stop, or he'd go way too far. "At your service," he murmured.

She snaked her arms around his neck, collapsing against him. "I thought you were the master."

"Mmm hmm. And don't forget it. I could just as easily tie you up and give you no satisfaction." Still holding her, he stood and carried her along the path. He wanted to get to the waterfalls before starset.

"But you wouldn't," she whispered, teeth closing around his ear.

No. She had his number. He would never be able to deny her pleasure. Delay, perhaps—to heighten her satisfaction when he gave it. Or to punish bad behavior. But never withhold.

. . .

Talia couldn't deny the pleasure of being carried by the great warrior. His massive chest and arms flexed with her weight, but he never seemed to grow tired. In fact, she was certain he enjoyed it, too.

She noticed the way he surreptitiously dropped his face into her hair and drew a deep breath, as if savoring her scent. Or how his fingers idly caressed her thigh. Now and then, he'd drop a kiss on her head or shoulder or one of her arms around his neck.

She admired the strong lines of his face, his constant vigilance of their surroundings. Tomis' protection made a gooey warmth flow through her entire being.

But it wasn't a feeling she could trust. Just because he wanted to keep her safe and alive, didn't mean he wanted her for his own. He'd made it quite plain he couldn't—*wouldn't*—claim her as a mate. Wouldn't breed her, despite the mounting desperation she felt to be satisfied in that way.

Damn him.

His refusal cut her more deeply than she cared to admit. She was nothing more than a job to him. Yes, he enjoyed aspects of the job, but he refused to take himself outside its confines.

He stopped and lowered her feet to the ground. "I won't make you walk, I just need to change your legs to the other side."

"I can walk now," she offered, although her body loathed to be parted from his, as if simply from skin to skin contact, it knew it might get satisfaction again soon.

"*No.*" Stars, she loved when he turned stubborn.

Instead of letting him pick her up with her legs to the side, she jumped to straddle his waist. His palms came up to her bare ass, still tingly and warm from the spanking he'd given her. She looped her arms around his neck and leaned her head close to his neck to make herself easier to carry.

Tomis muttered a curse. "I don't know if this is going to work, female," he said, but he started walking forward at the same pace as before.

"Why not?"

He kneaded her bottom with his hands. "Because I can't handle having that wet pussy so close to my cock, starshine, without wanting to be inside it, instead." He walked on, but his hands shifted restlessly. He propped her ass up with one forearm, freeing the other hand to stroke her buttocks, squeeze them, roughly. He groaned. "Stars, I can feel your wet heat through my pants. I want…"

"What do you want?" She traced the shell of his ear with her tongue.

He let out a huff of exasperation and dropped her to her feet. "Stop." He turned her around and slapped her ass. "I can't, starshine."

The crystals must heighten her emotions, as well as her physical reactions, because an irrational flood of rejection nearly split her open. Well, *veck* him. He could go *veck* himself for all she cared. She crossed her arms and clamped her teeth together, waiting for him to lead the way.

He studied her, uncertainty flitting over his expression. "Talia—"

She flicked her hand dismissively. "Go on. Keep walking. I'll follow my *Master.*" She said the last word with scorn, satisfied to see pain crease his brow. Good. He should be sorry.

And, yes, she was acting like a child, not that she remembered childhood.

Had she really been the daughter of the prince's master of arms?

A vague memory—shadowy and just out of her reach—had haunted her mind ever since Tomis had made his solemn gesture with his elbow bent, fist in the air. Something about it seemed familiar. It had jogged something. Not a memory so much as a feeling. Comfort. Safety. And, yes, the honor Tomis so often referred to.

Tomis frowned. "You can't possibly imagine that was a rejection, Talia." He gripped the giant bulge of his cock through his pants. "I've been in *vecking* agony for you since the moment I first saw you back in the prison. You know I want you."

"But you don't *want* to desire me. You're saving me for your prince."

His expression became an unreadable mask. He'd turned into the stoic soldier, an iron body ready to protect and serve. "Come," he ordered and reached for her hand. His grasp was gentle, though.

She attempted to remain sullen but soon forgot her grievance when the landscape opened to another mound of rubble—broken buildings, fallen walls, vines and determined trees growing over it all.

Tomis' watchful eyes took in everything. A frown creased his chin, but he said nothing.

She stopped, forcing him to stop, too. "So, they really killed every being?"

He tucked her against his side, as if to protect her from the past. "It's horrible, isn't it?"

"Sickening."

Tomis lifted his chin to a stubborn angle. "But they didn't kill *every* being. Not you. Not me. Not Prince Zander."

"Do you really think your prince can win against them?"

"Yes." His answer was so confident and swift she had no choice but to accept he believed. But how could it be possible? A young male who'd lived his life in hiding for the past fifteen solar cycles? How could he have raised enough force and might to bring down the species that toppled the entire structure of his father's kingdom? It didn't make sense.

"I want to see up close." She pulled away from Tomis and headed down the slope toward the rubble of the settlement. Of course, Tomis followed. "I hope Zander's plan to beat the Finn is better than yours to get me out of here."

He shrugged. "It's not my position to know *Prince* Zander's plan. Only to execute my orders. But I know he has prepared every day since his exile. And your father has trained him and molded him into as lethal a warrior as any of us."

Your father.

She shoved those words back. Hated that he assigned some stranger to her this way. "I don't have a father, Tomis. I told you that before." She tripped over a stone, and Tomis caught her elbow, steadying her.

"You do. And he hasn't stopped looking for you since the moment he heard you might still be alive."

She shook her head. She didn't need this pressure. To be someone's long lost daughter? *Hell, no.* She'd just won her freedom from Thurn. She sure as sun didn't need to be "owned" by some new male father-figure. *If* she even was his daughter, as Tomis believed.

"Just meet him," Tomis coaxed. "Meet him and Prince Zander. Keep an open mind."

"You promised you wouldn't take me against my will."

Tomis' extraordinary chest expanded, apparently with his overgrown honor. "And I won't. A Zandian never breaks his word."

They arrived at the site of destruction. The heaviness in the pit of her stomach felt like she'd swallowed an airship. The more she looked, the more her brain put together what each thing had been—pieces of a hovercraft, the walls of a house. *Oh stars.* "Tomis." She pointed inside the crushed hull of the hovercraft, where an adult and child-sized bones remained.

Tomis said nothing, his expression blank and soldier-like again. She thought he might try to pull her away or hold her. She was almost mad he didn't, although it had been her idea to see things up close. Maybe he wanted her to really understand what had happened to their species. So she'd join his fight against the Finn.

He reached in, plucking out what looked like a perfectly cut diamond. "A female," he said softly. "Mother and children." He plucked more diamonds out and held them out in his palm for her to see.

She shuddered, backing away. "How do you know? That's her jewelry?"

"Zandians mark their females when they mate. Pierce their skin and gift them Zandian crystal, that they might always be fertile and fed with the power that sustains us all. It's to show the male will always provide for his female."

She wrinkled her nose to mask the stir of longing his explanation gave her. This picture of domestic bliss didn't fit any reality she'd ever known. And, yet, something dreadful happened inside her as she stared at the winking jewels.

Recognition.

And with it came a terrible, horrible sense of loss.

As if a bomb struck that moment, she found herself on her hands and knees in the dirt, a sob of utter horror choking her throat. Icy prickles raced over her skin.

"Talia? Talia, what is it?"

She coughed, heaved, and, at last, the terrible emotion came out in a torrent of tears, blurring the ground in the flood.

The planet lurched and spun. Somehow, she ended up flattened against Tomis' hard body, her cheek pressed to his rock-hard chest.

"What happened?" He sounded alarmed. "What is it, starshine?"

"I had a mother. Oh, stars, I had a mother," she wailed against his chest. Tomis must be disgusted by the wet, ugly, sobbing mess he held, but she couldn't gain control. It was like something had cracked inside her, some inner shell, and beneath it lay a whole different person. A child with a mother. A mother who'd been pierced and adorned with crystals.

Someday you'll wear crystals like these, Talia. A beautiful female with long, auburn hair had let her touch the glittering gem below her belly button.

Why not now, mum-mum?

Little girls don't wear them, sweetheart. They are for mated females. Given by a mate.

"You remembered something? What was it?" Tomis' faraway voice sounded soft and soothing. His lips brushed her hair. His strong arms warmed her.

Yet, she couldn't find her way back to him. The implications of her memory still rocked through her.

Because having a mother meant losing a mother. And that memory was there, too, jostling just behind this one. The explosion of grief had accompanied it all, the anguish of losing her as acute as if it had happened yesterday. She experienced the terror of a small child, hustled with her sister through a crumbling palace, separated by a wall of rubble from her mother and an infant sibling.

She'd screamed and screamed to go back, tugged on the guard's arm to free herself, but he wouldn't let go. Like Tomis, he'd had a duty to protect her, and her desire to stay close to the place she'd last seen her mother didn't sway him.

"I lost her," she croaked against Tomis' bare skin.

He stroked the back of her head, massaged her scalp. "The Zandian star knows I understand."

Realizing he'd experienced this terrible pain, too, only intensified her suffering. No one should feel this. And, yet, her entire species had.

It wasn't fair. Wasn't right. She'd been loved. She'd known love. And had it all wrenched from her to serve a lifeless existence on Stornig.

Not anymore. She was alive, now. She was back on Zandia with an incredible male, capable of pleasuring, protecting, and comforting her. She was free. Or at least as free as she could be with Tomis around. And if she believed his promise, that meant he'd let her go eventually.

Why did that thought not make her any happier?

Tomis held Talia's trembling form, the salty scent of her tears slaying him. He wanted to grab a sword and slice off the head of anyone and everyone who ever hurt her.

And he would, eventually. He'd make the Finn pay for their evil terror. He'd do it for her mother and his own.

"Let's keep moving," he urged gently. "I have something to show you, and it's not far from here."

"You still know where we are?" She pushed away from him, her beautiful violet eyes red-rimmed. He stroked a lock of red-brown hair back from her tear-streaked face.

"Yes. I saw this settlement on the maps."

She turned and looked once more into the hovercraft's remains. "How do the Zandians care for their dead?" she whispered.

His throat closed. "We burn them. Their crystals with them. Then we scatter their ashes in water—a lake or river. Return them to the keeping of the planet."

"Do you still have her crystals?" Talia's voice broke, but her gaze was steady and brave.

He dug in his pocket for the little gems he'd tucked away when Talia had fallen to the ground. They sparkled when he presented them to her in his flat palm.

"Keep them," she said, a note of determination in her voice. "We'll scatter them next time we're close to water."

He managed a sad smile and pocketed the crystals. "Good. We're headed to water now." He laced his fingers with hers and led her in the direction he'd memorized, toward the twin waterfalls that served as the main attraction to this area of the planet. The bombed enclave had once been a quaint tourist town, providing lodging to visitors who came to see the planet's gift.

They walked in silence. He didn't want to disturb what appeared to be her deep contemplation of what they'd seen and what she'd remembered, although it took great resistance not to attempt to kiss away the furrow between her brows.

The sound of rushing water signaled he'd navigated correctly.

Talia lifted her head, peering toward the horizon. "What is it? A river?"

He smiled. "You'll see. Come on." He lengthened his strides, tugging her toward the sound. They pushed through dense jungle growth—sweet smelling flowering vines and thick tree leaves. The sound of the crashing water grew louder. At last they came to a clearing.

Talia's mouth dropped open.

Two hundred meter waterfalls crashed down crystal-embedded rock and crossed one another like streams on a perfectly engineered fountain.

A deep, round pool below collected the twin falls like a basin before the water spilled into the same river he'd washed Talia in before.

He kicked his boots off and unbuckled the belt at his waist.

Talia, seeing his intention, tore his shirt over her head, slipped his socks off her feet, and ran for the pool. "First one in wins!"

He let out a short bark of laughter, hopping as one pant leg tangled in his hurry to join her. "Wins what?"

But Talia had already discovered the secret gift of the basin. Her pouty lips formed a perfect O as she turned back to him. "It's warm!"

He grinned, her delight more pleasing to him than any satisfaction he'd ever received personally. He dove in after her, but not before he saw her eyes darken when she took in his naked form.

Feeling's mutual, starshine.

So mutual. The urge to breed her was growing by the minute.

In fact, the sight of her nude body sluicing through the clear water might be the most erotic thing he'd ever seen. She'd dipped down to wet her body to the neck and now stood in water to her waist, beadlets gliding down her throat, dripping from her perky nipples. Between her breasts. Not even the magnificence of one of his planet's greatest gifts to her people could drag his attention away from her beauty.

She waited for him to join her—a big mistake because all he wanted to do was drag her back to firm ground and *veck* her senseless.

Choosing restraint, instead, he dived past her, swimming toward the center of the cascades. "First one to the falls wins!" he called over his shoulder when he resurfaced.

She gave a shriek of laughing indignation and he heard her splashes behind him as she fought to catch up.

"Come here, starshine." He caught her wrist and pulled her through the water when he reached the entry point of one of the cataracts. "What do you think? Is it hot or cold?"

She bit her lower lip, the plump flesh trapped there begging for his kiss. "My bet is cold. The heat comes from underground."

He pulled them both under the spray.

Talia squealed as cold water beat down on their heads.

He grinned and drew a deep breath, pulling her underwater and away from the pelting drops. He opened his eyes, delighted to find she had, too. She swam looking at him, bubbles of laughter escaping her mouth.

He pointed in the direction of the other waterfall and she nodded. They both swam underwater, and he noticed a change in water temperature as they drew nearer. They came up under it and Talia gasped, shaking wet locks of hair from her face. "It's hot! One is cold. One is hot! I can't believe it!"

Seeing a ledge set into the rock wall behind the cascading water, he caught her hand and pulled her to it, lifting her from the water to sit on the slick black stone, worn smooth as the petrified hardwood Prince Zander used in many of the furnishings of his palatial pod.

Talia laughed and kicked some water in his face. "This is incredible!"

Warmth curled in his chest, satisfaction at winning her smile running deeper than he'd imagined it could.

"Any more surprises?"

He held up a finger. "One more, unless things have changed. I'll be back in a moment." He took a deep breath and dove down, swimming to the bottom of the deep stone hole. When his fingers touched rock, he moved horizontally, open eyes scanning for his prize.

There.

A huge wand of Zandian crystal. He wrapped his fingers around it and kicked until he broke the surface then swam to the ledge and handed it up to Talia. He didn't dare pull himself out of the water to sit beside her or she'd see the giant boner he'd sported for her since the moment he'd laid eyes on her.

And if she saw it, he might use it on her. Five hundred and twenty different ways.

So, no. He needed to stay in the water and keep her out of it. Or vice versa. Anything to keep their naked bodies apart.

She held the naturally formed wand up to the light. "What is this? A giant crystal?"

"Yes. The fall of the water shapes them. It creates a tumbling effect. They are only found here at Twin Falls, and they're considered sacred. They are never broken into smaller pieces. Wealthy Zandians often keep one over the door of their home, to bless it and amplify the light from the one true star."

A shaft of sunlight fell through the falls and across Talia's face, lighting her beauty. Her nipples puckered, seeming to point directly toward his mouth, as if begging for his teeth, his lips. "What is this *one true star* thing?"

He pointed to the glowing ball of light in the sky. "Our sun. That's what we call it."

"You make it sound like it's the Zandians' sun, alone."

Stars, those pouty lips.

"I think the original Zandians believed that. Before we knew there was life on other planets."

Blah blah blah. Why are we talking when we could be vecking?

He wasn't going to survive much longer without beating off to alleviate the pressure in his balls. His urge to breed must be amplified by the extensive crystal deposits beneath the falls. He cleared his throat. "I'm going for a swim. Enjoy yourself."

He ducked his head under the water, not even capable of hearing her musical voice one more time without closing his fingers around her knees and shoving them wide. Applying his tongue to that sweet little pussy of hers.

He swam under the falls and out to the expanse of the pool.
Away from temptation.

CHAPTER FOUR

The smooth crystal wand tortured her every moment she gripped it.

For one thing, the crystal activated the urge to breed so strongly, a fever crept across her skin, turning it hot and flushed. For another, the phallic shape of the crystal had her imagining an entirely un-sacred use for it.

Was it the same size as Tomis' glorious dick? Not quite. A bit smaller in both girth and length. Which made it quite perfect for self-pleasuring, didn't it?

Because the ache between her legs had grown too insistent to ignore.

Where had Tomis gone? He would help her with this ache, wouldn't he? He'd shown himself to be amenable to satisfying her needs, even though he mostly refused to satisfy his own.

She stood up, scanning for him but couldn't see much through the fall of the water. Well, she'd go and find him. A swim would do her good.

She attempted to leave the crystal on the ledge, but it seemed to beg her to take it along.

That was ridiculous. Crystals didn't beg. They certainly didn't have an opinion about being taken for a swim.

She forced herself to set it on the ledge and dropped down into the deliciously warm water.

She stretched her body and preened, adoring the luxury of this sacred site, then kicked off and swam under the falls, but immediately realized swimming was also a mistake.

Every kick of her legs activated her throbbing core. Her inner thighs brushed together, teasing but not satisfying her overwhelming need. She stopped, treading water, with the fingers of one hand curled between her legs.

Not going to work.

She would sink and drown before she ever satisfied the itch.

Where in the hell was Tomis when she needed him?

Oh, stars, the crystals would be the death of her.

She spun in a circle. She didn't see her savior anywhere. Desperation seized her.

Veck this, as Tomis would say. She simply couldn't wait any longer. She would die if she didn't get relief immediately. She dove underwater and swam hard, back toward the waterfalls, toward the ledge.

When she reached it, she pulled herself out, her wanton moans echoing off the cliff wall behind her.

Wand, wand. Where is the wand? Stars, she needed it. Right *there*. She frantically rubbed her clit with the wand, slid it against her flesh.

Not. Enough.

Changing the angle, she pushed the wand inside her tight entrance. It was too much, too fast, and it hurt, but she couldn't stop herself, either. She shoved it deeper, seeking relief.

Her moans grew louder, the answering echo making it sound like a chorus of females having sex along with her. Her eyelids drooped as she shoved the crystal ever deeper.

Come on, you vecking *crystal. It's your fault I have this urge. Can't you slake it?*

But it seemed it wouldn't. The crystal wasn't what she needed or wanted. Her body needed flesh. Male flesh, hard and unyielding. Pounding her into oblivion.

Out of nowhere, Tomis appeared, standing above her. Huge, dripping wet, and furious. Why was he wearing his pants again? They were soaked, as if he'd swum in them.

"What in the *veck* are you doing?"

She panted, hardly able to focus on him. "Defiling your sacred stone."

Tomis' eyes glittered violet as he unbuckled his belt. "You are not to pleasure yourself. I am your master. I determine when and if you receive pleasure. You know that. Now, you will be punished."

"Yes," she gasped. Punishment. Pleasure. Anything. *Please, just touch me now.*

He pulled the belt from its loops with a whoosh, the wet leather curling through like an angry sea serpent. "You want my punishment." It sounded more like a statement than a question.

"Yes," she admitted in a whisper. Or was it a moan? She didn't just *want* his punishment. She *vecking needed* it.

"I'm going to whip you, baby. Then I'm going to use that crystal on you in ways you never thought of. And, after that, I think I'll probably whip you again. Because, starshine, if I don't give that sweet little ass and pussy some attention, if I don't punish them until you scream, I'm not sure I'll survive the night." He wound the buckle end around his fist, shortening the animal hide strap to the length of her forearm. "On your knees, Talia. Forehead on your hands."

She assumed the position, her ass pointed in the air for his wicked wet belt. Yet, she wasn't afraid in the slightest. Tomis would make it good. Even if he caused her pain, he'd give her pleasure, too. He had, even when she'd hurt him and given him good reason to punish her. He was as needy as she was, and that meant she'd have satisfaction soon.

Stars, she hoped it would be enough to ease the mounting frenzy inside her.

Tomis didn't make her wait long. The first lash of his belt fell with a light slap. Just enough to leave a sting but no pain.

"Mmmm." Bliss.

He continued with the gentle kiss of animal hide, spanking her ass and the backs of her legs with his belt. And then he swung it harder.

She yelped at the line of pain, and her hips listed to one side.

He corrected her, bringing her hips back. "Hold still, little female." His voice was pure sex, the command soft and loving in contrast to how hard he'd whipped her.

Her thighs trembled. "That hurt," she warbled.

"I know. I've finished warming you up. Now comes your punishment."

"No," she said, but remained perfectly still in the position he'd placed her.

"You don't tell me no, starshine," he said, but he didn't move, either.

"Do it," she mumbled.

Tomis must have heard her because she heard the whoosh of air displaced by the arc of the belt, and it struck across her buttocks again, as hard as the last one.

"Ow," she whimpered, but didn't move to get away this time. No, she wanted the pain, craved the sensation of sharp torment blooming into warmth.

This was how Tomis acted on his attraction to her, and she loved it.

He whipped her, striking harder and harder, the wet belt turned into a fearsome instrument of castigation as it crisscrossed over her buttocks, the backs of her thighs. He spanked her until they both panted and moaned.

"Spread your knees, baby." His voice was so deep and thick, it was almost unrecognizable.

She widened the stance of her knees.

Tomis swung the belt between her legs, striking her pussy lightly.

"Tomis!"

"This naughty pussy deserves to be punished most of all, don't you think, starshine?" Another slap.

Tears sprang to her eyes, but, like the spanking on her buttocks, the sensation sparked even more desire. She wanted it harder, faster, higher, so it fell right on her clit.

"Tomis, I'm sorry."

"Oh, I don't imagine you are, starshine. But it doesn't matter, does it? You were caught trying to satisfy this greedy little pussy, and now, you're going to be thoroughly punished."

"Please." *Please* meant *more*, not *stop*. She didn't want him to stop. Not ever. She wanted him to fulfill the promises he'd just made of whipping her twice and using the crystal on her.

"Naughty, naughty pussy." *Slap slap.*

Heat flushed through her in waves. Her brain floated off while she surrendered to the vertigo that made her unsure of where her body even was in space.

"Tomis." A whisper. A plea.

Three more swats against her feminine folds.

"Now, do you know what happens to naughty females, Talia?"

"W-what?"

"We had to talk about it this morning. They get *vecked* in the ass. But, this time, we'll start with the crystal. You wanted to *veck* this crystal, starshine?" He ran the cool, hard gemstone over her stinging pleats, soothed the swelling and heat. He pushed the rounded end of the wand into her eager channel.

"Yes—yes."

"No, no. I'm just getting it lubed up, baby. This crystal is going in your ass."

To her great disappointment, he withdrew the wand and lined it up with the pucker of her anus. She squeezed, clenching against the foreign object.

"Open for it, my disobedient little female. I'm going to help you remember who controls your pleasure."

She didn't mean to open for it, but her body responded to his words, relaxing and opening of its own accord. The wand slid in, filling her. Not as much as Tomis' cock had earlier, but stretching her, nonetheless.

She let out a long, low, guttural moan. Stars, yes. Almost there.

"You like that, little female? You like when your master *vecks* your ass?" He twisted and pumped the wand.

"Need...just a little more," she gasped. "Please. Please, Tomis. *Veck* my pussy."

Tomis cursed and slapped her pussy. "You know I'm not going to do that, starshine," he growled, sounding angry about it.

"You have to," she gasped. "I'm going to die if you don't. I'm serious, Tomis. I need you so badly. Please, please, please *veck* me. You have to." Her words tumbled out in a frenzied torrent, need crystallizing to an urgency that couldn't be ignored. She was literally in pain, her pussy throbbing for him. "Please...please."

Tomis hissed out another curse, and she heard the squelch of wet fabric as he shucked his wet pants.

Yes! Oh please oh please oh yes.

He hadn't even touched her yet and she was pleading for her release. Nothing on the planet would satisfy her except his cock.

"Please, Tomis," she whimpered, even though he was already positioning himself behind her, the head of his cock bumping against her desperate pussy. "I need you so much," she sobbed. "I need it right now."

He sank into her pussy and she screamed her pleasure. "You need this cock?" He pulled away and shoved in again, pushing the wand deeper into her ass with his pelvis.

"Yes. Yes, please."

"Whose cock do you need, Talia?"

"Yours. Tomis'. My master's." Words spilled from her mouth in a frantic urge to appease him, to answer correctly so he'd continue. "Harder, Tomis. Oh please. I need you so badly."

"*Veck*, Talia!" He grabbed a handful of her hair and tugged her head back, using it to leverage deeper into her. The angle of his entry hit a place on her inner wall that sent her into spasm of ecstasy.

"More. Harder. There!" she screamed.

Tomis pounded into her, *vecking* her like it was part of her punishment, like she deserved every hard thrust for being such a bad girl.

"I need you," she sobbed, her internal muscles contracting around his length.

"*Veck*, Talia, *veck*!" Tomis roared, changing his grip to her hips for short, rapid thrusts that made her teeth rattle.

"More. More, Tomis."

He tipped her over onto her side, lifted one knee, and thrust into her from this new angle, this new position. With each stroke he plowed deeper, *vecked* her more thoroughly, until she was sure he planned to pound his very essence into her, leave her forever imprinted with his cock, so her body would accept no other male but him.

Yes. Have me. Take me. Keep me.

Somehow, she managed to keep those words to herself, even when Tomis came apart, shouting incoherent words as he plunged deep and came.

Satisfaction ripped through her. Her core squeezed and milked his cock as she unraveled, hips bucking, clit grinding, cries screaming from her throat. It wasn't only her body that celebrated Tomis' surrender to his lust. Some piece of feminine pride preened a bit, too. He'd taken her. Possibly bred her, despite his honorable intentions to save her womb for his prince's plans.

What if he succeeded in planting a young in her? The implications made her close her eyes with longing.

With sorrow.

Because Tomis didn't want to be her mate.

Vecking *hell*.

He hadn't meant to put his cock in Talia. To *veck* her so roughly, so thoroughly, that every inch of her body must be sore now.

But her begging, her pleading made it impossible for him not to claim her.

She lay beneath him, still trembling, but her sweet body limp and relaxed now. He'd brought her relief.

That had to count for something, didn't it?

No.

He shouldn't have bred her. She was Seke's *daughter,* for *veck's* sake. The only known living female of breeding age. Daneth, Zander's physician, probably needed her eggs to artificially inseminate and implant in human females, as he'd attempted to do with his human mate, Bayla. Or perhaps he'd wish to inseminate Talia with Zander's sperm.

Why did that thought enrage him?

He eased out of his beautiful female. The sight of his rainbow hued semen between her legs brought a jolt of satisfaction that greatly outweighed his guilt.

My female.

Mine.

But she wasn't his.

Her long lashes closed, and a flash of sadness crossed her face, causing a violent stab of pain in his chest.

He ran his knuckles over her cheek. "What is it, starshine? Did I hurt you? I'm so sorry."

Her eyelids blinked back open; violet eyes regarded him. He couldn't read her expression.

The wand. She was still in discomfort from the anal phallus he'd put in place. He gripped the end of it and eased it out.

Talia's body shuddered and relaxed. "Are you sorry?" There was a haunted quality to her voice that sent a spike of alarm through him.

"Sorry I served you when your body was in need? *Veck*, no, baby." He slid a hand under her knee to spread it wider and ran his open mouth along her inner thigh, tasting her.

She shivered. "I thought you were the master, and I was to serve you." Her breathless voice sent a fresh kick of lust through him, despite his glorious release.

"No, beautiful. You're to obey. I serve. My job is to protect you. Keep you safe. Satisfied, if I decide you deserve it."

Her lovely brown-violet eyes rolled back in her head, and she groaned, reaching for her pussy.

He caught her wrist and held it away as he used his other hand to stroke her clit. "You love being subject to my rule."

She arched, full lips parting. "I love the way you serve."

"Good, starshine. Then, you'll obey." He quirked a smile. "Or you won't, and I'll punish you."

Her pelvic floor squeezed and lifted as if a mini-orgasm had just run through her. "I already want more. It's the crystals, Tomis. This place..." Her head rolled fitfully over the rock floor.

His brows dropped. *Veck.* He hadn't meant to claim her the first time. She already needed him again? Stars. He was *vecking* incapable of denying her when she turned needy. He rubbed her swollen bud in circles.

"More," she panted.

Holy Zandian star! He slid his hands under her buttocks and brought her pelvis to meet his mouth. He flicked the sensitive nub with his tongue then clamped his lips over it and sucked, hard.

"Ooh—oh! Yes, Tomis. More. Please. *Please.*"

Oh stars, she was begging again. This female would be the death of all his self-control. He lowered her pelvis to the floor, drinking in the sight of his greedy little female half-sick with desire. Her eyes were dilated and glassy, cheeks flushed a pinkish-purple, hair twisted around her head. If Zandians had worshipped any deity, she would look like Talia. A goddess, made for *vecking.* Yielding soft flesh ready to be implanted.

He picked up the belt, shoving the desire to master her in front of the need to plant his seed. He rolled the strap around his fist until the length shortened to a short flap. Lifting one of her knees open, he slapped her inner thigh with the animal hide belt, leaving a neat, red rectangle.

She jerked against his hold, shuddering, her pelvic floor clenching again. She liked the pain.

Excellent. Because he needed to give her more. So much more. If he couldn't have this beautiful female, he sure as stars would master the *veck* out of her.

He slapped down her inner thigh then thwacked her dripping pussy. With one ankle held high in the air, he leathered one buttock thoroughly as she whined and moaned her approval. "Other side." His deep voice echoed off the cliff wall. He gripped her other knee, slapped the outside and inside of that thigh, spanked her buttock, then returned to her pussy.

Talia panted, her feverish gaze glued to his face. Her hands wandered to her breasts, and she squeezed them, pinching her nipples and moaning.

"Oh, baby, why did you have to do that?"

Stars, he couldn't be held responsible for all the things he was going to do to this incredible female. Not when she looked like pure erotic pleasure. Not when those sexy sounds came from her pouty lips.

"Tomis, it's not enough." Desperation crinkled her brow. She sucked her lower lip into her mouth, biting down.

He growled, wanting to be the one sucking that lip, claiming that mouth. In a flash, he was upon her, crushing her mouth with his, his tongue plunging deep, pumping in time with his hips.

His cock, stiff and heavy again for her, found the notch between her legs and slid against her slippery folds. He groaned at the torture of her. "Talia, you feel so good. I can't keep from putting my aching cock in you again. But aren't you too sore?"

She shook her head. "No, no, no, no. I need you now." Her words slurred with desire.

"You were so *vecking* tight the last time. I don't think you're used to Zandian cock."

She bared her teeth, sinking her nails into his forearms. "Give me. The Zandian cock."

He choked on a laugh and impaled her with a single thrust, catching her forearms at the last minute to keep her from sliding away from him with the force. He gritted his own teeth at the snug sweetness of her incredible channel. "You asked for it." He surged over her, pumping as if his life depended on it. As if both their lives depended on it. "I'm not going to stop *vecking* you until morning, now, starshine. You won't walk straight for three days when I'm done with you."

"Yes. *Yes.*"

"Oh *veck.* If I'd known Zandian pussy felt this good, I would've *vecked* you twice in the dungeon before I ever broke us out. Hell, I'd still be back there, *vecking* you senseless."

Talia's laugh sounded bitter, and her nails scored his back as she spread her legs wide and straight in the air in the ultimate symbol of offering. "You're getting the only Zandian pussy in the galaxy, warrior. How does that make you feel?"

"So *vecking* good, Talia."

Later, he would realize what a colossal mistake he'd made in objectifying her, making her seem like nothing more than the Zandian breeding machine his species required during the most intimate of acts. But her words only rang his already clanging bell, and he pounded her poor pussy as if he wanted to turn her inside out.

Her screams echoed off the walls of the cliff, mingled with his shouts until they reached a simultaneous climax, her tight pussy squeezing his cock, milking it, as he came.

CHAPTER FIVE

Tomis dragged his lips across Talia's jaw and groaned. "We have to get out of here, beautiful. Away from the sacred crystals."

They'd spent a fitful night near the waterfall, waking and breeding every few hours, as her body demanded. It was as if she was sick, and sex was the only cure.

"If we don't, I fear we'll never leave. We'll be trapped in time and space, mating on a continual loop until breeding season ends. This place will be the death of us both."

She groaned, too. Tomis climbed to his feet and pulled on his pants and boots. He tucked his hands under her armpits, helping her to stand. Her aching body unfolded with stiffness. Nearly every part of her felt tender, her ass and pussy abused by Tomis' belt and cock, her back and knees scraped and bruised from *vecking* against the stone floor.

"Talia." Tomis' face drooped with regret. "I was so rough with you. I'm sorry. I couldn't stop myself." He slid his shirt over her head with a tenderness that made her belly flutter. The crystal wand they'd used went into the breast pocket of the shirt. Her feet flew out from her when he swung her up into his arms.

She didn't even consider arguing. Walking could be an impossibility at the moment. Instead, she nestled her head against his massive shoulder, allowing the movement to lull her into a blessed stupor. Because she sure as hell didn't want to think.

She couldn't consider what her copulation with Tomis meant. Or how badly it would hurt if he still wanted to turn her over to her father and his prince after what they'd done. Why wasn't she worth keeping? It *vecking* killed her that he hadn't once considered mating her, piercing her with Zandian crystal and swearing to protect her and their children for the rest of his life.

Damn him.

Tears smarted her eyes, so she closed them, listening to the sounds of insects, the songs of the birds in the trees overhead.

She must have drifted off to sleep because an unexpected sound startled her awake—the laughter of children.

Tomis froze in his tracks.

"I didn't dream that?" she whispered.

He shook his head, creeping forward silently, head cocked in the direction of the little voices.

There—playing on the opposite side of the riverbank. Three children. *Zandian* children.

They wore little clothing, and the simple scraps they did wear seemed to be hand-constructed from animal hide.

Tomis eased her to the ground just as one of the female young caught sight of them and gasped. The other two—one male, one female—whipped their heads around to stare, as well. For a moment, no one moved. Then the children took off running, their bare feet sailing out behind them.

Tomis called out in the language he'd first used with her—what must be the Zandian tongue.

The male child threw a glance over his shoulder, but none of them stopped running.

"Come on," Tomis urged, plunging into the water. They crossed the river and followed the children. She noticed Tomis didn't run at his full speed. In fact, he more jogged along, keeping the children in sight but hanging back. He must have been concerned about frightening them.

The children cried out in their language.

"What are they saying?"

"They're calling for help." Tomis slowed to a walk, picking up her hand and lacing his fingers through hers. When he looked down at her, his eyes shone with excitement.

She couldn't help but smile back. "It's wonderful, isn't it? The species lives on."

He pulled their hands to his mouth and kissed the back of hers. "It's a miracle."

A moment later, their hands jerked apart, though, because three male Zandians appeared over a hill, all charging with weapons drawn.

Tomis stopped, shoving her behind him. He didn't draw his laser gun, though it would have outpowered their hand weapons, which appeared to be nothing more than sharp blades shaped as a spear, an axe, and a sword. He spoke again in Zandian.

This time, something about the words sounded familiar, as if the part of her brain where her first language had been stored turned on and was warming up.

Peace. He'd said something about peace. Or *friendship.* He lifted his fist toward the sky, elbow bent at a 90 degree angle. It was a greeting of some sort, the same one that had tugged at her memory the first time he'd used it.

The males jogged forward, weapons still held in front them. They stopped about ten paces away, eyeing them warily.

Tomis spoke, and, this time, she understood most of it. "Be at peace. We are friends. I am Tomis, of Prince Zander's royal guard. I came to rescue Talia from the capital." He stepped to the side to reveal her. "We seek an airship to get off-planet."

The tall but slender male sheathed his weapon and stepped forward. "I am Sankro. This is Elit and Banf." He gave her an appreciative up-and-down sweep that set her teeth on edge. The other two males also eyed her.

Don't even think about it, asshole.

Apparently breeding season didn't make her turn to mush over every Zandian male. Only the dominant warrior beside her.

Tomis' chest seemed to grow bigger, and he shifted back in front of her, as if to shield her from their view. She swore she heard a low growl from his throat.

But, *veck* that. He didn't get to act possessive when he wasn't even willing to claim her as his own. Wasn't he the one in a big hurry to turn her over to another male? She stepped around Tomis' huge frame and lifted her chin.

All three males stepped closer, and she had to force herself not to flinch. No, her body definitely had a preference. It didn't want to breed with any of the other males. Too bad her body it didn't get the memo about Tomis not being interested in mating her.

"I'm Talia." She attempted to speak in Zandian.

Tomis' eyes rounded with wonder.

The males drew even closer, the other two putting away their weapons as well. "Come. Meet our female," Sankro invited, looking only at her.

She nodded and stepped forward, knowing without a sliver of doubt Tomis would follow.

The males closed in around her, flanking her as they walked over the hill and down the other side. A crude structure nestled amongst a grove of trees. It appeared to be crafted of mismatched recycled materials—rubble from one of the bombed villages, no doubt. Thin slats of wood made up the roof, packed and fortified with dirt and chunks of moss.

In the doorway stood a female Zandian, not much older than Talia. Like the males and children, she, too, wore a simple covering of animal hide. The three young they'd seen at the river hid behind her, and she carried a tiny infant in her arms.

"Eslyn, look who we found!" Sankro called out as they approached.

Shock and wariness danced over Eslyn's pretty features, but she dropped into a curtsy.

Talia stopped and mimicked it.

"This is Talia," Sankro said.

"And Tomis." A prickle of foreboding at the way Sankro excluded Tomis crept up the back of her neck.

"Come in, the young just picked fresh yellow star berries."

They all pushed inside the ramshackle structure. Eslyn placed a bowl of fresh fruit on a makeshift table for everyone to eat. The young gathered around, staring openly at her and Tomis, creeping closer and offering shy smiles.

"This is Alyx, Ren, Teena and Solo." Eslyn pointed to each child as she named them off.

"How old are they?" The reverence with which Tomis regarded the young warmed her. He would make a wonderful father if he loved young so much.

What would happen if he'd managed to put a child in her belly? Would he still renounce her and give her over to his prince? Or would he make a claim?

Though she'd never had any interest in bearing children, a thick longing took over, coating her throat and tugging on her chest, as if some invisible string had been tied around her heart and cinched tight.

"Alyx is six, Ren is five, Teena is three, and Solo was just born. He's is a product of last year's breeding season."

Who was the father? Sankro, their natural leader? Talia eyed the males who took positions in the small hovel, blocking the door, filling the space with their large frames. It seemed all Zandians were much bigger than her. Even Eslyn was larger than Talia, nearly as tall as the males. So, her growth had been stunted from being away from the crystals.

She glanced from the children's faces to the males, trying to match them.

"We all bred her," Sankro said, guessing her question. "We are one family. All the children belong to all of us."

"Have you been hiding here since the Finn invaded?" Tomis asked, plucking a handful of berries from the bowl and offering them to her. "How did you escape?"

"Yes." It seemed only Sankro spoke for the males. "We were just children, all of us. Our parents hid us in an underground shelter together. Made us promise not to come out until we heard silence for at least three planet rotations. So we waited. It was nine planet rotations before it all stopped. When we came out, no being was left. The Finn sent patrols out in airships for a while, but we hid in the waterfalls. The heat of the water masked our body heat from their sensors, and they never found us. Now, they hardly ever patrol." His gaze fell on Talia and stayed, again sending a niggling of discomfort through her. "We didn't know there were any other Zandians alive."

Tomis dropped a proprietary hand on her shoulder. "There aren't many, but there's an enclave of Zandians who escaped the planet during the invasion, including Prince Zander and the king's master at arms. Zander has spent the last fifteen solar cycles building the means to take the planet back. He would be overjoyed to know any Zandians survived on-planet. Come with us, to his palatial pod."

They received Tomis' invitation with about as much enthusiasm as she had, sharing glances she couldn't read with one another.

Sankro dropped onto a bench made of a piece of wood propped over two stones. He waved them into similar seats around the table. "There are no airships to be flown off-planet. Did you think the Finn left anything of value lying around?"

"There's a graveyard of old ships a planet rotations' walk from here. I plan to construct one from the junk there."

Sankro's lip curled. "Good luck, friend."

Clearly he found that plan as lacking as she did, yet his derision brought up a defensiveness in Talia. "Tomis is a trained warrior," she said. "He knows what he's doing."

Sankro grinned. "I wouldn't be so sure. You're welcome to stay with us while he tries." This time, there was no mistaking the leer.

She glanced at Eslyn to see what the other female thought, but the new mother turned her back, bouncing her knees to rock the infant who didn't require soothing. The other males nodded.

"Talia goes with me," Tomis said stiffly.

She was one part relieved by his insistence, one part annoyed. He didn't own her. She wasn't the prize he got to carry back to his precious prince. She folded her arms over her chest. "I thought I had a choice?"

Tomis startled, shooting her a disconcerted look. "Once we're *off*-planet. I'm not leaving you here."

Sankro's lips stretched into a thin grin. "So you're not mated, then?"

She suddenly hated Tomis for not wishing to mate her.

Tomis scowled, the low growl issuing from his throat again. "We *are* mated."

She arched a brow. Oh, sure. How convenient for him to call them mated when other males took an interest in her but not wish to claim her for himself.

"Doesn't look like the female agrees," one of the other males—Banf, if she remembered right—said. He turned his narrow brown eyes on her. "Do you?"

She folded her arms over her chest, torn between keeping the other males at a distance and setting Tomis straight. "Tomis has other plans for me," she said stiffly. "But he promised I can choose my own destiny when the time comes."

"Well, choose it now," Sankro said, spreading his hands. "Stay here with us. Three males to serve two females. You'll be treated like a queen."

She bit her lip to keep from pointing out that their domicile lacked the luxury a queen might expect.

"You can't stay here," Tomis interceded, bringing his fist down on the table hard enough to make the bowl of fruit jump. "None of you can. The planet will be at war soon, and we must get the females and young away to safety before it begins."

It occurred to her that Tomis' backup plan had been simply to wait until the war started, which would leave her here during it, but she kept her mouth shut.

Again, their hosts exchanged glances she couldn't decipher.

"We'll take our chances," Sankro said. "We've survived this long without detection. We know how to stay underground and off their radar."

Tomis scowled. "Your young are the only Zandian children alive in the galaxy. I cannot, in good conscience, leave them in what could become a war zone."

Sankro stood and planted both fists on the table, leaning forward into Tomis' space. "Are you threatening to take my young?"

"No. I wish to take all of you. To *safety*. To ensure the females and young are not killed when the battles begin."

Sankro scoffed. "There will be no battles on this side of the planet. The Finn are not here. They are concentrated near the capital, where the crystal is easier to mine. We will take our chances. Talia, you're invited to stay, if you like."

She forced a smile. "Thank you, I will consider your offer," she promised, only to goad Tomis.

"Stay the night here. Both of you. We've never had company. It will be nice for the young to see other Zandians," Eslyn offered.

"We cannot," Tomis said, but she touched his arm. Maybe, if they stayed, they could convince the group to leave with them.

"Let's stay, Tomis. I could use the rest."

Tomis rubbed the back of his neck, his mouth pulling down at the corners.

"Please?" She gave him her best pleading eyes, remembering the power her begging had over him back at the waterfall.

It worked. He gave a weary sigh and nodded. "As you wish."

He was far more formal with her in front of the others. He didn't call her *starshine* or *baby*. Just as he'd renounce all claim on her when he brought her to his prince.

Damn him.

She stood from the bench, directing her attention to the oldest young. "I think I'd like to go for a walk. Would you like to show me around the area?"

All the young scrambled for the door, talking over each other so that she couldn't understand any of them. The older female took her hand and tugged her along. She laughed and followed, her wary warrior trailing behind, as if one of the young might harm her.

Let him *serve*, then. Let him protect her, and take her from Zandia to safety. She wasn't going to go to his prince, though. She wasn't the only female of breeding age anymore. There was Eslyn. And her two female young would someday bear young of their own. The entire future of the species no longer rode on Talia's shoulders.

Hopefully, she and Tomis would convince them to come along, and her warrior could bring them to his prince instead. Perform his duty with a different female.

Why did that idea make her want to run and leap into his arms, beg him to forget about his duty and take her back to the waterfall?

But no. If Tomis wanted to keep her, if he wanted to mate her, he certainly would have asked by now. He'd mastered her, had bred her in every position possible, had demanded her obedience and promised to serve. But this relationship wasn't about mating.

The sooner she got that through her head, the better.

⁓⋅⁓

"The hardest thing, at first, was defending against the wild beasts," Banf said.

They sat in a semicircle around a tiny fire, discussing the difficulties the survivors had faced in living without a shred of technology. All four of them shared the tales, seeming eager to articulate the stories they'd kept to themselves for so long.

Though he suspected Talia had lived through just as much or worse difficulty in her life, she offered sympathetic words and listened with rapt attention. Somehow, she'd become the focal point of the group, the children all gathered at her feet, the adults all vying for her attention.

She deserved every bit of it, but Tomis didn't like the way the males eyed Talia.

Of course, they'd be affected by breeding season as well, and if their female had just given birth, she probably wasn't participating in this season. Which meant all their interest fell on Talia.

Veck.

To make it worse, Talia didn't seem eager to leave. Did she want to be bred by those males?

The thought made him want to dismember them, one by one.

He gazed at her, face lit by moonlight and a small fire, holding Eslyn's infant. The awe and wonder on her face made him want to kiss her senseless. What if—he hardly dared think it—she bore his young?

Would it be such a terrible thing?

Possibly.

Master Seke would beat him into the ground for losing control with his daughter. A beating he could take. He'd been trained to endure all kinds of discomfort. But would his mentor accept him as a mate for Talia?

Probably not. Though there were few Zandians left. Surely Seke would want a more nobly born male for his daughter. And what if Daneth wished to use Talia as a vessel?

He ground his teeth, the idea of the species' physician examining or touching Talia turning him downright violent.

He needed to get a grip on his emotions. Talia wasn't his to claim. And she didn't even *want* to be claimed by him. She still resisted leaving the planet with him.

She and the rest of the group. He needed to convince them all to leave for their safety and the continuation of the species. Leaving two females of breeding age, and four Zandian children exposed to danger would be unconscionable.

CHAPTER SIX

Talia woke to the sound of children's voices. She'd slept with Esylyn and the infant on a soft mattress made of piles of animal furs. She'd attempted to refuse the bed, preferring to sleep outside, under the stars, with Tomis, but their hosts insisted.

In the end, she'd given in, only because she feared she'd beg and plead Tomis to take her again if she slept beside him, and she didn't want to humiliate herself anymore.

Yes, he'd proven willing to serve her that way, but the more times they bred, the more likely she'd conceive his child and the harder it would be to part from him when the time came.

She heard Tomis' voice outside, speaking jovially to the children. Stars, it caused her physical pain to hear him. All her life believing she was a human slave, she'd never pictured herself with a family. Humans didn't get to have families. If they bred, it was surreptitiously, and they were soon parted from their mates or children. Or they were bred by their masters and forced to raise a child of another species. So, she'd never wanted a mate or children. Had believed her life began and died with Thurn.

Now, having glimpsed what a Zandian family might look like, she wanted it with a desperation bordering on insanity.

Of course, it was probably just the crystals and her raging hormones, but knowing that made it no less intense. She wanted a mate. Young.

She wanted Tomis to pierce her with Zandian crystal, swear to protect and keep her forever. And *veck* if that didn't make her a pathetic, weak female.

She needed to put some starch in her backbone and get over this male. Today.

The animal-skin curtain hanging in the door separating the sleeping area from the rest of the hovel pulled to the side and Sankro, Banf, and Elit entered.

She sat up, pulling the animal skin to cover her body, though she still wore Tomis' shirt.

In a flash, Sankro arrived at her side, clapping a huge hand over her mouth and putting a dagger to her throat. "We don't want to hurt you or the warrior. All you have to do is tell him you've decided to stay here with us and send him on his way."

Veck that. All she had to do was scream, and Tomis would rip the three of them apart.

"If you don't, we'll kill your warrior and eat him for dinner. Understand?" He held up the laser gun Tomis had stolen from the guard back at the dungeon.

Ice sluiced through her veins, chilling the very center of her bones.

"Nod if you understand," Sankro said.

She nodded. He eased his hand off her mouth. "I-if you use that, the Finn will be able to locate us all." Her words came out shaky and weak. She darted a glance at Eslyn, but the female didn't look nearly as shocked or outraged as Talia had hoped. Stars, had she been a part of her mates' devious plan all along?

Tomis' booming voice carried through the hovel.

"Go and tell him now," Banf hissed, yanking her off the mattress and up to her feet.

"Remember, if he doesn't leave, he's dead," Sankro murmured against her ear. They both propelled her forward, out of the sleeping quarters.

"G-good morning." She cleared her throat. *Veck.* She had to make this convincing or Tomis would never leave her. She squared her shoulders and lifted her breastbone. "I'm not leaving with you."

Tomis went still, his dark gaze steady on her face. "Talia."

She held up her hand. "I want to stay here. You can send a ship for me when the battle begins, if you're worried about that, but I'm not. I've been away from the crystals my entire life. I need to stay here."

"Prince Zander has crystals—"

"I want to stay with them," she said firmly, knowing her words would strike a blow.

The pain that flickered across Tomis' face rent her in two, but she steeled herself against her sorrow. Tomis' life depended on her making him leave.

"You should go."

He took a step toward her, but she lifted her hand in warning.

"Don't. It's better if you don't. I appreciate what you've done for me, but I've made my decision. I need you to honor it, as you promised you would."

Tomis stepped back, his face turning to stone. "I see."

"Thank you for understanding."

"I don't."

She couldn't breathe. An enormous boulder pressed down on her chest, keeping the air from rushing in.

Tomis. She closed her lips against the plea. She hated wounding him, hated them parting this way, but she had no choice.

He took another step back then stumbled to avoid stepping on little Teena. "I'm sorry," he said gruffly, righting the child. "I'll be back for you all, when the battle starts." His gaze swept over the crowd of them, solidifying his promise.

"I'll count on it," she choked out, throat so tight the words barely came out.

He lifted his fist in the traditional Zandian gesture then bowed and backed out the door.

She rushed forward to stand in the doorway, watching as he jogged swiftly away. As if the sooner he put distance between them, the sooner her refusal would stop stinging.

I'm sorry, Tomis.

Sankro and Banf flanked her, pulling her back inside. "Keep quiet and out of sight," Sankro said gruffly. To Banf and Elit, he said, "I'll follow the warrior to make sure he doesn't circle back. If he does..." He touched the laser gun on his hip.

She covered her mouth with her hand, stuffing her fingers in her mouth to stifle a sob. This was all her fault. She'd let this group see her conflict with Tomis, know that they were already at odds about how far she'd go with them, and she'd given them ammunition to use against him. To separate them.

Stars, what if Sankro planned to kill Tomis, regardless? They wouldn't want him coming back for her, would they?

She had to stop him! She lurched forward, her body ready to fly after Tomis before her brain had thought of a plan. Banf and Elit each grabbed one of her arms and yanked her back. "Let's tie her up until the warrior has left the planet," Banf said.

The tight knot around her ribs eased marginally. Banf didn't seem to think Sankro planned to kill Tomis.

But her relief over Tomis quickly turned to panic for her own plight. The males wrestled her into the sleeping chamber and threw her on her belly, tying her wrists behind her back and her ankles together.

Tomis' shirt rode up, exposing her bare ass and pussy to the males.

One of them—she couldn't tell which—ran a finger over the curve of her ass. "He whipped her." Though her ass no longer hurt, there must still be a faint mark from Tomis' belt. "I told you that's how mates master their females. Not with their fists. I remember seeing it on a hologram once." She couldn't tell which one of them spoke, but a chill ran through her at the *not with their fists* comment. Had they hit Eslyn with their fists?

Two hands gripped her ass cheeks and pulled them roughly apart. "I'm going to take her here."

"Better wait for Sankro. If he's not first, he'll beat everyone down."

She squirmed, attempting to roll away from the assholes. So this was her destiny. *Veck-toy* for three completely isolated and stunted males. The urge to scream for Tomis rose once more, but she bit the mattress instead, muffling her sob of anguish.

Tomis wouldn't die today. That was all that mattered.

The rest of this nightmare, she'd survive, one way or another.

Sankro might think he was stealthy, but he wasn't. Tomis knew the male had followed him the moment he left their domicile. He didn't know what they'd done or said to Talia, but it was obvious something wasn't right. The fact that his laser gun disappeared that morning hadn't gone unnoticed, either.

They must have threatened to kill her or both of them if she left. That was the only reason he'd gone easily. He wasn't going to take any action that might get her shot.

But he sure as *veck* wasn't going to leave her on Zandia. They'd have to kill him first. His duty was to protect Talia and bring her home unharmed, and he intended to complete his mission. The sooner he lost his tail and could double back, the better.

He picked up his speed, jogging along the river. To extinguish his scent and hide his tracks, he crisscrossed the river several times. Finally, he climbed the rock outcropping beside the river, running silently along the top of it toward Talia. He passed Sankro, still picking his way along the river below, craning his neck to find Tomis. The laser gun rested on the male's hip.

As if the male had any idea how to defend himself in battle.

Tomis dropped from the cliff onto Sankro, throwing the male to the ground. One swift swing of his fist knocked him out cold. He picked up the laser gun and used it to smack Sankro's skull once more. Then, not wanting to waste a moment, he raced back to Talia.

Please let her be safe.

He almost hoped she really had decided to stay. That right now she was playing games with the young, or bouncing the infant. But he knew that wasn't the case. The stricken look on her face as she'd told him to go had been all the information he needed.

He raced along the riverbank, bounding over rocks and fallen logs, ducking under branches. He didn't slow until he reached the copse of trees where their lopsided hut stood. A long, thick fallen branch made a decent staff for fighting. He picked it up, breaking off the end with the leaves and twirling the weapon in his hands.

Keeping his steps silent, he approached the small building and entered, managing to get past the children playing outside without them noticing him.

Inside, Esalyn sat nursing the infant. Her eyes flew wide and lips parted, but no sound came out.

It was the scream from the sleeping quarters that made his heart fly up into his throat. He yanked the curtain down, swinging the staff as he entered. Banf and Elit had stripped Talia naked and bound her wrists and ankles. Banf had her ass cheeks pried open and was licking her anus while Elit stroked his cock and watched. A quick blow to Banf's head dropped him to the floor. On the return swing, Tomis caught Elit in the throat, sending the male flying backward, gasping for breath.

Tomis tore the leather ropes from her wrists and ankles and hauled Talia to her feet. She threw her arms around his neck with a sob that pierced his heart. "Forgive me," she murmured against his chest. "They said they'd kill you if I didn't make you leave."

"I know, starshine." With one arm wrapped around Talia, he jabbed the end of the staff into Elit's solar plexus to send him to the ground in a crumpled heap.

He pulled his shirt over Talia's head. "Come on." He led her into the main room. "You, too," he barked at Eslyn. Get the young. You're coming with us."

Eslyn jumped to obey, standing up with the infant still suckling and calling to the children outside.

"I'm sorry," Eslyn choked to Talia as he rushed them all away from the shack. "I couldn't fight them. Not with a newborn to care for and—"

"It's all right. Tomis came back for me." Her voice sounded strangled.

"Where's Sankro?" Eslyn asked. He distinctly heard a waver of fear in her voice, and it sent a fresh shot of fury careening through his veins. He hoped they ran into Sankro again so he'd have the pleasure of knocking the male out one more time.

"Up ahead with a broken jaw," he said. "I'll handle him if we see him."

Eslyn started to cry. "I'm sorry," she said again. "I wanted to go with you, but I knew they'd never let me. It was wrong, but I hoped you'd stay. Take some of the pressure off me as their only female."

"Hush," he said, catching Talia's horrified expression. "Both of you are safe now. I won't let anything happen to you or the young."

He kept them walking all day until they reached the airship graveyard. He hoped the maps he'd studied were correct. If they were, a working airship might be available in an underground hangar he'd seen. He led them to the entrance, barely visible to the naked eye, and worked on deciphering how to open it. After several long moments, he found a lever and tripped it, sending a giant metal door creaking open.

Thank the one true Zandian star.

An intact airship stood below. If they were lucky, it still worked and had enough fuel to get them off of the planet.

. . .

"Tomis?" Talia called from her lookout above the hangar. Tomis had not yet succeeded in starting the craft.

The warrior heard the alarm in her voice and took the metal stairs two at a time to arrive back on the ground level.

A few hundred paces away, Sankro, Banf, and Elit approached, appearing ready to commit murder.

He picked up the staff and swung it in a lazy circle in front of him.

"The gun," Talia urged, thrusting it into his hands. He'd given it to her when he put her on watch. "Use it, instead."

"We don't spill Zandian blood," he explained calmly, pushing it back. "There are too few of us left." He actually appeared cheerful at the prospect of fighting three against one. Or three against two, counting her, which, since she knew nothing about fighting, she shouldn't be. With calm confidence, he called out to the males, "Surrender."

Sankro laughed, and the three charged.

There was a blur of movement. The thwack of wood against bone. And three bodies fell heavily to the ground. Tomis shook his head. "Too easy," he muttered, as if disappointed.

A memory of her father came back to her. He'd been holding a similar staff, teaching a class to his warriors. She and her sister had begged for permission to watch, and at last he'd relented, but only if they promised to sit perfectly still and silent for the duration.

They had. Because it had been fascinating to see their father spar with every male. The quick, sudden movements. Their cries of agony when he dropped them to the mat. The easy way the males rolled when they fell and sprang back to their feet, ready for another knock-down.

It was an artform. Like a dance but with immense power behind it. She and...*Tara*. Tara was her sister's name. She and Tara had been fascinated.

She'd declared to her sister when they left that she planned to mate a warrior.

And here she had one.

Who didn't want to mate her. Because if he did want to, nothing would stop this male.

Tomis tied the males' wrists and feet and hefted the bodies one at a time, carrying them down the metal staircase and onto the airship where he buckled them into seats.

Eslyn flinched at the sight of them.

"They won't hurt you," Tomis rumbled. "I promise. You needn't have anything to do with them ever again, but it's my duty to bring them to safety, even if it's only to the dungeon of Prince Zander's pod."

That seemed to relieve Eslyn.

They boarded the airship, making the children comfortable as Tomis worked on starting it.

It wasn't long before a whir started up beneath the ship. "He did it!" She beamed at Eslyn.

The female smiled back.

Tomis boarded the ship at a run, commanding them to buckle every being in. They helped the children fasten their harnesses before snapping into their own.

The airship lifted off the ground, hovering and rising slowly out of the hangar. It didn't surprise her to discover Tomis was an excellent pilot as well as fighter.

The heads of the limp males rolled when the airship banked and shot into hyperspeed to exit the atmosphere. Eslyn stared at them, her expression a mixture of disgust and fear.

"Don't worry. If Tomis promised they won't hurt us, they won't. He'll protect us."

"You love him, don't you?" Eslyn asked quietly, so Tomis wouldn't hear.

She choked on her breath, her muscles seizing up at the question. With a quick shake of her head, she asserted, "It doesn't matter."

Confusion flickered over Eslyn's face. "What does that mean?"

"He doesn't want me."

"Yes, he does. You're everything to him. I see it in the way he watches you. The way he protects."

Pain sliced up and down her chest. "No. Well, he might, but he won't allow himself to keep me. My father is his mentor and master. He believes his duty is to return me to him and their prince and allow them to decide my future.

"Why would they decide your future?"

She rolled her eyes. "It's foolish, but, until they found me, it was believed there were no Zandian females of breeding age. They are worried the species will grow extinct, and I'm the key to keeping it alive. Of course, now there are two of us, and you've already ensured the future of our species with your sweet young."

Eslyn's brow furrowed. "He is noble, your warrior. Giving you up for the good of his species."

Veck noble. She'd rather have a selfish mate who wanted her only for himself. To change the focus, she lifted her chin at Eslyn's three mates. "Did you love any of them?"

Eslyn nodded. "All of them. Sankro most of all. But he grew abusive, and Elit and Banf followed his example. I still love them, but I knew the moment you and Tomis arrived I wanted to leave. I love our young, but living with the same few beings and no others for an entire lifetime became a torture. For solar cycles, I've fantasized about meeting just one other being." She smiled. "Now I've met two."

"We've been spotted. Hang on!" Tomis shouted from the front of the ship. The craft bobbed and swooped.

The children screamed, but with big smiles on their faces, as if it was all a game. Eslyn flung her arm out to protect them, though their harnesses were secure.

Laser fire sounded, some of it pelting the rear of the craft.

For the first time, her confidence in Tomis faltered. What if they were shot down? Would he be able to protect them all? Surely not. The Finn had entire armies.

The ship swerved, turned sideways then upside down. The young shrieked. Her stomach dropped to her feet. The ship flipped back over and darted from side to side. Thank *veck* she hadn't eaten much in the past planet rotations, or it would be all over the floor.

"Warrior Tomis exiting Zandian airspace. Six assets, three prisoners. Eight ships in pursuit and firing. Going into hyperdrive." Tomis spoke crisply into a communication unit, delivering information in a calm, concise fashion.

"Copy that. Dispatching assistance. Reading your coordinates." The voice that answered made her heart pound.

Her father.

She recognized his voice after all these years. Even with most of her memories of Zandia still missing. The sound was profoundly comforting. Like Tomis' ever-steady presence, it inspired feelings of safety.

Tears welled in her eyes. She closed them. It was all too much.

The ship surged forward, breaking through the atmosphere, leaving the light of the Zandian sun behind them as they sliced through blackness. Internal lights whirred and illuminated at their feet.

Tomis continued to move the airship in sickening swoops and lurches while laser fire whizzed past them.

"Verify coordinates," her father barked. Tomis replied with a series of numbers. "I have you in sight. We'll take care of your pursuers. Meet at the air base."

"Yes, Master."

More laser fire whizzed by, and an explosion of light and fire lit up one of the side windows.

Three more explosions followed in short order, but Tomis flew straight and smooth, giving her stomach a chance to settle.

They'd made it. Now he was taking her to the Zandian air base. Would she meet her father? Did she want to?

A knot tightened in her solar plexus. Once she was there, it would be harder to leave. Her father would want to reclaim her. The prince would want to make decisions about her life. While she no longer feared them or believed their intentions malevolent, she also wasn't ready to be claimed.

Look at poor Eslyn, controlled by three males for her entire life.

Was that what she wanted to happen to her? She'd just ended her lifetime of servitude with Thurn. In fact, she'd like to go back and shove a boot down his throat.

Yes, that wasn't a bad plan. Get some closure with Thurn and give her a chance to think about what she wanted. If she chose to go meet her father and Prince Zander, it would be on her own terms, not being brought in as an "asset."

CHAPTER SEVEN

Tomis landed the ship in the dock of the training pod where Zander kept his fleet of airships and his human army. He would have much preferred bringing Talia and Eslyn straight to the palatial pod, with its beauty and luxury. Give them a taste of the life Zander would probably offer them to stay.

The training pod—a former Ocretion death pod—was stark in comparison. Though Zander sent regular supplies, they'd been scrambling to provide for the sudden acquisition of the nearly two hundred humans who'd been slated for death when the pod was overtaken. There weren't enough beds or chambers for every being, though they'd distributed sleeping mats and blankets and provided food for the humans, who required constant sustenance.

No, he didn't like bringing the females and young here. It might frighten them. He'd overheard Talia's conversation with Eslyn, and he needed to get her alone, to correct her misconception and make sure she understood just how much he wanted her.

How could she believe that?

Just because he served his prince and species first, didn't mean he wouldn't kill or die for her in a heartbeat. Just because honor required he present her to her father and his prince didn't mean he didn't wish to take her straight to his chamber and pierce her with every bit of crystal his life savings would afford him.

He needed to be sure she understood. He unbuckled his harness and helped the females release the young.

The hatch slid open, and guards entered, hands on the hilts of their swords, though he'd been expected.

"Take those three to a prison cell until their fates can be determined." He jerked his thumb at the males who had come back to consciousness during the journey and now displayed varying degrees of anger and fear.

Rok, the captain of the training pod, met them on the dock, his lovely human mate, Lily, at his side. "You found her—them." His eyes traveled between Eslyn and Talia, taking in the young. Lily immediately engaged the young in conversation.

Rok correctly chose Talia and gave a slight bow. "Talia. Well met. I'm Rok. We escaped together as children. Our ship was shot down on Stornig."

Talia swallowed. Tomis moved to her side, wanting to draw her against him and lend her support, but she scuttled away.

It was a subtle movement, but it made the back of his neck prickle with foreboding. *Veck*, he needed to get her alone. To explain. Help her understand.

"I'm sorry, I don't remember. I don't remember much before Stornig."

A buzzer sounded, signaling the approach of another ship for landing. "We need to get inside before they depressurize. Come, all of you." Rok waved them inside.

Lily took charge of the females and young, ushering them off down the corridor before Tomis could stop them.

"All your reinforcements are returning intact." Rok dragged his focus back to the mission. "This should be them now. Lundric, Cambry, Tal, Seke, Jaso, and Janu all piloted." He named their chief of security and his human female, her human brother, Talia's father, and Rok's two Stornigian foster brothers.

"I really should see to the females," he said, staring down the now-empty corridor in the direction Talia had gone.

Rok's eyebrows drew together in a *what-the-veck's-wrong-with* you expression. "Lily will see to their needs. Master Seke and I need a full debrief now.

Right. A full debrief.

He sighed. Duty first.

~.~

"My name is Lily. I'm Captain Rok's mate." The copper-haired human female led them to a tiny office with two cots. "This is our medical unit. Is anyone hurt?"

They all shook their heads.

"Hungry? No, you probably don't eat. In need of crystal recharge?"

"Not yet," Talia answered.

"All right. Clothing, then. Fitting the children will be tough, but I do have flight suits that should fit you two." She pulled crisp white uniforms from a cabinet and handed a set to each of them. "My mother is handy with sewing. I'm sure she can convert some tunics into clothing for the little ones."

Eslyn and the children stared at everything, as if in total culture shock. "I'd like to wash up first, if possible," Eslyn suggested.

"Of course. We have a shower down this hall." She led them to the washroom. "Here are some towels."

Talia let Eslyn shower first and get the children cleaned up then took her turn. The water fell over her in a steady spray, but it did nothing to wash away her mounting panic about being there.

She felt like a prisoner—all choice removed from her. *Veck this.* She needed to get out of there. The sooner the better. Coming out of the shower, she bumped into two Stornigians. Short and stocky, with a set of vicious teeth, Stornigians weren't beautiful, but, to her eyes, they were wonderfully familiar.

"Hello?" She spoke in Stornigian. "You're from Stornig?"

They gave her identical wary glances. "So?"

"Any chance one of you could bring me there? To the Three Pits Tavern in Dumpler?"

She unwrapped the sacred crystal from the waterfall from Tomis' shirt and held it out. "I'll give you this."

The closest one snatched it from her hand. "Deal. Let's go." He looked around surreptitiously, like someone might see them and stop their flight. "I'm Jaso. This is Jano." They hustled her out of there, to the dock and into an old, rusted, and dented airship.

Before she had time to reconsider her decision, the ship had undocked, swooping out into the blackness. A communication from the pod blared over the loudspeakers. It sounded like Rok. "Where in the *veck* do you two think you're going?"

"On an errand. We'll be right back."

"The *veck* you are! You can't just take my ship on an errand whenever you want. What in the hell is going on?"

"Jaso wanted to get a drink at the Three Pits Tavern in Dumpler. Won't take long."

A long silence ensued. "Is Talia with you?"

"You guessed it. Don't ask us. She wanted to go and had the crystal to pay for it."

A string of curses ensued, most of which she'd never heard before, but apparently they didn't require answering because Jano flicked off the comms unit while Rok was still midstream.

This was it. She was going back to Stornig. To kick the crap out of Thurn and demand payment for all the years she worked there as a supposed slave.

Then she could figure out whether to return to her species and join in their flight for survival and repopulation of Zandia.

The terrible twisting in her belly would probably go away soon. The heartache? That might, too, although she didn't think so.

Tomis had been her one and only. She knew it without a shadow of a doubt. Too bad he didn't concur.

. . .

Tomis roared and threw his fist into the wall, denting the metal. Then he repeated the action.

On the third time, Rok caught his arm. He turned, ready and willing to fight Rok, the messenger of the *veck-all* horrible news Talia had left for Stornig with Rok's *vecking* foster brothers. He was ready to beat him to a bloody pulp for letting it happen, not just for being in the way, but the male threw his palms up in surrender.

"Peace, warrior. Females. I know—they're infuriating."

He drew his fist back once more, but Rok gripped his biceps, pushing his arm down. "Stop denting my *vecking* pod. If you want her so badly, *go after her.*"

Right. Simple advice, but sound. He'd go after her. But what then? She had chosen to leave, and he'd promised to let her. What would she think when he showed up ready to drag her back at all costs?

That wouldn't work. But maybe he could convince her to come. Say the things he should have said before.

"May I take a ship?"

"If you bring it back."

He whirled, already striding for the dock. "Clear me for takeoff."

"Feel free to kick my brothers' asses when you get there."

"Don't doubt it," he called over his shoulder before pushing the door open to the loading chamber. He threw a helmet on his head and stormed out onto the dock. He picked the closest airship and jumped on it, firing up the engines.

Gone. Talia was gone. He'd seen it coming. *Veck.* He should have prevented it. What an idiot he'd been!

He should have worked harder to disabuse her of the notion he didn't want her. Didn't need her. But what if, fundamentally, that wasn't enough?

He knew she cared for him. Or had that just been her hormones talking? No. She'd sacrificed herself to save his life. She loved him. He knew it.

He lifted off, setting the flight course for Stornig. Why in the hell had Talia chosen to run to the planet where she'd been enslaved? *Veck,* he would kill her former master if he got his hands on him. Was that why Talia had returned? To demand justice? Why wouldn't she bring him along to protect her. Didn't she knew he'd fight any fight for her.

Any fight.

Prickles raced over the skin of his arms.

Veck. He knew what Talia needed.

The answer hit him and, with it, all the life drained from his body. He had to choose her above duty. Above his species, his prince. Above honor. He had to be willing to fight for her, for them. Against his mentor and ruler, if he had to.

Was he willing to be Talia's warrior instead of Prince Zander's?

Hell, yes.

Because the alternative—losing her—was unthinkable. He couldn't live knowing he'd hurt her. Let her down. Abandoned her to the authority of anyone else.

She belonged to him. Hadn't she surrendered to him? Allowed him to master her—*begged* him to?

Yes. She was worth it.

He requested permission to land on Stornig. The air border guards charged him three steins just to land and another four to park his ship, but he didn't bother to bargain them down.

Stornig was a poor planet, known for shady dealings, swindling, smuggling, and underground business dealings of every kind. Captain Rok, along with his brothers Jano and Jasu, had been smugglers based on Stornig before being recruited by Prince Zander. Their adventures led them to be some of the best—and most wanted—pilots in the galaxy.

He leaped out of the craft, paid the fees, and asked for directions to the Three Pits Tavern, which he gleaned was the center of seedy business transactions.

Was this where Talia had grown up? The thought made him want to throat-punch the first Stornigian he saw. He restrained his fury, though, intent on only one thing—convincing Talia he was her mate.

On the way, Jano and Jaso passed him, skirting wide to avoid contact. He shouted a few obscenities and hurled a couple stones, but they weren't worth any diversion of his attention.

Inside the Three Pits, he scanned the tavern. Beings of every species jammed the dingy place, crowding the bar, standing around tables, spilling out onto an outdoor deck area. It smelled of stale brew and body odor.

An old, harried-looking Stornigian served drinks behind the bar. One of his eyes was swollen closed, and his lip was cut and bleeding. Beside him—*oh stars!*—stood Talia, coolly serving drinks, a smock tied over her white Zandian flight uniform. He'd loved her naked, and half-clothed in his shirt, but somehow she appeared even more delectable in the fitted suit, the fabric molding to her curves, setting them off in a way that made him want to hide her from the view of every other male in the place. She moved with efficiency and skill only the most experienced bartender possessed.

His heart thundered. It took all his willpower not to storm behind the bar, snatch her up, and carry her out of there. That wouldn't do any good, though.

Talia had chosen to come back here. She didn't appear to be under duress.

He slid into a booth in the corner to watch her, forcing himself to wait.

Stars help any being who laid a finger on her, though. He wouldn't be able to stand by if any being disrespected her.

She worked steadily through wave after wave of customers, until finally the place quieted down.

He sensed the exact moment she spotted him, the air in the tavern seeming to leave through the doors, the din of voices changing to a loud buzz. Or was that the blood rushing in his ears?

They locked gazes, her pouty lips falling open with what he imagined must be a gasp. She untied her smock and removed it, never breaking eye contact with him. She'd showered since he'd seen her last, and her reddish-brown hair fell in thick, glossy waves, which bounced and swayed in time with her hips as she crossed the room to him. His cock thickened in his pants, and he had to shift to accommodate it.

Talia arrived at his table and leaned both hands on it, staring down at him. Her breasts fell forward, pressed together by the frame of her arms as if presented just for his mouth.

He nearly trembled from the effort it took not to move, not to yank her down onto his lap and bite her neck. "Hello, starshine."

Her chin wobbled, and he cursed himself for being responsible for the vulnerability he saw there. "What are you doing here?" she asked warily. "You promised to let me go."

He attempted a nonchalant shrug. "I promised to let you, but I didn't say I wouldn't follow you anywhere and everywhere you went."

Her long-lashed eyes widened. "What does that mean?"

"It means I'm yours, beautiful. I promised to serve. I'm not quitting just because we're off Zandia."

She folded her arms across her chest, but not before he saw her nipples protruding beneath the fabric. "What about your prince? Did he send you?"

"No. I left his service. You're the only being I serve now." He finally permitted himself to reach for her, looping an arm around her waist and pulling her onto his lap.

"Tomis...what do you mean?" Her breathless voice so close to his ear made it hard to concentrate.

"I mean you're mine, starshine. Whether you like it or not. I may not have pierced you yet, but I claimed you back at that waterfall, and nothing will keep me away from you."

She wrapped a fist around one of his horns, and a shudder of pleasure made him yank her ass over his cock.

"You'd better know that touching me there is going to end with you getting *vecked* mercilessly against the first hard surface I can find," he growled.

She squeezed and tugged on the horn, and he nearly came in his pants. "What about my father?" she breathed in his ear. "And Prince Zander? What about the battle to take back Zandia?"

He captured the back of her head, holding her still as he grazed her neck with his teeth. "What about them?"

"You're leaving all that? For me?"

He bit down on the juncture of her neck and shoulder, hard enough to leave a mark. "That's right, beautiful."

She drew in a shuddering breath and he smelled, with horror, the scent of her tears.

"Starshine, no. Don't cry. Please, baby."

"You'd really give that all up for me?" She leaned her forehead against his.

"Yes. My life is nothing without you. Say you'll wear my crystal, Talia. Let me be your mate."

"Yes," she sniffed, pressing her body even closer to his.

He inhaled her scent, smelling the soap from her shower and underneath it, her own unique essence, sweet and wild. "I never should have pretended I'd give you up. It would have been an impossibility, even if I'd wanted to. You're mine. You'll always be mine."

"You're mine, too." She squeezed his horn. "And I require servicing."

Tomis attacked her mouth, biting her lower lip, twining his tongue with hers. "*Veck,* female. I thought my need for you would relax once we were off-planet. But it's only worse."

She kissed him back feverishly, apparently forgetting where they were or not noticing the elderly bartender stared at them with grudging approval. "It's worse for me, too," she said huskily. "Do you think it will always be this way?"

"I hope so." His hand slid up her inner thigh. "Come to the airship I borrowed. I need you alone."

"All right." She stood up and smiled, so beautiful she took his breath away. "Come and meet Thurn, my former master."

He growled, hands closing into fists.

"Easy, warrior. I already gave him a black eye." She shrugged. "He found a girl out in the desert and saw it as a windfall. My life wasn't all that bad. He taught me a trade and three languages. Took care of me when I was sick. Protected me from every patron here who wanted to use my body. He was a poor substitute for my real father, but I think he loved me in his own way. Even if he did use a lie to keep me bound to him."

He arched a brow. "You came to forgiveness far faster than I will." He unfolded his legs, adjusting his aching cock as he stood.

"Let it go. Take me to my real father, I'm ready now."

He went still. "You're willing to meet him?"

"Only as your mate."

Warmth exploded in his chest, filling him with more love and pride than he believed he could take. She hadn't wanted to be delivered to her father because she belonged to him.

"I won't keep you from your duties, Tomis. Knowing you were willing to give it all up for me is enough."

He yanked her into him, crushing her lips with his. "I love you, Talia. Only you."

She melted into him, her soft form supple and yielding. "And I love you, warrior. Now, let's go. I think you promised me a hard *vecking*."

He growled, palming her ass and squeezing as they started across the room to meet and bid farewell to Thurn.

His mate.

Stars, how did he get so lucky?

CHAPTER EIGHT

Talia gripped Tomis' hand far harder than she meant to, hesitating outside the door to Prince Zander's Great Room in the palatial pod. Her body felt deliciously tender in so many places after endless hours of lovemaking and her freshly pierced nipples, ears, and cheek. But her emotions were as raw as her body, and she didn't feel ready to meet Seke.

They'd gone to the training pod first, to return the airship, then traveled on with Rok and Lily to meet Prince Zander and her father.

"Wait," she whispered, digging in her heels as he tried to lead her through the door.

Rok and Lily bumped into them from behind.

"Sorry. I...uh...forgot something."

Lily touched her shoulder. "I know what it's like to meet family you don't even remember," she said. "I ran from it at first, too." She looked through the open doors, her gaze landing on two human women—one older and one with an infant in her arms—who had the same coppery hair and green eyes she did. "But, next to Rok, they're the best thing that's happened to me."

She hooked an arm through Talia's free elbow. "Come on. We'll go in together."

A mist blurred her vision as she walked in beside her new mate and friends.

The conversation in the room stopped, and the scarred warrior in white standing beside Lily's mother jerked his head up, eyes locked on hers. "Talia," he rasped.

She swallowed, hard. "Father?"

He strode forward, opening his arms.

For a moment, she didn't move.

Tomis squeezed her hand. "It's all right, starshine. You don't have to—"

She rushed forward, falling into her father's embrace, rediscovered memories jostling around her head. She remembered his deep voice. The strength of his arms. The straightness of his back. The warmth of his hug.

Tears wet her cheeks, and she sensed, by the tightness of Seke's arms, how much emotion he choked back.

"Talia. I thought you were dead. I'm sorry I never found you."

"You found me now," she said against his chest. "Tomis found me."

He seemed reluctant to release her, but, after a long moment, he did. He raised his forearm toward the ceiling to greet Tomis. "Thank you. For rescuing my daughter. I am forever in your debt."

Tomis bowed. "And I, yours, for my upbringing. And because I have mated her."

The room erupted with cheers of congratulations. Seke thumped Tomis on the back, and the handsome Zandian who'd been standing with Lily's sister did as well.

Tomis bowed to him. "My lord. May I present my mate, Talia, daughter of Master Seke."

Zander inclined his head. "Welcome Talia, and congratulations on your mating."

She curtsied. "Thank you, my lord. And thank you for sending Tomis to rescue me."

Prince Zander's lips quirked into a smile. "Tomis sent himself. Not that I wouldn't have dispatched a mission for your rescue."

She gazed up at her warrior, who tucked her back against his side, as if she belonged nowhere else. "Is that true?"

He nodded, once. "One look at you, and I was willing to give my life for your rescue. Are you surprised?"

"No," she whispered. Of course she wasn't. Tomis was her hero. Her protector. Her mate and master.

He leaned down and brushed his lips across hers. "Are you all right, starshine?"

"Yes," she murmured. "I'm perfect."

ZANDIAN PET

CHAPTER ONE

For a sex slave, there were worse gigs than Prium's Intergalactic Lounge, aka sex emporium.

Mina stretched, arching her back and pushing her hips in the air before giving the fluffy blue tail in her ass a wiggle. She had seven males of three different species watching her window as she wriggled around behind the laser glass for their entertainment.

The work at Prium's was nonstop, which some might find tiresome, but after five years closed up at Durhock's, she found the stimulation invigorating.

No, not the sexual stimulation. That part had never done anything for her. Personally, she didn't see what it was about sex that made males lose their minds.

One of the males watching rubbed his hands over his own man-nipples, and she took the cue and squeezed her breasts, lifting one to lick the nipple. She'd had years of training in turning males on.

The time Mina had spent as Durhock's pet wasn't overly taxing, though. All she'd had to do was obey his every command and look beautiful naked. Wear the collar, stupid fluffy ears pinned in her hair and a tail plug in her ass when he had guests. Service them when he'd ordered it. Service him when he'd demanded, but that wasn't often. He'd had so many sex pets, they were mostly for display.

Show cats, the human slave, Leti, used to call them.

Leti. *Veck,* Mina missed her. She didn't know what happened to her friend after her Bangardian master Durhock—the idiot—choked to death eating a piece of dried fruit. They all were auctioned off with the rest of his belongings. All she knew was Prium bought her for his sex emporium two lunar cycles ago, and there she was.

She caught the eye of one of the males and crawled slowly forward. *Come into my cell.* Some slaves preferred to dance and prance around alone to being selected for use by a customer, but not her. The more interaction she had with other beings, the greater her chance of figuring her way out of this place. She needed information, and she wasn't going to get it rubbing her own lady-flower behind the laser screen.

No, she couldn't have asked for a better place to be than Prium's. Locked away in Durhock's home, she'd never had a chance of escape, no hope of finding out anything about her species, if any of them still existed. But here? Hundreds of beings came and went every planet rotation. She'd personally serviced forty already, which meant she'd heard all the news of the galaxy.

She already confirmed she wasn't the only Zandian left alive. According to the Ocretion businessman who'd left that morning, Prince Zander survived and had amassed a small contingent of other survivors on a pod parked in Ocretion airspace. Maybe she was too optimistic, but she believed if she could get herself there, she'd be welcomed.

Her father had been the king's Master Warrior, after all. That had to count for something. She'd lived in the royal palace before the Finn invaded. She remembered Prince Zander, already a handsome and skilled warrior in training with her father at the time of the invasion. And her father had probably died defending the king and queen.

So, now all she needed was to break out of the emporium and hitch a ride to Ocretion airspace. Which most would say was impossible, but if she'd learned anything from her father, it was focus and determination. *There's nothing you can't do,* he used to tell her and her younger sister, Talia. *Decide what you want, or what needs to be done, and never let your mind wander from that goal.*

She wouldn't imagine her father's opinion of her means of getting to her goal. Trading her flesh for knowledge. For opportunity. She couldn't let the twist of shame free from the pit of her stomach. Someday, when she was free, she could take it out and examine it. For now, she'd do what she needed to do.

And she'd already made it one step closer to freedom. No, two. After careful study, she may have figured out a way to short out the laser wall that kept her caged. All she needed was a Zandian crystal.

Unfortunately, she hadn't seen one since her planet was invaded by the Finn when she was just eight solar cycles.

The male she'd been attempting to lure in fisted his cock, watching her.

She licked her lips and sat back on her heels, curling a finger to beckon him in.

I can suck that cock for you, ugly Ocretion. Come in here so I can seduce you into taking me with you. Straight to Ocretia. Or her airspace, anyway.

. . .

Erick doubled back twice before landing his ship. Some *vecker* had been following him. He wouldn't put it past the Finn to hire every mercenary in the galaxy to tail Zandians now that they knew Prince Zander had armed himself.

For now, he thought he was clear. Even if he wasn't, they weren't going to find anything out from his visit to Prium's Intergalactic Lounge, the swanky sex club on the neutral planet of Aurelia, which was one of the reasons he'd chosen to stop there.

The club featured every flavor of copulation in the galaxy with just about any species.

Don't want to participate? No problem! You can watch. At least thirty sex rooms had an invisible laser wall open to the lounge. He didn't know what type of customer requested those rooms. Did it cost more to have your activity on display? Or did you get a discount? He'd never asked. Exhibitionism wasn't his thing.

Prium's was the place he stopped to let off steam during breeding season. When his biology raged at him to find a female and plant her with his seed. Too bad there weren't any Zandian females left to implant.

At least, he'd believed there weren't until two short planet rotations ago when two stunningly beautiful females had arrived in the palatial pod, leaving every male there senseless with lust. Which was why he'd chosen to get the hell off the space pod.

The females weren't available, anyway. Talia, Master Seke's daughter, came already mated to the warrior Tomis, and Eslyn seemed to be in relationship with three other criminals brought in from Zandia. Although judging by the rumors, she wished to shed herself of those males, which left every warrior in the pod clamoring to take their place, offering to share her like her previous mates had.

Sharing wasn't Erick's style, though. Even though he'd never had a relationship, he knew that instinctively about himself. He'd be a possessive *vecker.* If he had a Zandian female, he'd fight every male in the galaxy for her.

A stray *nelot*—one of the furry mammals usually kept as pets on Aurelia—curled around his ankles, blinking up at him. He bent and scratched its ears. "Sorry, I don't have any food for you, little one. Zandians don't eat often." Only once every ten planet rotations, to be exact. Unless they were parted from Zandian crystal, the stone at the core of their planet, which gave them energy. The valuable gemstone behind the Finn's invasion and massacre fifteen solar cycles ago.

The electronic doors sparked and zapped as he stepped through, but since he had no weaponry, he entered unharmed. The moment he entered, his muscles tightened with the anticipation of release.

Veck, he'd never needed to blow off steam more.

He'd just lost 750,000 steins of Prince Zander's money.

In the years since the Finn took their planet, Erick had earned or helped Prince Zander earn millions through investments and business dealings. Wealth the Zandians desperately needed to wage war to regain their precious home. Wealth they'd used to buy airships and weaponry.

But he'd just come from his meeting with a broker empty-handed, his investment gone.

"Forgive me, Master Erick," Behn, the pock-faced Eglentian broker who had put together the deal for three galactacarriers had said, twisting a giant Zandian crystal ring on his finger. Erick had traded him that crystal solar cycles before in another deal. "At this point, all I can tell you is that the deal has been delayed."

Delayed his ass.

Although Behn had hidden it well, Erick recognized signs of his distress. The trickle of sweat running from his ear to his high ruffled collar, the ring twisting.

Erick's fingers had twitched over the handle of his sword. He may be Prince Zander's business and trade advisor, but he'd been warrior-trained by Master Seke, right along with the rest of them. No Zandian had gone unschooled except the very elderly, no matter what their role in the palatial pod was. They had a planet to recover and precious few of their species left alive.

Losing the bid to take back Zandia was unthinkable.

In the end, he'd left Behn alive, taking the crystal ring and an ancient Venusian talisman from his desk as collateral. It wasn't Behn's fault the seller had swindled him. Erick had left him with dire threats about recovering his funds. Not that he had much hope of ever seeing that money or the three galactacarriers.

The loss was a huge blow. They had precious few resources to win their planet back. It was a shame he preferred not to shoulder. He needed to salvage this situation because reporting his failure to Zander was not an option.

But until he eased the throb of his cock, avidly campaigning for him to storm the pod upon his return and spread the legs of one or both of those new female inhabitants, he wouldn't be able to think.

So, Prium's it was.

He skipped the lounge, pulsing with a hypnotic reverberation designed to lower one's inhibitions. It didn't help the heaviness in his loins. He went straight for a bidding room, where he could view holograms of the available females and purchase an hour or two with one.

Prium, himself, was behind the counter, and when he saw Erick, he saun- tered over. Tall, slender, and pinky-white skinned, with pale, almost silver eyes, Prium, like most Aurelians, possessed an austere beauty. Even the males appeared feminine, with long, delicate fingers and elongated skulls. He wore a flowing, fur-lined robe in pale yellow and had intricately embroidered slippers with curling, pointy toes. "Welcome to Prium's, Master..."

"Erick."

"Master Erick. Yes, welcome back. I have just the female for you today."

Something about the way Prium said it, or the assumption behind the words, made the back of Erick's neck prickle. His hand drifted to his sword belt, but, of course, he'd stowed all weaponry in the ship. *Excrement.* He hated being unarmed.

"No trust me, you'll love my newest acquisition," the glamorous pimp drawled.

Erick had a personal rule about never believing any being who said *trust me*, so he kept his face impassive and waited. Why had *he* been targeted by Prium for this sales pitch? He wasn't a frequent customer, nor a heavy spender. Something about it felt off, like a setup.

Prium launched a hologram, and it all became as clear as Zandian crystal. Not a setup. Ice flashed through his flesh, followed by prickles of heat. His fingers cranked closed into fists.

Prium has a Zandian female.

It took every ounce of control not to throw himself at the peddler of flesh and choke that smug look right off his face.

A *Zandian female* being kept as a *sex slave*?

Over his dead body. He would *vecking kill* Prium for dishonoring one of his species. Never mind the fact that enslaving a Zandian was illegal because his species was recognized by the United Galaxies.

But he'd negotiated hundreds of deals. Knowing better than to show any emotion, he gave the hologram a bored glance. "Interesting. Where did you find her?"

The hologram rotated, and prickles raced down his arms. Though her hair had been bleached to a human shade of reddish blonde, he recognized the female.

Taramina. Seke's other missing daughter.

"Her name is Mina. I bought her in a lot of slaves from a private collection. Aurelian. The previous owner used them as pets."

Oh no. He did not *vecking* say that.

Erick swallowed down his rage. His nails bit into the flesh of his palms, but he forced a calm he didn't feel to radiate from his shoulders, his face. Plastering on a bored countenance, he said, "All right. I'll give her a try."

"No privates with this one. You can only have her in a mainstage cell."

Every cell in his body revolted against that idea. He needed to get the female alone. Not to *veck* her—he couldn't touch Seke's daughter, not unless he wanted a quick death at the hands of the Master at Arms.

"How much for a private?" Now, he looked too damn eager. Damn, he hadn't wanted to show his hand.

Prium's generous mouth stretched into a toothy smile. He hadn't been fooled to begin with. "Stage cell only. She's one of my top exhibits."

Vecking hell.

"Fine. Why don't you show her to me?"

Mina dragged her gaze away from the scene going on in the cell directly across the lounge from hers. Prium's featured every kind of sex, from clean and clinical to rough and mean, with every fetish in between. The human female across the cell was new—not a trained slave—and she screamed and cried as two males had their way with her. Apparently, this sort of scene was a huge draw because every spectator in the lounge had shifted to watch it play out.

She should use this time to case the room, look for opportunities. But her gaze kept zipping back to the cell with the unfortunate slave. The Ocretian males had her arched over the padded bench, one shoving his malehood into her mouth as the other pounded between her legs. They took turns slapping her breasts, her face, her thighs.

The quickening between Mina's thighs made her stomach twist. She shouldn't be aroused by this girl's torture. It was sick and wrong. It must be because it was Zandian breeding season. At least, she thought it might be, if she remembered the cycles right. Once a year, for a period of weeks, all the females on her planet went into heat. She'd only been a child, but she remembered her parents locking themselves in their room for hours on end during breeding season, with the result being a new infant sibling.

But she'd always had a slightly different take on sex than the human slaves. She didn't *enjoy* it, *per se*, but she didn't find it as distasteful as some slaves.

Obedience came easily for her, or at least feigned obedience, because she'd always known she'd escape. Maybe that was the difference between her and the humans. They had no hope of ever escaping their fate. Humans were not recognized as free beings anywhere in the United Galaxies.

She stole another look at the cell across the way. The males had flipped the sobbing girl over on the bench, and one of them whipped her with his belt while the other took a turn with his cock in her mouth.

Again, something twisted in her belly, heat kindling between her legs. She didn't want to be whipped like that. Not by those males. But in her most unacknowledged fantasies, she served a slave master worth obeying. Not one like Durhock, but one who paid far more attention. Who controlled her every move, paid attention to her. Punished her. Rewarded her. He'd be big and muscled, like her father had been. Capable. Masculine.

But that was ridiculous. A worthy slave master wasn't her goal. Freedom was.

The door to her cell opened, and she whirled to face it. She hadn't expected any customers, since they were all engaged watching the threesome across the way.

Prium, himself, stepped in and then her breath caught. Behind him, ducking to get through the doorway, hulked an incredible male. One with the same color skin as hers and two horns on the top of his head.

A *Zandian* male.

When he saw her, his nostrils flared, and brown eyes turned violet. The stubby horns thickened and leaned in her direction, but his face remained blank, if not slightly disdainful.

Her own physical reaction to his presence was so instantaneous and complete, it overwhelmed her. Her breath whooshed out of her chest, thighs began to quiver. She caught his scent, which made her head swim and the room rock under her feet. Moisture trickled from her clenching pussy down her leg. She had to use the wall to hold herself up.

"On your knees, pet," Prium commanded with a frown.

The lounge owner loved that she'd been trained as a sex pet, almost as much as he loved the color of her skin, her species exotic for a slave. He showed her off to all his best clients, demanded a parade of her tricks: the leash and collar, the way she crawled and licked fingers.

She didn't move, not out of a show of will, but because her brain couldn't process the command, and when it did, her legs didn't obey her brain.

Prium scowled, and she regained her head, dropping to her hands and knees and crawling toward the Zandian, but not before her owner produced a leather tawse.

The Zandian gave a miniscule shake of his head, brows lowered, and she halted halfway there. Immediately, his expression went blank again, eyes sweeping the cell with a disinterested air.

"Get over here and greet your master for the hour," Prium hissed.

Her throat closed, not at Prium's anger or the certainty of punishment. It was because of the Zandian. Some unknown emotion surged up and choked her, now, some vulnerability or desire. Or was it grief? Did seeing him remind her of all that she'd lost? What she'd become?

Don't cry.

She never cried. Hadn't in years.

She hadn't seen a Zandian since the airship carrying her, her sister, and a Zandian boy crashed escaping the invasion and she'd been captured as a slave. She forced her knees to move forward, crawled to the Zandian, who Prium had ushered to the padded bench in the middle of the cell.

He didn't wear the traditional Zandian dress of a white tunic and leggings. Instead, he wore an expensive and perfectly tailored black flight suit with a sword belt, empty of its weapon, at his waist. All customers were disarmed when they entered Prium's.

She arrived at his polished animal-hide boots and dropped to her heels, kneeling before him. Her nipples pointed forward, tight and achy.

Prium stood over both of them, glowering down at her. "Mina, this is your master for the hour."

The Zandian didn't meet her gaze. He didn't ogle her body, either. Instead, he seemed to stare at a spot above her left ear.

"Elbows on the bench," Prium clipped, patting the space beside the Zandian. "You know how I deal with disobedience."

She slid into position, registering the tension in the male beside her, though he outwardly showed none.

Prium drew his arm back, but the Zandian surged forward and caught his wrist. "I'll do it." His voice was deep and resonant. It sent a flash of fire through her body, coating her with tingles of heat. It couldn't be just his presence that had this effect on her, could it?

Was this what happened between members of her species during breeding season? That might be part of it, but there was some other power to him. A familiar energizing power. One that gave her strength, too. *Zandian crystal.* She almost gasped when she realized. He must have one on him.

She'd forgotten how good it felt. How clean her body ran with it nearby, not needing to eat food every day the way she had since she'd been away.

Well, this planet rotation improved every minute. She turned her neck to scan his fingers for rings, but saw none. Nor did he wear any necklaces or bands around his wrists. Perhaps in his pockets? She'd have to check them while she serviced him.

Prium nodded and handed the Zandian the animal hide tawse—a wide leather strap, split in two at the whipping end. "Make it good, or I'll give her double when you've gone."

There. The surge of interest again. Like she'd had while watching the human girl getting whipped in the cell across the way, only stronger. More excitement, less shame. Because this master, the male before her, was exactly the sort she had fantasized about.

Whip me, Master.

"I'll make her sorry."

Her pussy clenched.

The Zandian's knuckles whitened where he held the tawse, though his expression was one of boredom. He stood and positioned himself to her left, drawing the tawse back.

Excitement raced through her. Fear, too, although she'd never cowered from punishment before. Something about having a worthy master made punishment completely different. She wanted to please him.

Badly.

But she didn't have time to examine that insanity, because she needed to keep her wits. This male may provide her best opportunity for escape.

His arm swung, and he struck her with the tawse.

She went up on her toes, her breath screaming in, belly hollowing out with the pain. Even as her buttocks twitched in response to the blow, her pussy clenched and released. Heat poured down her limbs.

More.

She wanted more from him.

He obliged. Another smack of leather caught the undersides of her cheeks, sending her clawing for the edge of the bench. The strap jostled the tail in her ass, adding a level of squirmy sensation to the pain. Not quite pleasure, but heat and desire coiling together into potentiality.

She couldn't help the whimper that escaped her throat.

Prium stood at the door, watching the punishment with a smug smile.

Suddenly, with such a delicious, worthy master standing behind her, respecting Prium became impossible. She childishly wanted to make a face or an obscene gesture with her hands. He was nothing compared to the male wielding the strap.

The tawse slapped across her buttocks again and again, and she dropped her forehead to the bench, forcing herself to breathe through the burn and pain. On and on her temporary master went, spanking her thoroughly with the forked paddle until tears smarted her eyes.

After at least a dozen strokes, the Zandian dropped the tawse and fisted her hair, pulling her head back roughly. He brought his face down to hers, brows knit, mouth turned down. "I'm sorry."

Her heart fluttered. He'd grated the words directly in her ear in Zandian, the language she hadn't heard in fifteen years.

～·～

Anger at having to hurt his beautiful female coursed through his veins. Yes, he was calling her *his female,* even though she was nothing of the kind. She belonged to him for this moment. He'd been named her master, and he intended to treat her with the care and protection a master provided his charge.

With his lips at her temple, her scent assaulted him. Not the scent of her arousal—stars, he smelled that, too, and it nearly turned him into wild beast. But she smelled like Zandia. Like home. Like honeyflowers and morning dew. The joy and wild pleasure of his youth. Of his first discovery of a female's lush body.

He had to stop himself from nipping her ear, or dragging his mouth down her neck. Tasting her.

His female's legs and bottom shook from her punishment, but stars, his body trembled too—like the very cells vibrated being near her. The effort of keeping his lust in check proved too great.

But he couldn't show his attraction. Not now, not here. And, somehow, he had to get out of this cell without *vecking* her. She was a Zandian, not some human slave. Even more, she was the daughter of one of Zander's most respected advisors. Master Seke would kill him if he debauched her.

Still holding her pale hair in a rough grip, he hauled her upright. Her bare, striped ass nested against his legs, sending a fresh shudder of desire through him. The heat from her well-spanked flesh radiated through his trousers, and his cock lurched against her back.

Veck if she didn't mold her back to his front, arching those perky breasts up like an offering. He wanted to fill his hand with those breasts, pinch and rub her nipples until she squirmed.

But he had a wretched audience. Not just Prium, but a lounge full of assholes had gathered in front of their cell to watch him punish Tara. Or Mina, as she went by here.

And if he wanted to get her out of this place, he needed to blend in. Just a typical customer, here to use and abuse a slave. So he made a show of shoving Mina down to her knees. She dropped obediently into a submissive posture, palms on her thighs, eyes lifted to him, as if waiting for his command.

Fury that she'd been trained this way didn't outweigh the surge of lusty power and pleasure the sight of her naked at his feet brought.

The door to the cell swished closed, and the asswipe, Prium, left, apparently satisfied with her punishment.

Mina studied him with long-lashed blue-violet eyes. He had to catch his breath at her beauty. Her father's irises were the same unusual color, but on her, it was exquisite.

He hoped she'd understood him when he apologized.

When the warrior Tomis found her sister, Talia, she had forgotten their planet and language entirely. She'd blacked out everything that had happened to her before being put into slavery. Erick hoped the same wasn't true for Mina.

He sank onto the bench. His fingers started to curl into fists to keep from touching her, but he forced them to relax. To hide his mounting need to throw her down and *veck* her until her teeth rattled, he channeled his desire into rage and glared down at her.

Her beautiful eyes widened, confusion flitting over her face. She licked her lips, and he tightened his to keep in a groan. Her gaze darted to his horns. They felt taut, and surely were leaning toward her. Did she know what that meant? Did she remember how the males of her species showed their interest?

It was easy to gauge hers. Despite her captivity and the forced nature of their interaction, her nipples were hard as the points of crystals, the scent of her arousal a heady perfume.

She rose to her knees and stroked her slender hands up his thighs, sultry invitation in the softness of her face. *Holy Zandian star*, she was about to suck his cock.

He frowned, and she froze. She was well-trained. That shouldn't turn him on so much, but it did. He loved her responsiveness.

Well, what else was he going to do in here with her, if not let her suck his cock?

He snatched her arm and hauled her across his lap, landing a slap on her perfectly rounded buttocks.

It was a mistake. The moment she was in position, so much of her bare flesh in contact with his body, her perfect pussy in view between her slender legs, he went wild.

He'd only meant to inspect her backside, make sure he hadn't done too much damage with the wicked tawse, but now he couldn't help his hand from lifting and falling, smacking her round globes with gusto.

His cock shoved against her hip, aching for release and this was the only way he could think to get it, without actually taking it out and *vecking* her every orifice. *Twice*.

So he spanked her, hard and fast, loving the way her bottom bounced and bobbed over his lap, the little cries she made. She wore nothing but a collar and a fluffy blue tail attached to a plug in her ass, which danced and wagged with each smack of his palm.

One of her hands curled around his ankle to stabilize herself, and the touch made his cock surge against his flight pants.

"Please," she squeaked in Zandian, sending a wild glance over her shoulder.

"Hush, slave," he barked in Ocretion, the commonly spoken language in the galaxy. They were putting on a show. No need to have their audience activate translators, even if it was highly unlikely for his language to be an option.

He checked his gleeful aggression, running his hand lightly over the welts on her ass. They should heal quickly, although her body was petite, like her sister's, from living away from the nourishment of Zandian crystal energy.

The scent of her arousal had grown stronger, as if she, too, found spanking to be an acceptable substitute for sex. He gripped the base of the tail and twisted it. She moaned, and her thighs fell open in an invitation for his touch.

His fingers arrived at the cleft between her legs before he even knew he meant to stroke her there. Her pussy dripped with moisture, the plump folds of her sex parted for his fingers. He circled her clit. With his other hand, he pulled the plug out, stretching her around it, then plunged it back in.

She cried out, her fingernails digging into his ankle.

Stars, she liked it. She was so easy to pleasure.

Never, in all his solar cycles of stopping at Prium's during breeding season, had he experienced a female like this. So responsive, so accepting of anything he tried.

Of course, he'd never had a Zandian before.

And he couldn't, now. It would be against her free will.

But giving her pleasure wouldn't be a sin, would it? She deserved release after the terrible whipping he'd given her. After the way he'd continued to punish her with his hand.

He shoved two fingers into her sopping channel as he *vecked* her ass with the tail plug.

When she spread wider for him, her muscles tightening around his fingers, anus squeezing around the tail, he grew desperate for the taste of her. He pulled his fingers out of her and grasped her hips, lifting them into the air and rearranging her so she straddled him. Her torso rested on his legs, fingers splaying on the floor.

Tucking his hands under her thighs, he lifted her dripping cunt to his mouth and licked into her.

Veck, yes.

Home.

She bucked against his mouth as he tongued her honeyed slit, affixed his lips over her little clit, and sucked the stiff bud. He sucked her outer lips, nipped them. Made his tongue stiff and penetrated her with it.

She squirmed and whimpered, desperation pitching her cries higher.

He lowered her hips back onto his lap, her legs splayed wide around his torso, pussy opened to him, ass straight up. In this new, enticing position, he delivered another half dozen spanks. Then he shoved his thumb into her pussy and pumped the plug again.

"Naughty pet," he rumbled. "Now you're getting your little red ass fucked." He used the Ocretion word for sex, instead of the Zandian term.

"Y-yes," she warbled, squirming and humping his lap, her nails digging into his ankle.

"You're lucky I don't fuck it with my big cock, instead." Stars, he'd lost his filter. Or was this part of the act? He wasn't sure anymore. The lines blurred into a mess of color and sensation.

"Please," she whimpered. "Please fuck me with your big, Zandian cock."

Veeeeeeeeck.

His eyes nearly flipped backward in his skull. He pulled his fingers out of her pussy and lit her ass on fire again, spanking hard and fast, forcing his breath out through his teeth.

"Please, Master!"

By the one true Zandian star, he would not survive this test. He shoved her off his lap. She landed in a heap at his feet, her reddish-blonde hair falling in soft waves over her face. He wanted to gather her back up in his arms, beg her forgiveness for treating her so cruelly, but touching her now was an impossibility.

His body shook, about to combust. Need overpowered all rational thought, all care. He closed his eyes and rubbed his face.

When he opened them, his beautiful female was on her knees, unbuckling his belt.

~.~

She didn't know what in the hell was wrong with the Zandian. One minute he was using his tongue in a way no male had attempted on her, giving her the most pleasure she'd ever experienced, the next, he'd shoved her to the floor.

If it weren't for the purple glow of his eyes and the stiffness of his horns, she might think he didn't find her attractive enough. But he did.

So, what was the problem?

She didn't wait for permission this time, certain if she could get his malehood into her mouth, she'd be able to satisfy him. She was trained for pleasure, after all.

His hand snapped out and caught her wrist, but not before she'd wrested his cock free of his pants. The huge purple shaft sprang out, bobbing in front of her, a drop of rainbow-hued precum on the tip.

Not wanting him to stop her, she opened her lips wide, and engulfed as much of his length as she could fit. His hand went slack, and he let out a choked shout, brows slamming down, even as his cock thrust deeper. He fisted her hair. At first, she thought he would pull her off his cock, but he just held her head immobile for a moment, indecision playing over his expression. Then he used his grip to move her forward and back over his cock.

He thrust too deep, choking her, bumping the back of her throat. Her eyes smarted as she struggled to relax her gag reflex and let him inch in even more.

"Was this what you wanted, little slave? A throat-fucking?" Some slaves would be offended by such taunts. In the past, with other males, she'd ignored such talk. She wasn't a sexual being, so she had no shame. She'd existed in her head, not her body. But the Zandian made her feel *so much*. Every centimeter of her body flushed for his touch. Every nerve ending tingled. Being near him brought on the insistent ache between her legs, the throb of her nipples. His words only made her burn hotter.

She loved the way his eyes blazed like bright jewels, locked on hers as he pumped his thick member into her mouth. Need coiled in her belly; heat flooded her core.

And then she remembered her task. *Find the crystal.* She shoved one hand under his balls to cup them as the other bunched in his pants. She closed her fingers around the material, tugged and pushed at it as if in the throes of passion.

Yes. *There.* She felt the hard stone—a ring. A very large ring. And another piece, as well.

She sucked hard, fisting his cock, moving it in concert with her mouth as her other hand emptied his pocket of its treasure.

But where to hide it? She wore no clothing. No orifice was safe while he was in the cell with her. Under the rug, then. It was the only possible place. Hopefully, he wouldn't step on it and discover her treachery.

The Zandian clenched his jaw, his thighs tensed and shook as his hard shaft pistoned in and out of her mouth. He caged her head and held it still as he plunged deeper, all the way down her throat. "*Veck,*" he spat. "*Veck-veck-veck.*"

She recognized the Zandian curse, similar to the Ocretion word *fuck.*

His balls tightened and then he came, spurting ribbons of hot cum down her throat. Her eyes watered, but she swallowed it down, choking a bit. He pulled out the moment he finished, dark torment coloring his eyes. With the tail of his tunic, he wiped her face, his thumb sweeping away a stray tear. She held still for his ministrations, arrested by his intense gaze.

He scooped her up by the armpits and lifted her then deposited her lengthwise on the bench, on her back.

She hadn't had a chance to hide the jewels yet, but she did now, her hand skimming the floor until she found the edge of the rug to tuck them under.

The Zandian gripped her thighs and spread them wide, straddling the bench to face her lady flower. He cupped her ass and lifted her hips to his mouth, licking into her with a fervor that made her flexed feet shoot out to the sides, knees straight. Her nipples ached and throbbed, clit pulsed in time with them.

Yes. This.

More.

All these years as a sex slave, and she'd never orgasmed. She'd thought perhaps Zandians didn't. What did she know? She'd been only eight when she was separated from the last Zandians she knew and taken to Aurelia.

But the desperate coil of desire in her core had her undulating her hips against the Zandian's mouth, shoving her clit against his tongue. Needy whimpers came out of her mouth.

More. More.

He'd brought her to this point last time before she made the mistake of begging him to fuck her ass and he'd thrown her off his lap. Maybe he needed it to feel forced. Like she didn't want it. But no, he worked hard for her pleasure now, his mouth almost frantic between her legs, as if he would devour her.

Stars, she was close. So close. Even without the experience of an orgasm, she knew.

She choked on a breath, thrust her breasts toward the ceiling. Lights flashed before her eyes as she hurtled over the edge into orgasm. Her channel spasmed, clenching and releasing in quick bursts. She wrapped her legs behind his neck and squeezed, trapping his head between her thighs as she gasped and sobbed through her release.

When her vision returned, her eyes sought the Zandian's. If anything, he appeared even wilder, sweat beading at his forehead, his horns a darker purple.

He shook his head as if angry with her.

But what had she done?

He flipped her body again, lifting and arranging her like her weight was nothing to him. He folded her waist over the bench, ass high.

More spanking, then.

He smacked her ass four times, alternating cheeks, then pulled out the butt plug with the fluffy tail and threw it across the room. The metal hit the wall with a thud.

"You keep teasing me with this ass, Mina," he growled and spanked her again.

Hearing her name spoken in his rough, broken voice did something twisty to her insides. It sounded intimate, like he knew her—exactly who she was. But he couldn't. And the whole reason she'd gone by Mina instead of Tara was because she became someone new when she left Zandia.

Was that what disconcerted her? Being fucked by one of her own kind?

Because he *was* going to fuck her, finally. His cock stuck straight out of the top of his pants, as he walked to the wall dispenser and took a palmful of lubricant. He rubbed it over his cock with quick, impatient jerks as he walked back.

A shiver ran through her.

She'd been fucked in the ass plenty of times. By many different species, all kinds of cocks. But a spike of trepidation surged at the knowledge that this male planned to use her that way.

It wasn't just his huge cock, although it would certainly stretch her. It was more. Again, did she assign more meaning to this coupling because of his species?

Yes.

Because he was the one. The male from every fantasy.

A male worthy of giving her flutters.

And she didn't even know his name. Had already stolen from him.

She would make it right when she got to Prince Zander. He would know how to find this male and she'd return what she stole.

The Zandian parted her cheeks and rubbed lubricant on her anus then lined his cock up with it. He sank into her.

She normally ignored all sensation during sex, but it was an impossibility with him. She felt every inch of him stretching her wide, filling her. She moaned, confused by the intensity, the discomfort, the overwhelming pleasure.

When his loins met her ass, she grunted at the pressure of her thighs over the bench, and he immediately pulled up, lifting both their bodies, pivoting, and pushing her to her hands and knees.

He shoved her head into the fluffy rug and held her down as he knocked into her ass. It was utterly degrading, dominating and... *so incredibly hot.*

So this was sex.

Real sex. Not going through the motions as a slave.

Now she understood.

She wanted... *more.* She wanted all of it. Everything this male could give.

The Zandian grunted behind her, taking her hard, his fingers bruising on her hips, thrusts rough and deep.

Her pussy clenched on air. She wished he could give her his cock there, too.

Tears stung her eyes—not from pain, not from anything definable. They just accented the intensity of the experience. Being taken so thoroughly. With so much passion. Having her desperation match his. Her need and desire swallow her whole.

The room tilted and swooped. Her vision blurred. Shouts and screams echoed off the walls, but she hardly realized they came from her until her throat grew raw from crying out, calling over his roar.

He pounced over her, shoving her all the way to her belly, covering her body with his larger one as he came. She must have orgasmed too, or maybe hers had happened earlier, it was hard to tell with his cock stretching her ass and nothing in her pussy. All she knew was that she was floating somewhere. Nowhere. Existing beyond existence. Soaring.

She was pleasure embodied. Satisfaction.

The Zandian molded his body over hers and forced a hand under her hips. The moment he cupped her mons, she came again. She bucked, anus tightening painfully around his huge cock, pussy squeezing and fluttering against his fingers.

So this was what she'd been missing.

"I'm sorry, sweet Mina," he murmured in Zandian in her ear. "I'm so *vecking* sorry. I didn't mean to take you like that." His lips brushed her jaw. "I'm going to get you out of here. That's a promise."

Warmth cascaded through her chest, along with a sense of safety she hadn't felt since she was a child. But no. Safety was an illusion she had to fight.

She couldn't wait around on a stranger's promise, even if he had the same skin color as she did. No, she'd stolen his ring. She'd make her own escape.

. . .

Erick wanted to keep his body wrapped around Mina's forever, but his time was up. The lights flashed to red, warning him he'd gone over.

Besides, if he stayed any longer, he was going to end up with his cock buried in her again, and he'd already shamefully defiled her twice.

Veck, Master Seke would chop his balls off if he found out what Erick had done.

He eased out of the soft, pliant female beneath him, wishing he had a blanket to wrap her in, a way to tend to her. But instead he had to walk out of her cell, leaving her naked and abused, with the eyes of two dozen males watching her. Maybe even—his fingers curled into fists—getting in line to have the next turn with her.

He shoved his dick back into his pants and stalked out without a backward glance, mainly because he knew if he looked back it would be impossible to leave. Nothing stopped him as he strode purposefully out of Prium's, knocking past other beings without seeing them. How much money was he carrying on the ship? Not enough, he feared. But he'd negotiated hundreds of deals over the years. He'd convinced beings to take far less than they wanted for their goods. This would be no different.

Except it *was* different. He'd lost all the indifference within him, the cool, manicured calm that allowed him to broker deals. Never negotiate from desperation. It was his number one rule. Always be willing to walk away.

But there'd be no walking away from Prium's. Not without Mina.

He already stood to lose the 750,000 steins on the galactacarriers. He wouldn't go home without something infinitely more valuable to all of Zandia. A female.

Wait— *veck* that. This bargain wouldn't be for Zandia. It was personal. He'd had a taste of Mina, and he'd never be able to breathe again without her by his side.

Of course, she may want nothing to do with him once she had her freedom. To imagine her undying gratitude after the way he'd held her down and *vecked* her senseless would be idiocy. Her *ass,* no less.

What in the stars had he been thinking?

He hadn't been. He'd turned into a beast with no brain at all.

But he'd make it right. He'd find a way to get her out of there. He entered his ship and pulled the soft animal-skin bag filled with Zandian crystals out of the safe. These were rough crystals, used mainly for laser gun technology rather than as jewels, but he might be able to make Prium believe otherwise.

He shoved them into his pocket and... No.

Behn's crystal ring and talisman were gone. He must've lost them from his pocket while claiming Mina. He'd never been careless in his life. He always kept his mind and eye on things of value, but apparently not around her.

Served him right.

Maybe he could recover them when he collected his female. After he brokered the deal of a lifetime.

Forcing his breath to slow, he brought his mind to the single-pointed focus: *get Mina*. Seke had taught him self-discipline.

The least he could do was use it to get the warrior's daughter back.

Prium registered his entry with a wide smile. "Back for more?" he called out when Erick arrived within listening distance. "They enjoyed your show." He waved a bejeweled hand toward the audience in the lounge.

Erick didn't mean to look, but his eyes darted to Mina's cell.

Vecking hell!

She'd curled up in a ball on the rug with her slender back to the laser screen. Had he hurt her? He'd cut off his own balls if he had.

Prium followed his gaze, and his thin lips stretched into a toothy smile. "You wore her out, didn't you?" The male gave him a speculative up and down sweep of the eyes. "You were *exceptionally* rough. Unexpected..." He tapped the tips of his polished silver claws together. "I had to give her a short rest after you. She'll need stamina for the five males in queue to use her."

His throat closed, choking back a roar of rage. "How much?" he growled.

Prium arched a white-haired brow. "I beg your pardon?"

"To buy her for personal use. I have Zandian crystal to trade, or I can have steins delivered to any intergalactic account within seconds."

Prium showed his interest in the dart of a forked tongue from the corner of his mouth. But he said, "I am not a broker. I do not trade in slaves. I only buy them."

"You're keeping her illegally. Zandians are recognized by the United Galaxies as free beings. She cannot be held against her will by any being."

Prium brought his slender fingers to his chest with affected innocence. "Zandian? No, I think not. She's a human with unusual skin coloring. Zandians are far bigger." Again, the up and down perusal of Erick's large body.

It was all he could do not to fist Prium's elegant robe and shake the male until his teeth rattled.

He pulled out the bag of crystals. "Your choice. Give her to me now and get something in return, or have her taken by the intergalactic police and pay a hefty fine on top of losing her."

Before Prium could answer, the lounge erupted in chaos.

A spray of laser sparks cartwheeled from Mina's cell, pelting all the beings in the lounge with scorching light-drops.

He ran without thinking, eyes trained on Mina's slender silhouetted figure.

Clever female.

She'd used the Zandian crystal to refract the lasers. She wasn't waiting for him to buy her—she'd chosen her own escape.

He grabbed a fistful of the stones from his pouch and pegged one into the cell next to Mina's, and the one next to that, creating more chaos to cover for her.

A guard surged past him, laser gun drawn. Erick grabbed the weapon, slamming the guard's wrist into his knee to dislodge his hold. A slash of the side of his hand into the male's throat dropped him to the floor. He used the gun to shoot out the lights, aiming and firing with careful precision, until the entire place fell into darkness.

Zandians could see in the dark, but Aurelians might not. He dashed off in the direction he'd seen Mina go—not toward the entrance, but down a corridor. Perhaps she knew another exit.

Laser sparks flashed around the bend. He sped up and arrived in time to see her rolling through an elevated window, the laser glass sparking in showers away from Behn's ring.

"Wait, Mina!"

He'd never fit through that window. How did she even get up there? He jumped to look out, but all he saw was Mina's fleeing back.

Damn. How would he find her?

He ran back up the corridor. Another light had been found, and it cast dim shadows around the lounge. Figures darted back and forth. Calls and shouts filled the room.

"There's the Zandian!" a guard yelled, pointing at him.

He shot out the new light and raced for the main entrance. Laser fire screamed past him, ricocheting off the wall and the floor next to his feet. These guards were not trained in expert aim by Master Seke, thank the stars.

The two guards at the entrance aimed their weapons at him. He could probably shoot them both before either one figured out how to fire their guns, but he didn't want an intergalactic murder charge to follow him back to Prince Zander.

Instead, he lobbed another crystal through the electronic doors, sending sparks flying in all directions. It was enough of a distraction for him to plant his foot in one guard's stomach while he bashed the face of the other with a right hook.

He ran for his ship as an alarm screamed and the pound of running boots sounded behind him.

Where are you, Mina? Veck.

He remotely activated the hatch door of his small spacecraft and dived through, smacking the button for it to close before he jumped behind the controls. He had the craft off the ground at the same time the hatch slid shut, but some guard, imagining himself brave, had attached himself to the outside of the craft.

He twisted and tilted the small ship, gunning it with power and sending it in wild circles until the idiot guard fell. Now to find Mina.

"Activate thermal scan." He watched the screen light up with the heat prints of every being below, but none matched the size and shape of his little Mina.

Wait—*there*.

Two beings were in a junky old spacecraft zooming away at top speed. He redirected his craft and followed, but they'd hit the edge of the atmosphere and their ship shimmered, preparing to warp.

"No!" he shouted, but it was too late.

The little airship disappeared, destination unknown.

"*Veck!*" He smacked the control panel once, twice, a third time.

He'd lost her. His Mina. He hadn't even had a chance to make things right between them. Didn't get to bring her to her father, restore her to the elevated position she deserved at the palatial pod. She'd be *vecking* royalty there. Could choose from any male in their species.

Except that had him gritting his teeth. The thought of other Zandian males competing for her attention brought a surge of aggression pumping through him.

What was it about this female that turned him into a savage beast? He didn't remember feeling this way about any female, even as a hormonal youth. But he'd been off-planet during what would have been his first breeding season. He'd spent the year in an alien-exchange study program on Ocretia, which was the only reason he was still alive after the Finn invaded his planet.

He had to find Mina. But how? And what would he say to her father when he returned? Did he dare say he'd seen her? But then he'd have to explain where and how.

And that, on top of telling Zander he'd lost the three-quarter million he'd invested in galactacarriers, made him never want to go back.

Perhaps he should stop somewhere first to lick his wounds and figure out how to deliver his news.

Yes, stopping at the major galactic trading post outside Ocretian airspace wouldn't hurt anything. It may even be where Mina headed.

CHAPTER THREE

Mina held the laser gun to the head of the small Stornigian pilot. She'd grabbed his weapon from his holster when she found him, half-drunk, outside his rickety airship. His eyes had bugged out, but she wasn't sure if it had been from the gun or her breasts bobbing in his face.

Still stark naked, she'd attempted to make up for her vulnerable appearance by using a mixture of force and the promise of reward to get him to fly her the hell out of Aurelian airspace.

He seemed more amused than scared or angry, so it was probably the hope of reward that had motivated him.

She hadn't promised sex. She'd offered the strange talisman she'd taken from her Zandian's pocket.

But he probably hoped for sex.

She wouldn't be above using it if she had to. Actually, that wasn't true. She didn't want any male touching her. Not when she could still feel the heat of the Zandian's hands cupping her ass. The marvel of his tongue between her legs. The skitter of her pulse at his heated, violet gaze.

Since their encounter, the idea of giving herself to any other being repulsed her. Oddly, she felt she belonged to him. He'd risked his life to save her.

She hadn't stayed to gawk, but caught glimpses of him attacking a guard and shooting out the lights as she'd made her run for it. Stars, she hoped he'd made it out safely. She hadn't meant to endanger him—had never, in a million sun cycles, dreamed he would come to her assistance so quickly and *capably*.

And damn, he *had* been capable. Though he hadn't been dressed as a warrior, he used his body like one. She'd forgotten the elegance and grace a trained fighter carried. Seeing him brought back memories of her father taking his warriors through their paces in the movement studio. The power and precision of each kick or lunge, the clarity of intention, the dance of bodies so clean it looked choreographed.

Her chest tightened with an ache she hadn't felt in years—the sting of losing her father and the rest of her family. She'd give anything to see just one of them right now.

The Zandian had woken that homesickness in her. He'd ruined her for any other destiny. And while she regretted leaving him behind—not waiting to ensure he got out safely—at least he'd strengthened her resolve and given her the means to achieve her goal.

"We're in Ocretian airspace. Where to now, beautiful?"

She shifted on her feet. This part she didn't know. "I-I'm looking for a pod docked in the airspace here."

"Let me guess, it's full of beings who look like you?"

Hope quickened. "Have you seen a being like me before?"

The Stornigian smirked. "I've seen a few. I know where their pod is." He lifted his chin at a large floating structure in front of them. "Doubt they'll let me dock without an invitation, though."

She frowned. "Take off your tunic."

He grinned and twisted to look over his shoulder at her. "So we're doing this now?"

She glared, but the merriment in his eyes said he only teased. She waved the laser gun. "Now."

He started to pull the tunic off too quickly, and she jerked the gun level to his head. "Easy, beautiful. I'm just doing what you asked me to."

She nodded, once. He moved more slowly this time as he removed the tunic and held it out to her. She gripped it, unsure how to put it on without lowering the gun or shifting her gaze from her prisoner.

"I'd offer to turn my back for you to get dressed, but I think I've already seen everything you have," he drawled, letting his eyes drift lower. Despite, the taunt, he did turn back to the controls.

She took a step back and pulled the tunic over her head with one arm, keeping the gun trained with the other. With a little struggle, she wriggled one arm through the hole then switched the gun to the other hand and donned the other sleeve. She unbuckled the stupid pet collar she'd worn and dropped it on the floor. "All right. Call them."

He flicked on the comms unit. "I don't know their channel, but if I fly close enough, I expect they'll hail me."

Stars, she hoped he wasn't tricking her. She tossed the strange bit of jewelry she'd taken from the Zandian onto the control panel. "That's for you."

"I'll take the ring, too." His teasing drawl was gone, replaced by a note of sharpness. In fact, he seemed far less drunk than he had when they left Aurelia.

She pinched her lips together. If he was, in fact, bringing her to the Zandian pod, she'd have no need for the expensive crystal. Surely, they would take care of her. If he wasn't, that meant he probably had a plan to overpower her, anyway, and could take the treasure himself. Wouldn't it be better to hand it over and established a little good will? He had enabled her escape, after all.

She unscrewed the ring from her thumb and dropped it on the control panel, too.

Both treasures immediately disappeared into his pocket.

An image flickered on the comms screen, and she nearly wept with relief. Zandians. Three of them, dressed as royal guards, broad-chested and proud, gazed out at them. "Identify yourself immediately," one of them barked.

Her prisoner fiddled with the comms unit, adjusting the color of the picture before them, bringing the flickering image into focus. "They can't see you. My lens is broken. Identify yourself."

Her throat went dry. She opened her mouth, but no words came out.

"I repeat, identify yourself immediately."

She answered in Zandian. "My name is Taramina. Daughter of Seke, who was Master of Arms to King Zander."

The guards looked at each other. The one who had spoken gave a low order to another, who disappeared. "Hold your position," he said curtly in Ocretion. "Do not fly any closer without authorization."

"Understood," her prisoner muttered.

Damn. What did it mean? Did they not believe her? Perhaps they were finding someone to verify if Seke was a made-up name.

She waited without breathing for what felt like forever. Then the missing guard reappeared with—oh stars—could it be?

"Papa?" Her voice choked with tears, eyes filled.

"Tara?" he peered at her, unseeing. "Get the picture up," he barked at the guards. Yes, definitely her father. She'd remember that calm authority anywhere.

She laughed, moisture spilling down her cheeks. "Papa, it's me. I didn't know you'd survived. I just got free, and we need to dock."

The head guard reached for a control on his panel, but her father held a finger up.

"Your mother's name?"

Emotion bombed her chest, the past colliding with the present in an explosion. "Becka," she whispered. "Is she—"

He gave a short shake of his head, and her hopes were dashed. "No. I'm sorry. I just had to be sure." He nodded at the guard, who hit a button, and the gates to the dock opened like wings.

"Your ship is cleared for docking," the guard clipped.

Her pulse raced as their ship landed on the dock. She tugged the Stornigian's tunic down, wishing it covered more.

"There are pants in the closet in the bunk room," he said.

She narrowed her eyes, trying to decide if he planned any tricks. But he wouldn't have brought her all the way here if he wanted to ambush her now. "Thank you."

She darted into the room he'd pointed to and threw open a cupboard. As he'd promised, she found a pair of pants, and she tugged them on. They were too short and fit her like a pair of tight stockings, but it was better than going out half-naked.

Someone pounded on the ship's door.

"You'd better get it," the Stornigian said drily.

She managed a wan smile and handed him his gun. "Thank you for bringing me here."

He shrugged. "It's not every planet rotation I get taken hostage by a naked Zandian princess."

A smile tugged her lips. "I'm not a princess."

The pounding on the door grew louder. He lifted his chin. "Open it."

She drew a long breath to steady her nerves and hit the button to operate the hatch. Zandian warriors parted and swarmed forward, surrounding her, propelling her straight toward the male waiting on the other side.

Her father.

At first, she could scarcely move, scarcely speak, but then he opened his arms and she was eight solar cycles again, running into her father's arms. He engulfed her in an enormous hug, and she wept against his tunic.

She'd done it. Had escaped slavery and found her way home.

~.~

Erick docked his ship on the Zandian palatial pod and disembarked. He'd delayed his return home an entire planet rotation, not because he had anything to do, more because he didn't want to face Zander and Seke.

But the time had come. Shame nipped at his heels, swirled through him like a fog addling his brain. It paralyzed his mind, kept him from finding any solutions to his problems.

If only he'd acted with more honor when he saw Seke's daughter. Or required more of a guarantee from Behn. But he hadn't done either of those things, and now he had to face the beings who cared.

He headed into the pod without seeing anyone of importance. Good. He needed a chance to use the washtube and get his head on straight. He avoided passing the Great Hall on the way to his chamber. Prince Zander would be in there, sitting on his throne, hearing from members of their species. It was the one planet rotation per week when he opened the pod to any Zandian to use the crystal baths, speak with him, and dine with them.

That was one of the reasons Erick had chosen this planet rotation to return home. Zander and Seke wouldn't have time to question him.

He stepped into his room, but it didn't afford the sense of comfort he usually derived from returning. It seemed empty, as if something was missing. But when he tried to identify what, all he came up with was the beautiful female he'd lost on Aurelia.

And he was losing his *vecking* mind.

He stripped and stepped into the automatic spray of water, closing his eyes and letting it rinse him clean. Wishing it would cleanse his guilt and shame.

The automatic dryer came on, blowing hot air across his skin. He squeezed his eyes closed at the sensation. For some idiotic reason it reminded him of having his cock in Mina's hot mouth, the way she'd swallowed him down, watching him like an obedient slave.

But she hadn't been an obedient slave, had she? She'd stolen the crystal ring and Venusian talisman from his pocket and used them to escape. Which made her fifty times more enticing. The beauty was as smart and capable as she was skilled and seductive.

Even if the galaxy had a million other Zandian females, he doubted he'd ever find one more captivating than Mina.

Ignoring his cock, which now ached thanks to his thoughts of Mina, he stepped out of the washtube and dressed in clean white palace finery. He couldn't avoid seeing Zander and Seke forever.

With any luck, the weekly meal would be about to start, and there wouldn't be time to report. He walked into the great room, only to find the chatter louder than usual. Beings stood, making the transition between Zander holding court and gathering at the enormously long dining table, set with the weekly feast their chef, Barr, prepared.

So bent on preparing himself for what to say to Zander, Erick didn't realize the cause of so much animated conversation until Tomis stepped to the side, revealing...

No. It couldn't be. Had Talia bleached her hair?

But Talia stood next to Tomis, which meant...

As if she felt his stare, Mina lifted her beautiful eyes at the same moment he went stock still, arrested in the entryway to the Great Room.

"Erick," Seke said, observing the direction of her gaze. His barrel chest appeared wider than ever. "Come and meet my firstborn, Tara. She found her way here yesterday, all on her own. Both daughters returned in the same week, can you believe it?" The baffled wonder in the scarred warrior's face made Erick's chest tighten.

Keep walking, idiot. Or at least say something.

But he literally couldn't make his body move or his tongue speak.

Seke, normally as sharp and attentive as they come, didn't seem to notice. Or maybe he just thought Erick was ogling. "Tara, this is Master Erick, Prince Zander's business and trade advisor."

Mina lowered her blue-violet eyes—so much like her father's—and dropped into a demure curtsy. "Pleased to meet you, Master Erick."

Veck, he loved hearing his name on her tongue. He'd been sorry he hadn't given it to her before. *But what is her game?*

His breath scraped into his chest. He stepped forward on wooden legs and bent his arm at a ninety degree angle in the traditional Zandian greeting. "The pleasure is mine, Lady Tara."

"Tara escaped from Aurelia where she was a house-slave."

A *house*-slave. Not a sex slave, or sex pet. Pain lanced his chest. Not for himself, but for Mina—or Tara—whatever she preferred to be called here. She didn't want others knowing how degraded she'd been, so she'd lied. He couldn't blame her. How would a young female tell her father she'd been defiled in every way imaginable? It would destroy a male like Seke, who would want to find every male who'd touched her and make him pay with his life.

Hell, it made him want to do the same. At the very least, he should go back to Prium's and bash the pimp's pearly white teeth in. He should have done it when he was there.

"It's illegal to keep Zandians as slaves. Aurelians should know that." Somehow, he provided the smooth, educated commentary expected of him with Mina just a few steps away. Her intoxicating scent drifted to where he stood, reminding him of how it felt to bury his nose in her hair. To speak with his lips right up to her ear. Which made him recall all the dirty things he'd done to her. All the things he still wanted to do.

All the things her father would kill him for doing.

"Yes and I'd ask you to file an intergalactic complaint but her sole owner died a few lunar cycles ago, which is how she got away."

Don't look at her. *Don't.*

He couldn't because, if he did, he might show every thought splattering his brain. "I will still file it. It's important we put the Aurelians on notice that Prince Zander will take every action for any abuse of his species."

Stars, what a *vecking* hypocrite. What action had he taken on behalf of his species? The *veck her hard over a bench* one? Or the *use her mouth as a veck-hole?*

Prince Zander waved a hand to invite the milling group to sit at the banquet table.

His instinct told him to place himself as far away from Mina as he could. But when a swarm of males crowded in, every eye bright and eager to catch hers, he changed his mind. He'd be damned if he'd let any of them move in on his female.

Fortunately, his status as trusted advisor allowed him to sit near Master Seke and, therefore, his delectable daughter. He took a seat across from her. Next to her would be too close. He wouldn't be able to trust himself if her scent was up in his nostrils, her soft body within grabbing distance.

Thankfully, Seke took the seat next to her, and her sister, Talia, took the one on her other side.

~.~

Erick.

That was her Zandian's name. *Master* Erick. The prince held him in esteem. That knowledge shouldn't send little wings of excitement flapping in her chest, but it did. She'd known he was a worthy male, even though he'd turned part beast in the cell with her.

She'd never dreamed he'd be here, but then, she hadn't realized almost every Zandian still alive either lived on Prince Zander's pod or visited it weekly for the crystal baths. She'd been treated to one when she'd arrived the previous planet rotation, and now felt like a completely different being.

But she felt like a different being in many ways. Like a being she didn't even recognize.

Her sister, Talia, reached under the table and gripped her hand. "It's hard to re-integrate, I know," she murmured.

Relief poured through her as she squeezed her sister's hand gratefully. It was almost easier that Talia hardly remembered her. Her younger sister had either lost her memory when their ship crashed during their escape, or had blocked out her past as a protective mechanism. Either way, she had only rediscovered their father and fellow Zandians three planet rotations ago. Even speaking Zandian sometimes challenged her.

Talia was right. After planning her escape for fifteen years, Mina found her new freedom almost more difficult than slavery. She didn't know how to be a presentable member of Zandian society. She acted a part without a script. The only being who knew what she'd been before her arrival was Erick.

And, for some reason, that bonded her to him even more.

She hadn't told her father she'd been used as a sex pet—it would've killed him. Instead, she'd made up the story about being a house-slave to Durhock.

She'd been afraid Erick would out her, but he hadn't. Of course, he probably wasn't in a hurry to tell her father what he'd done with her at Prium's. He'd followed her lead, and pretended they hadn't met, after a quick recovery from his obvious initial shock of seeing her. His gape had gone unnoticed, since nearly everyone on the pod had reacted the same way. It turned out, there were only three Zandian females alive. At least females of mating age. Her sister, Talia, who already had a mate, and Eslyn, a quasi-prisoner who was being punished by Prince Zander for helping to kidnap Talia.

Her punishment had just been announced by Zander before dinner. He'd assigned her to be reconditioned into Zandian society by three of his warriors. They'd escorted her out, the dark promise of punishment burning in their expressions.

Mina had found the idea of the conditioning arousing—especially considering it would come from not one male, but three—but hadn't been able to imagine any male touching her except Erick.

She'd wondered—had it just been because he was Zandian that he'd aroused such a passion in her? But despite the constant deluge of eager attention she'd received from nearly every male in the palatial pod since her arrival, she'd only been able to think of him.

And now, here he was, sitting across from her, radiating tension and hunger and something else. Anger?

While one part of her brain reasoned he had no cause to be angry with her, the other sped off imagining how he might *condition* her. Would he shove her to her knees and feed her his cock again? Or bend her over and whip her ass before fucking it roughly?

She squeezed her thighs together, arousal building in her core. It was wrong to think of being used that way. She wasn't a pet anymore.

She stole a glance at Erick.

He paused, mid-bite, his eyes locking onto hers. A frown marred his features, but there was no mistaking the tilt of his horns in her direction. Whatever was running through his mind, he wanted her.

He and most of the males in the room. Which was nothing new for her. The new was being in a position to accept or refuse their advances. Hell, she was in the position to look around the palatial pod and choose for herself. Pluck out a partner for pleasure, if she desired.

And, strangely, she did desire. Erick had awoken a side of herself she hadn't known existed. Maybe it was breeding season, maybe the crystal bath she'd had, but her body thrummed with an overwhelming need, an ache only one male could slake.

Kicking off her shoe, she sought his leg with her bare toes. She knew she'd found the right limb by the way his hand jerked at his food and his brows lowered. She inched her foot higher, following the inside of his calf to his thigh.

"I have a question," Talia piped up beside her, directing her attention to their father. "Why does everyone still refer to Prince Zander as *prince*, when his father is dead?"

"I will claim the title when I reclaim our planet," Zander answered from the head of the table, making Talia blush.

So he hoped to retake Zandia. *Interesting.*

"Although I suppose it is confusing now that we have a new prince in the palace." He turned a loving gaze on the bundle in his human mate's arms.

Lamira shifted their tiny half-breed, and a dozen servants surged forward, offering to hold the tiny new prince. From what Mina had seen, that infant would never pass a single moment out of some being's arms. The entire pod lived and breathed for their newest royal.

Even Eslyn's children seemed highly revered, despite the fact that their fathers were in the dungeons below. In addition to the three warriors who took charge of Eslyn, the young had dozens of other Zandian adults eager to step in as guardians and teachers.

Mina's foot arrived at the apex of Erick's thighs, and her toes wiggled along his hard length, trapped against one thigh.

His horns thickened, and he swallowed convulsively.

Beside her, Tomis stroked Talia's thigh, his fingers traveling higher and higher, his horns as thick and hard as Erick's.

What would her sister think of her past as a sex slave? She wanted to tell her but couldn't risk their father finding out.

What did Erick think of her now? She got the sense he was ashamed of his behavior at Prium's. Hell, he'd even apologized to her at the time. Maybe his lust had taken him by surprise, too. If there were no other Zandian females around, his reaction to her might have been as surprising as her reaction to him.

She found the head of his cock and squeezed it with her toes.

~.~

What was Mina's game?

If she didn't stop stroking his cock with her little foot, he'd never be able to leave the table because his malehood was at a full salute.

"So, Tara," —he cleared his throat— "how did you find our pod?"

The conversation didn't stop her toes, although he swore he saw reproof at his question.

"I heard of it a few lunar cycles ago and made it my intention to get myself here. I'd hoped I'd be able to beg for assistance from the prince, but I had no idea my father had survived the invasion."

She looked over at her father's scarred face. He had one hand buried in his human mate's hair, but he froze when she looked at him, an apology in his expression.

Now her little toes stopped, and she dropped her foot to the floor, which shouldn't have come as such a disappointment.

"I don't mind about your new mate," Mina said softly, and the table went quiet around her. She flushed as if she hated the attention.

This was the same female who'd goaded it back at Prium's. He *vecking hated* seeing her out of her element. Wanted to do everything in his power to make her comfortable, although he couldn't, for the life of him, think of what that might be. He offered Mina what he hoped was an encouraging smile.

Seke's mate, Leora, lifted her green eyes.

"I'm happy you found a new mate, Father. It's strange for me to see you with her, but I don't mind."

Talia nodded beside her. "Me neither." She shrugged. "Of course, my memories are incomplete anyway."

Leora inclined her head with regal grace. It was easy to forget she was human and had also recently been a slave. "I'm grateful for your acceptance."

Everyone seemed relieved when Zander stood, indicating the dinner was over. Mina jumped to her feet, although she couldn't go anywhere because she was immediately boxed in by a half-dozen interested males.

Separated from her by the table, there was nothing he could do to aid her. If she even wanted that.

What did she want from him? Had she just been torturing him because she knew he couldn't do anything at the dinner table? Was this her form of sexual payback for what he'd done with her?

"Excuse me, I'm very tired. It's been a long few planet rotations." She elbowed her way through the crowd.

He slipped out of the Great Hall ahead of her, taking the corridor toward the sleeping chambers and waiting around the first corner. The moment she rounded it, he stepped into her path.

"Erick." She stopped with an audible inhale, her pale hair falling forward into her face.

He advanced. One step then another.

She retreated. Not out into the corridor to the Great Hall, but backing up to the wall.

In a second, he was upon her, pressing her small, lithe body up against the smooth pastel plaster, dragging his open mouth down the column of her neck.

He hadn't meant to pounce, hadn't even known he'd intended to, but the moment he had her caged, his senses exploded with everything Mina. When she lifted one leg to wrap around his waist, his last thin thread of control snapped. He palmed her ass cheeks and ground his heavy erection against her core.

"Were you punishing me, beautiful pet?" He thrust his clothed cock into the notch between her legs, registering the dampness coming through her fine white leggings. "Did you want to make me sweat in front of your father? You know he'd *vecking* kill me if he found out what I did to you, don't you? One word from you and my life would be over."

It thrilled him to know she held the balance of his life in her hand, as much as it seemed to thrill her to be handled roughly by him. He thrust again, hammering her ass against the wall. "You're going to let me do it again, though, aren't you?"

It was unbelievably bold, but he'd made Zander's fortune with his skill at reading beings. He knew when he was going to get his way. *How* he'd won this victory, he had no idea, but he'd won it.

Her lids drooped, full lips parted as her head lolled against the wall.

"I'll take your pretty pussy this time, beautiful. It's what I should've done in the first place, not that I ever meant to claim you at all. I swear on the one true Zandian star, my only goal was to get you out of there."

She wrapped her fists around his horns, sending a jolt straight to his cock. "I believe you." Her husky tone made him even wilder.

He thrust against her alluring heat again. "You didn't wait to be rescued, though, did you, sweet female?" He nipped her neck. "You saved yourself. But you stole from me, naughty pet."

She used his horns to bring his mouth down to hers. "You'll have to punish me."

Holy star of Zandia.

He picked her up, and she wrapped her other leg around his waist as he carried her to his chamber, where he slapped his palm against the scanner to open the door. Mouth locked onto hers, he saw nothing on the way to the sleepdisk. His fingers roughly squeezed her ass as he stumbled forward and launched them both horizontal.

He tore her leggings off and attached his mouth to her core, taking his first pull of what he'd been missing every minute since they'd parted the previous planet rotation. "*Veck,* yes, Mina. You taste so good."

Her answering cry matched his urgency. She rubbed his horns, yanking his head tighter to her hot pussy. He suctioned his lips over her clit and sucked while she thrashed beneath him.

He broke his kiss. "You're so wet for me."

"Yes...*yes,*" she moaned.

"Too bad I can't let you come."

"Wh-what?" She leaned up on her elbows, her beautiful lavender skin flushed a shade of reddish purple, eyes glassy.

"This is punishment, remember?"

Her slow drink of breath went straight to his cock. Hell, the idea of punishing her went straight to his cock because, this time, he had her permission.

She wants this.

Nothing made him harder than the idea of Mina willingly placing herself in his hands. Offering that sweet ass up for the lick of his belt.

He yanked off his tunic and undershirt and threw them over his shoulder. Her clothing went next. He backed off the sleepdisk and grasped under her knees to yank her core to the edge of the bed. Right where he wanted it—no, *needed* it—when he finished punishing her.

He took his time unstrapping his sword belt, measuring the flicker of excitement in her eyes against the flinch of fear. Stars, if he saw any sign that his words or actions were too much, or that they threw her into distasteful memories, he would drive his dagger through his own hand. But she showed only interest, even encouragement.

He wrapped the belt around one hand and picked up her ankles with the other, holding them high. "What happened to the ring you stole, Mina?" He snapped the animal hide across her buttocks. He was relieved her skin showed no marks from the whipping he'd given her the previous planet rotation.

She jerked at the impact. "I traded it to a pilot to get here."

He nodded. "That was a good use for it. But if you'd waited for me, I would've flown you." He spanked her with the belt again.

She tightened her buttocks against the punishment. "I know," she panted.

He stopped and raised an eyebrow. "You know? You *knew?* Why didn't you wait, then?" He whipped her again. She jerked, her knees bending and making her bottom bob. He loved this position because he could make eye contact during her punishment.

"I don't know," she gasped, turning her head away, as if to avoid his gaze.

"Look at me." He slapped the belt.

"Too much," she gasped.

He stopped the belt mid-swing, jerking it back. "Too much, beautiful?"

She closed her eyes.

"Look at me."

Her lashes flew open, but she didn't meet his gaze, instead rolling her head from side to side, as if in pain.

Veck. Had he hurt her? He hadn't meant to use much force behind the strokes.

"It was too intense—what you drew from me," she blurted. "I'd never responded that way with a male before."

Triumph galloped through his chest, but he hid it, not wanting to break out of the role of master she'd let him seize. He whipped her three times in quick succession.

"It was easier to run."

Her courage kicked him in the gut. The sheer vulnerability it took to reveal herself to him stripped away his defenses, too. He dropped the belt. Not bothering to take off his pants or boots, he pulled out his cock and lined up at her entrance.

"No running this time. But I need to hear you say you want this, Mina. I don't want to hate myself for forcing you a second time."

"I want it. Give it to me, Master."

Oh stars. Lust rocketed through him, tightening his balls. He was going to come the moment he entered her.

He grasped her ankles and spread her legs straight out to the side. "You keep these legs wide, knees locked, pet, understand?"

If he'd had any doubt about whether she enjoyed his domination, he saw it in the squeeze of her pussy and anus, the shudder of bliss that ran through her body. She nodded. "Yes, Master."

He channeled all the pleasure of hearing her call him *master* into his first thrust, growling as he pinned her wrists above her head and buried himself deep into her sopping channel. "Oh *veck*, pet. So good. I don't know how I survived my whole life without access to this sweet *vecking* pussy."

She rocked her pelvis up to meet his thrusts, rubbing her clit along his shaft as he entered. He pistoned in and out of her, driving deeper and deeper until her eyes widened, riveted on his face. "Please, *please*," she whimpered, still holding her legs straddled wide and straight.

"Do you need to come, beautiful?"

"Yes... *yes*."

"So do I." He slammed harder and harder into her as his balls tightened. "Hold your breath, pet."

Confusion flitted over her face. He adjusted one hand to cover her mouth, leaving her nostrils open so she could choose herself if she wanted to obey.

She did. Her ribs stiffened as she locked down her breath.

He *vecked* her hard, plowing with enough force to shake the sleepdisk. His orgasm ignited, exploding through him in a rush of heat and glorious release. He thrust in to the hilt and stayed deep. "Come, Mina," he managed to gasp around the roar erupting from his throat.

Her body convulsed, jerking beneath him. He pulled his hand away from her mouth, and she drew a huge, ragged breath, pussy squeezing and releasing his cock like a tight fist. Shock, fear, pain, ecstasy all danced over her face as she came and came.

When her muscles stopped squeezing, her body went slack, knees bending, head lolling to the side. Tears leaked from the corners of her eyes.

Oh stars.

~.~

Her body had exploded into a million pieces—in the best possible way. Like some mad spiritual awakening, their sex had shown her the universe from a larger perspective. Pleasure pulsed through every cell, and yet she'd flown out-of-body at the same time.

The orgasm left her blown open, naked. Not in the no-clothing sense, but stripped of every barrier, of every defense. Even of what she'd held closely as her definition of self.

Erick eased out and grabbed the corner of his coverlet, yanking the beautiful spidersilk across her naked body.

She rolled to her side, dazed by the intensity of her experience.

"I'm sorry, Mina. Did I hurt you? Are you all right?" He fitted his body around the back of hers, wrapping an arm around her waist.

"I'm not hurt." Her voice sounded far away.

"I'm so sorry, sweet female. I've done it again, treated you like—"

"It was wonderful."

He went still behind her. "You're not upset?"

"No, just… stunned. Overwhelmed. How did you know what would happen when I held my breath?"

He leaned up on one elbow, stroking back the strands of hair that fell over her face. "I'm a depraved male. I've spent far too much time in galactic brothels, seeking something I never found. Until you."

His words warmed her chest. The previous planet rotation he'd shown her fierce domination and rough sex. It had driven her wild, and she'd wanted more, but she hadn't known the male behind the hard muscle and expensive clothing. They'd had no pillow talk. Now, his charm made him even more irresistible. Which scared the life out of her. She'd left her days as a sex pet behind. She didn't know who she was now, but it wasn't Mina. The reversion to her childhood name was symbolic of a bigger change. And if she let herself fall for this devastating male, she'd be consumed by him. She'd never figure out who she was.

"Well, I'm grateful for your habit, since it enabled me to get free." She kept her tone light, didn't acknowledge the claim he appeared to be making on her.

"With great damage to my male pride, I must say. I'd imagined myself the hero, bringing you back safely and receiving your father's commendation, perhaps even his blessing to mate you. Instead, I'm sneaking around corridors to catch you up and carry you back to my chamber like a thief. Like the sex fiend I've always been."

She sat up, smiling at his rueful tone. "Poor thing." She crawled off the sleepdisk. She needed to get out of his room, away from his addictive presence.

He stood as well, but he walked around the sleepdisk and put his hands on her waist. "Where are you going?"

She flattened her palm on his muscled chest. "You can't keep me prisoner, warrior. Remember what you said? One word from me, and my father will have your head."

He drew back as if she'd slapped him, dropping his hands to his sides. "I would never force you, Mina." His jaw flexed. "Will you not forgive me for what I took at Prium's?"

She swallowed against a tightness forming in her throat. "I *liked* it, Erick." She hid her face from him as she pulled on her clothing.

"So, what is this? You're going to hold it over my head…forever?"

She tugged the fitted dress down over her leggings. "No." She walked to the door and pushed the button to open it. "We're not doing this again. Mina no longer exists."

She held her head high and somehow managed not to look back as she strode out of his room. A sense of wrongness niggled in the back of her mind, like she'd just made a huge mistake, but she ignored it.

This couldn't go on. Not if she wanted to be free of her past.

CHAPTER FOUR

"A name, Behn." Erick placed his laser gun on the desk between them in a not-so-subtle hint. He'd told Behn he'd return in three planet rotations for his carriers, but he wasn't surprised to find they hadn't magically appeared.

The broker blinked his eyes rapidly, chin trembling. "I-I don't know. The manufacturer said they were stolen, but he's making you new ones. They'll be ready in five moon cycles."

Erick gave a short shake of his head. "I need them now. Who stole them?"

Behn mopped his brow with a square of spider silk. "I have no—"

He lunged across the table, pressing the butt of the laser gun against Behn's forehead. "Give me. The name."

"I-I heard it was Neo Lin, the collector. But I cannot verify such information."

Erick pulled the gun away from Behn's head. If he'd suspected Behn of stealing the money or the carriers himself, Erick would've killed him, but the male was too soft for that kind of treachery. He'd been caught in the middle of a bad situation, same as Erick.

"Who have you told about our arrangement?" He'd been firm from the beginning that no one could know the Zandians were buying the galactacarriers. Not that the Finn weren't already on notice.

"No one. I swear."

"Good."

"I beg you not to say I sent you," Behn called after him as he left his elegant office.

Erick didn't dignify it with a response. He returned to his ship and set the course back to the pod.

Then he allowed himself to check the security feed on the pod for Mina's location.

There. He found her in the Great Room, with the other females in the pod, playing games with the three young Tomis had brought from Zandia.

These holograms were the extent of his interaction with Mina since she'd walked out of his room four nights ago. Erick's chances of ever getting Mina—or Tara, as she went by at the pod—alone again seemed to drop each planet rotation. She'd been avoiding him at every turn.

The better part of him wanted to respect her wishes. He understood—she wanted to bury her past as a sex slave. But *veck* if he would let her bury *him* with it. Or rather, he'd accept her burying his shameful part, if only she'd consent to letting him into her new life. He wanted to know Tara as thoroughly and intimately as he'd known Mina.

And it wasn't just about sex. Their chemistry was incredible, that was true. Not a nanosecond had passed since he'd claimed her that he didn't long to have her smooth skin under his palms again, coax those sexy moans from her lips, or make her cry out in pleasure as he sank into her wet heat.

But his attraction to Mina went far beyond her glorious, nimble body. He admired her courage, her strength. Tara was every bit the warrior her father was. And when they'd been together in his chamber, he'd been electrified by her presence. It was as if the piece missing from his life all this time had fallen into place. He used to think he ached for Zandia. Or his parents. But the hollowness in his core filled just being near her. It was as if his purpose crystallized—and it was to be worthy of Mina. To protect and provide for her. To be her mate.

Unfortunately, she didn't feel the same way.

For four planet rotations, he'd stalked her about the pod, attempting to lure her into conversation or gain even a moment of her attention, but she always dodged him. His only dim satisfaction lay in the fact she hadn't engaged with any other males, either.

Thank *veck*. As it was, he wanted to throat punch every male who looked at her. Her father excepted, of course.

But her apparent dissatisfaction with her new life bothered him even more. His female observed the workings of the pod without engaging. She stared out windows more often than spoke. Even now, she smiled and engaged the children far less than the other females.

Something was wrong.

Mina had wilted in her new environment and his need to fix anything and everything bothering her eclipsed all else. Even his problem with the missing galactacarriers.

. . .

"If you weren't Master Seke's daughter, I think you already would have been carried off over one of their shoulders," Bayla, the pregnant human mate of the pod's doctor remarked, lifting her chin toward the three guards crowding the doorway to the Great Room.

Mina had joined the other females of the pod—Bayla, her sister, Lamira, and Leora to mind the three young from Zandia while their mother was undergoing her "reconditioning."

Mina forced out a laugh. The male attention didn't bother her—she'd been a sex slave for the past five solar cycles, after all—but she had no interest in any of the warriors, no matter how big and strong and masculine they may appear.

She wanted Erick. She'd seen him in action during her escape—he was as much a warrior as any of these males. And so much more. Intelligent. Refined. With a little prompting, she'd learned from her father that Erick had generated millions of steins for Prince Zander through investments and trade. In fact, his business prowess was the sole reason the Zandians were now positioned to take back their planet.

Unlike her former master, Dorhock, who considered himself something of an investor, Erick didn't exhibit the healthy ego she might expect from a being so potent.

"Don't look now," Talia murmured. "But one of them is coming over."

She stifled a sigh.

The guard cleared his throat when none of them looked at him. "Do you females need anything?"

"No, thank you, Derk," Lamira answered, beaming a smile up at him. "But we'll let you know if we do."

Mina had never seen a human female in a position of power before. Granted, Lamira didn't lord over any Zandian. Instead, she presented a friendly, we're-all-the-same-status attitude, which seemed to make her popular with servants and warriors alike. Her status might be the same, for all Mina knew. The human still wore a slave's collar, although it was bedecked with hundreds of Zandian crystals and was probably worth a fortune.

Derk adjusted his sword belt. "Right. Very well." He stood a moment longer before he swaggered back to his post.

"I feel like a collector's prize," she muttered. She adopted an auctioneer's tone, "Step right this way for a glimpse of the one and only single Zandian female alive!"

Talia snickered. Leora sent her a sympathetic look. "Breeding season makes it even more difficult for the males here. You have to remember, they've been without females on this pod for fifteen solar cycles."

"How long have you all been here, then?"

"I've been here one solar cycle. I was the first slave they brought in for breeding," Lamira said. "Your mate's idea." She winked at Bayla. "Then Zander bought my mother as a gift to me, and assigned your father as her master. It didn't take them long to mate. Zander found my sister, Lily, next. You haven't met her yet—she's mated to Rok, the pilot training Zander's human army. Next came Bayla, also brought on for breeding."

"Actually Master Daneth hoped to implant me with a Zandian egg, but the experiment didn't take." Bayla patted her belly.

Mina liked the human, who seemed more similar to her than her own sister. Probably because she carried the air of open sexuality trained into sex slaves. "So, he had to use the old-fashioned method?"

"Yes. He didn't mean to, because he thinks his genes are too old, but it happened, anyway."

"There's also Cambry, a human warrior, mated to a Zandian," Lamira said.

Mina sat up straighter. "A female?"

"Yes. She's part of the human army. Her mate, Lundric, killed another human defending her. Woe to any male on the training pod who even thinks of harming her—not that she can't defend herself." Lamira grinned.

"So your sister and Cambry are on the training pod? Is Lily a warrior, too?"

"Yes."

"I want to go there." She hadn't meant to say it out loud. The words had almost ejected themselves from her mouth. But they were true. The palatial pod held nothing for her. She wanted to crawl out of her skin most of the time, not knowing what to do with herself, who to be. Hating the secret she carried of who she used to be. Hating how out of place she felt.

Hearing they allowed females to train as warriors thrilled her. This was what she'd been born for. It made sense—she was the daughter of a warrior. And she wanted to be of use to Prince Zander, to aid her father. He was over on the training pod now. She wanted to go there to be with him.

"Good luck with that." Talia's tone was dry.

"What do you mean?"

"I mean there's one thing more important to the Zandians than taking back their planet, and that's ensuring the species won't go extinct."

Her brow furrowed. "So what are you saying?"

"The chances of Zander or Father letting you into any dangerous situation are nil. You and Eslyn and I are the only—"

"I'm not capable of breeding," Mina interrupted. "I've been hormonally modified to not conceive. For another two solar cycles, at least." She'd refused to let Master Daneth examine her when she arrived, or they would have known. "Maybe I should make that information more public—it might cut down on my admirers."

The females gaped at her, and she realized what she'd revealed. Only sex slaves were given hormonal implants to prevent pregnancy. Other slaves' owners expected breeding, even encouraged it to multiply their holdings.

"I'm sure Daneth can reverse it, if you want," Bayla offered.

"No. I want to train with the warriors, not stay around here and make babies. No offense," she added, realizing how insulting she must sound. "It's just... I've spent the last ten years caged. I want *out*. I never expected to trade one cage for another."

"I'll take you to the training pod." Erick's deep masculine voice boomed from the arched entryway, sending tiny shockwaves through her entire body. She would know the sound anywhere. It created a riot of emotion in her. Thrills, mostly, followed by dismay. She couldn't let this male take her anywhere. She'd ended things with him several nights ago.

Which didn't mean she hadn't thought about him nearly every moment of every planet rotation since.

Erick entered the room but hung back, giving her actual space, even though he'd just invaded her psychic space in every possible way. Leave it to him to offer the one thing she couldn't refuse.

Of course, any other warrior would take her. Or would they? Perhaps not, if Prince Zander forbade it. But Erick was an esteemed master here. He came and went as he pleased. In fact, the guards who'd been gathered at the door had dispersed, as if his mere presence sent them packing. Or maybe he'd actually ordered them away. She wouldn't put it past him.

Talia and the humans looked between the two of them with interest. Because she wanted to minimize their opportunity for observation, she surged to her feet and met Erick where he stood.

"When?"

He inclined his head in a show of deference. The chivalrous male who turned to beast in the bedroom. *No, don't think about him in bed.* Do *not* remember the way he looks with his shirt off. Or the rough command of his touch.

As if he knew her thoughts, one corner of his lips kicked up, his brown eyes deepening to purple. "Anytime. Now, if you like."

"Yes. All right. I'll just grab my things." She hated how breathless she sounded. It certainly wasn't because she was excited about being alone with Erick. Definitely not.

He didn't step aside, forcing her to crowd against his large frame to get through the arched doorway. Her tummy and arm grazed against his hard muscle, sending skitters of heat racing along her skin. She pushed past, not daring to look up into his face for fear she'd stop and drag his lips down to hers.

This was a bad idea. Still, it was better than sitting around entertaining someone else's young all day. She jogged to her chamber and packed the few items of clothing the pod servants had provided her. She, Talia, and Bayla had put in an order for new clothing, but it hadn't arrived yet.

When she exited her chamber, she found Erick waiting outside, leaning against the wall with a casual grace.

"Ready?" He took her bag from her, even though it wasn't heavy.

"Yes." She fell into step beside him, stealing a sidelong glance at his handsome face. Why had she decided she couldn't be with him? It seemed silly now that he was here again by her side and she could breathe again.

"What's the purpose of the trip?"

They fell out of stride when her step faltered. "Does it matter?" she asked tightly.

He held up his palms. "*Veck* no. I'm just glad to have a chance to, ah, be of service."

"You mean to get me alone."

He grinned widely. "That, too."

"I already told you—"

"Yes, I heard you. I won't force it."

Too bad. She rather enjoyed the way he forced things. And though it was wrong and backward to think it, her life had been cleaner when she had very few choices.

"That doesn't mean I won't employ every means of persuasion I know."

She stopped walking, putting a stride between them before he caught on and turned.

"All pleasurable, I assure you."

"Erick, this isn't going to work." She shook her head and started to reverse her direction.

He lunged and caught her arm. "Wait." When she looked pointedly at his hand holding her arm, he immediately released her. "What if I promise not to touch you for the entire trip?"

She raised an eyebrow. "Zandian's honor?"

His lips quirked, as if he already knew he'd won. "Zandian's honor." He lifted his fist at a 90 degree angle.

She resumed walking, unsure if her disappointment stemmed from his promise or her own lack of resolve.

~.~

Erick had never been so conflicted about winning a bargain before. Not touching Mina would be torture, but it was one he deserved. His behavior with her had been reprehensible from the beginning.

This would be a good chance to show her they had a connection that went beyond sex. Prove that he could be a mate to *Tara* as well as to *Mina*.

He led her to the dock and onto his ship. It wasn't one of the new battleships Zander had bought for war, but his old travel ship. The same one Master Seke had used when he taught him to fly fifteen solar cycles ago.

He waved her into the co-pilot's seat. "Buckle up, little warrior."

She paused on her way to sit. "Why did you call me that?"

"I saw you escape from Prium's Emporium. It took courage and strategy—*discipline*, your father would say."

"Do you think he'll let me join the army?"

It took all his own discipline not to crush the controls under his palms. Not to shout, *over my dead body*. This was important to Mina. He heard the hesitant way she'd asked it, the lift of hope when he'd called her a warrior.

He opted for a diplomatic reply. "I'm sure he'll appreciate your desire to help."

"That wasn't an answer."

He loved that she was such a straight shooter. She deserved his honesty. "No, it wasn't." He lifted the airship off the dock and eased it out the hatch. "Tara, your father suffered terribly for these past years. He thought his entire family had died on Zandia and blamed himself."

She went still, twisting in her seat to stare at him. "Why?"

"He saved Prince Zander—got him safely off the planet—but I suspect he always wondered if he could've saved you and Talia instead. Or your mother and baby sister. I don't think it was possible, or he would've done it, but that hasn't stopped his anguish."

She swallowed, audibly.

"So I'm just guessing he'd be loath to put you in mortal danger again if he can help it."

She turned away, staring out at the air traffic around them. He maneuvered the ship through the congestion of Ocretian airspace, heading away from the planet, toward free space.

"You're looking for a purpose, aren't you?" Finally reaching space, he set the coordinates and powered the ship into warp speed.

Mina's fingers tightened on the armrests. "Yes," she croaked. "How did you know?"

He shrugged. "You probably dedicated a lot of brain space toward navigating your escape from slavery. Now that you've achieved your goal, I suspect there will be an emptiness until you figure out how to fill it." Mina made a choking sound, and he finally gave in to the temptation of looking at her. *Veck.* She'd pressed a fist to her mouth, as if stuffing a sob back down her throat.

He swiveled his knees toward her and opened his arms. "Come here. I know I promised not to touch you, but—"

She unbuckled her harness and stumbled toward him. He caught her by the waist and pulled her onto his lap, tucking her head under his chin and stroking her silky hair. His heart squeezed for her.

"I'm sure you feel like a stranger in your own life, right now."

"Yes!"

"You'll find your purpose. I know you will. A female as smart and capable as you will surely find a way to help the Zandian cause, if that's what you want to do."

"It is," she sniffed. "I can't stand sitting around the palatial pod doing nothing. It kills me."

"I understand. You don't have to."

She wrapped her arms around his neck. "Thank you."

He closed his eyes and breathed in her scent. His palm coasted up her back, rubbing a slow circle.

Mina shifted her weight, swinging her leg around to straddle him.

He choked on the sudden intake of breath. What in the hell was she doing?

She rocked her pelvis, rolling the heat between her thighs over the bulge of his cock.

He groaned and palmed her ass, yanking her hard against his heavy length. "What are you doing, little female? I promised not to touch you."

"Well, you already broke your promise, didn't you?" Her breathy voice dripped with seduction. Tara had turned back to Mina.

No. He shouldn't impale her with his cock and make her ride him until she screamed. He'd given his word. And he needed to prove to her he could be trusted. And that——

Oh *veck*.

In a single, fluid motion, she pulled her top off and tossed it to the floor, still undulating over his lap.

He squeezed one breast, holding it captive for his mouth. The sound that came from her lips turned him rock hard. He sucked and pulled on her nipple, grazed it with his teeth.

"This isn't what you wanted," he managed to say hoarsely.

He couldn't even hear if she answered. Not when the sight of her semi-clothed body submerged him in the deepest pit of lust. One hand rubbed her ass crack while the other kneaded her breast.

He needed her naked. Now. Mina let him guide her to her feet so he could tear her leggings and panties off, get at that sweet spot between her legs.

In two seconds, he surged up and had her flattened over the dash to the left of the ship's controls, one hand wrapped around her throat, the other cupping her mons, his middle finger working her clit. "*Veck*, Mina. Don't let me do this."

Except he'd already pulled his cock out, already had the head rubbing over her dripping entrance.

She wanted it, too. There was no denying it. Still, if she told him no, he'd find a way to stop himself. Somehow.

"Last chance, beautiful. Say something or I'm taking what I desperately need."

Her only answer was the press of her soft ass back against his loins.

He shoved deep and let out a broken groan. *Veck*, yes.

"This," he rasped. "*This*, Mina. This is what I need to live."

"Stop," she panted.

What? His breath caught under his ribs as his next thrust stuttered to a stop. *Now* she wanted to stop him?

"Stop talking. Start fucking." She used the Ocretion word for *veck*.

Ah, thank the stars. "*Start* fucking?" He slammed home, protecting the front of her hips from bruises with his forearm but still punishing her with each stroke. This female would be the death of him, for certain. He couldn't get enough of Mina, couldn't control himself around her, couldn't imagine one planet rotation without thinking of her incredible presence.

With each thrust, he shoved her up to her toes, plowed deeper. Stars, she felt good. He adjusted the position of his arm around her waist and wiggled his middle finger over her clit.

Instantly, her muscles spasmed around his cock. She threw her head back on a scream as her orgasm gripped her. Her entire body shuddered and jolted with the intensity.

He jerked back and buried himself deeper, deeper until one continuous cry came from her mouth and the spasms ended. He brought his lips to her ear. "That's good, little warrior. I'm glad you took your release early because I'm not nearly done with you."

She fell back against his body, and he lifted her, his cock still embedded in her wet heat.

He dropped back into the pilot's chair. "Now, you're going to dance for me." He gripped her hips and lifted and lowered her ass, sliding her up and down over his throbbing malehood.

"Oh...uh..." Her sex sounds killed him.

He wrapped a hand over her lips and pressed a finger inside, needing to do something with that sexy mouth.

She sucked the digit, still emitting muffled cries around it.

"*Veck*, Mina, *veck*. So good..."

She arched her back, tossed her head, sending her pale reddish-blonde hair spilling down her slender back. "Mmph, mmph, mmph," she crooned.

Unable to pump as hard and deep as he needed, he spun the chair around and launched them to their knees on the floor. She fell forward onto her hands, and he slid out of her.

He slapped the inviting target her ass made. "Are you feeling your *fucking* yet?" He smacked her again.

"Y-yes," she warbled.

"I think I'd better spank this ass before I get back on it."

"Why?" Her husky voice revealed no fear.

He adjusted his position to her side to get a better angle at spanking her. With one arm wrapped around her waist, he held her steady and applied his palm hard and fast.

"Ow! Ooh, ow! Sorry, Master!"

"What are you sorry for, pet?"

"Whatever I did to offend!"

He laughed but didn't stop his steady onslaught. "I don't require a reason to spank you, other than that you have a perfect ass and my palm loves to show its appreciation. If I were to punish you, it would be for shredding all my control every time I see you." He spanked her even harder, slowing his cadence. "But you must like to see me undone, don't you, sweet female? Isn't that why you goad me into it every time?" He caught her on the backs of her thighs, and she yelped. "Isn't it?"

"Yes!" she blurted.

He stopped and rubbed her twitching buttocks. The heady power of sexual domination flowed through him, and with it came a swooping appreciation for the female who'd given her submission. Beautiful, brave female. His.

He wrapped his fist in her hair and pushed her head down until her chest and head hit the floor, ass still high in the air. "You're lucky I don't have any lubricant with me, or I'd fuck your little red ass raw, pet."

She whimpered.

"Give me that pussy."

She spread her knees wider, arched her back like the perfect pet. If he thought too much about it, he might grow enraged by the fact she'd been trained this way by some other male, but all that really mattered was that she surrendered herself—willingly—to him.

He rubbed the head of his cock over her slit, satisfied to find her still dripping for him. Not that he would've had a problem with applying his tongue there for hours if she needed it.

He sank into her sweetness. "Naughty pet, destroying your master with his need for you."

She gave a choked cry as he shoved hard and held her from flying forward by the hair.

"You need me to *veck* you hard, pet? Need my Zandian cock filling you until you can't take any more?"

"*Yes*," she cried.

He let out a string of Zandian curses and beat his cock into her. Stars swam in his vision. His thighs tensed, balls lifted and tightened. He roared, pounding against her ass as his rainbow cum shot into her.

When his vision cleared, and he took in the sight of his little female, collapsed and trembling beneath him, he scrambled off her and scooped her into his arms.

Oh excrement. He'd gone way too far again, hadn't he?

But Mina laid her head on his shoulder and gave a contented hum.

Thank the stars.

He carried her into the tiny washroom and set her on her feet in the old-fashioned manual washtube. He turned on a warm spray of water and shucked his clothes to join her.

His poor female leaned against the wall as if her legs wouldn't hold her. He squirted a handful of cleanser in his palm and rubbed it over her, exploring every curve, every crevice, earning more happy humming from his female.

When he'd thoroughly cleaned her, he turned off the water and wrapped her in a soft towel.

"How do you feel, pet? Are you sore?"

Her pretty lips curved. "Yes."

"Sorry for what you incited?"

"No." She shook her head, and his heart twirled in a triple pirouette.

He stroked her cheek with the backs of his fingers. "Good. That will help assuage my guilt."

"Too bad. I like you guilty." Head held high, smirking, she sashayed past him, leaving him staring after her once again.

CHAPTER FIVE

Mina grew nervous about her father's reaction to her plan as they docked on *Zandian Freedom*, the ugly training pod. "Where did you get this thing?" she asked to distract herself. Industrial and gray, the metal structure was clearly more utilitarian than homey.

"The pod? It was an Ocretion death pod. Lamira's sister, Lily, was sentenced to death on it and her mate, Rok, shot it down to rescue her. Our army in training consists of the slaves and prisoners they found on board." He put an atmospheric helmet on her before pulling one on for himself.

"Hmm. That was handy." Her voice echoed in her ears as it played in their joint comms. "They receive a full pardon only if they swear fealty to the purple king?"

Erick grinned, apparently not offended by her dry assessment. He somehow managed to appear handsome and debonair even with the helmet. She doubted hers had the same effect. "Exactly. The humans weren't really Rok's aim, but Lily insisted on saving all of them." He opened their hatch, and they jumped down to a metal platform.

"I'm looking forward to meeting Lily," she said. "And Cambry."

He gestured toward the door to the pod. "Female warriors like you." His understanding made her heart beat faster. "I'm sure you'll find them charming. You're not prejudiced against humans like many Zandians were to begin with."

She raised a brow. "Were they? Why? Zandians didn't keep slaves."

He stopped outside the door, as if he didn't want to talk about humans once they were inside. "No, but our only interactions with humans, if any, were with slaves, so there was a general consensus they were not worthy of respect. If Daneth hadn't been desperate for Zander to breed before we go into war, we probably never would have introduced humans to our mix.

"Do you like them?"

"Yes. Not much difference, if you ask me. More emotional, and physically weaker, but they seem just as intelligent. They'll contribute to our effort." He hit the button, and the door slid open to reveal a small antechamber. They stepped inside and waited until the door closed before pulling off their helmets and hanging them on the hooks on the wall. "Come on, pet. I'll introduce you around." His fingers brushed her hand, but he balled them and stuck them into his pocket, as if the very presence of her fingers beside his was too tempting.

She wanted to accept his gesture, considering the tenderness he'd shown after their rabid sex, but he was right. She wasn't allowing him to claim her as his mate, especially around her father, so she couldn't allow any public shows of affection.

"Erick, where are my galactacarriers?" A big, burly warrior met them at the door.

She registered a slight hitch in Erick's step right before she fell to a dead stop. Her mouth fell open, heart pounded in her chest. She recognized the male.

His gaze turned soft, almost sympathetic. He bowed. "Lady Tara, I'd heard you were found. You must recognize me. We escaped Zandia together as children. Our ship crashed on Stornig."

"You lived!" She fell on him, tears in her eyes. She hadn't known him before that fateful planet rotation. One of her father's guards had brought her, Talia, and the young male through the underground tunnels to an old outpost where he bundled them into an airship and made it out of Zandian airspace. Unfortunately, they'd been chased by a Finnian ship and shot down. She hadn't seen her sister, the guard, or the young male again until now.

He let her embrace him. "So did you."

"I'm sorry—I never even knew your name."

"Rok. A Stornigian smuggler wanted on three planets." He bowed. "And now a Zandian army commander."

She beamed. "Rok—Lily's mate."

He lifted startled brows. "Do you know Lily?"

"No, but I want to." She peered around him. "Where is she?"

Rok chuckled. "Hard to say. She's always somewhere making herself busy. Come, I'll show you around." To Erick, he said, "Where are my galactacarriers? We need to train the pilots to land and take off from them, not to mention pick six who will actually fly the carriers."

"I know, I'm working on it."

"I thought you said they'd be here last week."

"There's been a snag." Erick's voice tightened. The change was almost imperceptible, but Mina's body had attuned to his and she recognized the same clipped way of speaking he'd used with Prium. "I'll update you when I have more information."

They rounded the corner and met two human females. One had coppery hair and green eyes, almost identical to Lamira's. The other had a wild mane of wavy red hair, the front pulled back in small braids.

"Ah, here they are. Lily and Cambry, meet Tara, Master Seke's daughter."

Lily stuck her hand out in the human form of greeting then quickly withdrew it, probably realizing her mistake. "A pleasure to meet you," she said.

"Tara was interested in meeting you both," Rok prompted.

She drew herself up. "Yes, I'd like to join the army. To train with you for battle."

Cambry nodded. Rok didn't blink an eye, either. "Are you interested in flying one of the battleships?" he asked.

For some idiotic reason, she glanced at Erick, as if needing his opinion. But he wasn't her mate—his feedback had no bearing on her future. Even so, she appreciated his nod of encouragement. "Yes, I'd love to learn to fly."

"All right. You'll train in battle arts as well. You need to be prepared if you're shot down."

Shot down. Rok said it so casually. Well, what had she expected? This was war. And the danger was the reason the females at the palatial pod thought her participation would be denied.

"Wonderful."

"Great. Cambry, show her the training area. You and Lundric can take her through the paces."

"Yes, Master Rok."

⁓.⁓

Erick itched to follow Mina, to volunteer to oversee her training, but it would show his hand to every being on the ship. But why was that a problem? It would be a declaration of intent, not of completion. His female hadn't consented to mate him. Yet.

He started down the corridor and heard Rok chuckling behind him. "So, that's how it is, then?"

"*Veck* you."

More chuckling. He didn't care if he came off as a lovesick fool. Every Zandian who he'd witnessed before and after mating—Zander, Seke, Lundric, Daneth—had all exhibited irrationality, and bursts of emotion uncharacteristic of their species. He'd attributed it to the influence of the more emotional humans, but what if it was the natural response for Zandians during the mating process? Or a result of being without females for such a prolonged period before mating?

He trailed the females into the training room, where Lundric and several other Zandian warriors worked a group of humans through fighting exercises using wooden staffs instead of swords. Master Seke had taught them any object could become a weapon—if they only committed to swinging it.

Lundric glanced at the females—no, at Cambry. It took him a moment longer to notice Mina, but when he did, he walked over and bowed. Erick joined the group, itchy at having Lundric near Mina, even if he was already happily mated.

"Lady Tara, we heard from your father of your return. It means so much to him to have you back."

She inclined her head. "Thank you. I'm here to join Prince Zander's army and train with you."

Lundric didn't hide his shock. "Has your father approved this plan?"

Mina put her hands on her hips. "Why shouldn't he?"

Lundric looked to him for help. He winced, caught between his most protective male instincts and the desire to give his precious female anything and everything she desired. He was saved from answering by the appearance of Seke, himself.

Seke's startled gaze landed on Mina, then flicked to Erick. He strode over. "Is everything all right? Tara, what's going on?"

Erick started to speak, to help Mina, but she cut in. "I asked Master Erick to bring me here. I'm joining the army. I'd like to help win back Zandia."

Seke's face remained impassive, but Erick knew him well enough to notice the subtle signs of tension. "I see. I'm sure you can train with Lily in medical assistance."

"No." Mina stuck out her chin. "I'm going to learn to fly an airship and train in ground fighting in case I'm shot down. Master Rok already approved."

"Rok is not—" Seke appeared to visibly calm himself. "I am Master at Arms. All final decisions about where and how we use warriors will be left to me, and my decision is final. I cannot allow you on the front line of any battle —in the air or on the ground. You can find another way to help."

Mina's face flushed purple. "The final decision can be made at a later date. What is the harm in training me? If I'd had these skills before, I might have been able to fight my way to freedom sooner."

Smart female. Her words struck home, causing her father to wince.

"Shouldn't we ensure every Zandian is prepared, regardless of how we use them?" Erick offered. "Isn't that the reason you trained every being who survived the invasion?"

Seke's lips tightened. Only males had survived, so training females hadn't been a question, but he didn't respond with further argument. Instead, he met Erick's gaze. "You approve of this plan?"

Something sticky slogged through his veins. Thoughts rushed through his head. No just one thought—*Seke knows, Seke knows, Seke knows.* But that was stupid. Seke recognized Erick's interest in his daughter, that was all. He was asking Erick, as her potential mate, if he truly wanted Mina to train.

He nodded. "Yes. Not every female is content to be shut up for safe-keeping when there's a war to be won. Your daughter is a warrior. She escaped from slavery on her own, with no help from any of us. She deserves to train with our best."

He didn't allow himself to absorb Mina's grateful gaze because, if he did, nothing would stop him from pulling her against his side and presenting them as the united front he wished they were. Instead, he met Seke's angry one, holding steady under it. He believed what he said, even if the thought of Mina ever putting herself in danger made him physically sick.

Seke pursed his lips for a long moment. "Very well. Train. No sense in with-holding knowledge or skill from those we wish to protect."

All three females beamed at Seke for that pronouncement, and he had the irrational desire to one-up the Master Warrior just to earn the same grateful smile from his female.

But he needed to earn far more than a smile from Mina. He'd meant to earn her trust, to prove he respected her as Tara as much as he wanted to possess Mina. But, instead, he'd acted like an animal again. Stars, had he really shoved her to her knees and held her captive as he plowed her poor pussy into oblivion?

Yes. Yes, he had.

Sigh.

He needed to leave the *Zandian Freedom* until he got a grip on his base desires. Except, leaving Mina here—surrounded by virile young Zandian warriors—was an impossibility.

Still, what reason could he give for remaining? What business of Zander's could he conduct here? Especially when he needed to be out recovering their much-needed galactacarriers.

Excrement. He needed to face the sovereign and tell him the truth about the galactacarriers. The longer he waited, the more his guilt and shame ate at him.

That's what he would do—return to the palatial pod to explain to Zander. Then find an excuse to get back to *Freedom.* In the meantime, Mina would be happier here, at least, even if he couldn't be with her. That should count for something.

And she'd wait for him. Wouldn't she?

Veck, he didn't know. Did she recognize their true connection, or did she believe it was just about sex and breeding season?

Seke had always taught them to master their worst fears by leaning into them. So he'd just have to leave Mina here, around all the other warriors, and trust that he'd made enough of an impression on her that she'd wait.

And if she picked another?

I'll vecking kill him.

No. He'd fight for her, but he had to respect any decision she made. He owed her that much after the way he'd pushed himself on her three times now.

CHAPTER SIX

Mina lay on a rickety cot in a tiny closet of a room, every muscle aching from her first planet rotation of training. She missed Erick's presence. He'd left her in the training room, and then she found he'd left the training pod altogether —without saying goodbye.

She shouldn't be so offended. This should be what she wanted. She'd pushed him away, refusing to let him make any claim on her other than their sexual encounters.

And yet she craved his presence at nearly every turn. As much as she enjoyed her training—loved absorbing every bit of knowledge the warriors gave her—she somehow felt Erick should be there to witness it.

After all, he'd been the one to help establish her there. He'd brought her and argued with her father. She had to believe his opinion meant a great deal to her father, or he wouldn't have given in.

But then, that's what made Erick such a fine negotiator for Prince Zander. He had the silver-tongued power of persuasion. What would they be like, as a couple? What could she bring to complement his business prowess?

The image of her father's and Zander's docile mates floated before her mind, and she shoved it away. If that was being mated, she had no interest. Looking pretty and speaking demurely wasn't her thing. Not after being forced into a subservient role for so long.

No, she wanted to be out changing the galaxy. She wanted to be at Erick's side on his next mission. Helping him negotiate or strategize. What skills or traits would she need to join his efforts?

She couldn't think of any she possessed.

Too bad.

What had he been working on? A shipment of galactacarriers? Something had gone wrong. She remembered his tension when speaking of it. What caused her master stress?

Yes, she liked to think of him as her master. Not in the literal sense. But in the way he held her down and took her roughly. Every time. It was like he couldn't stop it—his passion for her took over and he couldn't help but abuse her body until his delicious needs were met.

She brought her fingers between her legs and stroked, not surprised to find her folds plump and wet.

A tap sounded on the door, and she jerked upright, straightening her clothes. "Yes?"

"It's Lily. I have some equipment for you."

She pressed her hand to the door and it slid open. She blinked against the lights in corridor."

"Oh, I'm sorry. Were you sleeping?"

She flushed. "Ah, not yet. I'd just laid down."

"Master Erick left these for you." She handed her several items, including what seemed to be an animal hide belt.

"What are they? Oh!" A dagger slid out of a hand-stitched sheath. The hilt glittered with Zandian crystal; the blade appeared razor sharp. "Master Erick left this? For me?"

Lily's lips twisted in a knowing smile. "He seemed reluctant to leave you here, but I don't think he could justify staying. His job doesn't require much time here. But he left this so you can communicate with him." Lily held out a wrist cuff. She'd seen them on many Zandian males. They must serve as communication devices.

"How does it work?"

"He said he programmed it to call him if you press this button." Lily pointed at a small blue button on the inside of the cuff.

She smiled deliriously. "Wonderful. Thank you."

Lily winked. "Don't thank me. Thank him. I'm sure that's what he's hoping for." And with that, she withdrew and walked away, her hips swaying with a confident swing.

Mina grinned. She liked Lily. She looked so similar to Lamira and Leora but had a fire all her own. One Mina hoped to match. She closed the door and turned on the light.

Should she press the button?

Oh, who was she kidding? As if she could wait even another minute to call him. She sank onto the bed and pressed the blue disk on the cuff.

A light beeped several times before a hologram sprang open. She caught her breath as Erick's image leaped into her tiny chamber. He lay in bed, head and back propped on a fleet of expensive pillows. A broad grin lit his face.

It sent tingles of awareness racing down her inner thighs, curling her toes.

"Erick," she breathed.

"I was beginning to think you wouldn't call."

"Lily just brought me your gifts now. Thank you."

"Where are you?"

"In my room." She flashed the cuff around to show him the tiny closet. "They gave me my own space, on my father's orders."

"Good," he growled. "Is the door locked?"

She smiled. "You sound just like him. Yes, it's locked."

"Did you like the dagger?"

"I love it. It's beautiful. Is it yours?"

"It was mine. Now it's yours. I want you armed at all times, all right, pet?"

"You're awfully protective for someone who thinks I'd make a good warrior."

"Just because I know you'd be good at something doesn't mean I want you at risk. If I hadn't known how important it was to you to get out and be of use, I never would've brought you there."

Her brows drew together. "How *did* you know how important it was to me?"

"Mina..." He took a breath, as if gearing up to tell her something he'd rehearsed. "I'm paying attention. I'm trying to show you that you're more to me than a good *veck*, but I always end up losing control around you."

Warmth curled around her ears, in her chest. "So I've noticed." Her voice turned flirty.

"I wanted to stay on *Zandian Freedom*, just to be near you, but I couldn't think of any good excuse to justify my presence. And then I thought about leaving you with my cuff, and it seemed like the perfect solution. A way for me to talk to you that doesn't end in me shoving you up against a hard surface and beating my cock into you until you scream."

Her pussy clenched at his crude words and the memories they invoked. She leaned back on the bed. "Oh yeah?" Knowing he wanted her gave her confidence a huge boost. She'd always known she was beautiful, she'd even known how to work her body and her beauty as a tool, leverage against Dorhock or his guests to receive better treatment than the other pets. But Erick's passion meant something altogether different. "You want to know what I was doing before Lily brought your gifts to me?"

His eyes flew wide, as if he knew what she would tell him, and it caused him alarm. "What?" His voice was hoarse.

She lowered her lids. "Lying here, on my back with my hand between my legs. Thinking of you."

He growled a curse. "No. That pussy belongs to me. No one gets to touch it but me."

"Too bad you're not here."

He sat up straight from the pillows, sweat glistening around his horns. "*Listen to me*," he grated. "Don't you ever *vecking* touch yourself unless I give you permission. I get to see every orgasm. If I'm not there to squeeze it out of you myself, then I'll be directing you by hologram. Understand?"

A shiver of excitement went through her, matched by a throb between her legs. She nodded.

He leaned back against the pillows again and squeezed his cock beneath his sleep pants. "Take off your clothes, pet."

She glanced toward the door, even though she knew it was locked. Somehow, knowing guards might be walking by outside her door made the idea even naughtier.

"*Now*, Mina."

Dearest Zandian star, how she loved it when he grew dominant.

She peeled off all her clothing except the cuff, which hung too loose on her arm.

"Prop the cuff away from you so I can see your whole body," he ordered, and she complied, arranging the cuff on a small wall shelf above the bed.

"Perfect," Erick groaned, his horns stiff. "What were you thinking about, pet?"

She licked her lips. "About how rough you get."

He winced. "I'm sorry. Did I hurt you earlier?"

She made a show of dragging her hand down her belly and curling her fingers between her legs. "You always hurt me. And I always like it," she purred.

He growled. "Spread your legs. Show me what those fingers are doing."

She obeyed.

"Are they as good as my fingers, pet?"

She shook her head, lust swimming through her veins like a powerful drug. "Remember that planet rotation when you showed up at Prium's?"

Erick sat forward again. "Yes?"

"Did you see what was happening in the cell across from mine?"

Confusion flitted across his features. "No. I only had eyes for you, beautiful."

"There was a human slave being whipped by two males."

His brows slammed down. "Oh no. Do *not* tell me you want two males at once, pet. I won't share. I can't."

She smiled at his vehemence. "No, I don't want two. But I wanted to be mastered like that. By a male worthy of my surrender. And then you showed up."

Erick's shoulder moved in the hologram, his hand out of sight. She pictured him fisting his cock, pulling it out of his sleep pants. "Are you saying you want me to whip you again, pet?"

Her eyes took a temporary detour, rolling back in her head with pleasure. She pulled up on her fingers and squeezed her thighs together around them. "Yes," she panted, thrusting her hips against her hand.

Erick groaned, eyes glued to her pussy, his expression pained. She heard the sound of him beating his cock with his fist.

"And then you missed it—back at the palatial pod."

"What happened, pet?" His breath rasped in and out like he was running.

"Zander assigned Eslyn to be punished and conditioned by three warriors."

"Again—I'm not sharing."

She threw her head back on her pillow, fingers undulating between her legs. The heel of her hand pushed against her clit as her middle finger breached her entrance. "Not the sharing part," she gasped.

"The punishment and reconditioning." He said it as a statement, not a question. "Little female, I'm going to subject you to the strictest reconditioning possible."

"Yes, *yes*." She arched up, pussy clenching as she reached orgasm. It was a pitifully small one compared to those Erick wrenched from her, but a relief, nonetheless.

"Kneel up," Erick commanded when she finished. His fist continued to glide up and down his huge cock. "Get on your knees with your face in the pillow, the way I like, beautiful. I need to see that ass I'm going to punish."

It was her turn to groan. She scrambled to obey him, her fantasy master who seemed to know exactly what she liked.

"Reach back and stroke that pussy for me and imagine I'm painting that ass red with my palm."

She whimpered as she obeyed. Her pussy dripped with moisture—more than she'd ever felt there.

"And then I'd have to pry those pretty cheeks apart and *veck* your tight little ass, wouldn't I?"

"Yes, Master."

Erick made a choked sound, and she lifted her head, twisting around to look at his hologram. Based on his expression, he was coming.

Warm satisfaction swirled in her chest, made her smile.

"I'm going to need you to record your fantasies, pet," he said, when he'd caught his breath. "Pick up the cuff."

She turned and retrieved the cuff, watching as he cleaned himself with a cloth and tucked his cock away.

"If you press the blue button and I don't answer, you can leave me a hologram to watch later. I want you to record every fantasy, everything you think you want your master to do to you. Even the things that scare you. Understand?"

"Yes, Master."

"Good pet." He blinked at her, and the lust began to clear from his face. "*Veck*," he muttered and dropped his forehead to his hand.

"What?"

"I was trying to prove to you I'm more than the asshole who wants to shove his cock into your every orifice. But, somehow, I just turned this into the same thing."

She smiled. "Maybe that's all I need from you, warrior."

His lips turned down. "That, my sweet, is my biggest fear."

. . .

Erick raked a hand across his face. How had he managed to *veck* things up with Mina yet again?

Reaching for something—anything—to get them back on stable ground, away from sex talk, he blurted, "I have a big problem I can't figure my way out of, pet."

Stupid, stupid, stupid. Now he would appear weak to his female.

She went still. "What is it?"

"Remember those galactacarriers Rok asked for?"

"Yes."

"I got swindled on the deal. The broker says they were stolen from the manufacturer, but no one has offered to make good on my 750,000 stein investment."

She whistled. "So that's what galactacarriers go for these days?"

"That's half the cost. I would've paid the remainder when I picked them up. And like Rok said, we needed them yesterday."

"So, is the manufacturer making more?"

"No. The broker says he doesn't have the capital to invest. Even if he did, it would take another nine lunar cycles, and we don't have that kind of time. I've put the word out to every broker in the galaxy, but no one can get me any others—used or new."

She twisted a lock of hair around her finger, her beautiful face thoughtful. "Do we know who stole them?"

He loved that she said *we*. Maybe sharing hadn't been a total fail. She'd aligned herself with him, wanted to be a part of solving it.

"Yes—perhaps. I got a name out of the broker. I have no proof to take to the United Galaxies court, of course. Based on my research, he's a reclusive, rich collector. He operates outside the law and is considered dangerous. He took the galactacarriers as payment for a debt, not because he needed them."

"So will he sell them to you?"

"I haven't had any luck getting an audience with him. Not to mention the fact that Zander doesn't have a spare 750,000 to make up for what I lost."

"First of all, *you* didn't lose it. Stop blaming yourself. Second, we'll get them back."

He blinked at her, unable to repress a grin. "That's my thought, too. I haven't told anyone yet because I want to fix it on my own."

"No. Throw away the *on my own* part. And you have told someone. Me." Her infectious smile lifted a weight from his chest. "What's the collector's name?"

"Neo Lin."

Mina stiffened. "I know him." The openness in her face shuttered, eyes deadened.

"You do?" Foreboding twisted through his gut. "How?" But he didn't need to ask how. If she knew Neo Lin, it was from her days as a sex slave. The days she wanted to leave behind.

"I may be able to get you an audience with him."

A chill sluiced through his veins. Whatever she was contemplating, it would involve returning to a world she hated, a role she hated.

"Never mind," he said. "I don't want you involved in this."

Anger flashed over her face. "What—are you my father, now, too?"

"No, but you want to be Tara. You left Mina behind. You've told me that, and I have yet to respect it. I'm respecting it, now. I would appreciate any information you can give me about Neo, but I won't have you involved."

She shrugged. "We'll see." The hologram flicked off.

Growling, he attempted to reconnect, but she didn't answer.

Veck it all. What had he done?

Erick paced the length of the palatial pod like a trapped animal. Mina hadn't answered any of his transmissions, which created a disquiet in his entire nervous system. Or perhaps that was just being away from her.

After three attempts to reach her, he left a hologram message promising thorough punishment if she did not contact him by the end of the planet rotation. Of course, considering her fantasies, she just might disobey to earn the consequence.

He still hadn't spoken to Zander or any other being about the galactacarriers. He continued to research Neo Lin, but the more he found out, the more dangerous the being seemed. An Ocretion, Neo's involvement was suspected in a large number of black market trades, but the authorities never managed to pin anything on him, mostly because all witnesses ended up dead. Whatever connection Mina had with him, he wouldn't allow her to use it.

"What's eating you, Erick?"

He startled at the sound of Prince Zander's voice. "My lord." He bowed.

Zander stood in the doorway of his war room. Erick had looped past the conference room three times in his restless roaming.

He faced Zander fully. This was the moment. He should tell him about the galactacarriers, let the young sovereign know how he'd failed him and his species.

He opened his mouth.

Say it.

"Something's been on your mind ever since you returned from Aurelia. What's going on?"

"I *vecked* Seke's daughter." Holy excrement. Really? *This* is what he chose to confess?

To Zander's credit, surprise only flickered for a moment at his blurted confession. "All right. So what's the problem?" Zander's brows knit. "Was it consensual?"

"Not exactly."

Zander shot forward, more of a warrior than four of his guards put together. He shoved Erick up against the wall and put a blade to his throat. "What did you do?"

He closed his eyes, signaling surrender. His loyalty ran far too deep to ever struggle or fight against the younger male, even if he thought him unjust. Which he didn't.

"I asked you a question."

"I found her in a brothel in Aurelia."

Zander's grip eased, but the intensity of his frown didn't lessen. "And?"

"And I only meant to speak with her, to get her out of there. But it's breeding season. I couldn't stop myself."

Zander released him with a shove, casting his eyes to the ceiling. "*Vecking* stars, Erick." Disgust was evident in his tone. "Seriously? How did she take it?"

He drew in a long breath, images of all the dirty things he'd done to her in that cell rushing back. But he couldn't summon the guilt he'd felt at the time.

All he saw now was his beautiful female admitting, I *wanted to be mastered.*

"She liked it," he murmured. "Stars, we both liked it. But she doesn't want her father or the beings here to know what she was. And she associates me with that part of her life now. The part she wants to leave behind."

The fury behind Zander's gaze extinguished, his fists unclenched. "I see."

Erick spread his fingers. "What should I do?"

"Zandians don't lie. I know you dabble in deception in your business dealings, but Seke doesn't. I don't see how you can keep this from him, even if Tara doesn't wish it to be known. You must tell him."

"It's not my secret to tell."

"You were involved. He'll see your silence as a betrayal."

"And he'll see my comportment as abuse," Erick mumbled.

"Maybe. But not if Tara vouches for you. I'm assuming you're the reason she's free?"

He sighed. "I wish it had been a glamorous rescue, but it wasn't. I'd planned to buy her, but she used a Zandian crystal of mine to disable her laser cage and escape on her own. I provided cover for her escape, no more. She slipped out of the galaxy before I could catch her and escort her here."

Zander's lips twitched. "You've finally met your match, haven't you?"

His hands balled into fists at his side. "What does that mean?"

"A female capable of getting under your skin. I thought it was only human females who made our species lose composure, but it seems the Zandian females have the same effect."

Damn the prince for his knowing smirk.

"You have my advice. I'm not making it an order, but I won't keep the truth from Master Seke if it comes up, either."

He bowed to the prince. "Thank you, my lord."

"I'm calling a meeting of all the advisors tonight. King Fluut of The Finn sent a warning to the United Galaxies that any planet coming to the aid of the rebels—that's what the bastard is calling us—will be cut off from all trade."

"So we reach out privately to every planet—offer repayment in the form of Zandian crystal if they provide assistance in any form—troops, ships, funding, information. You've laid the groundwork over the last five solar cycles. Now it's time to call in all favors. Talia's rescue drastically pushed up our timeline on war. We're heading into an emergency, and we need to know who we can count on."

Zander frowned but nodded. "Yes."

Erick noticed the hesitation there. Zander hated statesmanship. He would've preferred to be a warrior. Or the behind-the-scenes business being. Pomp and flattery annoyed him.

"You want me to take care of it? Communication would be better coming from you. I'd just be your ambassador."

Zander looked out the window. "Make a list of the most important planets. I'll take those. You contact the rest."

He bowed. "As you wish, my lord."

"What news of the galactacarriers?"

He rubbed his forehead, a sickening plunge twisting behind his solar plexus. "I'm still working on them, my lord."

Veck. It wasn't a lie, but it didn't sit well, either. Fortunately, Lamira appeared holding their young son, and Zander's entire posture went soft, his eyes warm on his mate.

"Thank you, Erick."

"My lord." Erick touched the infant's feet as he passed Lamira. "I honor your honor, young prince." He murmured the traditional greeting to their species' future ruler, the symbol of hope for their upcoming battle.

~.~

Maybe Mina had picked the wrong being to ask for help.

"You wish to bait a thief." Mierna, the old Venusian who reeked of alcohol, said, phrasing it more a statement than a question, as if she already knew the whole story without being told.

Maybe she did. Venusians were known for mind reading and fortune-telling. Mina had never been sure if it was actual ability, or just a cultural affinity for speaking in riddles.

From what she'd heard, Mierna was a pilot, part of Rok's original crew before he'd been reunited with the Zandians. Mina had climbed aboard the old ship where Mierna and the rest of the crew slept. Mina chose Mierna for two reasons: 1) She wasn't a Zandian, and Mina needed a different species for her plan, and 2) Mierna was female.

But maybe the female part hadn't been so important, though. As she eyed the being doubtfully, she wished she'd asked one of Rok's Stornigian brothers, or his giant one-legged friend from Elau.

Choosing a female had only been to keep Erick from getting his horns twisted over another being seeing her naked. Which was utterly stupid considering a) she'd been a sex pet for the past five years. which meant hundreds of beings had seen her naked, and b) Erick already knew that.

But he'd been possessive, even though she'd given him no reason to believe he had a claim on her.

I won't share. I can't.

And, for whatever reason, she cared about his reaction.

But she'd probably wasted too much brain space on the issue. The very reason this plan was possible was because he knew and understood her prior occupation.

As the Venusian stared at her with her giant, protuberant eyes, Mina shivered. She had the sense Mierna saw every *vecking* thought in her head.

"Yes, bait a thief. You call him, offer him a rare pet-trained Zandian female —the only one in all the galaxies. Tell him I belonged to Dorhock. He will remember me. Tell him you want to meet to discuss terms."

The old Venusian nodded once. "I will make the call and set up the meeting. But we cannot go alone. It will take an entire team to steal the carriers."

Relief flowed down her limbs. The Venusian *did* understand the plan.

"I know. Just get the meeting. Then we'll tell the others."

The Venusian took a swig of the foul-smelling liquid in her jar. "All right. Put on your collar, showcat."

Tingles raced up and down her spine. So. Venusians were the real deal. No being knew that nickname her human friend Leti had coined for Dorhock's pets. No beings except the other pets.

She stripped out of her clothing. She didn't have a collar and leash, but she'd found a rope that would work to tie around her neck. She sure as hell hoped this Venusian could be trusted. She knotted it loosely and held the other end out to Mierna. "Can they trace the transmission?"

"No, we'll record it and send it on a scrambled frequency. You know where to send it?"

"Yes. Well, not exactly. Erick said he can't find a way to communicate with Neo Lin, but I know a friend of his. And he should be easy enough to contact."

Mierna brought her jar to her lips and drank, guzzling until she drained it. It made Mina's stomach turn just watching.

The Venusian gave her a critical up and down sweep of her eyes. "Too tall. You look ready to kick my ass. Squat down. Hands and knees, or make a little ball."

Mina almost laughed at Mierna's directions, but she dropped to her knees, placing her hands palm up on her thighs as she'd been trained to do.

"Good." Mierna nodded. She flicked a button and faced a recording device. "This message is for Neo Lin. I have a very rare item for sale. I think you'll like it." The old female tugged on Mina's rope, shocking her with her strength. Mina flew forward onto her hands and knees, wincing. "Zandian female—one of only three left in the galaxy. This one has been trained as a sex pet by your friend Dorhock. Want her? Reply to my transmission with a meeting time and place." She smacked a button on the console, and the device light went off.

"Ow." Mina complained, rubbing the grit off her hands from the dirty floor as she stood up.

"Had to make it look real," Mierna said.

"Well, you didn't have to break my neck to do it," she complained as she worked the knot at her throat, but a reluctant smile tugged at her lips. This salty old female knew her stuff. She *had* chosen wisely.

"Now, you tell me where to send it, and we wait for the reply."

"Great." She pulled on her clothing and plunked down beside the Venusian at the control panel.

This crazy plan of hers just might work.

~.~

He'd officially lost his mind over Mina.

The female hadn't answered his calls or sent him any messages until that morning's, which had been cryptic at best.

She'd sent a hologram of herself, looking rumpled and beautiful and more than a little bit rushed. *I have a meeting with Neo Lin. Can you come to* Zandian Freedom *to talk about it?*

That was all.

No explanation of *how* she got a meeting. Or what she planned. And as relieved as he was to know she'd made contact, he still didn't like her being involved. Not if it meant she had to use her connections from the world she wanted to leave behind.

Worse, he apparently was incapable of not responding to a summons for her immediately, because staying at the palatial pod had become an impossibility—despite the fact that he hadn't finished contacting all the ambassadors in the galaxy to request support and assistance.

But getting the galactacarriers was just as important. Wasn't it? He couldn't even trust his perspective. Where Mina was concerned, he thought with his cock. He'd already proven that time and time again.

It didn't matter. He was getting on his ship just as soon as he finished sending the last transmission requesting a meeting. He could tend to the replies just as easily from *Zandian Freedom* as he could from the pod.

He wouldn't even consider the significance of his not choosing to tell any being why he was leaving or where he was going. If Zander needed him, he'd hail him on his comms unit. He wore the same arm cuff all the trusted advisors wore.

There. He'd finished the transmission. He tossed a few items into his travel case and stalked to the loading dock. The moment he got his ship into the atmosphere, his body started to relax. He hadn't even realized how tense his muscles had grown from being apart from Mina. Not hearing enough from her, not knowing what went on in that beautiful mind of hers.

Soon, he'd see her again.

His cells began to come alive, a low hum that grew louder the closer he drew to *Freedom*.

He'd punish her, of course.

She hadn't obeyed his request for her fantasies. And she'd involved herself in his problem when he'd told her not to. Of course, he'd have to be careful with how he scolded her for that one. His female hated being kept back from any kind of action. He'd have to explain to her first, that it wasn't because he didn't think her capable of protecting or taking care of herself, but because he wished to honor her desire to leave her past behind her.

But that was a laugh. He honored that desire only when it suited him. But when his body got anywhere near hers, he had no compunction in degrading her like the pet she'd been.

But she liked it. He had to remember that.

Except if this was a facet of herself she hadn't or couldn't accept, he'd never win. Unless she resolved her own internal struggle with shame and desire, she would dump him and Mina without a backward glance.

Veck.

"Master Erick, you're cleared for docking." The transmission sounded over the ship's comms. Warriors from *Freedom* had identified his ship and opened the hatch. He maneuvered the ship in and landed then put his helmet on to walk inside.

"Twice in one week. I can't imagine what could be drawing you here," one of the guards teased when he entered.

He wanted to punch him in the teeth, but he dug deeper to find a glimmer of humor. Or humility. "I'm sure there's not much competition on this pod."

Both guards laughed—way too heartily for his comfort. "Yes, they're lining up just to see her. But don't worry. She's stayed close to the human females for the most part."

Thank the one true Zandian star for that.

"Where is she?" he snapped.

"Training room. Where she always goes."

He forced himself to mutter his thanks and stalked to the training room. The moment he caught sight of his beautiful female, his pulse went wild. At the same time, something at the very center of his being quieted. Something he hadn't realized had been amiss, but it had. Ever since he'd parted from Mina.

She practiced with Cambry, and the red-haired human had her pinned to the floor, an arm twisted behind her back.

If Cambry had been a male, or even a Zandian female, his ever-present instinct to protect her would have surged to the foreground. But these two were well-matched. As he watched, Mina flipped Cambry onto her back and mimed a crushing blow to the larynx.

Both females smiled as they sprang to their feet and started circling each other. His cock swelled against his flight pants at the idea of taking Cambry's place. Tussling with his female on the mats. Throwing her to the floor and covering her body with his own. Pinning her wrists above her head as he positioned his—

Get your horns straight, Erick.

He didn't come to *veck* Mina. He came to find out about Neo Lin and the galactacarriers.

And Mina.

She looked over and caught sight of him, but her moment of distraction cost her a kick to the solar plexus. She flew back and landed on her ass.

He charged forward, but she was already scrambling to her feet, a broad smile on her face.

Thank *veck*.

She said something to Cambry and sauntered toward him, hips swaying in a seductive pattern. Every male—*every last male in the entire room*—watched, tongues lolling.

"You received my message."

He wanted to grasp her elbow and march her to her room where he could take out his frustration on the soft curves of her ass. Instead, he managed a polite smile, mostly for the benefit of their audience. "I did."

She hooked her hand around his elbow. "Good. Come on—let's gather the others."

The others. Right.

Spanking could wait.

At least another few minutes.

Mina worried her lower lip between her teeth. She hadn't told any being but Mierna her plan, but she had told everyone she hoped to involve that she'd need their input on a matter when Erick arrived.

"Is it time for the meeting?" Cambry asked, jogging up to them.

"Yes. Will you get Lundric and Rok? We'll meet in Rok's office."

Erick's gaze didn't waver from her face, and it held something she couldn't decipher. "What?" she asked when they headed down the corridor.

"You're more like yourself here."

Surprise popped like a bubble in her chest. "Am I? How would you know?"

She might have missed the flash of hurt on Erick's face before he masked it, if she hadn't fallen into his violet gaze. She pulled him to a stop. "I just mean... *I* don't even know who I am anymore."

Stubbornness streaked across his expression. "This is you. The female giving orders. Getting thrown to the floor and bouncing back up with a smile. The one so full of life she's bursting. I'm half-fascinated, half-jealous."

"Jealous of what?"

"Jealous of your time here. Disappointed that I had nothing to do with your new happiness."

Stars. Something fluttered loose in her chest. Did he really say that? "But you did. You brought me here. And argued with my dad to let me stay. He's not here, by the way. He left for the palatial pod just before you arrived."

Which had been a huge relief, because her plan would never execute if her father knew. She was still more than a little worried about Erick's reaction.

She squeezed into Rok's small office along with Rok's original crew: his two foster brothers, Jano and Jaso, Guardo, Depri, and Mierna. Lily and Rok, Lundric and Cambry, and Cambry's brother, Tal, all joined them as well.

"So?" Rok said. "What's the big mystery about?"

"First, let me say what I'm about to reveal is private information. No matter what we decide to do, none of this can leave this office. Not even to my father, understood?"

Only Lundric shifted uncomfortably, which didn't surprise her. His loyalties were with her father, his master.

"Lundric?"

"Zandians don't lie," he muttered.

"So don't lie," she snapped back. "Just don't tell him."

Lundric tightened his lip, but nodded.

She dared a glance at Erick, but he only appeared encouraging. Apparently, as dominant as he was, he didn't mind a female taking charge of a meeting room. Another point in his favor. "Yesterday, Mierna sent this communication to a trader named Neo Lin, the being who stole the galactacarriers meant for Master Erick."

She waited until the jerks of surprise and inquisitive looks at Erick had passed before nodding to Mierna, who launched the short communique showing Mina naked and on her knees behind the wizened Venusian.

Erick gave a strangled growl of anger.

Damn her face for heating. She was a warrior. She'd done what she had to do. Even so, she couldn't bring herself to look at him.

"We've received a response with his coordinates. He's invited Mierna to visit tomorrow. With her pet."

"No." Erick spoke before any other being had a chance to voice an opinion.

She slapped her hand down on Rok's desk. "You don't get to say *no* before you've even heard my plan." Now that she had fire in her gut, she matched his gaze.

A muscle in his jaw jumped. "Fine. Tells us your plan."

"Mierna brings me in. Preferably in a cage where we can hide weapons. The rest of you come along, either as additional prisoners—she glanced at Cambry and Lily—or as Mierna's guards. A backup team will hide in our ship and sneak out to search the premises. Once the galactacarriers are located, the pilots take charge of them, and we all fly away."

It sounded much crazier now that she said it aloud. It could only be their reverence for her father that kept them from scoffing.

"And if the galactacarriers aren't on premises?" Rok demanded.

"They are." Mierna used her cryptic sage voice.

Rok rolled his eyes, which made Mina like him. He was no-nonsense. He lacked the formality and pomp of the rest of their species. In fact, she liked his whole team. Somehow, it felt like she belonged more with them than with the Zandians. Perhaps because they each were oddities in their own way.

"So tell us, oh wise one, does this operation have a chance in hell of succeeding?" Sarcasm dripped in Rok's voice.

Mierna ignored it and tilted her head to the side, losing focus in her eyes. "A good chance, yes."

"What does *a good chance* mean?" Erick asked, then rolled his eyes to the ceiling. "I can't believe we're relying on a Venusian's predictions to make a decision."

"Eighty percent success. Maybe better."

Erick slammed his fist down on the arm of his chair. "So what's a partial success mean? We lose part of the team? That's unacceptable. I am not sending a female—or any being—in as live bait. That's insanity."

Mina's face flushed. She expected every male in the room to agree, but a silence followed Erick's outburst. "I am the only reason we were given the coordinates to his ship. He wants me. I know this being. If there's one thing I'm sure of, it's that he won't harm me. I'm nothing more than a rare object to him, but he cares more about his objects than anything else." She lifted her chin in challenge directly at Erick.

. . .

By the one true Zandian Star. Erick rubbed his temples.

Mina had him hamstrung. The mere *idea* of sending her into danger had his pulse skipping erratically, his hands clenched into fists. He wanted to bash heads of his imaginary enemies. Break necks. Shoot first and forget the questions.

But Mina *wanted* this. And denying his female anything she wanted sent his heart lurching out of his chest, made him ready to fall on his knees, promising to do everything in his power to fix it.

The fact that she'd come alive since she'd come to *Zandian Freedom* wasn't lost on him. His female was a warrior. She *belonged* in the fray. Whether he liked it or not.

"Do the rest of you believe we should go forward with this plan?" Incredulity crackled in his tone.

Guardo shrugged. "For the three galactacarriers necessary for our strike on Zandia? Yes. I'm in." He looked at the rest of Rok's crew. "We've successfully stolen or requisitioned goods with far worse odds."

"Yes, we have." Rok smirked. "But I'm reserving my vote until I'm sure Erick's not going to pull a sword from his belt and start fighting us all just to keep Tara safe."

The rest of the beings in the room swung their attention to Erick. He ground his teeth. "*Vecking* hell," he spat. "Fine." Somehow he forced the word out of his tightened lips. "But you'll answer to me in private for this." He glared at Mina.

Lily stifled a giggle, and he was pretty certain the rest of the group hid smiles, looking everywhere but at him and Mina, but he had his female pinned with his gaze.

A slow flush crept up her neck, but her blue-violet eyes turned more violet, and her nipples tented the front of her uniform.

Good. They'd both enjoy her punishment and then maybe he'd be able to move on and stomach this horrible plan.

"I'm in, then," Rok spoke up. "But I'm not comfortable taking all of Zander's top warriors on the mission. Lundric, you and Cambry will stay. My crew will go."

"What about me?" Lily asked.

"And me?" Tal interjected.

Rok rubbed his forehead. "Lily, I'd rather you stay, but you're part of my team. So, if you want to come, you're in."

"I'm in," she said firmly. She glanced over at Mina. "I'll go in a collar and leash, as well. I put my years in as a sex slave. I know the part."

It was subtle, but something in Mina's chest relaxed, as if she'd just exhaled, or dropped a piece of armor she'd been holding there. She smiled gratefully at Lily. "That would be great."

"I can go as a slave, too," Tal said. "It'd be hard to explain why you have a human along otherwise.

Rok nodded. "You'll go as Mierna's handslave. Guardo and Depri will be her crewmembers. Erick, Jano, Jasu, and I will be recon. We'll find the galactacarriers and fly them out of there. We'll need some kind of distraction to give the rest of you time to get out of there as well."

"An explosion near his collectibles will send Neo Lin into madness." Mierna used a singsong voice.

Erick was grateful for Rok's cool command because he couldn't think beyond *Mina will be in danger, Mina will be in danger, Mina will be in mothervecking danger.*

"I was thinking we could rig the slave cage with some kind of sleeping gas. In case I need a quick escape."

"Yes." He grasped the thin strand of safety that option provided. "Good idea. I know where to find a cage."

Mina's brow furrowed. "You do?"

He almost laughed. Was that jealousy behind her voice? Did she really think he'd kept pets before her?

Lily echoed it, tossing her hands onto her hips. "You do?"

"Yes, and neither of you want to know where I'm getting it."

Mina's eyes narrowed. "Why not?"

"Because it involves both your parents."

"Ew." Mina wrinkled her nose.

"Double ew." Lily concurred. "Yes, please leave us in the dark."

"Well, there's a lot of work to be done before tomorrow. Erick, you get the cage. I'll have the warrior Pal outfit it with a sleeping gas. He has one that's toxic to those who haven't been inoculated so you won't need masks. Lundric, outfit the group and my ship with all the hidden weapons you can come up with. Any questions?"

"No, Captain," they murmured as the group broke up.

Veck, he needed to be inside Mina. Everything could wait until he'd split those long legs of hers and wrapped them around his waist. And there was the matter of her punishment. He stood and grasped her elbow, directing her out of the office with a firm hand.

"Show me to your chamber."

She darted a glance at him, her cheeks coloring. After they entered her tiny room—which must have been a closet in a previous incarnation—she pressed her back against the door.

"Clothing off," he ordered. He'd meant to talk to her. To sit down and explain all his whip-tight emotions, but this was all he could manage. Punishment. Release for both of them.

Then, maybe they could talk.

When she didn't move, he advanced on her, caging her against the door with his hands propped on either side of her. "You heard me, pet. I need you naked. Now."

Anger and indignation seemed to war with lust in her eyes. She put her hands on his chest and attempted to shove him away.

He didn't move.

"You have no claim on me."

He fell back like she'd punched him in the gut.

And then he smashed his fist through the wall.

Mina stifled a scream, but she couldn't have been afraid because, instead of running away, she lunged for him, wrapping her arms around his waist from behind. "You're angry."

He punched the wall a second time. "Yes." A muscle jumped along his neck.

She must have felt it because she released him and stepped back.

He turned and followed, picking her up by the waist and pressing her against the wall, her feet dangling above the floor. "No. Not angry. I'm *vecking terrified.*"

They breathed together, nose to nose, both of them angry. Both of them needy. Her nipples brushed against his ribs, pointy and hard, even through their clothing.

"I never, *never* go into a negotiation with something to lose. That's my personal rule. I broke it at Prium's trying to buy you, and that was bad enough. But this? This is sending you to your *vecking* death. How do you think I'll be able to stand it?"

~.~

The fight went out of Mina in a whoosh.

Erick sounded too broken for her to resent his overstep. Her male was afraid for her. He needed soothing. If he wanted to let off steam on her ass, she'd take it. Hell, they'd both enjoy it, she knew with complete certainty.

"Put me down," she rasped, her lips almost up against his.

Although he was twice as strong as she—and angry—she knew she still held the reins. He eased his grip on her, letting her feet slide back to the ground.

Slowly, holding his gaze, she peeled her tunic off over her head.

His lids dropped, relief and lust mingling behind his eyes, quickening his breath. She cupped her breasts, squeezing and lifting them. Weighing them in each hand.

In a flash, Erick had her wrists pinned above her head against the wall. He slapped her breast.

She gasped at the shock of sensation, the sting followed by heat. Pain and relief melding.

He slapped it again. And again. Four times. Five. The pulse between her legs grew more insistent. Erick switched hands and spanked her other breast.

She moaned, sinking into the pain, surrendering to Erick's dark tastes.

He hooked his index finger in the waistband of her uniform pants. "What did I say about your clothing?"

She smiled and slid her pants and panties down until she stood naked before him.

The look he gave her body was mock-critical, as if she were a soldier reporting for inspection.

"Legs apart." He patted her mons. The moment she parted her thighs, he brought his palm up in a slap, spanking her pussy. *Hard.*

She cried out but didn't move. She sensed Erick was measuring her reaction. "More."

"You like that, pet?" He slapped her again and stepped in close, his breath hot on her neck. "I'm going to spank you so hard, pet." He buried his fingers in her hair and fisted them, tugging her head back. "You'll have so many marks on that ass tomorrow, they'll never question whether you're a real pet."

Her belly fluttered and leaped. One-third scared. Two-thirds excited. She was fairly certain he'd stop if she didn't like it, but not 100 percent.

Still, it was better not knowing. The danger and thrill of it only added to the tension.

"Now— *Spread. Your. Legs.*"

She widened her stance even farther, and he started spanking her poor pussy, fast and hard.

The room swooped around her as a wave of thick lust made her dizzy. She clung to his shoulders to keep from falling.

He gave one more slap then showed her his fingers, which glistened from her arousal. "Spanking always makes you wet, doesn't it, pet?"

"Y-yes," she admitted.

He sucked her juices from his digits, one by one, his horns twitching and thickening with each pull.

He unbuckled his belt.

A wanton sound slipped from her lips—half moan, half whimper.

He shook his head. "This isn't for your ass, pet. It's for your wrists. Turn around and put them behind your back."

She smiled and turned around, hitching her wrists together and wiggling her fingers.

Erick worked quickly, cinching the animal hide around her wrists and buckling it tight. "Now, climb up on the cot on your knees, facing the wall...perfect." He moved in behind her. She expected pain, but she didn't tense against it, just closed her eyes and waited.

Instead, his fingers slipped between her legs, rubbing along her dewy folds.

She leaned her forehead against the wall and arched into his touch, lifting her ass.

He growled. The pad of his finger circled her clit, and her breath hitched. Too soon, he pulled his hand away and let it fall with a smack against her ass.

"Oh!"

He spanked, slow and hard. Deliberate, measured strokes. The space between them gave her time to accustom herself to the pain, to convert it into pleasure. Her pussy dripped.

He dipped between her legs again, and whatever he found made him groan. He screwed his thumb inside her and used another finger to stroke her clit. "I'm going to eat this pussy all night long, pet. After I whip you, and *veck* you hard. And travel back to the damn palatial pod for your cage. Then I'm going to wake you up in the middle of the night with my lips suctioned over these lips."

It was too much. Between his finger-*vecking* and dirty-talk, she couldn't hold out any longer. Her ass cheeks squeezed together, and she lowered her hips, trying to take his digit deeper, grind her clit harder against his fingers.

He pulled his fingers away and spanked her pussy. *"No."* The word sounded harsh, stern. "You tip that ass back for your master's punishment. Do not come until I give you permission. Understand?"

"Yes, Master," she warbled.

He picked up the thin rod she used to practice sword play and whipped it against his palm. "Yes. I think this will be perfect for spanking my naughty pet, don't you?"

She couldn't muddle through an answer. Didn't know if she wanted to be whipped with the implement, so innocuous in sword play, but so frightening now.

"Seven strokes for all to see tomorrow. You'll wear my mark on you when you go in there, Mina, and you'll remember what it cost me to watch you do it." Without waiting for an answer, he whipped the crop across her ass.

She choked on her breath and accidentally knocked her forehead against the wall.

"Easy, pet." Erick burrowed his fingers in her hair and rubbed her head. Just a brief bit of comfort before he removed his touch and whipped her once more.

"Veck, Erick!"

"I know, pet. It hurts. Five more."

She clamped her teeth together and held tightly as he brought the rod down. The welts from the first strokes had grown more painful in the interim, like lines of fire painting her ass. He made neat, even lines down the lower half of her buttocks and one where her cheeks met thigh and then he tossed the rod onto the floor with a clatter.

"That's it, pet." He lifted her to her feet, wrists still bound behind her back. His large hands cupped her tender ass, and she flinched when he squeezed, but after a moment of rubbing, his massage took away the worst of the sting. "Thank you, sweet female. I know you're doing this for me. To solve my problem. That's what *vecking* kills me."

"You're not going to lose me." She meant she wouldn't die, not that she was giving herself to him, but the words were out. They were out, and she couldn't take them back.

"Promise?" His voice rasped against her ear.

"I promise. Are you going to *veck* me now?"

He gave a harsh laugh. "Yes, pet. The way you like it."

She wanted to ask how he thought she liked it, except she wasn't sure she'd like the answer.

Like a whore.

Like a degraded sex pet. The kind who wears a collar and kneels at her master's feet.

Exactly what she didn't want to be.

And she was right. Erick turned her to face away from him and shoved her torso over, so she stood, bent at the waist, her long hair falling down around her ankles. Her aching nipples brushed against her thighs.

He removed his cock from his pants and dragged the thick head through her juices.

She pushed back at the delicious contact. "Yes, please," she moaned.

He cursed and thrust, impaling her with his sizeable length.

It was perfect and not enough, and she had exactly zero control or leverage in the position Erick put her in. She had no choice but to let him direct the show, which he did. Grasping her bound wrists, he yanked her back onto his cock then released her forward. He continued, using gravity and her arms to leverage her.

"Are you sorry, pet?"

"Yes!" she wailed, even though she didn't know what she should be sorry for. She needed release, needed satisfaction.

"Sorry for punishing me this way? Making me suffer, caught between my need to make you happy and my need to protect you?"

She surrendered completely, her body a loose, ragdoll *veck*-toy for her master. The male who cared more about her than she'd imagined possible. "Erick," she choked.

He released her wrists and changed his grip to her hips, holding her immobile as he pistoned in and out of her.

"Yes, yes, yes," she chanted, her head bobbing at her ankles as he beat his cock into her. "Yes, Master."

"Come now, Mina!"

As if her body had been waiting for his command, her muscles immediately tightened around his malehood, squeezing and pumping,

Erick let out a string of curses and came, his hot seed filling her. He backed them up, still connected, and sat on the cot, pulling her onto his lap and murmuring endearments. "Sweet pet. Lovely female. So beautiful." He kissed her neck, her shoulder. "Thank you, beautiful."

She gave a sigh of contentment and leaned into his strong embrace. If only her world could be this small, this simple. The act of giving and receiving in a small closet.

Nothing more. Nothing less.

But they had a planet to take back. And galactacarriers to hijack.

Erick, too, seemed to know they were on borrowed time. He eased her off his lap and tucked her into the bed. "I'll be back late tonight. Don't wait up—you need your sleep."

Her mouth stretched into a pleasured smile. "Yes, Master."

He gripped her jaw and leaned over, claiming her mouth in a breathtaking kiss. "Be good, pet. Don't open the door unless you hear my voice."

"I won't," she mumbled, sleep already overtaking her.

CHAPTER EIGHT

Erick frowned and adjusted his cock. "Look at her and you die," he growled at Rok, who stood beside him.

They were surveying the two beautiful, naked pets in the cage loaded on Rok's ship. One human, one Zandian. The females wore nothing but collars, wrist and ankle cuffs—incredibly high-tech voice-activated ones he'd found with the cage back at Zander's pod.

"Ah, Lily and I need to have a private discussion in our room before we go." Rok's voice was rough.

"There's no time for sex. Keep your mind on the mission," said the male who'd made good on his promise to pleasure Mina with his mouth and tongue all night.

"*Veck* you. My mind isn't going to be anywhere but in that cage unless I get some relief," Rok snapped. He unlocked the gate on the cage. "Get over here, female," he growled.

Lily smiled and walked forward, shrieking as Rok tossed her over his shoulder and carried her back to his room. "I'll just be a few minutes."

"Take your time." Erick eyed his female, now alone in her cage. "Let's go over it again—"

"Erick. We've been over it four times already. I know how to release the gas. We double and triple checked to make sure all of us are now immune to it. I know how to get to my gun, fast. I know how to open the cage door. We're ready. Or we will be as soon as Rok is finished with Lily." She smirked.

Pal, the Zandian who had outfitted the cage with sleeping gas, arrived on board Rok's ship, dressed in black like the rest of the extraction and backup team members. No Zandian whites for this operation. Good, he was glad they'd have another Seke-trained warrior on board. Not that he didn't trust Rok's scrappy crew.

"Don't look at her," Erick growled.

"I wouldn't dream of it, Master Erick," he said smoothly.

The rest of the team entered and milled around, also tactfully averting their eyes. It was stupid of him to threaten them all. The last thing he wanted was for them to look uncomfortable around the "slaves" when they arrived at Neo Lin's, but he couldn't help himself. His need to shield Mina from other eyes asserted itself too strongly.

Rok returned from his chamber on the old ship, Lily once more hefted over his shoulder, giggling. He deposited her back in the cage and spoke into his collar. "Comms test. Primary team report."

Each of the members responded, their voices piped into the tiny devices in their ears. "Mierna ready and in position."

"Tal ready and in position."

"Guardo in position."

"Depri in position."

"Lily in position." She smiled at her mate, who swatted her ass.

"Mina in position." She folded her arms over her bare breasts and smirked at him, as if the cage was to keep him from touching her, rather than her being the prisoner.

He forced a smile. He couldn't deny the excitement coming off Mina in waves. She loved being a part of this mission, as much as it killed him.

"Extraction team report," Rok ordered.

"Jano ready."

"Jaso ready."

"Erick ready."

"And I'm ready," Rok said. "Backup team report."

"Pal ready with a team of four soldiers." The soldiers were human—newly trained—but they were armed and would prove useful. The plan was for them to remain hidden on Rok's ship unless needed. Erick just hoped they wouldn't be.

Rok buckled into a seat near the cage in the cargo hold. Erick did the same. "Let's fly," Rok commanded, and the ship lifted off.

He closed his eyes, striking all the images of tragedies that might befall them from his mind. Rok's scrappy team had succeeded many times without expensive ships or equipment. What worked for them was the same thing that he used in his negotiations. Having nothing to lose. Or believing they could get themselves out of any situation. He needed to adopt that mindset, too, if he was going to be of any use to this mission.

After what felt like three planet rotations, but in actuality was less than half of one, the ship docked on Neo Lin's pod off the planet Aurelia and they got into position, activating heat-masking sensors on their flight suits to prevent Neo's guards from accurately reading how many beings they brought.

Rok used his ship's sensors, controlled through his arm cuff, to scan Neo's ship. "There." He pointed at a dock below the one they were on. The outlines of the three galactacarriers showed on the screen.

"This is it," he murmured to Mina before taking his position in hiding. "I know you'll take care of yourself."

The smile that stretched across her face was so genuine, he kicked himself again for trying to keep her back from this mission. "Of course I will." She winked. "You too, Master."

Mierna, flanked by Tal, Guardo, and Depri, pulled the hovercage out of the ship. Mina and Lily sat on their knees, fingers twined around the bars in their attempt at pitiful and scared slaves.

Neo Lin's guards met them on the dock and escorted them to a reception area. Neo's ship was as expensive and beautiful as Zander's pod, only decorated with far more flash, which didn't surprise her. Neo cared about his possessions more than anything. They were a source of power to him, of identity and pride.

He'd been one of Dorhock's friends, one she was always assigned to service because he demanded her. It hadn't been about the sex or the quality of her skills. It had been solely because he, like Dorhock, knew and recognized her value in the galaxy.

I'll bet Prince Zander would pay any amount to recover the only female of his species still alive. Too bad he has no idea you're tucked safely in Aurelia.

He'd been stroking her cheek with the backs of his fingers as she'd sucked his cock, and she'd stopped, unable to hide her shock.

You didn't know? He'd grinned, as if being the one to tell her thrilled him beyond measure. *Dorhock knows. Why do you think he keeps you hidden away except for his most special guests? You're his prize possession. I've offered to buy you at least a dozen times, but he won't sell. Too bad, because you're as beautiful as you are rare.*

So, she had no fear of the reception she'd receive from the eccentric Aurelian. But she wouldn't put it past him to shoot Mierna and dump their ship to avoid spending any of his own money to keep her.

When the silver-haired Neo came in, he clapped his hands with glee. "Mina! My little Zandian pet. What a treat." He came close to the cage, ignoring every other being.

He was just as she remembered—ornately dressed, face painted in metallic silvers and rose, silver nails sharpened.

"I was furious when I couldn't find you at auction after Dorhock's death.

They must have traded you privately." He turned to Mierna. "Where did you get her?"

Mierna lifted her chin. "I stole her."

"And what makes you think I won't simply turn you into the authorities?"

"It's illegal to keep Zandians as slaves. Besides, the slave pet told me you'd pay." She rapped the cage with a cane that doubled as a concealed weapon. "Didn't you, pet?"

Neo's face lit up. "Did you, dear?" He reached through the bars to pinch one nipple.

Mina didn't flinch.

"We always had an affinity for one another, didn't we?"

Damn. She hated having the conversation broadcast to all three teams because she'd prefer Erick didn't hear she'd had past relations with this being.

But he must've known anyway. And he'd never judged her or been jealous of her past exploits. He only seemed possessive about any future males.

Guards on the dock have been neutralized. Extraction team heading to the underground bunker for the galactacarriers, Rok's voice reported in her tiny earpiece.

She rubbed up against the bars like a *nelot,* or *cat,* as her human friend Leti called them.

"Where's your tail, little one?"

She stuck her lower lip out like an infant. "I lost it, Master Neo. Maybe you'll buy me a new one?" She licked the bar of the cage, holding his silver gaze.

He chuckled. "How much do you want for her?"

"One million steins."

Neo barked a laugh. "Ridiculous. I'll give you ten thousand."

"No deal."

Galactacarriers located and boarded.

Mierna grabbed the cage and swung it around. "Come on, boys. We're leaving."

Mina didn't believe Neo would actually let her walk out without a counteroffer, but if he did, the timing couldn't be more perfect. It sounded like the galactacarrier extraction team was in position and ready to leave.

Neo grabbed the back end of the cage and whipped it back to face him. "Open the cage, and let me inspect her."

Mierna thumped her cane on the floor. "She requires *no* inspection. You can see for yourself she's in excellent health." The tiny Venusian drew herself up tall. "And you're already acquainted with her skill."

Neo whipped out a gun and put it to Mierna's head. "Open. The. Cage."

The entire team tensed, but no one dared move, not with the laser gun so close to Mierna's head.

Primary team, get out of there. Extraction team is ready to evacuate. Rok's urgent communication came through her earpiece.

"Open cage," Mierna said tightly.

Lily slowly lifted her hand to her hair then to the ceiling of the cage, where the trigger for the sleeping gas had been hidden. Using the guise of stretching her cramped body, she pushed it.

Nothing happened. *Veck*. Why didn't the gas work?

Neo kept his gun trained on Mierna but gestured to one of his guards. "Pull out the Zandian. Leave the human."

Lily tried to trigger the gas again.

"I'm coming, I'm coming." Mina kicked off the guard's hands and tumbled out of the cage then bounced to her feet, still playing cute. She heard the snick of the cage door closing behind her.

She wiggled her body between Neo and Mierna and threaded her arms around the Aurelian's neck. She licked a line up Neo's jaw. "You're going to buy me, aren't you, Neo?"

The male's face hardened, and he didn't take his eyes off the rest of her team, but he clamped a hand over her shoulder and shoved her to her knees.

She knew exactly what he wanted, and didn't hesitate to comply. Humiliation had always been part of the pet game, which she'd learned to play a long time ago. If he wanted to have his cock sucked while he held a gun on Mierna, she'd do it.

The gas hadn't worked, but they had other distractions in play. Erick would set off a bomb somewhere, and she'd knock the gun out of Neo's hand. Or bite off his cock. Or do whatever she had to do to get out of there with her friends' lives intact.

She pulled Neo's flaccid cock from his pants and fit it easily in her mouth, sucking and warming it with her tongue.

In the past she'd been able to disassociate from sex. No, that wasn't it. She had no positive association with it, so there'd been no need to disassociate. It was just one of the asinine ridiculous things Dorhock expected of his pets.

Now that she'd been with Erick, now that she knew true pleasure, understood the measure of sex—how gratifying it could be, how intimate, how incredibly bonding, she couldn't stand having her mouth on another being's cock.

And the fact that it was a small, soft cock made it even more disgusting to her.

But her job was to distract. To diffuse the situation until the gun left Mierna's head and her team could act. So she cupped Neo's four balls, and rolled her tongue along the underside of his pathetic malehood.

To make matters worse, Erick's voice came through on the comms unit. *Primary team, it's too quiet. What's going on in there?*

"Get rid of them," Neo snapped.

In a mind-boggling blur of simultaneous action, Mina slammed her wrist up against Neo's, sending his gun flying to the floor. He backhanded her, and she flew to the floor as his guards pulled out laser guns and shot at Depri, Guardo, Tal, and Mierna.

Depri fell, but rolled, taking a wound to the shoulder. Guardo attacked the guard closest to him. Mierna, Depri, and Tal scattered to take cover. Tal flipped the cage, with Lily still inside, to its side, using the floor to shield them from the laser fire.

Lily opened the compartment in the false floor and pulled out her own laser weapon, aiming and firing at Neo, but she missed.

Mina had scrambled to her feet, her cheek throbbing, and she ran for the cage, launching herself at it and using it to knock over two guards.

What the veck is going on in there? Rok's voice rose with urgency.

"Small problem," Lily muttered.

A shock stick struck Mina's back, and her body jerked and dropped to the floor, immobile, staring up at Neo's cold face. He picked her up by the armpits and dragged her toward the exit, barking a command for a guard to help him. One swooped in and grabbed her ankles.

No, she tried to scream, but her larynx was paralyzed, and her body didn't obey her commands. Laser fire flashed through the room, Guardo still fought in hand-to-hand combat. Miera lifted her cane and fired at the guard holding Mina's feet, and he crumpled to the ground. It didn't stop Neo from dragging her from the room and down a corridor into what must be his chamber.

To his comms unit, he said, "All units to reception. The Zandian has been taken. Kill the rest."

Oh veck! Mina! Don't worry, pet, I'm coming for you. Erick's determined voice came through.

But she couldn't answer him.

Apparently, Neo had to keep his sex partners prisoner, because he had cuffs attached at the head and foot of a low sleeping platform. He swiftly locked her in place as she stared up, unable to blink or move any muscle in her body. It was a wonder her heart still beat, lungs moved air.

Immediate backup requested for primary team, Rok barked. *Jano and Jasu, fly your vecking galacatacarriers out. I'm triggering explosions now. Pal, find the primary team and get them the veck out of there!*

On our way, Pal clipped.

Who is flying out the third galactacarrier? some being asked, maybe Jano or Jasu.

We'll leave it vecking behind, if we have to. Erick and I aren't leaving without our females! Rok snarled.

Copy that. Jano taking off.

Jaso taking off.

Explosions sounded through the building.

Neo turned a deadly gaze on her. Gone was the pompous, well-mannered collector. She was seeing the killer. "What is this, Mina? What are you after?"

"Lord Nin, the galactacarriers are taking off!" A frantic transmission came through some invisible comms unit on Neo.

His face contorted with rage, and he picked up the shock stick and hit her with the voltage again, just for spite.

The door flew open, and Erick took Neo down with a single laser shot to the head.

"Mina," he choked, taking in her lifeless form. He unsheathed his sword and sliced off her bonds then put his ear to her chest.

Not dead, she tried to croak, but nothing came out.

He scooped her up and ran down a smoky corridor.

Rok and Lily taking off in the third galactacarrier, Rok reported.

Thank the stars. That must mean her friends made it out. At least Lily had.

Guards rounded the bend at a run, and Erick fired twice, dropping them both. A true warrior. He killed four more on the run through the mansion and had to use the laser gun to shoot the panel of an electronic door that kept them from exiting. The bodies of sleeping guards lay everywhere on the dock, but her friends waited at the ship, hatch open. "Come on, come on," they urged.

Someone tried to take her from Erick, but he wouldn't let go.

The ship lurched into the air before anyone had buckled in, and Erick stumbled along the deck until he found a cot to lay her on. Beside it, Depri lay on another, tending to his own bleeding shoulder wound.

Erick injected her with something that took away the jangling of her nerve endings, the fire that had started in tiny pinpricks. He pressed a large Zandian crystal into her palm and closed his fingers around hers, helping her hold it against her heart.

Her body sputtered to life, and she lurched to a sitting position, coughing and choking in more breath.

Erick clapped an oxygen mask over her nose and mouth, and she sank back to the cot.

This wasn't how she expected to feel. Like the weak female who required rescuing. Like the one who'd been captured for sex. Used like a slave pet.

Gone was the strength and excitement she'd felt going into the mission. Buried under the guilt and shame that she'd sucked another male's cock. Had used her body like a slave's again. She wanted to beg Erick's forgiveness, but then that instinct made her angry.

Why should she apologize? She'd been doing what she had to do, like any other warrior there.

Why, then, did she feel so dirty?

She'd never once felt this way in all her years as a sex pet. This must've been the misery most of the sex slaves experienced. She'd seen it in the dead of their eyes. Their extreme distaste for what they had to do.

She'd never understood it.

Because she hadn't had her own desire awakened. Hadn't known what it meant to give her body of her own free will, to give and receive with a partner of her own choosing.

Now that she knew, it changed everything. And she hated how soiled she felt.

⁓·⁓

"Talk to me, Mina. Can you speak, now? Tell me you're all right." Erick didn't like the way Mina had receded before his eyes, as if her life force had drained. But her physical body looked better. Her color had returned. She could blink her eyes and turn her head.

Turn her head away from him.

Why wouldn't she look at him?

"Mina..." He tried to hold in the question raging at the forefront of his mind, but he couldn't. "What did he do to you?"

Mina's lips curled in disgust, and she rolled to her side, away from him. "Nothing."

"Mina—"

"It's *Tara*," she corrected.

And then he understood.

Veck it all. Something in there had caused Mina to feel degraded. Shamed. It brought back the life she wanted to forget.

He wanted to beat his head against the ship wall. To go back to Neo's and kill the bastard all over again. He'd let him die too easily. He should have caused some suffering first.

He laid a hand on her shoulder, but she shrugged him off. The rejection stung more than he would've thought possible. Of all the worst-case scenarios that had trampled his mind as he'd raced through Neo's following Mina's tracker on his armcuff and praying she hadn't been hurt or defiled, he'd never imagined this consequence.

Her rejection of him.

But he deserved it. He'd never treated her like anything but a sex object. He'd agreed to this ill-conceived mission, which had been necessary to solve his own shortcomings in business dealings.

He'd not only relished the sex pet in Mina, he'd put it to use. Offered her to another male.

The thought sickened him.

Yes, she'd thought she wanted this, it had energized her to be a part of an exciting and dangerous mission. And he'd accepted that as enough to justify the plan.

But he should have considered every angle. Should have known this might happen. Wasn't it his duty to protect Mina? She was his female.

Or he wanted her to be, anyway.

Now, he may have lost that chance.

Veck it all, this was bad.

"I'll...uh...just give you some space. Do you want anything? Any other being?"

She shook her head, still staring at the wall in front of her.

Damn.

He would've rather died back there than have this outcome.

CHAPTER NINE

Mina couldn't muster even a smile during the back-slapping and congratulations that went on back at the training pod. The mission should be considered a success. All three galactacarriers had been restored, and apart from minor injuries, no one had been hurt.

The teams tried to make her the hero, but she refused.

A hero doesn't get on her knees to service the criminal. She doesn't let herself get dragged naked to his chamber to be kept as his pet. She sure as *veck* doesn't need to be rescued and carried out lifeless by another male.

Another male who seemed to be suffering as much as she now.

He must be battling his own demons now. He'd never wanted to let her go in. Never wanted her to use her body as bait. He'd made it plain to her how much it cost him. But she'd insisted. And then he had to listen to her offer herself to another male.

A disgusting rodent of a male.

But as much as she cared about Erick and wished she could ease his turmoil, she couldn't. She couldn't see her way out of her own.

And the only answer she could see— the best one she knew—was to leave Mina behind.

She needed to get back to the palatial pod and figure out a life as Tara. Get to know her sister and father. Be without a male for a while until she knew her head from her ass.

Because she couldn't sort through her tangled emotions around sex and slavery and the things she'd done.

It wasn't Erick's fault.

But she couldn't be with him. Not now, anyway. Not until she knew who she was—away from her life as Mina.

. . .

Escorting Mina back to the palatial pod should have been an honor. At least she'd asked him. They were the first words she'd spoken to him since they returned from the mission.

But knowing she was returning in defeat, knowing she was resolved to permanently turn away from her life as Mina left him cold.

It meant he'd be shut out, too. Because he loved Mina.

Wait—that wasn't true. He loved Taramina. All the parts of her. He didn't see the distinction between the two. But she did.

She did, and that was all that mattered. He couldn't make her accept herself or her past. Only she could do that. And he couldn't convince her to keep him in her life if she'd decided to shut off an entire piece of herself. The piece with him in it.

The flight to the pod was silent, in the worst possible way.

The air hung thick and heavy between them. He wanted to give her space —knew she wouldn't want him to harangue her about her choice. Yet, he also felt the apology from her. The extra politeness. The sad pursing of her lips when she looked at him.

But, *veck* that. He didn't want her apology. He wanted her.

He just had to figure out how to get through to her.

And it wasn't through sex.

They needed some other connection. But as much as he tried to come up with something, he fell flat.

He didn't even know her Tara side.

Hell, she didn't even know her Tara side.

So, he'd have to help her figure it out. What would a bright, ambitious female find interesting on the palatial pod?

It wasn't caring for infants or plants. She wasn't wired the same as Bayla or Lamira.

Maybe he could find her a job in research and strategy for the big strike to take Zandia back.

His mind was working so hard on a solution, he failed to notice the same ship had stayed behind them at the same distance for quite some time.

Veck. How long had it been there? Had it registered the training pod?

He flicked on communications to the training pod.

"Rok, this is Erick speaking. I have a tail. I don't know how long it's been on me, but I suggest relocation of *Freedom*."

"Copy that. Can you lose it?"

"Yes, and I will, although there's no point. The palatial pod coordinates are well known. But this isn't the first time I've been followed. There must be a tracker on my ship."

Part of him hoped Mina would show interest. He could put her on the task of finding the tracker, give her a sense of purpose. But she just sat there like the carved statues that used to adorn the palace in the capital of Zandia.

"Get rid of it. We'll update the prince with the new coordinates."

He ended the communication and for the sheer sake of outflying his followers, he put the ship into turbo mode and zipped around Ocretion airspace several times before landing on the palatial pod. He would have the ship thoroughly searched for a tracking device, but he knew what it meant—war with the Finn loomed bright and close. And, if they were smart, they would strike first, now that they had the galactacarriers.

As uncomfortable as the flight had been, he didn't want it to end. He knew, instinctively, that the moment Mina walked off his ship, their relations would be over.

"Mina—Tara—" he called to her as she zoomed toward the hatch.

She stopped but didn't look back, just hung her head.

Seeing her so defeated *vecking* slayed him.

"I'm sorry."

"You don't have anything to be sorry for," she snapped, turning and slumping her back against the hatch. She pushed her pale hair out of her face.

It took all his self-control not to crowd her, not to get up into her space, cage her against that door, press his body against hers and remind her how good—how incredibly good they were together.

"I don't want to be purged along with whatever happened back there that you don't want to think about. I want to know Tara, too. Is that possible, beautiful female?"

There was a pleading quality to her gaze, but she shook her head. "Maybe... I don't know." Her shoulders slumped. "I don't know, Erick. But I don't think so." She turned back to the hatch and hit the button to activate the doors.

He waited until she'd left before he punched the wall, denting the metal with the force of his frustration.

He needed to let her go. She couldn't have been clearer. After all the times he'd failed to respect her boundaries, this time, he had to do the honorable thing.

Even if it killed him.

⁓⋅⁓

Mina hated herself for hurting Erick.

And she hated everyone in the damn palatial pod. She hated the adorable babies and the laughing children. She hated the doting servants and every male who went out of his way to talk to her or flirt.

She hated her sister for being happily wrapped into Tomis. No, that wasn't true. She was thrilled for Talia, even though she had baby fever and had started talking about her fertility and annual cycle.

Mina lay curled up in her sister's room on her hoverdisk, watching her try on clothing from the shipment of goods the servants had ordered for the two of them.

"Aren't you going to try anything on?" Talia asked, looking at herself critically in the mirror.

"I'll look through whatever you don't want."

"Daneth says we still have a few more weeks of breeding season and my chances are excellent. Even if I don't conceive this cycle, he can force a second season in a few lunar cycles, and I can try again."

"That's great."

Talia looked over and narrowed her eyes. "What's on your mind, Tara?"

"Nothing," she answered, too quickly.

Talia dropped the gown she'd been holding and climbed up on the hoverdisk. "You're lying. I know we don't know each other that well, and we're still getting reacquainted, but I know something happened while you were on the training pod, and you've been moping ever since. Was it something with Erick?"

Her face flushed, but she looked away. "No."

It wasn't. Not really. Except that was the part that bothered her the most. She'd thought cutting Erick out of her life would help her find her way onto a different path, but instead she just felt like a hole had been blown right through the center of her body. A giant gap remained, and it was a wonder she was still able to walk and talk. To breathe and eat.

"What did he do? Did he get too dominant? I can't tell if Zandian males are always so aggressive or if it's just breeding season. Or if it's the fact that they haven't seen a female in so long."

Her heart had picked up speed, despite her resistance to the topic. "Is Tomis dominant?"

Talia snorted. "Mmm hmm. Especially when it comes to protecting me." She mimicked his deep voice, "*I'm your master. When I give you an order, you obey.*"

Mina giggled. "And what happens if you don't?" She shouldn't ask that question. She really shouldn't. Except she really wanted to know.

"He punishes me." Talia waggled her eyebrows. "And he's damn good at it."

No, she didn't want to know. This was her sister, after all. Oh hell. Weren't sisters supposed to share about their sex lives?

"Erick's dominant, too," she admitted, then immediately wanted to cram the words back into her mouth.

Talia waited for her to say something else.

"I like it. A lot. But I'm having a hard time reconciling it all with what I did before."

"You weren't a house slave, were you?"

"You know I wasn't."

Talia slipped a hand over hers. "I'm sorry. That's one thing I was spared."

Tears burned her eyes, but she didn't want them. How had she gone from having no shame while she was a pet, to being crippled by it? Was it Erick who brought on the shame?

She'd associated it with him.

But it wasn't.

He'd never judged her. He'd been the one who had noticed she didn't feel comfortable here on this pod. Had tried to help her find a place on *Zandian Freedom*.

How had she forgotten that?

"Erick...Erick found me in an intergalactic brothel. He planned to get me out, but I ended up stealing his Zandian crystal and using it to bust out on my own." She smiled, a bit of her former courage, the sense of power she'd had returning.

Talia laughed. "That must've been hard for his male ego."

"A bit, but he took it like a champion." She turned and sat cross-legged, facing her sister. "Here's my situation. I like him—a lot. He definitely likes me. But..." She couldn't finish, because it sounded too lame to say out loud. *But he reminds me too much of the place I met him?* That wasn't even true. She'd been empowered, even as a slave back at Prium's and Dorhock's. It wasn't until she came to the palatial pod that she lost her strength. It was fear of her father's judgement. Or her sister's. Or other beings on the pod.

"But what?" Talia prompted.

"I don't even know. Actually, I think I just figured it out." She scrambled off the bed.

"Good. Figured what out?"

"Erick accepts who I was and what I've been. But I guess I didn't. Or I didn't believe anyone here would. So I tried to push him away. I know. It doesn't make any sense." She walked to the door but stopped when some being tapped on it.

Bayla's holograph projected into the room. "Is Tara in there? Your father is trying to kill her mate in the Great Hall. Come quickly!"

Her heart jammed up into her mouth. "What?" She hit the panel to open the door and flew out, followed by Talia and Bayla at a run.

In the Great Hall, she found her father crouched over Erick, pounding his fist into Erick's face.

"Stop!" she screamed, launching herself at her father. "Get away from him." She wedged her body between theirs and draped her torso across Erick's.

Leora shot forward from where she'd been shouting on the sidelines and caught her father's arm, pulling him back.

"Why weren't you fighting back? What in the hell is going on?"

When Erick just panted and looked at her with pained eyes, she understood. He thought he deserved this. Someone had told her father something—either what she'd done at Neo's or what had happened at Prium's, and he was exacting his own form of punishment.

She stood up and put her hands on her hips. "What do you think you're doing here?" she demanded.

Her father's jaw muscles twitched. "He forced himself on you. In a *vecking* brothel."

She didn't think, just swung her own fist and landed it squarely on her father's jaw. She knew he could've ducked. He was the Master at Arms, after all, but he let it fall. Maybe he was too stunned to believe his own daughter would punch him.

She advanced on him, swinging again. This time, he ducked. She jabbed a finger in the center of his chest. "You don't get to exact retribution on my behalf. You don't get to decide what's wrong or right about my sex life."

He flinched. She felt a ripple of shock go through the room, which had filled with a hushed audience.

"I am a grown female. I have a past, not so different from many of the females on this pod. I don't have to be made ashamed of it by my father or any other being who believes I was dishonored. I won my own freedom, and I make my own decisions, now."

She stopped and served a hard look to every being in the pod. "I'm a warrior, same as you. If I choose to use my body as a weapon for the Zandian cause, I'll do it, and I won't be made to feel ashamed for it. Not by any being." She looked over at Erick, who had climbed to his feet. "Including myself."

He opened his arms, his expression soft.

She ran into them, pressed her face against his solid chest, and let him squeeze the breath right out of her.

"Tara," her father began, rubbing his forehead.

"It's Mina. I go by Mina, now."

"Mina," he said softly, a touch of sadness in his tone. "That's nice. Mina, I'm sorry if it seemed I was judging... your experience. If you don't have a problem with it, neither do I."

Relief came so swift and hard, she burst into tears.

Her father's face flashed alarm, but Erick sifted his fingers into her hair and murmured endearments. "It's all right, pet. No one judges you. You can be anything you want to be here."

"I want to be yours," she choked, shocking herself.

"Good, because I was planning to do everything in my power to convince you to give me another chance."

"It's yours."

"Say, *I'm yours*."

She laughed through her tears. "I'm yours...I think. Let's try it out."

Erick's brows dipped. "I'm aiming for more than *trying it out*, Taramina. But I'll take that for a start."

~.~

Erick hooked his forearm under Mina's ass and hauled her legs around his waist. She looped her arms around his neck and let him carry her from the Great Hall and their spectators.

"You're a mess," she murmured, gazing down at his bloodied face.

"I'll clean up in the washtube."

"You might need a visit to the crystal baths, too."

He nipped at her breast. "All I need is you, beautiful."

"Talia said Tomis punishes her."

The suggestive lilt to her voice made him chuckle. His pet was angling for his dominance. "I'll bet she isn't nearly as naughty as you, pet. Does she get her ass *vecked* after her spankings?"

Talia squeezed her thighs together around his waist, squirming.

"Don't think I won't make you pay dearly for walking away from me. Especially after I finally completed a heroic rescue of you."

She laughed.

"I know you prefer to rescue yourself. I would've preferred it, too, sweet female."

He entered his chamber and walked straight to the washtube, bringing them both in without removing any clothing.

"Wait!" The water spray started. Mina giggled. "You're crazy!"

He ripped her loose blouse from her body and slapped a breast. "Crazy for you, pet. Too crazy to wait to get you naked."

"That doesn't even make...oh!" He yanked her leggings down and nipped her inner thigh. "Sense." He kissed and nipped up her inner thigh, but the water level had risen too fast, and it covered his head. He stood, lifting his head out of the depths of water and laughing.

She tugged at his clothing. "Not fair."

"Oh, it's never fair between you and I. Remember? I'm the master, and you're the pet. I'm the male who smacks your ass and makes you scream. The one who gives it to you exactly the way you like to get it. Right, pet?"

"Y-yes, Master." Her eyes glazed over with lust.

He claimed her mouth just before the water level covered their heads, and he kissed her right through the submersion. He was still kissing her when the water began to drain. He whirled her to face the wall. "Brace yourself, beautiful. And stick that ass out for me." He quickly shucked his clothes as she moved into the position he described.

There wasn't much room in the washtube, but he managed a few slaps of her ass before he lined his cock up with her pussy's sweet entrance and pushed in.

"Oh stars, pet. It's better every time. I will never sink into your wet heat without believing it's the only thing keeping me alive."

She giggled. "I don't think my pussy is *that* special."

"Oh it is, beautiful. Believe it." He withdrew and thrust into her again, sending her up to her toes with the force.

"Is this my punishment?" she asked, voice husky.

"No, pet. This is just me letting off some steam." He wrapped his fist in her hair and pulled her head back as he shoved his cock in deep again. "By the time this night is through, I promise every inch of your body will have been punished... and rewarded." Another hard shove. "And this is just round one with your sweet pussy. I plan to pound you so hard, you won't walk straight tomorrow, and I'll have to spend the entire day kissing it better."

Mina's knees buckled.

He caught her around the waist, stabilizing her hips for his thrusts. In and out he pistoned, eyes rolling back in his head with the pleasure of it all.

"F-fuck me, Master," she gasped, reverting to the Ocretion word for sex.

He loved it. Somehow it sounded more crude, invoking memories of the brothel where he'd first claimed her.

"I'll fuck you," he growled. "I'll fuck you long and hard and teach you that there's no way you can live without me."

"I can't," she agreed. "I can't live without you."

His heart exploded with satisfaction. Three more strokes and he came, his shout echoing in the washtube. The shower was on the oil cycle, spraying their bodies with a fine mist of aromatic oil, and he used it to slide his fingers down her belly and rub the sensitive bundle of nerves at the apex of her sweet pussy.

She went off, clawing the wall of the washtub, screaming, "Yes, yes, yes, yes, *yes!*"

"Yes, you'll be my mate?" he challenged her, slapping his loins against her ass with another hard thrust.

"Yes," she moaned.

"Yes, you'll let me pierce you?"

"*Yes.*"

Now his own knees almost buckled, but with relief. He dropped his mouth to her neck and kissed and sucked his way to her shoulder. "That's good, pet," he purred. "I promise I'll figure out everything in the universe that puts light into your eyes and deliver it to your feet."

"Erick." Her voice sounded choked, so he pulled out and whirled her around. Her arms shot around his neck as she blinked back tears. "I know you will," she whispered. "That's why I love you."

He leaned his forehead against hers, not kissing her, just breathing her breath. "I love you so much, Taramina, daughter of Seke."

EPILOGUE

Pal squared his shoulders and rechecked his weapons as they disembarked the spacecraft. They hadn't been followed on this trip—both he and Erick had been watchful. He walked behind Erick and his mate, where he could keep an eye on the two of them and any potential threat.

Prince Zander himself had commanded Pal accompany Erick as his royal guard on the emissarial trip to the planet Jujo. Erick usually operated solo, but since he was taking his new mate along, he required protection.

If they'd asked Pal—which they hadn't—he would've suggested they leave Tara on the palatial pod, where she could be protected. Especially after what happened on their last mission.

But apparently there was nothing Erick would deny his mate, and she wanted to be a part of the political machination.

For his part, he was honored to have been chosen. Although flying with them was as awkward as the last mission, when he had to avoid looking at Tara, and the human, Lily, who'd been naked except for collars around their necks.

Being in a small space with a Zandian female during breeding season—one who didn't belong to him—frayed his control. At least, here at the Emperor of Jujo's palace, he'd be able to breathe without getting a hard-on.

Or maybe he wouldn't.

As they entered through a downpour of lights in every color, a show designed to make it seem like the colors rained down on the guests, they passed through an atrium filled with glass cages. Each one contained a scantily clad female, moving her body in time with a rhythmic pulse.

Veck. He adjusted his cock.

He wondered how Tara felt about the show, considering she'd been used this way—illegally—by an Aurelian collector and later a pimp. Her attention seemed to be drawn to a human female—the most beautiful he'd ever seen.

She had long, thick black hair and caramel-colored skin. She wore a pair of black boots up to her thighs and a matching collar, with nothing in between. Her hair had been twisted into two knots on the side of her head, and two long tails tumbled from the knots. Giant dark eyes, framed with ridiculously long lashes, took in everything around her as she swayed seductively to the music.

The human's movements hitched when she saw his party, and while he'd love to say it was from his sheer masculine magnetism, the female had eyes only for Tara. Her lush mouth spread into an ample smile, punctuated by deep dimples. She slowly lowered to a wide-kneed squat, undulating her hips in the most distracting fashion.

He cleared his throat, trying to get a handle on his raging libido.

All too soon, they'd glided past the enchanting creature, but when they reached the ballroom, Tara stopped and touched his arm.

"The mission has changed, Pal."

He arched his brows. "It has?"

"Yes. Erick and I can protect ourselves. Your job is to extract Leti, that human female, and bring her to our ship without the Jujo knowing we were behind it. Can you do that?"

His sense of honor warred with desire. Zander had ordered him to protect Tara, not steal a human slave.

A very *female* human slave with the nicest pair of breasts he'd ever seen. *Lickable* breasts.

Erick was capable of protecting his mate, wasn't he?

And it wouldn't take him long to devise a plan to free the human. He just needed to make sure no one knew the Zandians were responsible.

He bowed. "As you wish, Lady Tara. Extracting the human will be my pleasure."

HIS HUMAN POSSESSION

CHAPTER ONE

Leti advanced from her slow undulations in the glass cage to put on even more of a show for the emperor's guests streaming in under a shower of colored lights. She swayed her bare ass, strutting around in her thigh high black boots, which were the only thing she wore, unless you counted the matching black collar and inch-long fake lashes.

Standard petwear in Jujo.

She didn't pay attention *at all* to the purple, horned giant of a warrior circling silently around behind the entertainment cages.

He's coming for me.

Her friend Mina had sent him. Mina had entered the palace with two warriors of her kind—lavender skinned and packed with muscle. Leti couldn't remember the name of their species. Had Mina ever told her? Had her friend even known? Mina had believed—because Dorhock told her—she was the only one left in the galaxy. He used to glory in owning a female of an extinct species. Said it made her worth a fortune, if he ever decided to sell. Too bad for him, he'd choked on a piece of fruit before he could sell any of his prized pets. She and Mina had been auctioned off for next to nothing with the rest of his assets.

To provide the purple warrior with cover and to keep from showing the kick of fear and excitement rushing through her, Leti pressed her bare breasts against the glass and coasted down, then turned and gave an ass-jiggle fast enough to set the floor on fire. Only months of experience dancing in the ill-fitting high-heeled boots kept her from falling on her ass.

The male had disappeared from her vision. He *was* coming for her, wasn't he? No, she knew he was. He had to be. Mina's appearance was the first good thing that had happened since she arrived in the Jujo hellhole.

Tzatzu, the emperor of Jujo, treated his pets far worse than Dorhock did. He punished Leti harshly and only fed her when he deemed her performance good enough. She was given to a different guest every night. Sometimes more than one.

It was business to Tzatzu. He wasn't actually attracted to the female slaves he kept. She wasn't sure any of the Jujo were, which meant her one weapon—the only weapon a human female in captivity possessed—didn't work there.

She couldn't sex them up.

But now she had a way out. And the purple warrior, he'd be a different story. She saw the way he adjusted himself when he watched her dance. Well trained and restrained, his face had shown nothing, but his cock couldn't lie.

The main lights went off and a burst of smoke exploded in front of her cell. The colored pin lights still glittered around the room, illuminating the plumes of gray in an eerie dance.

This was it! She whirled and rushed for the door to her cage. The electric barrier buzzed and disappeared and she launched herself out, only to slam into the huge warrior as he came in. Her breasts hit his chest at the same time his hands clamped around her upper arms like iron shackles.

Even though she'd fully expected the male, her breath caught in her throat and died at the sheer size and power of him.

The scent.

Spicy and masculine, with a tinge of smoke and flint.

In a single smooth motion, he picked her up, turned and dropped her a few feet to the ground below, jumping down after her. She waited for him, but he caught her upper arm once more, as if afraid she might run away. No, actually, it was to haul her along, because, *damn*, he ran fast.

They streaked out through a back entrance she hadn't known existed, staying close to the domed wall. The warrior slapped a small air mask over her face and yanked her back against his solid form, head cocked like he was listening. She willed her racing heart to slow, shoved back the dread of being caught. It would mean her death.

And the warrior stealing her hadn't said a word. Was she right to trust him blindly? Just because he'd come in with Mina?

A dozen guests of some tiny species tromped by while they waited in the shadow.

She took shallow breaths into the mask, not sure if it contained poisoned gas or oxygen. It smelled clean, but the fact that the warrior didn't use one put her on edge. No, Mina sent him. She'd already made her choice—all she could do now was trust.

Even if Mina was now a slave to one of her own species, Leti would rather be enslaved with a friend than in the Jujo shithole. But her friend hadn't appeared subjugated. She'd been dressed like a princess in regal finery and she seemed...*damn happy.*

The warrior's cock twitched against her lower back, reminding her that her earlier assessment had been correct. This male was one she could influence. He appreciated her human form. And she knew how to service his malehood. At least she did if it was similar to the shafts of other various species she'd sucked over the years.

"Good girl. Thank you for staying quiet," he murmured in her ear and blood rushed to the apex of her legs.

Apparently she, too, could be influenced by sex. That was new. Was it his deep velvety voice? Or was it his impressive size and stature?

She'd have to be careful with this one. She'd lose her game if she grew greedy for his affection. She'd seen it happen time and time again with Dorhock's pets. It never ended well. That's why she had a personal rule to never get emotionally attached. It just provided one more way she could get hurt.

He borrowed her face mask and took a pull of oxygen, then replaced it and gripped her arm again, propelling her forward until they ducked into the rear entrance of a hangar.

Inside, scores of airships were docked side by side. He angled her body behind his, walking swiftly to one. Despite his huge size, his boots moved silently on the stone floor.

The sound of a communication transmission nearby caused him to pull up short, again, shielding her body with his.

"All unstationed guards to the atrium," a voice clipped.

Her disappearance had been discovered.

"Yes, Captain," the guard who could only be a few paces away from them, just around the corner, answered.

The warrior held her still until they heard the door grind closed, then he hustled her up the ramp onto a gleaming new ship. He spoke into his comms unit. "The female has been safely extracted to the ship."

"Nice work," answered another deep male voice. "Stay with her there. We can handle things in here."

"Copy that." He ended the transmission and turned to her. His gaze skittered to her bare breasts, then lower to her bare sex, lasered free of hair.

She made a show of perusing his body like he studied hers, letting her gaze land on the enormous bulge in his pants.

He scowled as if he hated what he saw, but she had enough experience to know the look. He thought he couldn't have her. He'd done his duty rescuing her and now he thought he was stuck standing guard with a boner hard enough to crack marble.

Tend and befriend. That was her second rule of survival as a slave. Reward the male who saved her, keep his interest as long as she needed his protection.

She turned on all her weapons. She snaked her arms around his neck, rubbing her breasts against his broad chest as she swayed her hips in a slow dance.

His body went rigid, horns stiffened. "What are you doing?" he choked. His cock lurched against her belly, hard and impressive in size.

She kept up her swaying, brought her lips to the patch of skin above his collar. "Thank you," she breathed. "For saving me."

She wasn't above playing every weak submissive female card she had.

"Get off me," he ground out through clenched teeth.

Something about his irritation made her all the more determined to seduce him. She stood on her tiptoes and nipped his ear.

"*Stop*, female," he growled. Reaching behind his neck, he grabbed one of her wrists, disentangling it from his nape. In two seconds flat, he slapped a pair of prison cuffs on her wrists and had them magnetized to the wall in front of her.

His huge hand clapped down on her ass.

The stinging blow went straight to her core. Her pussy clenched, excitement zinging down her inner thighs. She'd jumped on impact, but put herself back in position for him.

More, please.

This played perfectly into her game. The act of punishing could be erotic for a male. It wasn't that she wanted him to continue because of her own arousal.

At all.

No, creating any kind of bond with her master was the key to an easier existence as a slave. Sometimes even to survival.

It seemed to work. His hand cracked down again and again, the loud slaps echoing off the metal walls of the ship, his harsh breaths betraying the effect it had on him.

She tried to ignore the effect it had on *her*, but every smack sent a fresh sizzle of excitement through her body. She twitched her thighs together to alleviate the throb in her clit.

He stopped and roughly squeezed one of her buttcheeks with an audible inhale. "You're aroused." He sounded surprised. "So it's true that human females enjoy pain?"

She struggled to catch her breath. "Some."

~.~

Some. Paal fought back the blinding need to *veck* the little human until she screamed. That's what she wanted. She'd been trying to play him, rubbing those taut nipples all across his uniform. What was her game?

Still, he couldn't resist sliding his fingers between her legs to feel the arousal he'd scented from her. Glorious nectar dripped from her swollen folds. His pulse kicked up three notches.

She jerked but held still for his touch, same as she had when he'd spanked her. Inhaling in deep, measured breaths, she leaned her forehead against the cool metal surface.

Stars, she was beautiful. He couldn't deny what her surrender did to him, even as part of him rebelled at falling into her trap. Whatever that trap may be. He didn't like a female who used her wiles to ensnare a man. Females like his mother.

"Some females or some pain?" He barely recognized his voice.

"Yes." Her husky laugh went straight to his already hard cock. "Both."

Because touching her dripping pussy drove him wild, he pulled away and slapped her ass again.

Holy Zandian star, he had no idea spanking a female could be so satisfying. *Damn.*

He slapped again. Each crack of flesh on flesh, every sharp intake of breath she gave made him dizzy with lust. The bloom of his red prints on her caramel skin gleamed, attesting his ownership.

Veck if he didn't want a slave of his own. Too bad their ruler, Prince Zander, didn't allow the keeping of slaves since he'd mated and freed his human female.

"Why don't you put me on my knees, Master?" Her voice dripped sex woven into temptation. "I'll show you my thanks."

He grasped one of her pigtails and growled, "I'm not your master."

Un-vecking-fortunately.

Despite his assertion, he demagnetized the handcuffs from the wall and refastened them behind her back. Then, he backed himself into a nearby flight chair and pushed Leti to her knees before him. Because, hell, she *had* offered, hadn't she? And even though a smarter warrior would lock her in one of the ship's cabins to remove all temptation, he was just dying to know how that lush mouth would feel around his thickened cock.

And—*oh, stars*—the female knew exactly what she was doing! She had been perfectly trained, because she sat back on her booted heels and parted her thighs to give him the full view of her dewy sex right before she leaned forward and opened her generous mouth.

Her plump lips closed around the head of his cock and his eyes rolled back in his head.

Need.

Want.

She took him deeper, her tongue stroking the underside of his rock hard member.

Veck, yes!

He grabbed the two buns on the sides of her hair, the ones that held her pigtails in place, and yanked her forward, over the full length of his shaft.

He hit the back of her throat. The incredible female's eyes widened, but she didn't even choke. She swallowed him down, all the way, until her glossy lips hit the base.

Veck. Yes.

"Leti," he choked. "Is that your name?"

She lifted her tawny brown eyes to his, the long fake lashes a ridiculous frame to such exquisite natural beauty. She pulled off his cock and licked her lips. "Leticia, yes. Leti for short." As soon as she finished answering him, she engulfed his cock with her delicious wet heat again.

What in the hell was he doing? He'd been sent by Prince Zander to protect his species' most precious resource—a Zandian female of child-bearing age—and here he was in his ship getting his cock sucked by a human slave.

A *vecking* beautiful, talented, *dangerous* human slave.

Dangerous because she was up to something, for sure. And the gleam in her eye told him she understood exactly how much power she wielded in that talented, perfect, cock-sucking mouth of hers.

The need to take all control from her, to dominate her completely, rushed through him like a powerful drug.

He caught her by the throat and pushed her back, off his cock. He spun her around and lifted her bare ass and sex in the air.

This. Yes.

The heady rush heightened at the sight of her pinkened ass. He needed more of that.

He spanked her, hard and steady. The position wasn't good, so he shifted to straddle her, facing away, so he could bend over and slap her rounded globes. He knew he was spanking hard, and stars, the girl really hadn't done a thing to deserve it, but he couldn't help himself. It felt so *vecking* good.

She started to emit tiny whimpers and her bottom clenched, as if to avoid the pain.

"*Veck*, I like spanking you, female." He hadn't meant to admit it out loud, but she probably deserved the explanation.

He liked it so much, he imagined whipping her with a strap of leather. What stripes would it leave? How would it sound? Would she cry? What if he slapped that leather strap right between her legs?

Oh *stars*. His head swam.

He spanked her pussy with his hand, lightening the intensity of his swing.

She screamed.

Veck yes.

He spanked her there again. And again.

"Hurts, Master," she whimpered.

His balls tightened. He returned to her plump cheeks, spanking harder. If she kept calling him *Master* in that pained little voice of hers, he'd come all over her ass.

But her skin turned a hot shade of red under his palm, and his conscience nipped at him.

"I'm sorry, little slave," he murmured, rubbing her ass swiftly. "I spanked you hard, didn't I? Want me to *veck* it better?"

For one second she didn't answer, and he had to deal with the careening guilt and disappointment. Because he wouldn't force himself on her if she didn't want it. She may be a slave, but she wasn't *his* slave.

But then she let out a held breath. "Yes."

Thank veck.

He got on his knees behind her and shoved his flight pants down to further free his throbbing malehood. He already knew how wet she was, so he entered her without preparation.

He let out a growl of pleasure at sinking into her wet heat. "I'm warning you, human, I'm going to *veck* hard."

There was no holding back. The need to claim her, to own her, to *vecking ruin* her barreled through him like a ship going warp speed.

He pistoned in and out. "Naughty human for tempting me." He plowed in deep, smacking her hot ass with his loins with each in-stroke. "Naughty slave for trying to seduce me. Why would you do that?"

She didn't answer, not that he expected her to. How could she when he used her so ruthlessly? On and on he *vecked* her, gripping her hips to hold her immobile for his high velocity thrusts.

"Naughty, naughty little female for making me want to come all over your pretty face." He reached around and cupped one of her breasts, squeezing tight. "All over these perfect breasts."

In and out he jacked, all rational thought gone, replaced only by the need to turn the little female inside out.

He wanted it to go on forever.

Couldn't take another second.

She was too hot. Too tight. Too juicy. Too *vecking* pliant.

His roar echoed off the ship walls as he plowed deep and stayed there, filling her with his Zandian seed.

As a sex slave, she'd be modified not to conceive.

That idea shouldn't piss him off, but it did.

He didn't want to ever pull out, so he gathered Leti up onto her knees, her back against his chest, his hand caged around her throat.

"Human, you just short-circuited my mind," he growled in her ear, inching back and then tapping her sweet ass again. "I wish I could *veck* you all night long."

She trembled, perspiration dripping down her back, her breath making her rounded breasts bob.

He stroked his thumb along her frantic pulse. "Are you all right, little female?"

When she didn't answer, he pulled out. "Release cuffs," he voice commanded the handcuffs, and they dropped to her calves. He moved swiftly, picking her up by the waist and backing into the chair.

He settled her on his lap, his lips finding her shoulder. He knew next to nothing about females, even less about human females. He'd never even *vecked* before, but it had been a meteoric first attempt. And what he'd seen in the old Zandian holograms looked nothing like what he'd just done. No, they'd shared something far more bestial and raw. Something other species do.

He stroked Leti's back. "I was too rough. Forgive me, beautiful."

"I'm fine," she said, but her voice shook and she attempted to stand up from his lap.

No. *No, no, no, no.* He held her fast. He didn't like that one bit. Was she running from him? He hoped to the one true Zandian star he hadn't traumatized the beautiful creature. He hadn't meant to be so cruel but hurting her had made him delirious with lust.

Which might mean something terrible about him.

Or it might just be how sex felt. Hadn't she admitted some human females find pain sexual?

"Look at me." He didn't even know this side of himself. This male who suddenly had to soothe. Was it not enough to possess the little human female's body? Now he wanted her soul, too?

When she looked, he quirked a sympathetic brow. "More than you bargained for?"

The proud little thing kicked up her chin. "Of course not."

He couldn't stop the smile tugging at his lips. Her inner steel made him want to go a second round with her. What would it take to break the beautiful creature?

No, he didn't want to break her.

Yes, I do.

Veck. He really did.

———

It wasn't the pain that had her reeling. Yes, her ass burned, but that would pass in an hour or two. It was the effect the horned alien had on her.

Every time she thought she was getting somewhere with him, he'd flip the game. She'd found herself incapable of "pleasing" him other than surrendering to his rough desires. Rough desires that awakened an incredible fire within her. And left her without any form of defense.

Like an empty hull.

Who in the hell was she, if not the over-sexualized pet who worked every angle to keep her feet dry? Though the warrior hadn't threatened her with anything worse than his hand on her ass—and he'd already apologized for *that*, she'd never felt so vulnerable. So unprotected.

He held an arm around her waist like a tight band until she stopped struggling. When she wouldn't look at him, he pinched her chin between his thick digits and turned her. His purple-brown eyes searched hers, forehead wrinkled up in sexy confusion.

She forced her armor back in place and put a purr in her voice to keep it from wobbling. "You know my name, warrior, but I don't know yours. Unless you wanted me to call you *Master*."

She hadn't missed his excitement every time she called him that. This male loved the idea of having his very own female to punish and fuck.

The thing was, she'd been used by every sort of male, of at least a dozen species. Some had been rough. Some had hurt her.

But no experience compared to what she'd felt with this male.

She *wanted* him to hurt her as much as he'd seemed to want to inflict pain. She'd craved his every slap, every thrust, even though the intensity behind them was too much. No, not too much. Exactly right.

She loved the brutality behind the warrior's dark interest. Maybe because she felt he, too, lost control. Not to her, but to his own dark desires to possess her.

Something snapped behind his eyes. Irritation. He disliked when she flirted with him. Even though his attraction to her was undeniable. "I've changed my mind," he said cooly, pushing her off his lap. "You will call me *Master*."

She tried to ignore the staggering disappointment at being released, despite the fact that only a moment before she'd been trying to escape his touch and scrutiny.

A comms unit near his collar crackled. "Trouble in the ballroom. We're exiting through the back. Do you copy, Paal?"

She tensed. Did that mean Mina was in trouble?

"Copy that. Preparing for takeoff," her warrior answered.

Paal. So that was his name. Strong and sturdy like him.

She watched in fascination as he sprang into motion. He clapped the handcuffs back on her wrists and pinned her once more to a nearby wall before he took the helm of the ship and started the engines. The doors swished open and Mina and the other purple warrior rushed in.

Thank the sweet mother Earth.

"Take off," the other warrior barked at Paal. "I will report to the prince." He disappeared into a separate room.

Mina cocked her head at Leti, her glance sweeping over her position and resting on her ass, which must be painted bright red. "Looks like things didn't go so well for you, showcat."

A laugh burst from her lips at the old nickname, even as tears speared her eyes. Mina had been the only other pet at Dorhock's she'd liked. The only one with half a brain and the same instincts for survival as Leti. They'd used humor and sarcasm to make their situation bearable, and relied on each other for safety and the small comforts.

"Buckle up for takeoff, Lady Tara," Paal barked.

Mina ignored him and rushed over and reached for the cuffs, but she couldn't budge them. "How do you release these handcuffs, Paal?" she called.

"Are you buckled? I'm taking off."

She grabbed Leti's wrist as the ship swooped into flight, throwing them both to the side. "Uh, no. I wasn't. The cuffs, Paal?"

"I'm sorry. No time to wait."

The ship swooped again and Mina knocked into her.

"Maybe let him fly for a minute," Leti muttered. "Are we being chased?" She didn't want to die just yet.

"Someone tried to assassinate us, so Erick killed him first. Then the Emperor suggested we leave before we disturbed his party any further," Mina summarized.

Leti digested that information. She'd gone from abused sex slave to escaped slave on the run with three purple-skinned beings who were wanted dead.

She decided it was still an improvement. Her life may be in more danger now, but at least her sanity would remain intact.

Unless she made the mistake of tangling with Paal again.

But more importantly, "Who's Erick?"

She swore Mina blushed. "My mate."

Genuine happiness filled her chest. Her friend had found freedom and love. Miracles really could happen for a pair of pets.

"How did you get on Paal's wrong side?" Mina asked, quirking her brows at Leti's still smarting ass.

In the cockpit, she saw Paal stiffen, clearly listening. Mina followed her gaze with a curious gleam in her eye.

"I wouldn't necessarily say I got on his *wrong* side." She weighed her words. "More that he's the sort who'd rather take—forcibly—than have it offered."

Paal's spine straightened, the back of his neck radiated tension.

Mina gave an exaggerated expression of awe. "Really? I wouldn't have guessed that of him."

Were the tips of his ears turning a darker purple?

The ship banked again sharply and she had a feeling it had more to do with Paal's irritation than any real need to fly that way.

"Paal, how do you release these cuffs?" Mina asked again.

"Release cuffs," he grumbled and the cuffs sprang open.

"You do realize humans are far more delicate than Zandians, don't you?" Mina scolded him.

Her casual treatment of the whole Paal thing helped Leti tamp her rioting emotions down.

"She experiences far more pain and won't heal as fast as a Zandian, either."

Zandian. So that's what they were called.

Still Paal did not turn around, but he answered stiffly, "She did not lacrimate."

"Lacrimate?" Leti repeated.

"He means cry." Calling to the cockpit, Mina said, "That doesn't mean you didn't hurt her. *Ohhh.* You meant *take* forcibly." She stared at the rainbow-hued jizz between Leti's legs.

That made Paal turn. When he caught the direction of Mina's gaze, he surged to his feet, his expression wooden. "I apologize, Lady Tara. She was not mine to claim or to punish." He bowed.

"Mina," her friend corrected.

"Lady Mina," he amended.

Lady Mina? Whoa. Her friend had really risen in station since finding her kind.

Mina walked to a closet and produced a white tunic, which she tossed Leti. "Don't apologize to me, apologize to *her.*"

"He already did," she mumbled. "I'm fine."

"She is your friend. I should not have..." he stopped and swallowed, probably remembering in vivid detail all the things he'd done to her. She sure as hell couldn't forget them.

She tied the tunic around her waist. It was short, only coming to her upper thighs, leaving an ample amount of flesh showing between the top of her boots and the hem. Paal glared at her legs as if she were tempting him on purpose again.

And just like that, her sense of power returned.

That's right, warrior. I have the goods that make you lose control.

"I'm thinking she will require a Zandian sponsor for the prince to grant her assylum. I guess I'd hoped for a happier partnership between you two." She shot Leti a conspiratorial glance, one Leti knew all too well.

Her friend was telling her to make nice with this male, because he could be her ticket to freedom, or at least safety.

I fucking tried.

She'd tried her best, but the male resented all her attempts. He must think she was trying to play him.

Well, she was.

"Why wouldn't you be her sponsor?" Paal cast Mina a wary look, mistrust simmering beneath his stern gaze. There was something else, though, too. He wore the awareness of a trap being sprung.

Another surge of power went through Leti.

That meant Mina's plan had worked. Because if the warrior didn't want her, he would shrug and tell her to find some other being. But, instead, conflict vibrated in the tense set of his shoulders, the firmness of his jaw.

And damn if his gaze didn't keep flicking to the apex of her bare legs as if he wanted to see where he'd just spent.

"Well, I think Prince Zander hopes to mate his warriors to every available female to ensure the continuation of the species. Especially before the war." Mina gave an innocent shrug. "Also, I'll be traveling quite a bit with Erick on official ambassadorial business."

A muscle flexed in Paal's jaw and his horns twitched, but he simply nodded stiffly and bowed.

Mina waited until his back was turned before she tossed Leti a smile. "Come on." She hooked a hand through Leti's elbow and led her toward a washroom in the rear. "You look underfed, and although you certainly look adorable with your, ahem, rainbow decoration, we should get you cleaned up and comfortable. There are clothes in the back and a washroom. Did you hate the food on Jujo?"

"The emperor made me earn it," she muttered. She couldn't resist a glance over her shoulder as she left and found Paal had also turned, a deep frown etched between his brows. Did the warrior actually care?

She smiled, winked, and snapped her pigtails as she whirled back, earning an eye roll from the purple-skinned warrior.

A flutter of something foreign winged through her chest. Excitement? Interest? Whatever it was, she'd better watch herself around Paal. The last thing she needed was emotional involvement. It violated her personal code of slave conduct. She'd learned from the tender age of six never to care for anyone or anything. And if you do, for some reason, take a shining to someone or something—never let it show.

Because if they know what you love, they know how to hurt you.

CHAPTER TWO

Zander paced the length of what had become his war room. Seke, his Master at Arms, stood against a wall, arms folded across his chest as they waited for Erick's hologram to fully appear.

It flickered and then projected into the room from the ship he'd taken on a diplomacy trip to Jujo. His incoming transmission had been marked urgent, which worried Zander.

"My lord, we were attacked," Erick said as soon as the conference began. Thank *veck* his business advisor knew how to get straight to the point.

"Taramina?" Seke barked. His concern for his daughter, Erick's mate, was immediate.

Zander kicked himself for allowing Erick to take her. She was one of only three female Zandians of childbearing age alive.

"She's fine. We all are." Again, Zander appreciated Erick's concise report.

"What happened?"

"There was a party after the banquet and during the entertainment, a being fired a laser from a balcony. I returned fire and killed the would-be assassin, a Finnian."

"How did the assassin miss?" Seke asked.

"I'd assessed all possible threats and vulnerabilities to our position when we were seated." Erick left it at that, but the rest was clear. He'd kept Taramina and himself safe. Though Erick ran all of Zander's business and financial dealings, he'd been trained as a warrior by Seke, same as all of the remaining Zandians. He would know what to do when under attack.

"The emperor insisted he didn't know how the male got on planet and swore he hadn't given permission for any attack, but I have my doubts. I informed him the time had come to choose sides. If he chose to support the

Finn, we would cut them off completely from the supply of Zandian crystal when we take back our planet.”

“And?” Zander prompted.

“He asked for time to consider his position. I gave him until the next planet rotation. I asked that his show of support come in the form of military aid.”

Seke nodded. “Good.”

Erick shrugged. “We’ll see. Any word from the other leaders?”

“We’ll brief you when you come in,” Seke cut in, before Zander could answer, reminding them both that the communication could be hacked.

“Of course.” Erick nodded.

“Anything else?” Zander asked.

“One small detail.”

“What is it?”

“We’re returning with a stolen human slave. A female pet of the emperor. Mina knew her.”

“How is that supposed to help diplomacy?” Zander snapped. He seriously didn’t have the *vecking* time or patience for this sort of excrement.

“Her disappearance should not be linked to us. Paal freed her.”

“It had better not. I don’t care what she means to Tara, one human isn’t worth jeopardizing our entire *vecking* war effort.”

“Of course not, my lord.”

He ground his teeth. “She’ll be Tara’s responsibility.”

“Yes, my lord. I’m sure Mina understands.”

Mina. Yes. He’d forgotten she preferred to be called the latter part of her name now.

“Be sure she does.”

Erick bowed and ended the transmission.

He turned to hear Seke’s assessment. “Well?”

“It’s not a good sign. We should assume they’ll back the Finn.” The grim lines around his Master at Arms’ face showed his age more than ever. “The pressure Erick applied is good, though. The trouble is that most planet leaders believe us incapable of winning this battle. And we’re even less so without their support.”

Zander’s fingers tightened into a fist. “They’ll support us after they see our firepower in the first strike. Erick can offer them one last chance to throw in with us.”

He had no other choice but to believe it. Because any other outcome meant the final extinction of his species.

———

Paal docked the ship on Zander’s palatial pod. The scent of the human female still lingered on his clothing, his hands. He wanted to get close enough to her to smell *his* scent on *her.*

Veck, it had felt good to spend between her legs. If he'd known sex with a human was this satisfying he would have sought one out a long time ago.

Except that idea didn't quite ring true. He didn't want any human female. Just this one.

This one, whom he didn't trust as far as he could throw. Who used sex as a weapon, along with her other conniving female wiles to attain a purpose.

No, he needed to avoid her tempting presence. She was trouble.

Erick strode to the door and opened it, waiting to escort his mate out.

Why couldn't there be more Zandian females like Lady Taramina available? Except he couldn't imagine treating a Zandian female the way he'd just treated Leti. Zandian males are dominant, but they don't disrespect their mates. At least not that he remembered—but he was young when he left.

Leti had taken it. He'd left her shaken, but she hadn't complained, even when she could have.

And had she actually blushed when Lady Taramina had demanded his apology?

The blush looked so pretty on her—so unlike the confident swagger she hid behind. He'd seen a glimpse of something real there.

And he'd liked it.

No, he'd *vecking* loved it.

He hung back in the ship, waiting until they'd exited. He needed to be out of the same breathing space as Leti so he could get his head on straight again.

But...excrement. The three of them stood waiting just inside the pod.

"Paal, do you wish to take charge of Leti, at least temporarily?" Lady Tara asked.

"Me? I cannot."

Leti leaned into one hip and twirled her silky dark hair around a fingertip with mock innocence. Even though she now wore a pair of leggings, her long legs jutted out from the too-short tunic, and the black boots only served to remind him how she'd looked naked. Though he willed himself not to, his mind instantly conjured the image of her kneeling at his feet, those peach-tipped nipples stiff as spikes. Why hadn't he paid more attention to her pretty little breasts?

And suddenly, he was hard as stone again, desperate for a do-over with the crafty human.

"Why not?" Lady Tara pressed.

His brain stuttered and stopped, which irritated the hell out of him. "I have nowhere to keep her, for one thing. Nor do I think it's my place to take guardianship of a female. Not unless the prince decrees it."

"I understand," Lady Tara said easily. She turned to her human friend. "Don't worry, there are plenty of warriors here. They'll be fighting over who you call *Master*." She hooked a hand through her friend's elbow and tugged her down the corridor of the palatial pod.

Master.

Instantly, the image of Leti on her knees servicing him morphed into one of her lush body being used by other males. Multiple males—at once.

Rage rose up in him, scalding his throat. His fingers closed into fists.

"Wait," he called, but his voice cut out. "Stop."

The three stopped and looked back.

He stalked forward, catching Leti's arm. "I will take her. Just until Prince Zander gives his word."

He might have celebrated his decision had he not caught a conspiratorial smile pass between Leti and Lady Tara. Then he suddenly felt the fool.

He'd just been played by the lovely female.

Again.

She wanted to trap him, ensnare him into doing her bidding.

He wouldn't have it. Dark anger bubbling, he marched her to the lift down to the guards' quarters and into his small but comfortable chamber.

"You'll stay here," he snapped, thrusting her inside but remaining in the corridor. "You may not leave without my escort. There's a washroom in the corner. I will have food sent to you."

"Where will you be?" She loosened the knot of her tunic, allowing it to fall open.

His cock surged against his pants as if he hadn't just had her in the ship. He ground his molars.

He would not allow her to make him the fool.

She opened the tunic wider, slipping it from her shoulders. Her taut nipples stood as proud and haughty as she did. They were even more perfect than he'd remembered. A little darker. More insolent.

He closed his eyes, debating whether to step inside and lay down the law. Show her exactly what would happen to females who used their bodies to tease. Except he knew how that would end—with him plowing into her every orifice. And then she would have won, wouldn't she?

Instead he stepped back, pressing his palm against the sensor outside the door to close it. Leti wouldn't be able to leave. Only the servants would be able to enter to bring her food.

Dammit.

He couldn't have servants going in her room!

What if she tried that little strip tease temptation with one of them?

Most were quite old, but they wouldn't be immune to her charms. Hadn't Prince Zander's human mate wrapped the servants around her finger while she was just a slave? Before Zander had fallen to her allure?

Veck.

No, he'd have to bring her food himself. No being would ever be allowed to see his female naked ever again.

And he *didn't vecking care* that she wasn't his female and he had no intention of keeping her or succumbing to her beauty!

He marched back upstairs to report to Master Seke.

———

Leti walked around Paal's chamber. It was spacious but simple, constructed of the finest materials, like the rest of the palatial pod she'd seen. The walls were a rich plaster with color mixed in—pale yellow and a deep teal. The shelving units were made of exotic hardwood or perhaps bone. Despite the fact that they were on a lower level of the pod, Paal had an outer room with a window and a small faceted crystal suspended in the middle of it sent prisms of bright light dancing around the room.

Hands down, the room—and the pod overall—presented the most lovely and cheerful surroundings she'd ever been in. Neither Dorhock's Aurelian home nor the Jujo palace compared.

She tried the door even though she knew it would be locked. She wished she had a bit of wire to play with. She'd learned the art as a child, when she'd been kept in a cell with twenty other girls until they were old enough for sex slavery. They were kept in a portion of the industrial factory where they'd been born and taken from their parents. They were let out once a day for exercise and all the girls would pick up little scraps of wire from the ground to bring to her.

She taught herself to weave the wires into complex, three dimensional shapes, which became toys for the children.

Well, she might suffer from boredom here, but it sure beat the factory cell. She wouldn't be uncomfortable in Paal's chamber. She pulled off the high heeled boots which were too small and had left her feet a blistered mess and sank onto the floating oval-shaped bed in the center of the room.

Pure bliss. The mattress was firm, but the finely woven fabric of the coverlet was like a dream against her skin. She could barely believe she was in a place so comfortable.

When was the last time she'd had a good night's rest? Not since Dorhock's death. The Jujo Emperor had kept her busy entertaining his guests until days and nights bled together. She grabbed snatches of sleep when she could, but had only made the mistake of falling asleep while entertaining a male once.

She shuddered and wrapped her arms around herself at the memory of the punishment, but she pushed it away fast. She simply couldn't allow herself the luxury of self-pity — it made her weak. She needed all her wits about her to navigate this strange new existence and make sure she was never, ever taken advantage of again.

That kind of punishment wouldn't happen here. Mina wouldn't have tried to connect her with Paal if she thought him cruel.

And what he'd done in the ship? That hadn't been mean.

It had been *hot*.

Though her body ached from his use, she couldn't wait to get him that aroused again. Because even if she'd been reduced to nothing but an object—his possession—in the moment, having a male that aroused by her, that passionate, couldn't be a bad thing. And the sweet mother earth knew she'd enjoyed it. Far better than she'd ever enjoyed any male, or female for that matter.

Paal liked sexual control.

So... did that mean he wanted her to submit? Did he need a meek female who did everything he asked? Or was it the act of *wresting* control he loved? Should she keep goading him into punishment?

She rather thought the latter, although maybe it was her own preference tainting the issue.

She curled up on her side, not bothering to reach for a pillow or climb under the blankets. The crystal amplified light cast sparkles on her bare skin. She sighed and closed her eyes. Finally safe to sleep, for the first time since Dorhock's death.

———

Master Seke's blue-violet gaze bore into Paal, probably seeing far more than he wanted to show. Paal had gone straight to his superior to debrief on the mission, and had to confess his abduction and new guardianship of Leti.

"Humans are not to be kept as slaves, per Prince Zander's decree," Master Seke said, watching him far too carefully.

He drew a measured breath. "I understand, Master."

"Do you? It's a rather complicated situation." Like Prince Zander, Master Seke had a human mate. "To keep human slaves dishonors the prince's mate and disrespects the hundred-fold humans who have pledged their lives to our cause. They have been promised freedom on Zandia when we reclaim her. And yet they must be subject to Zandian rule. Trained to function in our society. As such, it is best if they are bonded to a master— one or more Zandians willing to serve as the human's sponsor or guardian. One who will be responsible for their behavior."

His chest went rigid. He didn't want to be locked into a lifetime of responsibility for the little feline of a human who he didn't even trust.

"In a sense, that leaves the human in a subjugated position, similar to that of a slave, because they must conform and obey or they will lose the right to remain with us. Yet they should have the freedom to change guardians or masters to prevent abuse and give them the opportunity to find contentment with us."

And now again, that sense of panic swam through him. The same one he'd felt when Lady Taramina said warriors would fight over Leti. He may not want responsibility for her, but he didn't want any other males having access to that beautiful body and vibrant personality, either.

"So they can just...pick a new master? Anytime?" Paal's hands fisted at his sides.

"I expect they would petition the prince to approve any change. Prince Zander has not made any formal decrees yet, but once Zandia is won, he will need to put a policy in place for handling and integrating the humans."

Paal forced himself to swallow over the band around his throat. "I see."

Seke cocked his head. "The emotional nature of human females can bring out long-dormant... *desires* in Zandian males. Perhaps you are experiencing this?"

He forced himself to release his breath. "Something like that. Yes, Master."

"Creating a bond between yourself and the human is the key to winning her obedience. It's not a difficult process."

Paal waited when he didn't elaborate.

Seke rubbed his face, signalling his discomfort.

"It's quite easy to punish a human female. Dr. Daneth has researched it thoroughly, but I imagine it's not hard for you to intuit?"

"Right. Yes." Holy star, he didn't want to have this conversation with his mentor and boss.

Seke appeared relieved. "Good. Then with proper attention and care, your female should become quite pliant."

Quite pliant.

Why did that sound so distasteful? Did he want Leti pliant? Or was the heaviness still in his balls about the act of bending her to his will? Not wanting any other male to command her. Not wanting her to bend to any other male's commands.

"Thank you, Master." He stood and bowed.

Master Seke did the same. "Stop by Dr. Daneth's lab. He can provide you with... er, training materials."

Paal stopped by the kitchen to request a tray of food be prepared by Chef Barr, then, because he couldn't resist his curiosity, paid a visit to Dr. Daneth.

Unfortunately, the visit did nothing to alleviate his hard on for his human. If human females were aroused by pain, he sure as hell found the thought of giving it arousing. Dr. Daneth gave him a box of spanking implements and devices. He cut short the explanations because his own imagination was already running wild. He didn't need Daneth to make it worse.

He returned to pick up the tray of food, having refused Chef Barr's offer to deliver it personally, and headed down to his chamber, imagining all the myriad ways he'd train his human to surrender to him.

He found her naked, curled in a ball, asleep on his hoverdisk. Two conflicting desires rose up and battled within him. The first was nothing new — to wake her to round two of his cock in her perfect pussy, banging her until she screamed. The second was far more foreign. The need to care for the fragile human.

He set the food and implements down on the small table inside the door and moved silently to the sleepdisk.

She was even more beautiful in her sleep. Or rather, watching her sleep gave him the chance to fully study her. Her skin was flawless and smooth, full lips pouty, even at rest. She'd curled her hands into fists at her chest, lending her a childish vulnerability that tugged at his heart.

Her bottom still bore the prints of his hand, which also made his chest constrict. He'd been far too rough with her.

And then he saw her feet.

Outrage rocketed through him. His little human's boots had mangled her poor feet! Blisters puckered nearly every surface and her toes were scrunched up as if they'd been forced in too-small footwear for a long time. He remembered her comment to Lady Taramina about the emperor forcing her to earn her food.

Suddenly the idea of Leti being subjugated by any being made him want to smash things. She may be human, and therefore an inferior species, but she shouldn't have been made to suffer. And considering she'd pranced around in those boots without a single wince, he knew she'd suffered far worse in her lifetime. It was a wonder she'd become so resilient after the life she'd led.

He ran one fingertip lightly over her marked ass. How badly had he hurt her today? Shame at his previous excitement to do it again pushed in all around him.

Her long fake lashes fluttered open and she stiffened for no more than a few seconds before her seductive mask slid into place and she rolled her shoulders open to give him the full view of her golden breasts.

His disappointment was almost as palpable as the surge of lust that shot through his body.

She sat up and caught his hand, placing it right between her legs, over her bare pussy. "Hello, Master."

He growled at the softness of her petals under his fingers. Not wet yet— no, she'd just woken up. He growled, too, at her bold seduction attempt. He hooked his free hand behind one of her knees and pushed it wide.

One slap of her pussy was all it took to make her wet. Her eyes flared, nipples peaked. She slid to her back in a clear invitation.

He brought his palm up between her legs again. "You don't offer your pussy to your master, little slave. Not when it's already mine to take."

Her belly fluttered and he found himself fascinated by the lip of her navel. How would it look pierced?

But that wasn't right. He didn't want to *mate* this female. He just wanted to punish her.

The urge to dominate rose up strongly in him. He rolled her to her belly and grabbed a handful of her ass roughly. "Tell me, beautiful. Are you still sore?"

"Mmm." Her answer sounded more like a purr. "A little, Master. Not much." She pushed herself up to her elbows, no doubt to show off the beautiful line of her back. "Enough to remind me where you've been." The huskiness of her tone had him slapping her legs apart. Or maybe it was the words.

Stars, the girl knew exactly what to do and say to drive a male wild!

As if to prove his thought, she arched her ass up and gave it a little waggle.

It was all the invitation he needed. His palm crashed down on that tantalizing flesh.

Yes.

It was as satisfying as he'd remembered. Maybe even more. He kept spanking, loving the little gasps she made, the way her hips writhed on the sleepdisk, the tightening of her back and arms.

"Stars I love to hurt you," he confessed, still slapping hard. It bewildered him, this need to punish her.

Why did she let him?

Oh, excrement. What choice did she have? She was a *vecking slave*. And that made him an asshole.

Except no. She didn't mind. He *knew* she didn't mind. It made her wet. He scented her arousal. And she liked the attention because it was sexual and sex was her commodity.

Not wanting to take the spanking too far, he stopped and rolled her over to remove the temptation. Still, he had to feel those hot globes, the evidence of his domination. He slid his palms under her hips to cup her ass and brought his mouth to her wet pussy.

He licked into her, parting her lips with his tongue, tracing the inside flaps.

She cried out, her hips popping up from the sleepdisk. He pulled her tight against his mouth, stroked her clit with his tongue until it swelled enough to suck.

One of his horns came in contact with her inner thigh, sending a jolt of sharp pleasure straight to his cock. He rubbed it on her as he licked, moaning his own pleasure as she squealed hers.

Of course his female was smart. She intuited the significance of his horns and reached down to grip them both, squeezing and releasing them.

He stopped licking, delirious from her touch.

"Master," she purred, an awed appreciation in her tone. "Your horns get hard for me, too."

Unwilling to give her the upper hand, he forced himself to pull back, out of grasp, away from his worship of her incredible pussy. He slapped one of her breasts.

"Hands behind your head. Legs wide," he barked.

A little smile curved her lips. "Yes, Master." She obeyed, putting her glorious body on full display for him.

"When I tell you to get into position, this is the one I mean. Understand?"

Her eyes gleamed with interest. It might be his undoing. "Yes, Master."

"I want you to hold this position until I tell you to change it or I move you myself. Understand?"

She nodded. "Yes, Master."

"If you move before I tell you, I will punish you."

Her gold-flecked brown eyes held his as she purred, "How, Master?"

The little vixen. Of course she knew he liked to punish.

He fingered his sword belt. "I will take this off and spank you until you scream."

She shivered, but it was excitement that flared in her gaze. "I understand, Master."

"Good girl." He walked to the box of implements he'd brought in and selected two devices designed for pleasure. Or sexual torture, in this case.

He disinfected the first one with the wipes Daneth had provided, then tested it. It sprang to life, vibrating and whirling. Perfect.

He slapped Leti's wet folds. "I'm going to show you what happens when you try to tempt me with that naughty pussy."

She jerked but held the position, panting. Her firm breasts were lifted and spread wide and they bobbed with each short breath.

He slapped her once more before inserting the long phallus into her channel until the smaller whirling part met her clit. Then he turned it on.

She shuddered, her mouth dropping open, toes curling.

Those poor little toes. He'd address them later.

He stood back and folded his arms, watching the effect of the device on his female. Her golden skin flushed with color and she began to make micro-movements with her pelvis.

"How does it feel to be teased, beautiful?"

She said nothing, but her large round eyes turned pleading, fixed on his face.

He slapped her breast. "I asked you a question."

"I-I don't know." It struck him as a fairly honest answer, so he let it go.

"I'm curious how long it will take before you start begging me for relief."

She licked her lips. "Master wants me to beg?"

He gave a sharp shake of his head with a frown and she closed her pretty lips. "No. Your master wants to see you crack. I'd like to know what lies beneath that sexy facade of yours."

Another shiver raced through her, but she clearly took his words as a challenge, because the chink in her armor, the one that allowed her confused arousal to glimmer through disappeared and she turned it into a show, rolling her pelvis up and down and changing her expression to some version of an orgasm face.

No. *Veck* that.

He wanted the real thing.

He cleaned off a second device, the same sort of instrument, but one designed for her ass. It was shorter, but rounder, with a handle on the end.

Her eyes widened when he approached with it, but she kept up the hip thrusts.

"Lift both legs in the air, Leti."

She complied, keeping them spread wide. It wasn't what he'd imagined, but so much better.

"Mmm. That's a pretty sight."

Her belly flexed and stretched with heavy breaths. Her juices dripped down her crack. He used a pump of lubricant and coated the device before screwing into her tight anus. At first he thought Daneth must have been mistaken—that the device was the wrong size for a human female, but then her body accepted it.

He pumped it in and out of her, watching her lose composure. Her eyes glazed, jaw went slack.

When she started making pleading little sounds, satisfaction pounded in his ears. He reached up and pinched one of her nipples, holding on and tightening.

She screamed.

He changed to the other nipple, all the while pumping the vibrating plug in and out of her ass while the other thick phallus owned her pussy.

"Please?" She sounded hoarse. "You want me to beg, Master? Please, please let me come."

"Oh you'll come." He shifted position to grip both devices and he started to *veck* her with both of them, deep and hard. "You'll come and you'll come and then you'll beg me to make it stop."

Alarm flashed over her face just before she came for the first time. Her legs spasmed out of control, flailing around in the air. One would have kicked him in the face had he not dodged.

He chuckled, enjoying the heady sense of control he wielded, along with the front row seat to the most beautiful display of female orgasm—of any species.

When it passed, he tsked. "You didn't hold position, love. Now I'll have to punish you."

She panted, clearly still out of her mind with her climax. "No... wait."

He unfastened his sword belt and let the scabbard drop to the floor. After doubling it, he lifted her ankles in the air and swung. The animal hide struck right over the anal plug, sending it deeper as she tightened around it.

"Ung."

Yes, her masks were gone now. All he saw was arousal and alarm—an intoxicating mix, especially on his delectable female.

He applied the belt several more times, enjoying the way her legs flexed and bottom bobbed, trying uselessly to escape it.

He lowered the belt and ran his thumb over one of the marks. "I wish I knew how much you could take, little female. You mark so easily." He lowered her ankles. "Into position," he barked, like a Master at Arms giving orders to his proteges.

She responded as a well-trained subordinate, snapping her legs and elbows open.

"Good girl." He thrust his thumb into her mouth and she sucked without being told. "You'd best never anger me, love. I'll wear that pretty ass out with my belt."

She made an unintelligible sound around his thumb.

"And then I'll finish with my hand." Stars, he loved to talk about hurting her. "Which is worse, my belt or my hand?" He removed his thumb so she could answer.

She shrugged, writhing on the sleep disk, stuffed full of vibrating devices. "D-depends on how you use them. You could make me cry with either."

The thought of making her cry both sickened and aroused him. Would he enjoy her tears? He didn't think so, and yet somehow desperately wanted to know.

He settled, instead, for sucking her breast.

She panted and shifted beneath him. He didn't realize what she was about until her mouth closed around one of horns.

He shouted, nearly coming in his flight pants.

"*Veck*," he growled. He jerked up to see if she'd come out of position, but she hadn't. She'd simply contorted her neck to reach him. He fisted the horn and squeezed with a bruising force, trying to regain his control.

"You want to suck your master's horns?"

The little she-devil nodded, batting those long eyelashes at him.

He shook his head slowly. "You don't get to suck until your master orders you to suck. Don't ever take without asking. Understand?"

———

What. The mother-Earth-loving fuck?

She stared up at the massive warrior, noting the change in his eye color from brown-purple, to bright amethyst. Hunger seeped from every line of his face, showed in the stiff, thick knobs of his horns, which leaned toward her.

And yet he would deny himself pleasure if it meant giving her an inch.

Crazy alien.

But nothing within her rejected him. No, something hot and full flowed through her, from her. She fucking loved his dark, dangerous passion. The one that made him need her as much as she, apparently, needed him.

Because sweet solar light, her body was on fire! If he didn't remove the vibrators soon, she would lose her mind.

Never in her existence had she known sex could be this visceral, this raw, this intoxicating. Oh, she'd had some "clients" who were tender, and some who aroused her. But no man, alien or beast, had ever reduced her to this quivering mass of need, dying for his touch, for her own release. She was ready to beg again. And she meant drop all pretense at pride and seriously beg for him to stop. Or go on. She needed release. This was fucking torture!

"Please, warrior—Master." Her brain wasn't even working anymore. "Giant horned male. Paal," she babbled, words flying out of her mouth before she could reel them back in.

"Please, what? Please may I suck your horns?"

All right, no. But she'd do anything he demanded to get some relief. "Yes!" she sobbed. "Please let me suck your horns. Let me please you, Master. I'm so good at it."

His expression closed, some of the fire in him visibly dampening. "I know you are."

Why did he sound disappointed? Did he resent that she'd been previously trained? That she'd been with so many other males?

She tried it a different way. "Teach me what you like, Master. Train me."

He rubbed his thumb across her lips, a storm brewing under his assessing look. Then he moved, lightning fast, to pinch both her nipples at once. He pulled them taut, forcing her to arch off the sleepdisk and follow him.

"Come, Leti." A quiet command.

Her body responded. She bucked, pussy and anus squeezing hard around the vibrators, thighs quivering. He released her nipples and the stinging heat there amplified her release. The relief was enormous and short-lived, because the damn contraptions still held her hostage.

"Please, Paal," she begged.

He shook his head, a stubborn look coming over his face. "Punishment."

She writhed on the bed. "This is my punishment?"

He arched a brow. "Are you holding your position?" A sharp warning in his tone.

"Yes." She sounded sulky now. She had managed to hold the position despite her restless movements.

"Yes, little human. This is your punishment. For being such a *vecking* temptation to me."

"It's not my fault I've been trained."

He slapped her breast. "I will untrain you. I want you real."

Real.

The word bounced around in her head, setting off explosions of thoughts she couldn't handle. What in the hell was real? Who was the real Leti? She'd never been allowed to be anything during sex but what her master molded.

All she knew how to do with Paal was figure out what he wanted and give it to him.

Except he wanted the only thing she didn't know how to give.

Her.

A sob escaped her lips. She wasn't crying. Tears hadn't formed, but she felt like wailing. Or did she want to yell?

And all the time, Paal watched her with that glimmering gaze of his.

Unable to take even one more second of it, she did something she'd never, in all her twenty-five years as a slave, done. She cranked her leg and kicked her master.

She aimed for his balls and put as much power into the kick as possible, but she was a fool. A trained warrior isn't slain by an opponent in plain sight. He easily sidestepped and caught her ankle, using it to deftly flip her to her stomach.

She expected retribution. Something terrible—worse than the belt, but he only gave her a light slap on the ass.

"Just for that, I should leave those in all planet rotation," he rumbled, but in the next moment, he turned off the vibrators.

Relief swept through her, leaving her utterly limp.

Paal coaxed the devices out of her and dropped beside her on the bed, draping an arm around her waist.

She couldn't make herself move, not even to turn. Although whether she would have turned to him or away, she wasn't sure.

He nuzzled her neck, kissed behind her ear. "This is how I want you, beautiful. Trembling and wrung out and a little bit raw."

Now tears speared her eyes, although she couldn't imagine the reason.

She didn't cry often—usually only under extreme punishment, which she did her best to avoid. Why would hearing these soft, murmured words from her new master bother her?

He inhaled sharply and rolled her to her back, concern pinching his brows. "Are you hurt?"

She shoved at his chest and attempted to roll away, but he pulled her even closer, until her body met every hard line of his. Her pussy squeezed, still ripe for anything the warrior demanded. He coaxed her face up and brushed his lips across hers.

She stopped breathing.

This tenderness from him—it was so much worse than his rough demands.

Dangerous.

Because it felt so. Damn. Good.

And slaves don't get it good. They don't fall in love with their masters and they don't trick themselves into believing anyone actually cares. Or, if you can get a master to care, you certainly don't offer emotion in return.

Another panicked sob rose in her chest.

She pushed even harder against Paal. Tried to get a reaction out of him. Maybe if she struggled enough, he'd punish her again. Finally take her the way they both knew he wanted to.

Yes.

He flipped her onto her back and pinned her wrists beside her head. "Easy, beautiful. I just want to kiss you. I'll only make it hurt if you want me to." He was teasing her, trying to lighten the mood, but she didn't bite.

She simply turned her head away. Her stomach rumbled and he frowned.

"I forgot—I brought you food." He eased off of her and walked to the table beside the door, where a covered tray lay. He carried it back to her. "Are you hungry again? Humans have to eat all day long, right?"

She couldn't hide her smile at his misconception, relieved that the topic had changed. "Not all day. But at least twice. Three times if we can get it."

He scowled. "You'll have all the food you desire here. Any time." He sounded almost gallant and despite her desire to scoff it away, his assertion produced a curl of warmth in her chest.

He removed the lid from the tray, revealing a plate heaped with all kinds of colorful, but foreign food. "We grow human food. From the original Earth. Our chef knows how to feed humans." Picking up a beautiful red berry, he held it to her lips.

She took a bite and juice ran down her chin.

He watched it dribble, then startled her by surging forward and licking it off.

"Oh!" She hid a smile and dropped her eyes. "When do you eat, Master?"

Irritation flickered over his face. "Once a week. And I don't think you should call me *Master*."

"Why not? You like it, don't you?" She almost produced her mock innocent, sex-kitten voice and expression, but at the last minute veered into normality. Although admitting she'd made this concession for him niggled her.

He busied himself scooping a flat bread in some kind of green dip. "Zandians don't keep slaves. I am your guardian or sponsor. Not a master."

She leaned forward to take the bite he hadn't offered yet, knowing he liked to watch her eat.

Sure enough, his horns twitched and his gaze stayed glued to her lips.

"What's the difference?"

"The difference is while you must conform to Zandian society and obey Zandian rule, you are not a prisoner." He used the same stiff tone he'd used when he'd apologized for fucking her.

She gave a harsh laugh. "As if there were any place in this galaxy where a human can be free."

"I mean, if you are unhappy, you may petition for a new guardian." He fed her another bite when she lifted her chin for it.

"Unhappy how?"

His frown deepened. "It is undetermined."

She rather loved when he turned stiff and formal like this, only because it meant he was uncomfortable. A mixture of relief and unease permeated her senses. Her instincts had been right—the Zandians were a fair and kind species. Being under their rule meant her situation had vastly improved.

Yet the idea of disengaging herself from this male sent a chaotic spiral of wrongness through her chest. She may not understand him. She may not find him easy to be with, but she was drawn to him like a magnet. She craved his touch, no matter how rough. Her body responded as if he had always been her master. Or as if he was her body's only true master.

But she didn't need him to know any of that. She batted her long lashes at him. "Maybe I'll petition for a master who lets me suck his horns."

Paal crushed the soft pouch of liquid he'd been holding in one hand and a sweet-smelling juice sprayed all over both of them.

She squealed and jumped up, laughing.

"You're going to get spanked again," his deep voice growled, but a smile tugged his lips as he lunged for her, catching her around the waist. "You want the horns, you'll have to earn the right to suck them." His hot breath feathered across her ear.

She giggled, struggling against him to be free, pleasure blooming everywhere he touched her.

He carried her into the washroom she'd meant to investigate after her nap and thrust her into a washtube. "Clean yourself, human. I want your hair down and the smell of Jujo washed from your skin."

"I don't smell like Jujo," she grumbled, but moaned with pleasure the moment a warm spray of water drenched her from every side. "Don't eat my food!" she called out over the spray of water. "I'm going to finish all of that."

Paal chuckled. "I won't eat your food, ridiculous human."

She smiled and leaned back against the washtube surface. She was starting to get somewhere with this male.

Although the fact that he was also starting to get somewhere with her, too, should be something she worried more about.

CHAPTER THREE

Paal didn't know what to do with his human. Part of him still rebelled at having her. He was a warrior, for stars' sake, and his species was going to battle —within a few planet rotations if he read the signs correctly.

No one had said for certain which day they would strike the Finn to drive them off their planet, but judging from the acceleration of preparations going on all around him, it had to be soon.

He wouldn't even be around to train the human to conform to Zandian society. *Veck,* he might not even survive the takeback. There was a chance none of them would return.

And yet the idea of even releasing her from his room—from his sight— made every cell in his body rebel.

Already her sweet, exotic scent filled the chamber, was on his tunic, his sleepdisk. His fingers. He closed his eyes, savoring the memory of having her spread wide, giving over to her urgent need to come.

How could he even think about sending her away after he'd seen *that*? Impossible!

The washtube finished and he heard the door swish open. Part of him thought he should leave now, because knowing her clean, naked body stood just a few feet away made him want to barge into the washroom, bend her over the counter and force himself on her again. *Veck,* if he didn't want to claim her tight backhole this time, now that he'd seen how the anal plug had undone her.

He adjusted his cock in his pants. Not yet. He hadn't even allowed her to finish her meal. Nor had he seen to her wounded feet. And a tour of the pod might be in order.

He suddenly wondered what the spunky human would think of it.

He'd lived on Zander's pod since puberty and the minute he'd come here, he'd never wanted to leave. He'd hated the times he had to return to visit his mother at some new domicile she'd taken. With some new male she'd seduced.

He was supposed to be grateful to her because she'd taken him and left Zandia to live with an Igorian just before the Finn attacked. Yet he'd never found it in him to thank her.

All he ever remembered was the look on his father's face as they left. His utter devastation at discovering his mate had decided a miner couldn't provide enough for her and her son. And seeing his father so ruined had ruined him, too.

And so, with the logic of the 9-cycle-old he'd been, Paal had blamed her for Zandia's demise. For the deaths of his father and every friend he'd ever had. And he'd been stuck watching his mother suck up to the ugly, rich Igorian, who within a few lunar cycles she realized wasn't as wealthy or generous as she'd expected.

From there, she'd found a Niteean, then a Gambordian. But, because a surly adolescent interfered with her scheming, he'd long since been delivered to Master Seke for military training. Which was the best thing that could've happened to him.

Leti emerged, long hair hanging down over her bare breasts. The picture might have tempted him but he caught the knowing gleam in her eye as she twirled a section of the shiny dark locks around one finger. "Is this better?" She cocked a hip and used the ends of the section to tickle her bare nipple.

A growl rocketed from his throat. He cut the distance between them in a single stride and gripped the back of her hair. "Yes." He tugged her head back until she gasped and had to follow. "Better for pulling."

Anger flashed in the gold of her eyes before she hid it. "Master likes to control."

Dammit if he didn't want more of that anger from her. More of anything genuine beyond her *vecking fake* seductive excrement.

"I do." Still holding her prisoner by her scalp, he cupped her mons, delighted to find her wet again. His middle finger dipped into her slick heat. "Tell me what it does to your pussy."

A flush of color tinged her cheeks. Surely a sex pet wouldn't be embarrassed? Angry, then. He realized, with a start, that she might have learned to be the first to offer up her body, because it allowed her more dignity than having sex taken from her. His little pet was no victim, despite her slave status. She'd kept that one small granule of control.

And he was an asshole for not letting her keep it. And yet her attempt at seduction was like the scrape of metal to his nerves. Every time she asserted her sexual power, he had to take it back.

Part of it was the game, a need to dominate and conquer. But part of it was something deeper, more personal.

He profoundly mistrusted the female.

He didn't want to be made a fool of, like his father had been. Or all those other males his mother had used.

He shoved a second finger in his squirming female, using the heel of his hand to grind against the place Daneth had told him would arouse her.

Her lips tightened but one of her hands flew to cover his, pushing him deeper, rubbing his hand against her.

"Does this pussy get wet when I make it hurt, Leti?" He rasped in her ear.

She struggled against him, her backside writhing against his aching cock. "I don't...want it to," she admitted.

He laughed and released her. "That's probably the first honest response you've given me." Picking her up by the waist, he lifted her pussy to his mouth and gave it a soft kiss, then lowered her down again.

Her knees buckled under her and he had to catch his wobbling female to keep her from dropping to the floor.

Alarm shot through him. "Are you ill?"

She lurched out of his hold, toddling toward the food, once more. Head bowed, her hair fell in a curtain, hiding her face as she selected a berry.

"Are you that hungry?" he demanded. Stars, he needed to learn how to keep his little female nourished.

She didn't look at him when she spoke, and her words sounded grudging, like she didn't wish to say them. "No, I'm just a little...affected."

Affected?

Ah, affected. By *him*.

Another honest moment. His heart squeezed with the sudden urge to soothe and care for his female. He rummaged through his clothing and produced an undershirt. He brought it to her where she stood, eating, and pulled it over her head. She threaded her arms through the holes with an air of surprise. Had no one ever taken care of her before?

That idea both enraged him and solidified his determination to see to her needs. Whether he ultimately kept her or not.

The shirt hung to her thighs but the material was thin enough for him to see her dusky nipples through. He picked up the flight tunic she'd been wearing earlier and helped her into it. "Put on those leggings you found on the ship, I don't want any other being seeing those legs when we leave this chamber. I'm going to shove my fist down the throat of any male who looks at them."

A genuine smile touched her lips. Not artful or calculating. Pretty. As if she liked the compliment of his jealousy. But just as quickly as it appeared, she turned away, hiding herself from him.

"You're not wearing these any more, either," he declared, holding up her boots and dropping them into the waste chute where they were whisked down to incineration.

Leti pouted. "I looked good in those boots."

"You looked *vecking* amazing," he admitted. "But they wrecked your feet."

She let out a surprised laugh and looked down. "You've been looking at my feet?"

He nodded. "I'm going to bring you to the Prince's doctor for treatment."

Her full lips opened and closed soundlessly. Then she laughed again. "Master, I never know what to expect from you."

His face split into a satisfied grin. "And that's how it should be. Come," he held out his arm. "Are you finished eating?"

"Yes," she said, but shoved another cracker in her mouth and gave him a sly grin. "Almost."

"You'll never be denied food here, Leti. Zandian promise."

A flash of vulnerability flickered across her face, but she covered it with a toss of her hair over her shoulder. She hooked her hand through his elbow. "Where are we going, Master?"

He would've thought by now the kick of lust that shot straight to his cock every time she called him *Master* would've diminished, but it hadn't. He gritted his teeth and rearranged himself again. He'd have to *veck* her again soon, or he wouldn't make it through the rest of the planet rotation with his sanity intact.

Damn the little temptress.

He led her up the lift to the main floor, straight to Dr. Daneth's lab.

"Ah, the new arrival. Come in. Sit there on the table."

Leti obeyed and Daneth peered at her with a clinician's interest. "Appears healthy. I'd like to do a full examination—"

"*No*," he interrupted. No *vecking* way he'd have Daneth inspecting his human. She'd have to get naked for that and then he'd have to kill the doctor.

Daneth arched a brow. "Zandian males do exhibit radical possessiveness when it comes to human females." Despite Paal's refusal, the doctor appeared to be approaching her with a needle.

"What are you doing? I brought her here for her feet, not for your testing."

"A simple genetic screening will allow us to determine how she will breed and which warrior would be the best—"

"She's not here for breeding." His teeth almost broke from clenching them so hard. "Look at her *vecking* feet."

"Out of line, warrior," Daneth warned. At the look on Paal's face, his expression softened. "Paal," he explained, "I can delay the exam for now, but you know it's required for any newcomer to the pod. All arrivals need a full physical exam to assure their safety and that of the other residents." He gave Paal an even gaze. "I will treat her with the utmost respect."

He worked to calm his temper. Daneth was right. He may not be Paal's superior, but he certainly ranked far higher as Zander's trusted advisor. He forced a stiff bow. "Please, doctor."

A tap sounded at the door, and it slid open before the doctor answered. The doctor's pregnant female mate, Bayla, stood in the doorway.

"Oh, forgive me, Master."

The doctor's normally wooden face instantly softened, his eyes caressed the bump of Bayla's belly. "Not at all. Come in. I could use your help."

Bayla, a rosy-cheeked, dark haired human, brightened, casting a curious gaze at Leti. "What can I do?"

"Prepare to clean and treat this human's wounds."

Bayla dropped a curtsy. "Of course, Master."

Daneth picked up one of Leti's ankles and turned her foot to each side, visually examining the wounds. "Subject shows signs of vesicles and abrasions, likely from wearing ill-sized or restrictive footwear." He touched a particularly angry red area and Leti jerked. "Some infection present. Proper cleaning, bandaging and local antibiotics should resolve the issue within a week, provided the footwear is discontinued."

Relief swept through him. "So it's not dangerous to a human? I know they are an inferior species."

"Your female shows no sign of stress or systemic illness, although I'd still like to give her a thorough—"

"No."

Daneth shrugged, but didn't argue further because his mate came to stand by his side.

"Hi, I'm Bayla," the female offered Leti with a soft, friendly tone. "I hadn't heard of your arrival."

"I just arrived." Leti lifted her chin at him. "He stole me from the Emperor of Jujo." She hesitated a moment, then added, her voice softer and a little uneven, "He...rescued me, that is." She looked at Paal for a moment, and her expression was something he'd never seen on her — almost worried, perhaps? But before he could analyze it, her typical haughty, strong expression was back.

"Ah. Lucky you. Zandians make great masters."

He stiffened. Hearing females discuss his gender in generalities set his teeth on edge. Too much like his mother.

Bayla went on, chattering as she wiped an antibiotic cleanser over Leti's feet. "They seem to find human females pleasing once they get used to us." She winked. "Sounds like you already have this one halfway to a piercing ceremony."

His stomach knotted.

No.

No *vecking* way.

He would not be the prize won by these scheming females.

"What's a piercing ceremony?" Leti asked, her gaze swiveling to his face.

He forced his lips to move. "It's for mating. But your friend is wrong." He allowed scorn to splash over his expression. "I would never mate a human slave."

———

It shouldn't have hurt.

Hurt implied she cared, and she definitely *did not* give a shit about this arrogant Zandian bastard. As if she wanted to be mated to a fucking purple alien!

But it wasn't like the Zandians who had human mates seemed like they thought they'd downgraded. Mina's mate had doted on her, and even the strange doctor couldn't stop looking at his pregnant mate.

So if Paal found her so repulsive, it probably wouldn't be too hard to find another Zandian who would actually *enjoy* her extensive training as a sex pet. Why in the hell should she waste her talents and efforts on this one?

And it had already been made clear that she wasn't stuck with him. Mina had been trying to help, but she'd set her up with the wrong purple horned man. She'd just find herself another. It took way more than a scornful master to get her down.

A helluva lot more.

The doctor released her with some of the antibiotic cream and the directive to return in three planet rotations for him to recheck the wounds.

"I will need a full workup, though," he called after them as Paal directed her by the elbow out of the room.

Paal didn't answer.

Funny that a male so irrationally possessive should also find her not nearly good enough.

Paal led her back to his chamber, hurrying her through the colorful corridors without giving her a chance to see much of anything. He pressed his palm to the plate outside his door and it slid open. He scooted her inside but didn't follow. "Stay where you won't get into any trouble. I have things to do."

"I won't get into any trouble outside your—"

The door slid closed in her face.

She tried to open it, but apparently it was programmed only to respond to Paal's handprint. Damn the warrior.

Too bad. For a few minutes there, she'd actually imagined she might have more freedom with the Zandians.

Maybe Mina would come and set her free.

She returned to the tray of food, eating not out of hunger, but for sport. Because she'd never tasted such delicious food and it was hard to stop scooping it into her mouth.

She'd probably give herself a bellyache, but she didn't care. What else was there to do?

———

Zander sat at the long oval table in what had become his war room. All his advisors sat with him, alert. Ready for battle.

This was it—the moment he'd spent a lifetime training for. Most of the males in this room had devoted their lives to preparing him for it. Having females in the room was altogether new, but with so many lives on the line, he needed his mate's gift of sight. Rok and Lundric's human mates were trained warriors now, and Taramina had taken a lead role with Erick's diplomatic efforts.

Erick stood up to speak. "As most of you know, my sources report King Fluut continues to lose control of his empire. Very few Finnians linger on what's left of Finn, their home planet—the toxins there are too strong after the last mining explosion. Fluut's failed bid for Shanli seriously reduced his troops and weaponry. They are expected to pull out of that engagement by the next lunar cycle. We need to strike before they return to Zandia."

Rok cleared his throat. "Strike where?"

Seke stood up and projected a hologram of the galaxy. He pointed to Shanli. "I propose a two pronged attack. We strike their fleet that's residing in the airspace above Shanli, and at the same time we take out Fluut himself on Zandia."

"Do we have enough ships for both offensives?" Rok asked. "I mean, I know what we have, but I don't know what we're up against in the Shanli airspace."

"We will be outnumbered, but unlike the Finn, our ships are new and our soldiers fresh. They've suffered major losses. Morale will be low. It's the perfect time to strike," Zander explained.

Seke enlarged the hologram of Shanli airspace. "They have only one main galactacarrier left. It's three times the size of ours, but that makes it slow and heavy. We park our galactacarrier here, in cloaking mode." He pointed to a position behind the Shanli moon. "We stay in the gravitational pull of the moon and follow it around until we're in perfect position. Then, we send a torpedo straight for the carrier. If all goes well, we won't even use any of the small fighter ships."

Rok nodded soberly. "Is this my assignment?"

"Yes," Seke replied. "You'll accompany Prince Zander. I'll lead the Zandian invasion because I remember the layout of the capital better than either of you. I'll need no more than one-third of the troops to sack the palace and eliminate Fluut."

"And if they're prepared for us?" Lundric, his Chief of Security asked.

"Considering the assassination attempt on Erick and Mina, they probably will be," Seke offered. "All the more reason to strike now."

"Who will remain here?" Lium, his tactical engineer asked.

"We'll leave the females and young." Zander looked at Rok. "Send over any of the humans on the training pod not fit for combat. We'll consolidate here with a skeleton crew."

Rok cast a glance at Lily. "You and Cambry should come here as part of the defense team. I don't want you on the front line."

Cambry, Lundric's fiery red-headed mate, opened her mouth, but Lundric cut in. "Agreed."

Cambry ignored him, appealing to Rok. "I can fly a fighter ship as well as any of your men."

Lamira stirred beside Zander and he waved them quiet.

"You and Lily will be needed on this pod," Lamira predicted. Her beautiful green eyes had the unfocused glaze they took on when she was seeing with her inner eyes.

A cold hook of fear ripped through his solar plexus. "Why?" he demanded.

Lamira stared unseeing out the window. Finally she shook her head. "I cannot see. They will lead something important here on the pod."

Cambry didn't appear convinced, but Lily, Lamira's sister nodded.

He didn't *vecking* like it. Leaving for war was hard enough knowing he might not return, but thinking his mate and young might be in danger while he was away flayed his chest open.

"Who will be in charge of defense here?" Lundric asked.

Zander hesitated. "I'm considering Paal, from my royal guard. He's taken over security here since Lundric went to the training pod."

Erick nodded. "He's proven extremely capable."

Lundric concurred.

"All parties will meet danger," Lamira said.

A ripple of disquiet traveled through the chamber.

"And success?" Lily asked the question probably in the forefront of every being's mind.

Lamira went quiet once more.

The tension in the room grew palpable the longer his mate remained silent. Finally, she said, "The chance for success is there."

"And the chance for failure?" Lium asked.

Lamira bowed her head. "Also there. But more energy for success."

He'd hoped for more practical information from Lamira, but she had no control over her visions. All he could do was include her and accept whatever nuggets she handed him. She'd been the one to see that the rough and tumble smuggler Rok would be the Zandian who trained and led his army, and she'd been right.

"When do we strike, my lord?" Lundric asked.

"We move into place after nightfall tomorrow. We'll strike the following planet rotation." He stood, indicating the meeting had ended.

Every being surged to their feet, bowing to him before they exited.

Lamira stayed back, plucking a few dead leaves from the fruit tree she'd planted in a pot in the corner.

The underlying sense of dread at leaving Lamira and his tiny son unguarded mounted. "I should send you away," he said. "I'll seek diplomatic sanctuary for you and little Zander at the United Galaxies."

Lamira shook her head. "I will be needed here as well. This isn't the time to hold back any resource. If you want Zandia we go all in. Every being, every risk. That's what it will take."

The cold dread swam through him. "You've seen this?"

She nodded. "It's the only path to success."

He closed his eyes against the blinding pain produced when he thought of losing one of them. "Zandia means nothing to me without my family."

Lamira stepped closer and put a hand on his chest. "We'll be there. Win it for us, my lord. Give your son his birthright."

He caught her nape and melded his mouth over hers, claiming her with his lips, his tongue, his teeth.

"I love you," he murmured.

Tears glistened in her eyes. "Don't." She pushed his chest.

"Don't what?"

"Don't kiss me like it's goodbye. Go and win Zandia for us."

He forced a smile and leaned his forehead against hers. "I will. Zandian promise."

———

Paal stood outside his chamber, not quite ready to enter. He never should have taken on the guardianship of the female in the first place. Keeping her locked in his chamber wasn't a solution to his dilemma of not trusting her but not wanting to give her to another.

If only Lady Mina had taken guardianship of her! Then the searing jealousy that rose everytime he imagined her in the care of another male wouldn't be an issue.

His fingers twitched over the hand panel that scanned his palm. He'd had more food sent to Leti at sunset, but he should let her out now. He couldn't lock her up forever. What would he tell Lady Mina?

He needed to make a decision—keep her or let her go.

With a grumble, he pressed his palm to the panel and braced himself as the door slid open. He expected to find Leti naked again, or in some form of seduction. Instead, she surprised him by darting past him without a glance.

He snatched her arm and when she whirled back, he saw the fire in her eyes that he so loved. Immediately, every cell in his body fired.

Claim. Conquer.

Love.

Love? No—where did that thought come from? Ridiculous.

"Where do you think you're going?"

"Am I your prisoner?" She arched a brow, telling him she'd perfectly understood her situation on the pod. She may not be completely free, but she wasn't a slave anymore. Not under Zander's rule, anyway.

"No." He sighed and released his hold on her arm. "You're not. I'm sorry, I won't shut you in again. Not unless you prove disobedient."

Her upper lip twitched at the last part, but he let it go.

She spread her hands. "Listen. No hard feelings, but it seems like maybe this was a bad idea. Mina meant well when she gave us a push together, but it's clear I'm not up to your standards. It's fine. You shouldn't be obligated to be my master or guardian or whatever."

His heart beat faster in his chest, breath raked in and out with far too much effort.

He should be thrilled by her understanding of their situation. They weren't well-suited. It wasn't going to work.

Why, then, was he dying to pick her up and throw her back in his chamber? Bind her on his sleepdisk and never let her leave again?

Instead, he stood paralyzed, caught by indecision, and Leti—clever female that she was—pressed her advantage and flounced away, down the corridor.

Veck.

He let her go, watching the sway of her hips as she moved, the lines of her long legs. Even bare-footed, in a plain Zandian flight suit, she screamed sex.

Not until she disappeared into the lift did he realize he couldn't very well let her wander around the pod unescorted. He should at least keep an eye on her.

Except he knew where that would lead. Any time his gaze was on her, he wanted his hands on her, too. His mouth, his tongue. Why hadn't he *vecked* her a second time when they returned to the pod? He was an idiot.

He forced himself into his chamber, but nothing about it seemed familiar anymore. Her scent and the aroma of food coated everything. The sleepdisk reminded him of how she'd looked lying naked, legs spread on it. The wash-room reminded him of the way her hair looked down, fresh from the washtube.

Damn.

Maybe he'd just go make sure she hadn't gotten herself into any trouble. Not that the pod provided much opportunity for that.

He took the lift to the main level of the pod and exited. The sound of female laughter reached his ears and once more, every cell activated.

Leti.

Had he even heard her laugh before? He wasn't sure, but he knew without question the musical sound had come from her pouty lips. He rushed forward, into the Great Hall and choked.

His female stood, *balanced on another warrior's shoulders,* gazing up at one of the Zandian crystal amplifiers used to bring light to the room. Two other warriors—Ronan's damn cousins —stood on either side, their hands gripping her upper calves, stabilizing her.

All three guards' horns were thick and extended, pointing toward *his* female.

"*Leticia,*" he barked.

She whirled and lost her balance.

He surged forward, jockeying with the other three males to catch her. His female showed no fear, though. Like an acrobat, she'd tucked and dropped neatly into the arms of Ronan, the tall scarred warrior who'd had her on his shoulders.

———

Leti met the gaze of her master. His eyes were wide with shock and—could it be—fear? Had he been afraid for her?

That idea shouldn't send such a surge of satisfaction through her.

But he didn't want her. He'd already made it plain. Maybe she needed to make it plain to him that he really did.

She leaned forward and dragged her tongue up the side of the neck of the male holding her. "Thank you for catching me."

Rage flashed over Paal's face, his eyes blazing pure purple.

Good.

She craved his attention, no matter how backward it seemed. After being discarded and locked up all afternoon, feeling his intense arousal gave her a surge of power.

"*Mine*," he growled like a primitive sub-species, snatching her from the other warrior's arms and tossing her over his shoulder.

"Says who?" demanded Tarron, the biggest of the three cousins she'd just met.

Gaining their interest had been child's play. Too bad she felt none of the thrill, none of the intense attraction Paal drew from her.

Paal hadn't stopped for a second. "I rescued her. She belongs to me."

"I'm not sure she knows that," Ronan, the charming one, muttered.

"I'm going to teach her," he growled.

For the first time, a frisson of fear traveled through her body. How angry had she made the warrior?

The Zandians seemed like a civilized species, but the doctor had said females bring out a strong possessiveness in them. Could she handle his rage?

He kept her on his shoulder and didn't say a word on the ride, and she didn't dare goad him into putting her down and letting her walk.

In his chamber, he dropped her unceremoniously to her feet. "Take off your clothes."

She hid her fear, and managed not to appear seductive as she obeyed. She kept her movements swift and succinct to avoid further enraging the warrior.

Paal rummaged in the box of implements he'd brought in earlier and produced an animal hide strap. He struck his palm with it as if testing its bite.

Her belly fluttered and pussy clenched. She'd been beaten by far worse implements in her life—by far crueler masters—but something about the angry Zandian had her quivering.

She should do something to diffuse his anger before the whipping. But what? He resented all attempts at seduction.

A challenge, then. She walked boldly forward and shoved her hands down his pants, grasping the base of his cock.

Paal's horns shot straight out, in perfect concert with his cock. His mouth opened, and he let out a feral growl. "You want my cock?" His words came out raw and rough, voice deepened. "You'll get my cock, little female." He backed her up against the wall and lifted one of her thighs, aiming his cock like a thick weapon at her core.

"Yes," she breathed, wrapping her legs around his waist. It wasn't a lie or a manipulation, no matter how it had started. She desperately wanted his shaft. Her body hummed for it. Purred for it. She needed him to claim her as badly as she'd needed him to take her away from those other warriors. "Give it to me."

"I'll give it to you," he warned, thrusting deep inside her. "You're going to get it so hard, you'll forget your name." He withdrew and thrust again. "How you got here." Another hard slam. "Where you came from." He drove her against the wall, but she barely noticed the discomfort. "All you will know,"— another thrust hit so deep she thought he'd split her— "is who owns you."

She tried to moan her agreement, but the sounds from her mouth were incoherent. Pleasure and need coiled up together, wrapping her in a net of white hot desire.

"Not enough," Paal growled.

She opened her lids long enough to see his tormented face, eyes screwed up with effort, like he was trying to hold back the climax they were both hurtled toward.

"Need more," he growled, fucking her faster now, pumping in and out like his life depended on it. "It's never *vecking* enough with you." He slammed hard and shouted and the heat of his essence filled her.

Her muscles clamped down on his and she climaxed, too, but he cut it short.

"No." He pulled out, fisting his cock and spilling the last bit of his rainbow-colored cum on the floor. "No pleasure for you. Not when you *vecking* tortured me out there." His eyes flashed a warning and he lifted her by the waist and tossed her on the sleepdisk. "Standing on that male's shoulders," he growled, picking up the animal hide strap he'd dropped when she grabbed his cock. "*Licking his neck?*"

She scrambled back on the sleepdisk. "I'm sorry, Master."

She really was. In that moment, she only wanted to please him. He'd shown her the extent of his passion and need for her and it had far exceeded her hopes.

He lifted his chin. "You will be sorry. Roll over."

"Master—"

He tucked his fingers under her pelvis and flipped her to her stomach. "Do you have any idea what I wanted to do to those males?"

Every second of the scolding nourished her on some level she'd never been fed. This went beyond any sexual power she'd wielded with other males. It wasn't about gaining his interest or getting him hard.

This warrior was ready to fight for her. The menace in his tone suggested maybe even kill for her.

"I'm sorry, Master. I won't do it again."

He shoved a pillow under her hips, lifting them for her punishment.

She covered her ass with her hands, not because she was scared—well, maybe she was a little scared—but more to slow him down. Get him to talk more before he whipped her.

He snatched her wrists and cinched them together in one of his large palms and then the whoosh of the strap swinging through the air preceded the first hard *thwap*.

"Ow!" she jumped and listed to the side. "Master, please."

"Mmm." He made a sound of satisfaction and whipped her again.

A second line of fire seared just below the first one. It was nothing in the scheme of things. It wouldn't hurt for long, wouldn't harm her, and yet she let up a protest. Maybe because she thought he'd like it. Maybe because she knew she could.

She rolled and wriggled and gasped as he brought the leather strap down again and again across her buttocks. "Ouch! That hurts, Master. Please."

He didn't stop. Didn't hold back. "That's right, pretty female—beg. I *vecking* love the sounds you make when I hurt you."

So she whimpered. Mewled. Gasped. Cursed.

It hurt but it also satisfied her on every level. Like his passion, his anger, this whipping showed her the depth of his emotions. She loved his raw response to jealousy, loved feeling the bite of his retribution.

And maybe because her orgasm had been cut short, it made her grind against the pillow, the need for release growing with each stinging stroke.

And when it truly grew too intense—when the pain got on top of her, she begged in earnest. "Paal, please! It's too much."

And, miraculously, he somehow recognized the difference. Understood when it had gone far enough, because he immediately stopped, tossing the strap onto the sleepdisk beside her head.

"Forgive me," he murmured, his huge palms gripping her ass. He squeezed her cheeks roughly with a ragged groan. "Whipping you gives me such pleasure."

She closed her eyes, physical relief rushing through her limbs as the soft glow of satisfaction at his words melted something in her chest.

He shoved her legs wide and licked a long line from her pussy to her anus.

She jolted, would've popped right off the sleepdisk, but he held her down, licking around her anus, shocking all sorts of sounds from her lips. It was pleasure and embarrassment and more of that growing need all at once.

"I can smell your nectar, Leticia. You haven't been *vecked* enough yet, have you?"

"No," she whined her admission.

"Good." His weight disappeared from the sleepdisk and she started to get up from her position, but he barked, "Don't *vecking* move."

Her pussy clenched, excitement zinging through her. She stilled, every nerve ending on high alert, waiting to see what came next.

"I *vecking* loved the way you humped that pillow while I whipped you, beautiful. Show me again. What were you doing?"

She reached to slide her hand between her legs but Paal caught her elbow. "Uh uh. You don't touch yourself. Only I get to control when and how you get pleasure. Understand?"

"Yes, Master."

"Good girl."

He shoved his hand under her pelvis and—oh stars!—placed one of the vibrators just beneath her clit. It whirred to life, sending bolts of electric pleasure down both her legs. With one hand on her ass, he pushed her pelvis down over the device. "Grind down, female. Show me how those sweet little hips move when you're aroused."

She let out a fevered moan and obeyed, rubbing her clit over the device, her breath growing labored.

"That's it," his rumble was warm and coaxing. "I love the way this ass moves." He pried her cheeks apart. "I can't wait to *veck* it."

Oh sweet mother Earth.

She'd been afraid of that.

———

Paal pumped a generous amount of lubricant into his hand and coated his cock, then applied more to Leti's tight little pucker.

Stars, it was so wrong, but he loved seeing his marks on her ass. He'd long forgotten his anger, satisfaction at Leti's complete and utter surrender replacing his fury with a powerful sense of pleasure.

He shouldn't have whipped her so hard, but it couldn't have been all wrong. It couldn't have, because his beautiful female lay there, wriggling over the vibrator as if she craved the same release he so desperately desired.

And it was never enough. Every time he touched her, he craved more. Every minute he came near her, his emotions careened more dangerously out of control.

"You're going to take my big Zandian cock in that tight little hole, aren't you, female?"

She whimpered when he pressed the head of his cock up against her sphincter muscles. "Yes, Master."

He applied a little pressure. His beautiful female pushed back at him, opening her muscles to let him enter. He went slowly, easing in, loving the little hurty sounds she made as she accommodated him. "That's it, beautiful female," he encouraged.

Her little moan of pleasure made it nearly impossible not to shove the rest of his length forward, but he held back, taking his weight on his arms planted beside her.

"Master." A pleading voice.

"That's it, Leticia. Open for your master."

He shifted to work a hand beneath her, checking to see that the device was still in contact with her clitoris. He rolled it around as she panted and mewled beneath him. Finally, finally he fed every inch of his cock into her. The heat of her chastised flesh met his loins and the fronts of his thighs, the tremble in her legs made it hard not to pound into her.

"So good," he grunted. "You feel so *vecking* good."

"Yes, Master. Please."

"You need your master to *veck* your ass, Leti? Remind you who owns this luscious little body?"

"Please, Master."

Stars, her whimpered begging would be the undoing of him. He drew back and pressed in, again and again. When her begging turned incoherent, her mewls took on the high-pitched urgency signalling her orgasm, he let himself crest the peak again.

"Come, Leti. Take your pleasure, if you can."

Her body shook beneath his as he drilled into her and released once more. He shuddered when she tightened around him, sobbing out her release.

"Good girl," he murmured into her hair, lowering himself over her. "So yielding. So beautiful."

Her breath came out in another sob, back shaking with its ragged release.

The need to take care of her came over him and he eased out and went to the washroom to clean himself and dampen a cloth.

She remained exactly as he'd left her, still bent over the pillows, her whipped and *vecked* ass in the air, her legs spread, limbs limp.

"Sweet female," he crooned, gently wiping his seed from between her legs and ass. "Are you all right?"

"Yes, Master," she mumbled.

He pulled the pillows out from under her and jockeyed the bed linens down to cover her. Daneth had given him an anesthetic spray, in case he wished to pierce her and he retrieved it. Humans were delicate. His female was probably in pain now, and he hated her to suffer because he'd lost control with her.

He applied the spray, startling her up out of her post-orgasmic reverie.

Her hand flew back to her ass. "What was that?" The fear in her expression disturbed him. She'd been so mistreated in her lifetime that she suspected only harm.

"Be of ease, little one. It's to take away the pain. I regret any suffering I caused you."

She blinked, her eyes bright with moisture.

Ice cold alarm rang through him. Why was she crying? Had he hurt her more than he knew?

She turned her face back toward the bedding. "Thank you, Master." Her voice sounded choked.

He'd wondered whether he'd enjoy breaking her and now he knew the definitive answer. He *vecking* hated it. His strong, proud female should never be broken, especially not by him, the male entrusted with her care.

"Leticia, sweet female." He knelt beside her on the bed and gently rolled her over. "What have I done?"

She pressed her lips together and shook her head, blinking rapidly.

"Forgive me. I'm not used to being near females—especially not human females. Every moment I spend with you—"

To his utter shock, she threw her arms around him and tucked her face against his neck. "I regret any suffering I caused you, too."

He let out an astonished laugh as he pulled her in close and stroked her silky dark hair. A kaleidoscope of emotions flickered through him, but the primary one was the deep satisfaction evoked by holding his little female in his arms. Nothing had ever felt so right. The softness of her bare skin, her scent, the way she fit so perfectly against his chest. He kissed her hair, savoring the moment.

He'd been mistaken before—a fool. There was nothing he wanted more than to keep this little female as his own.

CHAPTER FOUR

Leti woke to the sensation of heat against her backside. A heavy arm draped over her waist reminded her where she was. Her warrior was nested against her back, his large body curled around hers.

She hadn't pegged him as affectionate, but she'd been wrong. He may be dismayed by his intense attraction to her, but he seemed to be growing just as attached to her as she was to him.

She shifted and her bare ass pushed against his cock, which instantly surged against her sensitive skin. The anesthetic must be wearing off. Somehow, the return of heat and pain came like an aphrodisiac. The buzz of sensation grew more insistent, dampening her folds.

Stars, if she didn't know better, she'd think her new master had given her a dose of breeding hormones. She'd never wanted sex so often and with such desperation.

She slipped a hand down between her legs to take care of the situation and was shocked to find how swollen and wet she was. A whimper escaped her lips and she rocked her hips.

Paal's hand slid up to cup her breast. "Are you touching my pussy?" he grumbled through a sleep-thickened voice.

"The spray wore off," she told him. "It hurts again."

"Mmm." His fingers tangled over hers and he shoved one thick digit inside her. "And you need me to *veck* it better?"

"Yes, Master."

"Stars, every time you call me *master* I want to *veck* you senseless," he growled, rolling her to her belly and climbing over her. "You know that?" He rubbed the head of his cock over her juicy slit.

She laughed, a deep throaty sound that didn't sound like her. "Yes, Master."

He slid inside her and they both groaned. "You feel so good to me, Leticia. I lose my mind when I'm with you. Forget Zandia, I want to lock my door and *veck* you for an entire solar cycle."

She gasped as he thrust deep again. "Just one?"

"Five," he amended, pushing in again. "No, ten. Do males ever grow tired of *vecking* their females?"

"I don't think so."

It wasn't exactly true. Males never grew tired of fucking females, but the same one? Yes. Masters grew bored quickly in her experience. Why did that bring such a sharp sense of loss to her chest?

She had a rule. No emotion.

Somehow, after less than one planet rotation, she'd already indulged in her cardinal sin—caring.

And he'd made it plain he wouldn't mate her.

But none of that mattered when he wrapped his fist in her hair and tugged her head back. She loved his growl of dominance, his palpable excitement as he drove into her deep and hard. She moaned her pleasure, wanting it to go on forever, even as the need became too great to bear.

"I *love vecking* you," Paal rumbled behind her. "Feeling this hot little ass underneath me, that tight channel hugging my cock." He rubbed her scalp, burying his fingers in her hair before he fisted it once more. "This *hair*."

His reverence for her changed everything. Yes, she was still an object for his pleasure, still a possession, yet her effect on him was so plain. It was better than any choreographed seduction attempt she'd made during her stint as a sex slave. More true and honest and real a connection than she'd had with any being, since the time she'd been taken from her mother at the age of six.

Paal pulled out and lifted her hips in the air until she stood on her knees. She brought her weight to her hands but he pushed her torso down. "No. Like I first had you. On the ship. I'll never *vecking* forget how it felt."

Her breath caught—not at the sheer ecstasy of his re-entry, but at the starburst of pleasure his words produced. And then the ecstasy caught up to her. Her mind took off, soaring body turned liquid, nothing but a willing vessel to Paal's passion.

He gripped her hips and pounded into her until she screamed her need. "Yes, yes. Please, Master."

His roar met her screams, matched them, swelled even louder and then she was sure they both shot into orbit. Pleasure spiralled all around, like a net holding them together, as she collapsed beneath him, mindless and replete.

He rolled her back to her side, tight against him and kissed her neck. "Never enough," he mumbled as the arm around her grew heavier and he dropped back to sleep.

Never enough for her, either.

But that was because this wouldn't last. She needed to remember, to remind herself before she lost her heart as quickly as she'd lost her mind.

———

A thunderous crash tore Paal from sleep. A scream ripped the air and his body flew back, crashing against the wall behind the sleepdisk before dropping back to the mattress.

Leti.

His arms flew out to catch her, cushion her fall.

The moment he ascertained her safety, he surged from the sleepdisk, lifting her to her feet. "Can you walk? Put this on." He thrust a tunic at her as he yanked on his uniform and shoved his weapons in their holsters.

"Wh-what's happening?" His female was smart. Though shock sounded in her voice and her hands shook, she moved quickly.

He flicked on the light, but it didn't work. An alarm started up, blaring through the chamber, echoing off the walls. "I don't know. Sounds like an attack. Come." The pod tipped, sending them both sliding across the room.

He cursed and grabbed her leggings, but didn't wait for her to put them on, just handed them to her before he took her hand. The pod rocked back to its starting position, but the floor and walls shook.

The door wouldn't activate to open, but it had an emergency mechanical thrust which he used to jimmy it wide enough to get his shoulder through and muscle it open.

Meanwhile, Leti had hopped into her leggings.

"Let's go." He grabbed her hand again and they joined the other guards and servants running through the corridors for shelter.

The pressure in the pod changed, air growing thinner and noxious. *Veck.* His human. She wouldn't last long without sufficient quantities of oxygen.

Knowing the lift wouldn't work, he raced toward the emergency ladders, where a crowd already thronged. He pushed his way in to assist the weak and elderly, and the moment a gap appeared, held his hand out to Leti.

"Up, up," he encouraged and she scaled the ladder, her bare and battered feet sliding over the rungs. He followed her, stopping to give a hand to the next few Zandians before he returned his attention on getting his human to safety.

"We are under attack. Follow emergency procedures." Prince Zander stood on the landing, his mate and tiny young standing behind him. "To the fight ships," he barked at the warrior in front of Paal reporting for duty. When he saw Paal, he thrust Lady Lamira toward him. "Our atmospheric system has been hit. Take all females and young to the crystal bath—the oxygen is most pure there."

"Yes, my lord." He extended his hand to usher Lamira and her screaming young first, then hustled behind with Leti. They passed Erick and Lady Taramina on the way. "All females to the crystal bath," he relayed.

"That's for human females," Lady Taramina called over her shoulder.

"Wait, Paal." Erick caught his mate around the waist. "*Please*, go with Paal."

"Not on your life," she gritted.

Erick growled, but conceded, waving Paal on with his other two charges.

The pod shook and tipped again. The Zandian infant screamed louder and Lamira pressed his tiny head to her breast, making soothing noises. They ran through the corridors, picking up Bayla from Dr. Daneth. Eslyn, the other Zandian female on the pod, and her four young were being lifted through a busted door that looked like one of her mates—probably Granit—had smashed open with his fists.

"Bring them to the crystal bath—Prince Zander's orders," he barked to Damon, another of her mates.

"Right behind you."

Paal used the manual release to jam the door to the crystal bath halfway open. Leti took the infant from Lamira's arms so the princess could squeeze through, then handed him in.

Paal eased Bayla and Leti through next, then followed to allow Granit, Laake and Damon to secure their own female and her young.

"One of us should stay to guard them," Damon said. "What were your orders?"

"To get all females and young in here." Paal looking around. "Who are we missing besides Lady Taramina?"

"My mother," Princess Lamira said.

Veck. Master Seke's mate, Leora. "I'll go for her."

"I'll stay," Granit said.

"Thank you." Years of training with these warriors made it easy to negotiate in the moment of crisis.

Paal and Damon left the large, circular chamber at the center of the pod, dragging the door closed behind them.

He cast one last glance back at his little female and found her wide brown eyes on him. "You'll be safe here," he promised.

Stars, make it true.

Because leaving Leti felt like leaving a limb behind.

———

Leti dragged shaking fingers through her tangled hair and gravitated to Bayla's side, since she was the only being she knew.

They were under attack. That much frightened her. But even more terrifying was the notion that Paal—one of the prince's warriors—may never return.

No, she couldn't think that way. Paal had a gift for operating under turmoil. She'd witnessed it when he rescued her on Jujo, and she saw it now. His movements were quick and efficient, his manner alert and assured. He had the training and the background to thrive in these situations. He would take care of himself.

The constant buzz of a comms unit came from the huge warrior standing guard at the door. She couldn't hear everything—just terse fragments about fighter ships and engineering teams. The pod continued to shake and shudder as if it might collapse at any moment.

"You're Leti, Mina's friend," the prince's mate said, coming to stand close to her and Bayla. She bounced her knees and rocked the wailing baby.

"Yes... my lady?" She wasn't quite sure how to address a fellow human, who in any other realm would be a slave just like her.

"Lamira is fine unless we're in court. They're very formal there."

She tried not to gawk at the beautiful young mother. A million questions flitted through her head about how she'd come to mate the prince and gain her freedom, but now was not the time. Instead, she asked an inane question. "What is this place?" The room was circular with a domed ceiling. In the center of the ceiling a giant crystal had been embedded.

"It's the crystal bath," Lamira explained. "Zandians only eat once a week but they require regeneration from sunlight or Zandian crystal. Normally it would be too bright for our human eyes, but since it's night, we're safe. This room utilizes both. Zandians located all over the galaxy trek here to use this room on visitor's day. If they don't recharge, they grow weak or their growth is stunted."

She kicked herself for not knowing such basic facts about her new master's species. She'd been holed up sexing him without even fully understanding their situation.

"Who is attacking us?" She'd better start with basic facts.

"The Finn. They must know we plan to attack soon and are taking preemptive strikes."

"Is this it, then?" Bayla asked, twisting a lock of dark hair around her finger. "The war?"

Lamira's eyes went unfocused. "Yes. This is it."

"Have they called in the troops from the training pod?"

Lamira shook her head. "No. I don't know. They're chasing the battleship that attacked, but it was only one small craft. The hit was strategic to take down our life support systems."

Bayla's big eyes grew even bigger, her pale skin paler. "Will we survive?" she whispered.

Lamira again took on an unfocused look.

"She's clairvoyant," Bayla whispered. "Like the Venusians."

Leti couldn't imagine how a human with any kind of special gift or gene mutation had managed to survive Ocretion slavery, but it explained why she might be a valuable mate for the prince. Not that her beauty and gentle bearing weren't enough.

Lamira turned her green eyes on Leti. "Your help will be needed to fix the systems."

Her hand fluttered to her chest. "My help?" She shook her head. "I'm sure you have me confused with another being. I have no training in engineering or electronics. I've been used as a sex pet since my adolescence."

A commotion at the door brought their attention there. Granit assisted another being in, shoving it to the side, then helped an older version of Lamira through the opening. Paal stood on the other side, his gaze landing on her.

Lamira pushed her forward and called out to him, "Bring your mate to Lium. Her help is needed to restore oxygen."

Confusion clouded Paal's face. Good—at least she wasn't the only one who thought the princess had lost her mind. "Forgive me, my lady?"

"Take Leti to Lium. She will be the being who fixes the problem."

"I'm sorry—"

"I don't know how she'll do it," Lamira snapped, anticipating whatever protest Paal might give. "Just take her." Despite the order, there was an imploring look in Lamira's eyes, telling Leti she hadn't been in a position of power so very long. She didn't have the confidence of having her every order obeyed.

But Paal bowed. "Yes, my lady." He stepped through the opening and offered his hand to Leti.

She wanted to refuse. She already knew Lamira had mixed up her messages. There was nothing Leti could offer to solve an engineering problem. But she didn't dare refuse. Besides, she preferred to be at Paal's side if she was going to die.

He hustled her out of the chamber and they jogged through the corridor.

The air smelled horrible and burned her lungs. She coughed. "You know I have no idea what she meant—"

Paal held up his hand. "I know. Don't speak unless you have to—conserve your breath."

She nodded and followed his lead to a far end of the pod, where the smoke was thicker. He pushed her forward, toward an older, grizzled Zandian covered in soot and oil. "Master Lium, the princess says Leti can be of help. She has seen it."

She met his irritated glance with a small curtsy.

He waved her back. "Out of the way."

Right. That would've been her preference, too. Unfortunately, Lamira seemed to think differently. She backed up against a nearby wall to wait.

"I'm going to get you a helmet with oxygen." Paal's brows were low with concern. "I'll return shortly. Remember—conserve your breath."

She nodded again as warriors swarmed around discussing technical problems far beyond her understanding.

The prince arrived on the scene. "The hole is nearly patched—what's the progress on the generators?" He glanced her way, then did a double-take. "What is she doing here?"

"Lamira said she can help." The old engineer gave a dismissive shrug.

"And the generators?" Zander snapped, clearly finished with worrying about her presence.

"We need to rewire the atmospheric pressurizing system, but the panel has been crushed. It's impossible to open up and get in there. I can't see what I'm doing. I'm trying to do it by feel. I've sent Jax to get a pry bar, but I fear it will wreck everything inside if we force it."

Wiring. Feel.

Could it be?

No. That was silly. She didn't know anything about wiring electronics.

But the prince turned to her. "Why are you here?" he repeated the question as if Lium hadn't already answered it.

She shook her head. "I'm sorry—I know nothing about engineering, my lord. I wish I could help."

Zander gave a wave of impatience. "Why do you think you're here? What could you possibly offer?"

Ouch. Harsh.

But something forced her lips to move. "I'm good with wires." She coughed at the effort to speak.

He'd started to turn away already, but he jerked back. "Excuse me?"

"I mean, I know nothing about wiring, but I'm good at bending wires." Her face grew warm. "I used to shape animals and other little objects from the bits of wire in the factory where I worked as a child."

Zander grabbed her arm and pulled her roughly forward. "Move aside. Let the human reach in there. Her hands are smaller and she knows wires."

The old engineer cursed, but grudgingly pulled his arm out from around the panel. He looked at his hands as if they were new to him, then at hers. "True enough," he muttered. "But she doesn't have an inkling of the schematics behind that panel. How in the stars will she know what to do?"

"You'll have to talk her through what needs to be done."

Lium grumbled and barked an order at a warrior nearby. Paal arrived with a flight helmet, which he dropped on her head and fastened under her chin. Breathing immediately became easier.

She reached her hand behind the bent panel. "All right, what am I feeling for?"

Lium cut off a length of wire. "We need to bypass the diode..."

And he immediately lost her in a stream of technical speak.

When she shook her head helplessly, he snapped, "Just get familiar with what's in there. I have Jax fetching something I can write with."

She let her fingertips slide over the topography of electronics inside. Little bumps and ridges. Tiny poles and lines.

When the warrior returned with a flat board and some kind of primitive writing device, she watched as Lium sketched exactly what she felt under her fingers. "Your job will be to wrap this wire from here," he pointed to a tiny pole, "around this button here, and over to this one. You can't touch the wire and this pole here without getting shocked, so you'll have to bend a little hook like this, see?" He bent the wire into a crude hook. "And then loop it around without getting your finger in contact. Understand?"

She nodded and took the wire from his fingers, quickly fashioning a sturdy, thick hook that wouldn't slip off.

The engineer's eyes widened with interest. "You *are* quick with a piece of wire. All right, human, let's see what you can do."

She reached her fingers in. Without being able to use both hands, it took her awhile to wrap the wire, but she eventually fastened it to the first pole, around the second button. Now she just had to hook the third one without getting electrocuted. She waved the wire hook back and forth, trying to connect with the pole, but without the sense of touch or sight, it was impossible. Setting the wire down, she reached in to locate the pole by touch, then picked up the wire again. It was too flimsy for her to hook it on. She brought it back out and twisted several lengths of wire to reinforce it, ignoring the tense questions from the half dozen beings gathered around watching.

It was the first time she'd been the center of attention for anything besides her body, and it surprised her how much she wanted to succeed. Not just to save the pod and ensure the safety of everyone on it, but also to prove to herself that she had some value beyond sex.

There.

She hooked the end of the wires and immediately the lights flickered and came on. Generators hummed, the air system blew clean air into the room.

"She did it!" One of the warriors shouted.

Lium thumped her on the back, nearly knocking her down before Paal swept her up against his body in a tight embrace.

Prince Zander barked orders about finishing the patch on the outer shell, and clearing debris, but she only half-heard. Instead, in the cavity of the helmet, she listened to the amplified beating of Paal's heart, just beneath her ear.

Being held by him brought an unbelievable comfort. Emotions she hadn't thought she ever desired to feel ricocheted through her chest. She felt cherished by him, protected. She sensed his approval, his happiness at her success. He was proud of her. Maybe even impressed by her.

And it wasn't over sex.

A new hand touched her back and she reluctantly pulled away from Paal's massive frame. Prince Zander loomed over her, beautiful and regal. "What is your name?"

"Leticia, my lord." She dropped a curtsy.

"Thank you for your help. You have earned your place here with us and are welcome."

She never knew the gooey warmth that came with belonging. With being accepted into a group. Welcomed.

Her cheeks heated as she curtsied, once more.

The prince changed his focus to Paal. "Get her back to the crystal bath until the air has cleared. Report to me the status of the rest of the females and young."

"Yes, my lord." Paal looped an arm around her waist and ushered her away from the wrecked side of the pod, to the dome-shaped crystal bath room. With the power returned, the doors should be working now, but apparently the warriors had broken them with their rough handling. The huge warrior who'd stayed to guard the bath—Granit, she thought she'd heard him called— was struggling to refit the door into the mechanism.

"All beings safe?" Paal asked.

"Yes. How about out there?" All the faces of the females and children turned to listen.

Paal squeezed her. "Leti fixed the wiring and restored the power and the hole has been patched. Prince Zander ordered you remain here until the air is clear."

"And then what?" Bayla asked.

Paal shrugged, but Lamira spoke. "Then they go to war."

CHAPTER FIVE

Zander let out a string of curses in their native tongue. Three planet rotations and they would've taken the Finn by surprise.

Or maybe they wouldn't have. What if they had a mole and that's why the Finn struck this planet rotation?

He stood at the helm of the pod, where Seke and the rest of his advisors had gathered to both brief and counsel him.

"The pod is completely secure and flight worthy, my lord," Lium reported. "Just give the order and we can leave Ocretion airspace and put it in hiding."

He nodded. "And the attacker?"

"Dead. Single battleship, as far as we can tell. There was no sign of any other craft. The Ocretions supplied us with their recorded data, and it appears to have entered the airspace alone and without authorization," Erick said. "The Ocretions are, of course, swearing they had nothing to do with it and cooperating with our effort. That said, I'm sure they won't mind a bit when we relocate."

"And the target for relocation?"

"The Aurelian ambassador has agreed to keeping it in their airspace," Erick said.

Thank *veck* he had Erick to work the diplomatic channels, because his temper was far too frayed to do it well himself. "For how long?"

He met Erick's somber gaze across the oval table. "Indefinitely. They understand our plans and know the majority of us may not return."

"Have they offered any other assistance?"

"None. They refuse to break their vow of neutrality."

"Begin relocation immediately." Erick nodded and left the war room.

Lamira entered without their young. "What do you know?" he asked her, dispensing with any greeting.

"Only what you've already decided. You will strike immediately." His female had developed a quiet strength since she'd embraced her gifts as a seer. He drew from it, trusting she would warn him if his decision was wrong.

He bowed his head. "Yes." He turned to the warrior at the door. "All horns on deck—we meet in the Great Hall. Humans, too. Immediately."

The warrior pressed a button on his comms unit and projected the order throughout the pod.

Zander sank into a hoverchair for a moment of quiet before he addressed his beings. This was it. War.

———

Paal laced his fingers through Leticia's as they strode to the Great Hall. He wanted to be in contact with her at every moment—hated to leave her side. Probably because he knew they were about to be parted.

Veck.

What if he never saw her again? The thought ripped his chest open. Not for his own fate—he wasn't afraid to die. But for her. Who would care for her? What would happen if the Zandians couldn't return to the pod? Would the humans be returned to Ocretion slavery?

Probably.

That thought sickened him.

He hoped to the one true Zandian star Zander had made provisions for his own mate and the rest of them.

A throng had gathered in the pod, but Zander's throne stood empty. A tense silence reigned, only a few murmurs disrupting it. Every tight expression showed fear or anger.

Zander walked in swiftly and stood in front of his throne. "We strike tonight," he said without preamble. "You may have sensed the pod is already in motion. We will relocate to the safe airspace of Aurelia. All servants will remain. All humans will remain. The females and young will remain. I will send out a message to every Zandian in the galaxy and suggest they come to the pod for safe harbor until the battle is won."

Out of the corner of his eye, Paal saw Taramina make an irritated gesture, but Erick caught her hand and brought it to his lips.

"The training pod occupants have boarded the galactacarrier and battleships and are making their way toward our strike locations. The warriors on this ship will board the battleships we keep here." He scanned his warriors, who all raised their fists at 90 degree angles, pledging their undying fealty. "Two of you will remain behind to guard the pod. Paal and Ronan. Paal, you're the lead. Ronan is your second-in-command. You will have the two trained warriors Lily and Cambry at your disposal, as well as the brain power of the remaining female council." He nodded in the direction of Lamira and Taramina.

Paal's heart dodged from side to side in his chest, as if unsure whether to lift or fall. Staying with Leti was his greatest wish, and yet he'd trained his whole life for battle. To be left behind felt a bit like an insult.

As if Zander guessed his thoughts, he met Paal's gaze. "You are responsible for the sole future of Zandia. If anything happens to the occupants of this pod, our species may never survive. I'm sure you comprehend the enormity of your position."

Humbled, he bowed, as did Ronan. "I am honored to be chosen for such a duty." He meant it.

Zander nodded. "Say your farewells. We depart immediately." The prince turned to his own mate and wrapped her in his arms.

Most beings remained in the Great Hall, as if needing to cling to one another in this time of great uncertainty. Lady Taramina argued with her mate. Like Paal, she probably didn't want to be left behind.

Erick pressed a laser gun into Mina's hands. "Your father is the greatest Master of Arms our species has ever known," he said. "I know you'll defend this pod as well as any of the warriors left behind." He looked at Paal, as if for agreement, so Paal bowed. "I'll be grateful for your assistance."

Annoyance flitted over the female's face, but she nodded and pulled her mate's mouth down to hers.

Paal wrapped his arms around Leti, allowing his relief at not having to leave her to pour into the embrace. Now he needn't worry what would happen to his lovely female if the others never returned. He would see that every being on this pod remained safe and lived a long life.

No matter what it took.

———

Leti peeled off her dirty clothes, exhaustion seeping from her every pore. She'd stayed in the Great Hall with all the beings on the pod until all the warriors had departed. Paal had been busy receiving last minute instructions from Master Seke and even now still was out patrolling.

The sun had risen, but after being up most of the night, she couldn't keep her eyes open much longer. And that delicious washtube was calling her name. Having such a posh chamber to return to still made living on the pod feel like a luxury. Even if they were under attack. She stepped into the washroom and groaned when she saw how dirty and tired she looked.

She hit the button to open the washtube and stepped in. Warm water started to fill it, spraying from every direction and she stifled a moan of contentment. Abruptly the water stopped.

"What the—?"

The washtube door slid open, revealing her giant warrior looming in the opening. He stood naked, and his eyes glowed bright purple, amplifying the bald hunger scrawled all over his expression.

She smiled—a genuine smile, not a seductive one—and stepped back to make room for him. He lunged for her, but his hands were gentle where they settled around her waist. He kept walking forward until he'd pressed her against the washtube wall, every inch of his huge, hard body in contact with her softer one.

"Leti," he rasped.

That was all—just her name. And then he went silent, stroking his large hands over her, as if just discovering the topography of her body for the first time. The washtube filled with water and he kissed her just before it was time to hold their breaths, his lips sealed on hers, as if keeping her safe from drowning. When the water drained and the light spray of scented oil coated their bodies, he stroked her again, rubbing it in. When she attempted to reciprocate, he pinned her wrists above her on the wall and continued his massage.

As his touch warmed her, she forgot about being tired, forgot about the drama and trauma of the night. She knew only Paal. His touch, his beautiful body. Heat coiled in her core and her legs began to tremble. He stroked up her legs, along her inner thighs, but maddeningly avoided her aching pussy.

Releasing her wrists, he slid his hands down her arms, along her sides, over her ass. He knelt in the tiny space and stroked down her legs, even picking up her feet and gently rubbing them, inspecting her wounds.

After he'd set the second foot back on the floor, he hooked his thumbs around her inner thighs and pushed them wider. Then—oh stars—then, he brought his face to her pussy and licked into her.

Although his reverence had been awe-inspiring, and incredibly sweet, she hadn't been sure if she appreciated it more than his rough passion. But she didn't have to choose, because as soon as he got the taste of her, he lost all control. He flung her leg over his shoulder and flattened her ass against the wall, opening her petals for his mouth.

She moaned as he turned feral, penetrating her with his thumb as he sucked and licked her clit, her inner lips. He pushed one well-oiled finger against her back entrance and she flinched, still tender from his ass-fucking during the night.

He stopped and looked up with bright purple eyes. "Too sore, little female?" His voice was soft, not the hard, demanding tones he usually used with her.

She wrapped her fingers around his horns to pull his mouth back on her. "No, Master. I like when you make it hurt."

He treated her to another epic tongue-lashing, but then he slid out from under her leg and stood. "No," he said softly. "I don't want to hurt you, lovely girl. Not tonight—this morning—whenever it is. I only want to make you feel good."

She bit back the sigh his words produced. Keeping the barriers around her heart with this male was getting near impossible. Especially when he hit open the door to the washtube and swept her up into his arms, carrying her to the sleepdisk. He eased her onto her back.

"Spread for me, beautiful."

She bent her knees up to welcome him and he settled his hips into the cradle of her legs. He let her reach for his cock and guide it into her as their gazes tangled. Locked.

She held her breath, utterly destroyed and rebuilt by the intensity of the moment.

"I'm the lucky one," he murmured as he sank into her.

She arched her back and moaned.

"I didn't have to say goodbye to my female. I get to feel her beneath me one more time. Touch her sweet skin. Savor her taste."

"Paal." Now it was her turn to utter his name without any other reason than to say it. "Paal."

"That's it, beautiful. Say my name when I fill you with every inch of my passion." He rocked deep, with smooth, satisfying strokes. "Say my name when you take it deep."

"Paal." She reached for his horns, squeezing and releasing them.

Her warrior lost control, hammering into her with short, hard thrusts, his muscles bulging in his shoulders and arms.

"So good," she whimpered, matching the squeezing of her fists over his horns to his thrusts.

He roared and buried himself deep inside her, filling her with hot streams of his rainbow essence.

She squeezed her legs around his waist and took him even deeper, allowing herself to fly over the brink into bliss. Her inner muscles squeezed, inner thighs shook as she rubbed her clit down hard on the base of his shaft.

Paal jerked and shook her off his horns with an indulgent smile. "No nails in the horns, pretty girl. They're sensitive."

"I'm sorry," she gasped.

Again he rewarded her with the indulgent smile, his gaze soft and warm. "Don't be. I love to see you go over the edge."

"Paal," she murmured and he lowered himself over her, nuzzled her neck.

"You should sleep, beautiful."

She hardly noticed him easing out of her, covering her with blankets and kissing her forehead. Already she'd slipped into a restful sleep.

CHAPTER SIX

Paal patrolled the corridors of the palatial pod. He'd docked it in Aurelian airspace but he couldn't stop the itchy feeling they weren't safe. Every incoming transmission had his teeth on edge.

Since the docking the night before of two battleships from the training pod carrying the humans not fit for battle, all had been quiet. He'd had no word from Prince Zander or Master Seke, but they'd gone dark on purpose. If all had gone as planned, they were already in battle.

A communication buzzed through the unit it in his collar. "Ronan requesting permission to dock." The message had been received throughout the galaxy for any and all Zandians who desired protection to seek refuge on the pod. To avoid any foreign ships docking, he'd set up a meet location on Aurelia and sent Ronan to run transport.

"Permission granted. How many on board?"

"Twenty-two."

Twenty-two. Damn. It would require some logistics to find them all places to stay. Maybe he could hand this off to the princess. She would be the hostess in Prince Zander's absence, right?

He found the females in the Great Hall, where the majority of the pod's occupants had naturally gravitated since the strike. He searched out Leti first, his breath catching, as always, at her beauty. The way she'd met him the night before—open, giving, vulnerable—exactly as he'd always dreamed his female would be—didn't just make his shaft hard, but filled his chest with warmth.

The females looked over at him and he cleared his throat. "The first arrivals of Zandian refugees are docking. Twenty-two of them. I, uh, wondered if you wished to be in charge of their placement on the pod?" The shift in roles and responsibilities was awkward, at best. The humans from the pod had been given shared servants quarters, except for Lily and Cambry, who, as Zandian mates, were honored.

Lamira stood, but appeared unsure. Of course—no Zandian who hadn't already been acquainted with her would accept a human as their hostess and leader. Humans were enslaved throughout the galaxy. They were considered lesser beings.

Lady Taramina and the princess's mother stood as well. "Yes, we'll figure it out," Lady Mina said.

His gaze wandered to take in his female again. Her lips quirked at him—so *vecking* sexy. "Good. I'll have them sent in here, then." He spoke into his collar to give the order and a few moments later, two servants arrived with the group of newcomers.

"Paal! Son, how are you?"

His body went rigid at the sound of his mother's voice. Oh *vecking* hell.

He should've expected her. Why had he not predicted this?

Because she was the one Zandian he never thought would come running back.

He ground his teeth. "Hello, Mother."

Leti and the other females watched the interaction with obvious interest, which only compounded his annoyance. His self-absorbed mother should not be able to still get under his skin after all these years, but she had an uncanny knack for it. Jaw clenched, he stepped forward to offer each of his cheeks for her kisses.

"You didn't think your current mate could provide you protection?"

"I preferred the protection of my son. Your name was relayed as the commander of the pod, and I dropped everything to come."

Right. Or she'd decided to jump ship to something brighter and shinier once again.

As if his mother ever dropped anything for him. No, things must have gone south with her current mate and she was trolling for a new one. Too bad for her she was long past breeding age, or she'd have the pick of every Zandian warrior after the war. Assuming there were any left.

The other Zandians—mostly of the older generation, like his mother, had also entered, taking in the room with varying degrees of appreciation.

Diplomacy wasn't his strong suit, but he recognized Lamira's position was awkward at best, and foisting the bulk of this problem on her hadn't been fair. He cleared his throat.

"Welcome, Zandians. You will be safe here. I wish to introduce you to Princess Lamira, Prince Zander's mate and the mother of little Prince Zander," he waved his hand at the infant in Lamira's arms.

Lamira drew herself up and offered a regal curtsy. "Welcome, Zandians," she echoed his words. "I will speak to the servants to find accommodations for all of you. We hope this war will be short and decisive, but of course, we cannot know how long it will go on. Keeping the last of the species safe on this pod was Prince Zander's most fervent wish, so thank you for placing your-selves under his protection."

It was well-spoken, and the Zandians appeared to receive it politely. Word of Zander's mating to a human had probably already reached them prior to their arrival.

He stepped away, this time avoiding eye contact with his lovely female. Having his mother close put him in too sour a mood to wish to interact with any being.

"Master, wait," Leti jogged after him.

No. He didn't want to talk to her. Not now. Especially not with his mother watching. It wasn't her fault, but seeing his mother scraped his every nerve raw. He didn't turn, just waved his hand to shoo her away.

It was strange, but without turning, without her saying a word, he knew his dismissiveness hurt his little female.

Great, now he was turning into his mother—abandoning those he should be caring for.

But even being able to see his folly, he couldn't make himself undo it. Couldn't stop, and call her back. Couldn't change his emotional state to want to be around a female in that moment.

All he could do was walk away. And the faster the better.

———

All the air whooshed out of Leti.

Had Paal found her so inferior he didn't wish his mother to know about their relationship? She'd been careful to call him Master—so he could've intro-duced her as his slave. But maybe even taking a human slave was considered beneath Zandian warriors—what did she know?

Well, fuck him.

Two could play at this game. And she knew how fast he'd crumble if she turned her attentions to the other warriors in the pod. How convenient that the very three she'd flirted with were the ones chosen to remain behind.

Except flirting with them felt about as enticing as dropping a brick on her bare foot. She wanted Paal. Wanted things to be the way they'd been since the attack. She'd let down her guard and he'd met her there. It had been soft and easy. She'd felt honored by him and honored to be at his side.

Damn. She should've known heartache was the only consequence to getting emotionally involved.

———

Zander walked through the galactacarrier where warriors—human and Zandian alike— stood alert, prepared for battle. He cleared his throat. "I am grateful to each and every being on this carrier, and to those with Master Rok.

So much is at stake for us now. For the Zandians—our home planet. The only source of Zandian crystal in the galaxy. The only place our bodies receive the full nourishment they require. That planet is our birthright. The Finn took it from us unjustly. They killed our families and wiped out most of our species and tomorrow—" he paused, looking around at all of them. "Tomorrow we make them pay."

A cheer went up.

"I have waited, as most of you have, for this planet rotation. Our time to exact revenge. To take back what belongs to us. Our numbers may be small, but we are fierce! We have trained, and invested. We have the best fleet currency can buy. And we have the aid of the bravest humans in the galaxy!"

A slightly less enthusiastic shout went around.

"Tomorrow you fight by our side, and for that, I will ensure you have a safe place on Zandia. I will provide you protection against Ocretion slave traders. On Zandia, you will be able to settle, make a home. You will never have your children or parents or family ripped from your arms again. You will be treated fairly, with the decency and honor Zandians are known for."

A few humans nodded their heads.

"We must put our trust in each other now. Never lose your focus on the prize. We must win back Zandia."

Another cheer.

"Thank you. Get some rest, all of you. I need you at your best tomorrow."

Paal kept himself in the control room of the pod for most of the following planet rotation. He'd sent a coded communique to Prince Zander saying that they were safely docked, but otherwise communication with the troops had been cut off for everyone's safety.

He waited until long after dark to return to his chamber. If he was honest, he'd admit he was avoiding Leti, but it was easier to tell himself his job required him to work through the night.

He opened the door to his chamber and walked softly in the dark. Leti sat up and peered in his direction. Apparently humans couldn't see in the dark. "Paal?"

"Yes, it's me. Go back to sleep."

She laid back down but didn't close her eyes. When he shucked his clothes and joined her in the sleepdisk, she ducked her head under the covers, crawling down over his shaft.

Even though his cock instantly turned harder than Zandian crystal, he grasped her hair and pulled her head back before she could apply that temptress mouth to his malehood.

"Did I say you could suck it, female?"

"May I, Master?" she purred.

It annoyed him. He wanted a genuine reaction from her like he'd had the night before. Why was she always trying to seduce him?

He threw off the covers, pulled her across his lap and landed several hard smacks on her ass.

She had the audacity to giggle.

"Little human, if I want something from you, I'll take it. I don't need you to offer it. I thought you understood, but it seems you require another lesson."

She waggled her ass on his lap, her soft skin brushing over his throbbing cock.

He smacked her ass again. "Up."

She crawled off him and he stood from the sleepdisk, picking up his sword belt from the dressing table. He grasped her wrists and looped it around them, then pulled until she stumbled off the hovering bed.

He dragged her to a place where he had a hook on the wall for his sword and pulled her up until he could drop the buckle over the hook. She turned in a circle, body stretched up until she balanced on her tiptoes.

"Now that's a lovely sight."

Because he felt completely unforgiving, he sought the animal hide strap out of the implement box. She still sported a few marks from the last whipping he gave her, which ought to inspire his mercy, but it had the opposite effect. It excited him. Power rushed through his veins.

"Turn and face the wall, beautiful. You know I want access to that ass of yours."

He supposed if Leti had appeared frightened or cowed he would back down. But his female always seemed to relish his punishments, which made him all he more eager to deliver them. He started with light strokes, slapping the leather strap across her ass, loving the way she tightened her round globes and released them, the way she danced around and put herself right back into position.

Such a good little slave. He ought to be kinder. Instead he channeled all his irritation that had been buzzing through him since his mother's arrival, all his annoyance at Leti's sex pet act, all the stress of bearing the responsibility for the future of their species, into reddening her ass. He striped the lower half of her cheeks down to where ass met thigh. When he stroked the backs of her legs, she cried out with a different timber. "Ow! Master, please."

He recognized the difference—he'd crossed the line from painful pleasure into something more challenging. But still, he *vecking* loved hearing her beg, so he whipped her there again, And once more.

Then, to force himself to slow down, he stepped in and grabbed one of her heated cheeks, squeezing and kneading the plump flesh. "I like it when you make those hurty little sounds."

She made another sound—half whimper half moan.

He reached around the front of her hips to cup her mons.

So *vecking* wet.

His little female always got wet when he punished her. Victory roared through him. "Turn around," he commanded, his voice rough.

She swiveled, revealing her perky breasts, stretched and lifted by her arms overhead.

He rolled another length of the strap around his fist to shorten it. "I wonder what sounds you'll make when I whip these pretty little tits?"

She whimpered, her breath coming fast, eyes dilated. Her long hair fell over her shoulders. He brushed it back to get it out of the way. With a light flick, he slapped the strap over her right breast.

She whimpered.

"Mmm, that's a good one. Let's see if I can get another. Spread your legs wide, female."

She stretched her long lean legs as wide as she could to still balance on the tips of her toes.

He brought the strap up between her legs, spanking her pussy.

"Master!" He loved the alarm in her voice.

"Does that hurt, beautiful?" he purred and slapped it up again.

"Yes! Ooh. It hurts." She danced around, but he noticed she still returned to position, as if she wanted more.

His beautiful, sexy little human. Ack, he wasn't going to last much longer. He needed to get his hands on her.

He whipped her left breast, then her pussy, then the right breast again.

"Please, Master," she pleaded.

He growled and spun her around, dropping the strap. One hand cupped her soaking wet pussy as the other slapped her ass—hard.

Stars, it was so *vecking* satisfying to spank her ass. He spanked her hard and fast, his hand crashing down again and again as he rubbed her clit, then penetrated her with one finger.

She came the moment he pushed inside, arching up so her feet left the floor and she dangled from her wrists, a strangled scream reverberating in her throat.

He caught her around the waist to lift her wrists from the hook as he plunged his finger in and out of her while she came.

The moment she stopped, he propped her over the sleep disk and spanked some more, her ass turning rosy under his hand, though she only made soft crooning sounds.

"*Now* you will suck my cock, little one."

He dragged her from the bed and arranged her on her knees at his feet, closing his eyes for the moment of impact.

A shudder ran through his large frame at the shock of her hot wet mouth engulfing the whole head of his malehood.

"That's it, beautiful." He pushed her head forward, forcing her to take him deep. "Show me what you've got."

Like a good little slave, she swallowed him down, running her lush lips all the way to the root of his cock. She sucked hard as she pulled back, her tongue swirling over the underside.

One lick and his thighs were shaking.

He may pretend he possessed this little female, but in these moments, she owned him.

Maybe that's what he'd been fighting the whole time.

"Take me again," he rasped, his voice nearly unrecognizable. "Take me deep like that."

She took him deep. She sucked him like her life depended on it, and sadly, there probably had been moments in her existence when it had. But he couldn't think about that without wanting to go back in time and murder every *vecking* owner she'd ever had.

"Take it," he growled, holding her head in place with a fist in her hair as he *vecked* her mouth. Her clever hands twisted around the base of his cock, tightening, squeezing, scraping her nails lightly over the underside of his balls.

"*Vecking stars!*" he shouted. "*Vecking* Zandian star, the source of our creation and fuel of our existence!"

He came down her throat and she took it, swallowing it with a readiness that humbled him.

"Good little female," he crooned, picking her up after she'd licked him clean. He carried her to the sleepdisk. "You're so *vecking* good at that. How could I possibly want to punish you for doing what you've been trained to do?" He asked the question aloud, because she should know that he understood how wrong he was to hate that about her.

He settled them both on the mattress. She curled into his body, nestling her head on his shoulder and smoothing a slow circle over his pectorals. It didn't strike him as seduction, but of an idle caress, and he *vecking* loved it.

He caught her hand and kissed it.

"Are you ashamed for your mother to know we're together?" Her usually sultry voice faltered with insecurities and a hint of pain.

Damn. "No, it wasn't about you. I hate my mother."

"Why do you hate your mother?" Her question reached through the darkness and stung him out of his post-orgasmic bliss.

Something twisted deep in his gut. "I don't *hate* her," he started to say, but it wasn't really true. He did hate her. Or he hated many things about her. He also loved her, but she hadn't returned his love. Or at least that's how it felt.

As he searched for an explanation, he landed on the grudge he'd harbored for the last sixteen solar cycles. "She left my father. Broke him, completely. And then he died when the Finn invaded. I guess I never forgave her for that."

Leti returned to stroking her soft palm over his chest. She made a sympathetic sound in her throat.

"She always said I should be grateful because her leaving my father meant she and I were spared. We were off-planet. And I guess, in the end, she's right.

I wouldn't be a member of Prince Zander's Royal Guard if we'd stayed. My father was nothing more than a crystal miner."

"Playing the what ifs is a fool's game. You have to roll with what life brings you, that's what I've learned."

He pulled his little slave's body closer against his. *Veck*, he was an idiot, having his pity party over losing his father when she'd been through far worse in her lifetime.

"Your resilience humbles me, little female. I don't know why it also makes me want to break you."

She silenced him with her fingertips over his lips. "Don't." She pressed a soft kiss to his neck. "Don't question what you need to do with me and I won't question why I enjoy it. All right?"

Warmth rushed into his chest in swirls of appreciation for his wise little slave. "All right." He kissed the top of her head. "Get some sleep, little human. I know you need much more than I."

She nuzzled him and her body softened even more, molding to his frame, her breath slipping in and out evenly.

He closed his eyes, wanting to savor only the feeling of Leti's body against his. Forget about his mother, the war, or the precarious position of his species.

CHAPTER SEVEN

A touch on Leti's arm brought her attention back to the room. "Can you give me a hand?" Bayla was speaking to her. The females—Zandian and human alike—were playing with the children gathered in the Great Hall.

She gave herself a shake. "I'm sorry—with what?"

"In the lab. I want to check on the baby."

Great, another place to remind her of Paal's scorn. But she needed something to do, so she agreed. "Sure, of course."

She and Bayla headed to the lab where Bayla turned on pieces of medical equipment. One whirred to life next to the table, projecting a blank hologram.

Bayla hopped up on the table and handed a small hand-held instrument to Leti. "Just bring it slowly over my belly," she instructed.

Leti complied, and the blank hologram turned into a projection, flickered and transformed. "Oh!" Her breath caught as the image of the tiny fetus appeared floating beside them.

Bayla giggled, covering her mouth with her hand. "I don't really need to check so often, but I like to see her. She's so perfect, isn't she? Look at those little toes!"

Inexplicably, tears welled in Leti's eyes. She'd never wanted to have children, not that it mattered what she wanted. Reproductive capabilities were suppressed in all sex slaves. A child would be another emotional attachment—something to cause her great pain when it was taken from her.

But seeing Bayla's tiny fetus stirred some deep longing in her. Her chest tightened and twisted with pain at what she'd never have. "She's perfect," she managed to choke out.

"Do you want to breed?"

She choked on an inhale. Damn Bayla's directness. Pain—not just at not having babies, but at not having a mate who'd want to breed her— bounced around her chest before she managed to expel it all.

"No," she said firmly. "Never."

Bayla must've seen through her, because she shrugged lightly, slipping off the table. "You should have Daneth check to see if it's still possible. You know —just so you know."

Was it still possible?

Her uncertainty must've shown on her face because Bayla waved her up to the table. "Get up there. We can at least see if you still have a womb."

Curiosity won out over her desire to run away from the lab and never look back. She pushed herself up on the table, her palms damp with cold sweat.

Bayla took the small device and pressed it over Leti's abdomen. "Oh yes, you have a uterus, see?" She pointed at the hologram. "And what's that?" She dragged one section of the hologram to enlarge it. "Look," she pointed at a tiny round spot.

"What?" She tensed. Was it some implant they'd put inside her? Or some illness?

"I might be wrong..." Bayla frowned.

"*What,* Bayla?"

"That looks like an implanted egg."

Leti stared, still not sure she understood. "What are you saying?"

"A fertilized egg. The start of a baby."

First everything inside Leti went dead still. Then it exploded. She didn't realize she was sobbing until Bayla handed her a disposable cloth to wipe her tears.

"I-it's not possible," she sobbed. "I shouldn't be fertile."

"Some sex slaves aren't permanently altered. So that their masters can have the opportunity of breeding them if they wish. You might have been given something to suppress it for a number of years and now it's worn off."

More tears. A ridiculous amount of tears.

"I mean, I might be wrong! There's a blood test we can do. Do you want to try?"

She sniffed and nodded. "Yes, please."

"Okay." Bayla went to the storage cabinets and searched for a device. When she returned, she cleaned a spot of Leti's inner arm and shot her with it. Blood filled a cannula and mixed with some other liquid. Bayla popped it out and shook it. "We'll know in a few minutes. It measures an early hormone."

Leti's brain couldn't even function as she sat there waiting. Every time her thoughts came around to *I might be pregnant* it stalled and went dead.

After what seemed like an eternity, Bayla said. "Yes, you're definitely pregnant. And it's definitely Paal's. See?" She showed her a readout Leti couldn't understand, as she'd never been taught to read. "Daneth had Paal's gene sequence in his database." She grinned broadly. "You're having a Zandian young, like me."

Sweet mother earth. Pregnant!

"H-how old is the baby?"

Bayla grinned. "It's not a baby yet. But I'd say no more than a planet rotation or two. It's definitely Paal's, if that's what you're wondering."

Another sob went through her.

Paal.

The male she didn't want to care about.

And a baby she'd couldn't stop herself from loving.

What in the hell was happening to her?

———

Zander paced the dock of the galactacarrier. Three battleships had docked. He nodded to the pilots as they disembarked. His presence was important. He had to show them they were all in it together. That he didn't send them out to risk their lives lightly. But he couldn't think of a *vecking* thing to say to them.

And so no being spoke.

No one wanted to point out what had become painfully obvious.

Shanli had been a trick. A trap. A *vecking* mistake.

They'd waited in position through the night and into the next planet rotation, but the ships they'd identified on their radar weren't there.

Zander had ordered the battleships out to fire at the places their maps showed the Finnian ships, but they weren't cloaked.

They simply didn't exist. Or they may exist, but they sure as stars weren't anywhere near Shanli.

Which meant they were somewhere else.

Zandia.

And Seke didn't have nearly enough laser power behind him to fight.

And he hadn't answered any communication since that morning.

Veck, he'd waited too long to call his ships back. They needed to be traveling to Zandia now.

"Rok, as soon as the last ship is docked and accounted for, set the course for Zandia."

"Yes, my lord." Rok's expression was as grim as Zander's must be.

The war had begun and they were drifting out in Shanli with all the best ships and equipment with their heads up their asses.

By the time they got to Zandia he may have lost half his troops.

Vecking excrement!

"Let me know when they've all safely returned."

"I will, my lord."

———

Paal grumbled as he changed his tunic. Lamira had decided to uphold the tradition of a formal weekly meal in the Great Hall, despite the fact that they were at war. Leti was already with the other females, doing whatever it was females did.

He supposed it was smart, on Lamira's part. A distraction for the occupants of the pod. But for his part, he could do without it.

He'd spent the entire planet rotation and this one avoiding his mother, but now he'd be forced to not only see her, but to sit down and converse. And yes, he was acting like a ten cycle old.

Maybe he should just keep pretending he was needed on deck. His mother had been hard to dodge, because she kept seeking him out, asking a million questions about the pod and those who normally lived there.

It would be just like her to be seeking a new mate. Foolish and greedy old female.

He dragged his feet getting to the Great Hall, but arriving late was a strategic error, because he found a seat had been saved for him at the head of the table. Right next to his mother, with Leti on the other side.

May the one true Zandian star help him.

He bowed to the table before he sank into his chair.

"There you are, dear," his mother trilled. "It really isn't polite to keep the table waiting when you're the commanding officer."

As if his nails weren't already digging into his palms.

Like when his mother had arrived, he sensed Leti's avid interest in their interaction. *Veck.* If he were a real leader, he would send his mother away from the table for insulting him in front of others. No, a real leader wouldn't draw the criticism in the first place. Or would a real leader just brush it off?

Veck if he knew. Which probably meant he wasn't a real leader. Only when he had his little female pinned beneath him did he feel the way he wanted to. Powerful. Potent. Masterful.

Not the way he felt now, like little more than a defensive youth. Damn his mother for bringing out this side of him.

Fortunately, Barr, the pod's elderly chef, arrived with the food, with help from his servants. The meal featured human and Ocretion foods alike—a savory combination of fresh vegetables and fruits, grown right on the pod by Lamira, and the best meats available from Ocretia.

Leti only picked at her food. Strange, considering how eager she'd been to sample all the dishes when she first arrived. But perhaps she'd finally eaten enough. He didn't know how the human metabolism worked.

A niggling in the back of his mind warned him it was something else, but he pushed it away. He couldn't trust any thoughts he had about females when his mother was around.

A Zandian Paal didn't recognize sat beside his mother—another refugee, about the same age as her. The male was well-dressed and regally mannered, a fact that hadn't gone unnoticed by his male-eating matriarch.

She touched the male's sleeve and purred, "Did I tell you my son is the commander here?"

Ugh. He wanted to vomit. Now she was going to use his status to improve hers? Of course she was. She'd use anything.

On his other side, Leti watched everything.

The male turned to him and put his fist up in the traditional Zandian greeting. "I am Thon."

Paal returned the gesture. "Paal, of Prince Zander's Royal Guard."

"We appreciate your efforts to keep us safe."

Blah, blah, blah.

He forced a smile.

Watching yet another dance of seduction between his mother and a male made him sick.

His gaze drifted, as if attracted by a magnet, to Leti. Her skin appeared paler than usual and she'd stopped paying attention to his mother, frowning, instead at her food. When she realized he was watching, though, her temptress mask snapped into place. She took a slow bite of food, closing her lips around the fork in a way that had his cock surging against his flight pants. Now that he observed at her, he realized how incredible she looked, dressed in a beautiful white gown with a plunging V for a neckline.

Maddening female. Now he'd never stop staring at her cleavage. He wanted to *veck* that temptress look right off her face. Put her up on the table on her hands and knees and make a meal out of her. Then tug her hair back with one hand as he plowed into her hard enough to make her scream.

"Paal," his mother trilled. "Why haven't you introduced me to your human?"

Oh veck.

"What is she to you? Slave?"

Every being at his end of the table stiffened, Zandians and humans alike. They were in mixed company with a human as hostess and mate to their leader. Referring to humans' slavery seemed...gauche at best.

"Lidea, meet Leticia. Leti, my mother, Lidea. And no, she's not a slave. Zandians keep no slaves, by decree of Prince Zander." He employed formal tones and pitched his voice so everyone would hear. His mother could insult him all she wanted, but he wasn't going to give her the opening to target Leti. Especially if her purpose was to show off to some male.

"Mmm." His mother dabbed the side of her mouth with a napkin. "Be careful, then. She looks like she wants to get her hooks into you."

"Enough, Mother," he snapped.

Leti's lips curved into a sultry smile, and she made a clawing motion toward him.

Vecking hell. He needed to get out of this damn room.

———

After the meal, some of the old refugees pulled out musical instruments and started playing. The music was elegant. Soothing. All the older Zandians immediately brightened, some with tears in their eyes. Servants appeared from every corner of the pod, hovering in doorways to listen.

It struck Leti that she hadn't heard a single note of music since she'd arrived on the pod. She'd thought perhaps Zandians didn't listen to music.

Lamira stood and used a switch on her collar to amplify her voice. "I am delighted to introduce to you the musical group Crystal Prophecy. They were on tour in the galaxy when the Finn struck and have been quietly playing the music of Zandia in small gatherings ever since. They've offered to play for us tonight. Please feel free to remain here in the hall while the servants clear the tables for dancing."

Dancing.

What did Zandian dancing look like?

The band struck up the lovely melody again. The older male who'd sat next to Paal's mother, Lidea, extended a hand as if inviting her to dance. Other elderly Zandians got up in pairs, delight shining in the smiles on their wrinkled purple faces.

Despite her age, Paal's mother moved with light feet and grace as her partner spun her around the room. Leti found herself smiling despite her opinion of the female. She could see why Lidea got under Paal's skin. She struck Leti as superficial, selfish, and judgmental. And that was based on the way she treated her son, not the way she looked down at a human slave.

Leti didn't give a flying pile of excrement about that.

She didn't give a flying pile of excrement about much of anything except reconciling her thoughts around having a baby.

She didn't know the first thing about being a mother. But she'd learn. She'd spend time with Lamira and watch how she cared for her little halfling. And Bayla, when she had her child. She'd be the best *vecking* mother to her baby the galaxy had ever known.

She didn't have the slightest clue how to talk to Paal about it.

Hell, she didn't even know if she would.

There were moments, mainly after they'd been intimate, but also after the attack on the pod, when both their barriers had been down. She'd been herself with him and he'd shown a tenderness that had taken her breath away.

In those moments, she'd been a different person. Without fear, she found in herself a bounty of affection. She wanted to give to him, without limit. Not because he was her master, but out of genuine desire.

But he'd also been distant and angry. He'd rejected the idea of mating her and hadn't claimed her in any way in front of his mother.

If she were smart, she'd squelch that flicker of yearning that flared in her chest when she found out she'd be having his baby. He didn't want to mate her. She should find another male. An easier conquest. A Zandian who wanted to mate with a human and have a family. He didn't have to know the young was Paal's.

But that thought made her nauseous.

She didn't want a "conquest." She wanted the real thing.

What she had with Paal.

They stood up from the table to allow the servants to clear. She fully expected Paal to disappear immediately—he'd been eyeing the door from the moment he came to the meal, but instead he held out his hand to her, the same way his mother's suiter had.

"Would you care to dance?"

She reached for his hand, breath catching in her throat. Why should the simple invitation make the room spin and her knees wobble?

Because she was a slave and he was a beautiful, noble warrior. Because he'd been playing hot and cold since the moment she met him and she never knew where she stood. Because maybe she'd wanted this moment to arrive far too much for comfort.

He led her to the side of the room and gathered her hands in his. She didn't know the dance—had never partnered with another being before—but he made it easy. His confident, sure movements guided her. She glided around with him, turning to and fro, circling the room.

He leaned his head down. "I'm sorry about my mother."

She flashed a smile up at him. "She doesn't bother *me*, Paal. I've met far worse. I wish you wouldn't let her get to you."

His eyes followed her across the room. "Look at her now—throwing herself at a new male."

"I know." She made her face sympathetic. "But your father is already gone. Her betrayal no longer hurts him. Stop letting it hurt *you*."

Surprise flitted over his face. He looked over her head, still gracefully guiding her about the room. He remained silent long enough she was certain she'd offended him. But finally he said, "You think I should excuse her? Forgive her?"

Leti shrugged. "The grudge only hurts you. Your mother is a limited being. She probably didn't offer you enough as a parent. She certainly did your father wrong. But she is who she is. Resisting her only makes you tense."

Paal eyed her. "Great wisdom from a slave." He released one of her hands and spun her around beneath his other. When he stopped, she fell into his arms, dizzy. He held her quiet against him, not dancing. "I'm sorry—I didn't mean that to sound derogatory."

The edges of her lips kicked up in a smile. "Takes more than calling me a slave to offend."

Paal guided her back into the steps, circling the room.

"How do you think I became so wise? I learned at a very young age what I could control and what I couldn't. Most of it I couldn't, so I had a choice. Either live in misery, or figure out how to flow."

Paal was looking at her as if she were the most interesting being in the galaxy and she didn't want it to ever stop.

"Mina and I used to play games to make it easier. We'd take bets on silly things, or give stupid names to things. Anything to lighten the droll."

His look hadn't wavered. It sent a warmth right down to the white slippers she'd borrowed from Mina for the night. "All right, little female." He glanced over at his mother. "What will you bet my mother has that male in her chamber by the end of the night?"

She giggled. "Are you going to bet against it?"

He gave her a chagrined smile. "No. I fear it's inevitable."

"So let's bet on how long it takes her."

Paal threw back his head and laughed—a rich hearty sound that sent pleasure winging through every part of her. All the while, he kept perfect time with his feet—their feet, since he guided her steps, too. "Two more songs."

She shot a glance over at his mother to gauge how much physical contact she had going with her suitor. "I give it three. But I'm not sure I can keep dancing long enough to find out. I'm getting dizzy."

Paal laughed again and led her to a hoverchair where he sat down and pulled her into his lap. "We'll watch from here, then."

She melted into him, the heat of his body warming her skin. Their closeness made her bold. Maybe she would tell him about the pregnancy tonight. "Did you ever want to become a parent yourself?" she asked.

The comms unit in Paal's collar blinked. "Update required from palatial pod. Go to a secure channel."

Paal stiffened. "It's the prince." He stood, lightly setting Leti on her feet. "I'm sorry, I have to go. You'll stay to tell me who wins the bet?"

Disappointment blew through her but she forced herself to nod and smile. "Of course."

He grasped her nape and tipped her head back, brushing his lips lightly over hers. "Thank you for the dance."

Her heart proceeded to dance and glide around the room, spinning beneath his violet gaze.

"Thank you," she murmured.

So what if she lost her heart? Her old plan of never caring had ceased to exist the moment she found out she was carrying their baby. It was time to make up new rules.

———

Paal jogged to the flight deck and switched on a private communication line. "Palatial pod to carrier. This is Paal."

"Message received, Paal. This is Zander. Have you received any communication from the other troop?"

"No, my lord."

"Shanli was a diversion. There are no Finnian ships here. We are changing course for Zandia. We lost communication with the other troops. If you receive any transmission from them, I require immediate notification."

"Yes, my lord. Of course."

"Anything to report from the pod?"

"Twenty-two Zandian refugees have joined us. No other news to report."

"Good. You have your orders."

"Yes, my lord." Paal ended the transmission and sagged against the control panel. All the lightness of his evening with Leti drained away.

He attempted to connect with Master Seke, but like Zander, received no answer.

Veck.

Vecking bad news.

He hated to break it to Mina that her father had gone missing. To any of them. He definitely didn't want to return to the Great Hall with the news. Especially not when everyone had worked so hard to lift each other's spirits.

What had Leti said? You had to find flow. But flowing around the loss of this battle would be pretty *vecking* hard.

It would mean the end of their species. The next generation would consist solely of Eslyn's three Zandian young and Lamira and Bayla's two halflings. Hardly enough to repopulate. And if they lost their bid for their planet, there wouldn't be a place to repopulate, anyway.

No, they had to win this war. One way or another.

He just wished he didn't feel so *vecking* helpless stuck on the palatial pod while the rest of his species fought.

————

Leti watched Paal's mother slip away with her suitor after three dances. She'd seated herself beside Bayla to watch and she stood after they left. "I think I'll head to sleep," she murmured to Bayla.

"I'm exhausted too. I'll walk with you." Her new friend also rose and they left the Great Hall together, walking down the corridor in the direction of Bayla's chamber and the lift. They stopped outside Bayla and the doctor's chamber.

"You haven't told him yet, have you?" Bayla asked.

Leti shook her head. "No." She didn't want to go into all the reasons why she hesitated. "There's just a lot going on."

"Yes, but considering the uncertainty now, wouldn't it be better to secure your future? You're sure to get Paal to mate you when he finds out you're carrying his young."

Her stomach twisted. Bayla's line of thinking made sense logically. Under normal circumstances, it would've been her exact thought.

But these circumstances were far from normal.

Her heart was in play, and "securing a future" with Paal if he didn't want her felt dead wrong.

"Well, I think you should tell him, but it's up to you. I won't say any word until you tell me to." Bayla gave her a quick hug and opened her door. "Good night."

"Good night," she mumbled and stepped around the corner to the lift, only to run right into the solid form of her master.

And he'd never looked so fearsome.

Her stomach lurched.

Cold anger darkened his face. "Tell me what?" His words came out cold and crisp.

She attempted to suck in a shaky breath, but it didn't come. "I'm pregnant." She forced the words out over numb lips.

She wouldn't have thought it possible, but his expression darkened even more. "I see. A clever strategy to secure your future."

The corridor tilted. It was a wonder her feet stayed planted on the floor with the way her head swam. Clever? Strategy?

She tried to shake her head, but had no idea if she was successful. "No, that's not what this is," she managed.

But of course he would think so. Bayla had just said as much aloud.

His mother had accused her of strategizing at dinner.

And after growing up with a mother like that, of course he'd believe the worst.

In fact, it explained why he grew so outraged every time she tried to seduce him. He always believed he was being played.

He took one menacing step toward her. "No?" Ice splintered through his words. "Then what is it?"

And she supposed she had been playing him. Using her body as a weapon was the only trick she had in her bag. Since she'd been put into sex slavery, it had been her only means of survival. She'd used it at every turn.

But that was before Paal had made her believe something else was possible.

Well, she wasn't going to prove him right. She lifted her chin and jabbed a finger in his chest. "Fuck you—or *veck* you, as you'd put it. I'm not looking to secure a future with you. This baby probably isn't even yours!"

She stepped through the open lift door and smacked the button to close it. In the three interminable seconds that followed, she watched Paal's pallor turn from peach lavender to pale purple and the lines of his face go wooden.

Then, just as the door shut, it flooded with violent color. "What the *veck* do you mean—"

The door slid shut as she choked on a sob. She leaned her forehead against the door, forcing in a slow breath.

This was for the best.

This was definitely for the best.

She couldn't be with a male who didn't trust her. Who believed the worst of her in every moment.

Even if she deserved that belief.

She wouldn't harangue him into a relationship he didn't want.

She knew from the start what happened to slaves flawed enough to believe in love.

Heartbreak.

The only inevitability.

At least she got hers over sooner than later.

The door slid open and she ran to Paal's chamber. He'd given her a code to enter to get in and she used it. She rushed in to grab her things—which really consisted of a few borrowed items of clothing, then quickly left, running back down the hall.

Should she take the lift? No, what if he was coming down?

She raced the opposite way down the corridor, jogging through the maze of halls that made up the center level of the pod. She just needed to find a place to hide.

And she needed it quick—before the tears started to fall.

———

Rage rocketed through Paal. He slammed his fist into the wall beside the lift to keep himself from tearing after his female and demanding to know exactly what was going on.

This baby probably isn't even yours.

Was it true? How had she even been impregnated? Weren't all sex slaves altered to prohibit conception? Those who weren't breeders, that is?

Had she known she was carrying another male's baby whilst she tried to seduce him?

But if so, why not pretend it was his?

Nothing made sense.

All he knew was the sickening sense of being duped, being trapped when he'd heard her talking with the other human about securing her future made him certain he shouldn't follow her.

Whatever was in play here, it would end in disaster.

He'd be the chump his father had been, left cold the moment the situation changed or a better opportunity came along.

His own mother had seen it clearly that night at the weekly meal, hadn't she?

She looks like she wants to get her hooks into you.

He forced his feet to start walking and made his way to the deck, hoping to the Zandian star something—anything—would require his attention there.

CHAPTER EIGHT

Leti ignored the female voices around her.

Maybe they'd go ahead if she just left her head under the pillow.

Some being pulled the covers off her and gave her leg a little shake. "Come on, Leti. You can't cry in bed all day, even if it's the nicest sleepdisk you've ever slept on."

Bayla.

Sigh.

She emerged from under the pillow and shoved her tangled hair out of her face. Her eyes still stung from all the crying she'd done the night before. Or had it been an entire planet rotation ago? She didn't know how long she'd been buried in Mina's covers hoping to wake up to a new reality.

One in which it didn't feel like her heart had been put in shackles and whipped with an animal hide strap until it gave up and just stopped working. And, of course, that image brought memories of Paal rushing back to the forefront.

"Guess what?" Bayla sat on the sleepdisk by her feet, Mina near her head. "Mina has the ability to project holograms in her chamber."

Leti rubbed her swollen eyes. Bayla's words made no sense to her overslept mind. "Huh?"

"Holograms. For entertainment. Some of them are funny, too. Want to watch?"

"Oh. No, I don't think—"

"We're watching," Mina insisted, crawling up on the sleepdisk and sitting beside her. Bayla scooted onto the other side.

Leti had ended up at Mina's door after running from Paal's chamber, and had told her the long, sordid story.

"And guess what else?"

She shook her head. "I can't."

"I brought food. I know you haven't eaten for an entire planet rotation. That can't be good for the young. You need to keep your strength up." She pushed a bowl of sweet-smelling custard in front of her. "Try this. It's heavenly."

"I'm not hungry," she groaned, pushing it back.

"Try it," Bayla said more firmly. "You're going to love it."

Leti took a bite, only to stop the woman from talking any more. Her head ached with a vengeance. Okay, it actually was delicious. Sweet and creamy goodness. She took another bite.

"See? What did I tell you? Now, let's watch."

Mina flicked on a hologram depicting a Zandian family. "These are old. From when I was a child. Before Zandia was taken."

Leti sat up straighter, commanding her eyes to focus. Her friends were trying to help her. But watching the strong, good-looking male Zandian on the screen only reminded her of Paal.

So much more handsome. So much stronger. More capable.

She remembered how adept he was in a crisis. When he'd rescued her. When they'd been attacked.

She remembered the way he'd kissed her like he wanted to devour her.

Before she could stop them, tears spilled down her cheeks. "I'm sorry. I'm just not up for company."

"The hormones don't help," Bayla said kindly. "They can intensify your emotions.

She sniffed, wiping at a tear. "That must be it."

That, or she'd truly lost her heart to Paal, even while she thought she'd been protecting it.

"He's going to realize what a colossal mistake he made," Bayla said.

She shook her head. "No, he won't. I told him it's not his young."

"Why would you say that?" Mina demanded.

"Because... "

It sounded stupid now. "I didn't want him believing I got pregnant to trap him. Because I didn't."

"Of course you didn't. I don't even know how it's possible," Mina said.

"Me neither, but you should probably get checked out, too. You might be fertile, too."

The hope that bloomed in Mina's eyes made Leti remember what was more important. A tiny life grew within her. Her very own child.

And Paal's.

The damn tears started again.

"Let me ask you this," Mina said. "If Paal hadn't acted like an idiot and accused you of trapping him, would you have *wanted* to mate him?"

The tears came down faster. She wanted to lie and say no. Wanted to make that true. But she couldn't.

She nodded miserably. "I've never come alive the way I do with him. Not just sexually, but as a being. I feel real when I'm with him. Not a slave. Not a pet. Like there's more to me than just my body. He cared about what lay beneath it all."

She rubbed the center of her chest as if she could make the ache go away.

"Then just tell him the young is his. Give him some time to adjust to the idea and see what happens."

"No." She shook her head stubbornly. "I'm not going to tell him and I forbid either of you to tell him, either. Using the baby would be trapping him. If he wants to be with me, it needs to be without dangling a child in front of him."

Her friends looked at her like she'd gone mad.

"Promise you won't tell him." She screwed up her face into a severe expression.

"Only if you promise to get out of this sleepdisk and get into the washtube," Mina said.

She sighed. "Fine. Yes. I'm getting off." She dragged her heavy limbs to the edge of the sleepdisk and stepped off. "I'm going to the washtube."

She hoped to the stars it would wash off the darkness weighing down her very soul.

———

Paal smashed his fist through the wall of the flight deck. He'd already punched three holes in the wall in his chamber. It hadn't done a thing to take the edge off his nerves.

Leti had disappeared entirely. She'd moved out of his chamber and he hadn't seen her since. For the first planet rotation he'd been too *vecking* stubborn to ask where she was. But after another sleepless night without her—with her scent fading from his hoverdisk sheets—he was going mad.

He couldn't help but believe he'd made a terrible mistake.

If having Leti leave him—yes, she'd *vecking walked out* on *him*—made his chest feel as if it had been sliced open by a *vecking* laser gun, then would being trapped by her have been any worse?

It couldn't be.

Because, *veck*, at this point, he wished to the Zandian sun he'd been ensnared by that wiley female. He wished to the Zandian sun she'd sunk her claws deep into him and refused to let go.

Wouldn't that be far better than *this*? The empty ache of having her gone and not even understanding what had gone wrong?

Except he had a nagging, itchy sense he *should* understand what went awry.

Whatever it was, it had been his *vecking* fault.

The door to the flight deck slid open and Lady Taramina strode in, mouth tight.

Alarm rocketed through him. Had something happened to Leti? Did something go wrong with the pregnancy? Stars, humans were a weak species, what if the pregnancy killed her?

Lady Taramina just looked at him, cocking her head to the side as if she might decipher some deep meaning from the set of his horns.

"What?"

"You think you're too good for a human? Is that your hang up?"

He nearly choked on his own spit. "No! What are you talking about? Is this about Leti?"

Pure scorn danced across Taramina's face. "Of course this is about Leti. I want to know what your objection is to her. I see attraction between you two, sometimes affection. But it's like you fundamentally hate who she is. Is it because she was a sex pet?"

His throat tightened at the word *hate*.

He didn't *vecking hate* Leti. How could she say that? He loved her.

Holy Zandian star. Was that true?

Yes, it was.

He loved his little female.

Mina strode forward with long, purposeful steps. She stopped two paces in front of him. "Leti told me you mistrusted when she tried to please you. Like you thought it was a trick or something."

His stomach churned. The tingle crawling over his skin told him he was about to get his ass handed to him, but, like an idiot, he still hadn't put it all together.

"Let me tell you something, Commander. If you think a sex pet has any options available to her besides performing as trained and pleasing her master's every wish before he even wishes it, you're dreaming." She got up into his face, her eyes flashing a bluish-purple with anger. "So if you resent Leti working hard for your pleasure, if you think it's a sign you can't trust her, then you need to find yourself a different female." He swallowed under her furious gaze, so similar to her father's, it made him shift in his boots. "And furthermore, if you'd ever bothered to ask her *anything* about her life as a slave, you would know that her fertility has never been under her control. So the idea of her getting pregnant on purpose to trap you?" Lady Taramina made a scoffing sound. "Asinine." She started to march away, apparently concluding her lecture, but then she whirled back for another round. "And don't you think if she meant to trap you, she would've told you that baby was yours?"

"Is it?" he choked.

He'd gone *vecking* crazy not knowing. Wondering if he actually had a young growing inside his beautiful human right now. And the times he allowed himself to believe he did? The thrill had gone beyond any joy he'd known.

Lady Taramina hesitated for a split second, making his nerves go haywire. But all she snapped was, "What do you care?" before she sailed out of the chamber and let the door slide shut behind her.

Damn.

He made another hole in the wall.

He'd been a *vecking* idiot.

He needed to go and win his female back.

Whatever it took.

And Lady Tararmina was right—he didn't care if the baby was his or not. It didn't matter. He wanted Leti, regardless.

————

Leti sat in the kitchen with Bayla and the other human females, eating. Lamira appeared pale and tired. Her baby suckled her breast, one of his tiny hands wrapped around his own horn for self-soothing.

Her heart lurched at the precious sight.

Abruptly, Lamira dropped her spoon and stood up, eyes wide.

"What is it?" her mother asked sharply.

"I need to go to the crystal baths," she said, already running. The rest of the women looked at one another for only a few seconds before they dropped their utensils and went running after her.

"Are you finished, then?" Chef Barr called after them.

No one answered. Lamira entered the crystal bath, thrusting her infant into her mother's arms. "Wait here. I need quiet," she said.

The rest of them stood in a clump in the corridor, silent. Fear shot up Leti's throat, closing off her air.

Something bad had happened. Lamira had seen it.

Time inched by. It seemed like hours. No one moved. No one spoke.

Finally, Lamira emerged. She worked hard to swallow, accepting her fussing baby back without even looking at him. "Cambry and Lily, you're the last hope. Master Seke's troops were shot down in Zandia. Zander's troops are under heavy attack above Zandia.

"But the crystals have shown me where to find Fluut."

"You must find him. Take him out. Once he falls, the rest will concede."

Cambry, the most warrior-like of all the females, tossed her long red tresses back over her shoulder. "Tell me how to find him."

————

Paal stalked down the corridor looking for Leti. Not that he'd figured out what to say to her, yet.

She'd been sleeping in Lady Mina's room, he thought, but no one answered his knock. As commander of the ship, he *might* have the ability to open locked doors and he *might* have used that privilege, only she truly wasn't there.

He rounded the corner and found himself face to face with his mother and her new lover, Thon. For once, he felt nothing at being in his mother's presence. Maybe it was Leti's talk about flow, or maybe it was because his mother hardly seemed significant when he stood to lose his female forever.

"Have you seen Leticia? My female?" he blurted.

His mother stopped and looked around. "Well, no dear. Is something wrong?"

"Yes," he muttered jogging past her.

"What is it, Paal?" his mother called to his back.

"I was an idiot and I may have lost her," he said. He'd never been so honest with his mother about anything. One simply wasn't with a parent who found so many things to nitpick. But he didn't care what she thought. He didn't care if she approved of his relationship or not. He wanted Leti—needed her—and nothing was going to get in his way of winning her back.

"Commander Paal, we need to get this pod to Zandia straight away," Lily said, appearing breathless at the end of the hallway.

Except maybe this.

"What's going on?"

"Lamira has seen that all the troops are in trouble. Our only hope of winning Zandia is to fly in and take out Fluut in his secret location, but the battleships aren't made for long distances. We'll need the pod to get us close enough."

Vecking excrement.

He drew in a slow, measured breath. "Lady Lamira has seen this?"

"Yes."

"And you know where this secret location for Fluut is?"

"Yes."

Veck, veck, veck.

He'd made a promise to Zander to keep this pod safe. Flying it into the war zone was a direct violation of that order.

Yet not aiding the cause went against every cell in his warrior's body.

Lily must have guessed his dilemma. "Just get us close enough. Cambry and I will fly in and take out Fluut and you can get the pod back to safety."

Veck that. If he flew in that close, he'd be taking a battleship and going into Zandian airspace with them. Ronan could get the pod back to safety.

"All right," he clipped. "Get onto the dock and board your ships. We'll be warp speed in less than ten."

Lily gave a decisive nod and took off running in the opposite direction as him.

On the flight deck, he voice commanded the pod engines on. "Set the course for Zandia."

Instruments whirred to life, maps shifted and spun into place. "Warp speed to outer atmosphere."

He gripped the counter for the lurch as the pod shot out of Aurelian airspace.

He was going home.

They may not make it out alive, but at least they would die trying.

CHAPTER NINE

Paal fastened his helmet. "As soon as we take off, you get the pod as far from that fighting as you can," he instructed Ronan.

Once they'd arrived at the edge of Zandian airspace, the battle area became clear.

The galactacarrier was surrounded, defending itself against assaults from all sides.

Paal had to repeatedly remind himself of their mission, because the urge to try to save his fellow warriors nearly slew him. But Lamira had seen where Fluut lay in hiding and she saw that killing Fluut would end the war.

He couldn't second guess his decision making now.

What he could and would obsess over was leaving without fixing things with Leti.

"Battleships cleared for takeoff," Ronan said.

"Battleship One heading for Zandia," Cambry said.

"Battleship Two heading for Zandia," Lily said as soon as Cambry's ship had disappeared out the docking gate.

He waited for Lily's ship to disappear, then spoke into his comms unit. "Battleship Three heading for Zandia."

"May the one true star of Zandia watch over you," Ronan murmured the ancient benediction over the comms unit, sending chills racing along Paal's skin as he sped toward his beautiful planet.

"Ronan." He couldn't stop himself.

"Yes, Commander?"

"If anything happens to me, I want you to tell Leticia, my female, that my only regret in life is not mending things with her before I left."

Ronan didn't answer.

"Ronan?"

"Tell her yourself when you get back," the young warrior challenged.

"You heard the message. I want you to promise me you'll see that she's protected. She's—" he swallowed back the tightness in his throat. "She's carrying my young."

Ronan cleared his throat. "Copy that, Commander. You have my vow on Zandian honor."

"Thank you."

He focused on the controls. As they entered the Zandian atmosphere, the battle near the capital became clear. Zandian battleships swarmed in the airspace above the—*oh stars.*

"I have a visual on a crashed Zandian ship," Cambry reported. Their troops had suffered severe losses.

"I see it, too," he answered. "Stay the course."

Two fighter units swooped in behind them.

He flipped his craft upside down and fired, hitting his target. The enemy ship plummeted, smoking, to the ground. He kept firing, rotating back, but Cambry had already taken the other ship down.

"Nice shooting, Red."

"Not so bad yourself," the human answered. "Now let's get the hell away from here and find that mine. Cloaking up."

"Cloaking engaged but I'm not sure it works," Lily reported. "You're still on my radar."

"These ships are designed to see each other to prevent accidents. Let's hope it hides us from their technology."

They flew in a triangle formation and shot around the side of the planet to the largest crystal mine. There, Lamira said Fluut had taken residence, believing he was undetectable and protected by the Zandian crystal, the hardest substance in the galaxy.

Too bad for him the crystal itself had spoken to their princess.

He closed his eyes and sent a silent message to Leti. *Wait for me, little female. I'm coming back and I'll fix everything. I promise.*

When they drew close to the mine, enemy ships appeared out of nowhere, firing on them. "Incoming from every side!"

"I see them. Still trying to line up to drop my bomb," Lily said, but she was surrounded by three battleships.

"Abort and fly hard," he warned, ducking and dodging his way around the ships crowding him, trying to keep Lily's attackers in his sights.

Cambry was spinning and firing indiscriminately, which actually was a perfect tactic, as she took out two of their ships in the process.

And then she went down hard.

"*Veck!*" He dived for her, turning on his magnetic force to slow her careening fall. He caught her just before she hit, but his ship exploded in flames before they touched down.

———

Leti watched Lamira where she stood at the window of the Great Hall, staring out into the inky blackness around them. They'd removed the pod from Zandian airspace, moving in cloaking mode at a slow pace toward Aurelia.

From what she could tell, no being wanted to leave Zandia at all. Every heart had been linked to that planet, whether they were human or Zandian. Whether it was to a being fighting for Zandia's freedom, or whether it was because Zandia was home.

For her part, the unrelenting jaws of fear had snapped down around her throat the moment she heard Paal had flown off on a suicide mission meant to save them all.

Without saying goodbye.

But why would he say goodbye? They had nothing to say to each other. She was done with him. She'd left, and with good reason. He would never trust her, would always believe she was a conniving pussy-trap like his mother.

Still, knowing he might never return changed everything. Every. Damn. Thing. So many thoughts ran through her head. Things she would like him to know before he died. That he'd been the only male to ever get a genuine response from her body. That his kindnesses to her were the only ones she'd ever known from a master. That she'd give anything to be in his arms whirling around the Great Hall one more time.

Tears smarted her eyes, but she blinked them back.

No. She wouldn't cry for him yet. He still might make it back.

"What do you see?" Leora whispered to Lamira.

Lamira shook her head. "The outcome is still undetermined."

"Is there nothing we can do to help?" Talia, Mina's sister, asked.

"Not yet," Lamira murmured. "Wait—perhaps. The ships above Zandia have nowhere to land when they're out of fuel. If we signal them and let them know our location, we could become their base."

"We're a poor substitute for a galactacarrier," Eslyn, another Zandian female observed.

"Yes, and it would put us in great danger. I don't know if we can convince Ronan to take us there." Lamira tapped her lips with her fingertips.

"Aren't you the princess?" Leti had to ask. She didn't know how things worked here, but there seemed to be a disconnect. "Wouldn't he have to do what you command?"

She lifted her shoulders, uncertainty on her face. "I'm also human. And a female. And I have the sole heir to the royal line on board. He may feel his duty to Zander outweighs obeying me."

"Well." Leti stood. "Wouldn't the first question be whether we can contact the battleships at all? Perhaps we should ask Ronan to try."

The rest of the females must have been as anxious as she to do something, because they moved as one out of the Great Hall, heading to the flight deck to talk to Ronan.

Ronan appeared somewhat over his head. He was a young, affable warrior with an easy smile. He swallowed at the sight of seven females—three Zandian, four human—spilling into his territory. Lamira, Leora, Bayla, Eslyn, Talia, Mina and Leti crowded into the room.

Mina explained the situation when Lamira hesitated.

"So you want me to send out a communique? That would alert the Finn to our location and make us a target as well?" There was indecision on his face. Poor male was in a terrible position.

"Isn't there some way to send out a coded message? Something our ships would understand but the Finn wouldn't?" Leora asked.

"I know," Talia said. The lovely Zandian was Mina's sister, so Leti took an instant liking to her. "What if it's not a message at all? We broadcast something for entertainment, like a hologram theater. And our troops will recognize our voices and understand."

"That is so stupid it just might work." Mina grinned at her younger sister who had also only recently found her way back to her species.

The females began to speak at once, throwing out their ideas for the theater performance, but Ronan reached out and touched Leti's shoulder. "May I have a word with you?"

Oh hell.

Ronan was one of the three cousins she'd flirted with to anger Paal. She sure hoped he wasn't hoping to get intimate with her now.

He led her out of the chamber and into the corridor. But the handsome young warrior appeared uncomfortable. He gripped his hands behind his back. The tips of his ears colored darker purple. "Paal begged me to give you a message if he didn't return. If you wish to wait and hear it from him—"

"No," she cut in, her heart suddenly galloping. "What did he say?"

Ronan cleared his throat. "He said to tell you his only regret in life was not mending things with you before he left. And he asked me to protect you and the unborn child at all costs." Ronan bowed and backed away.

Tears smarted her eyes. "Thank you, Ronan. I'm glad you told me," her voice choked.

She wanted to stay and help the other females, but her feet carried her away, running down the corridor to Paal's chamber.

She opened the door and tumbled in, falling on the sleepdisk and breathing deep. Remembering his scent. His touch. The tremble-inducing things he'd done to her in that chamber.

Please come back, Paal.

I need you.

It was true. She could no longer pretend not caring about others was the safest way to go.

She cared. Hell, she loved Paal. And leaving him had been a mistake.

So he had to return safely.

Not just for the baby.

For her.

CHAPTER TEN

Paal threw himself out of the burning battleship and ripped open the door to Cambry's ship. As soon as he saw she was alive and moving, he raced back to his craft. He needed to get the *vecking* bombs off the ship before they exploded in the flames.

If they had any hope of still taking down Fluut, they'd need the firepower.

"What are you doing?" Cambry screamed when he ducked back into the burning craft.

Another ship crashed into a hill just beyond them. "That's Lily. Go get her," he ordered. "I'll meet you both there."

Cambry pulled a laser gun from her waistbelt and nodded, taking off at run.

He ducked through the wreckage, holding his breath to keep from drawing in too much smoke.

In the belly of the craft lay the big weapons. The ones they'd hoped to bury Fluut with. He needed at least one of the bombs.

An explosion sounded nearby.

The weapons on Cambry's ship. He didn't have much time.

Eyes smarting, lungs burning, he reached the armory and managed to pry loose a large torpedo bomb. Hefting it over his shoulder, he scrambled out.

Light and sound burst behind him, launching him into the air and throwing him several meters.

A high-pitched whine sounded in his ears.

His ship exploded. One more second's delay and he'd have gone up with it.

He staggered to his feet and found the torpedo a few meters away. Once again, he balanced it on his shoulder and took off at a jog for the third burning craft.

When he arrived, he found Cambry and Lily dragging a torpedo between the two of them, away from the burning ship. Clever, capable females. Why had humans ever become a subjugated species? Clearly they were equal to his own.

"Well done," he praised.

The females let it drop to the ground between them, panting. "What are we going to do with these?"

"I'm going to walk to that mine and drop them down the *vecking* hole."

Lily giggled, a sort of hysterical sound.

A slow smile spread across Cambry's face. "All right. Let's do it."

"I'll go," he said. "Alone. It's a suicide mission."

"*Veck* that," Cambry said. "You can't carry two bombs. We all go."

He rubbed the soot from his forehead. "Fine. Let's move."

———

They wouldn't hold through the night.

Zander's pilots were exhausted. They'd been fighting all planet rotation against impossible odds. He still had no contact from Seke or any being from the other troop.

He'd been inching—literally *inching*—the galactacarrier toward Zandia during the battle. If Seke's pilots were out there fighting, they might use the carrier as a resource if he could get close enough. That, and he wanted to be within the atmosphere if they went down.

Because yes, it looked as if they'd eventually be shot out of the sky.

Rok's urgent commands to his pilots came through his comms unit.

He changed the frequency to their other channels, hoping to pick up something—anything—from the troops fighting on Zandia.

He stopped when he heard the idle chatter of females.

His female, to be exact.

Every nerve ending in his body went to full alert. What was this? They were telling stories. Or were they acting out a holo-play? He attempted to get a hologram of them, but it wasn't available. Just the sound.

They were offering a signal. For him? Were they in trouble? He started to trace the signal to a location.

"But I like my male to know there's always a place for him to come home to," one of the females purred.

Ah.

Not a distress signal. A beacon. Leading their pilots home.

Which must mean Seke's troop was still fighting but needed help. Their base ship must've gone down.

Well, he'd have to get the galactacarrier over the damn planet to unite their efforts.

He armed the galactacarrier with all the firepower left. He'd have to use it up now, saving none for when he arrived.

It was a risk he'd have to take. He'd rather die on Zandia than out here in unclaimed airspace.

"Battle fleet, return to mothership," he ordered. "I repeat, battlefleet, return to mothership immediately."

Rok's fighter pilots swooped and turned, zooming back to the galactacarrier.

Zander readied all his weaponry.

It was time to go home.

———

Paal laid the torpedo near an air vent to the mine. They were miles from the mine's entrance, but this was the slope Lamira had described, with the exact scar on the side. Fluut was directly beneath them now, if Lamira's sight could be trusted.

"This is the spot," he murmured, keeping his voice low even though no one appeared to be in the area. They'd hiked for hours to get there, and he'd had to take turns carrying both the torpedos to give the humans a rest.

"Now what?" Lily asked, wiping sweat from her brow.

Paal stared down through the vent into the abyss. "Now we drop them down. Simultaneously, if possible. And then we run like hell."

The females nodded. They arranged the two torpedos side by side near the edge of the vent and positioned themselves behind it. "On the count of five." He bent down and placed both palms on the bomb.

"Five?" Cambry asked.

He couldn't hide the flash of irritation at the question. "Yes, why?"

She grinned. "Humans say three."

"Aw. Five is a sacred number for us. On the count of five. One...two...three...four...five!" He pushed hard and his torpedo toppled over the edge. He started running the moment the job was done, waiting only to make sure the females got theirs over the lip of the vent.

All three of them ran hard and fast down the slope of the mountain. They ran and ran until he realized something surely should've happened by then.

"Hold up."

The three of them slowed to a stop and stared at one another, panting.

He cursed. "Stay here. I'm going back."

"What are you going to do?" Lily asked.

He pulled the laser gun from his belt. "Shoot it." He jogged back up the hill to the vent, half expecting the bomb to go off any moment, but it didn't.

Peering down, he had no idea where to shoot—all he could see was inky darkness. He positioned himself on his belly, letting his head hang into the crevice and blinking as his eyes got used to the lack of light.

After a few agonizingly long moments, shapes came into focus. He spotted one of the torpedos where it had landed on a ledge not far down.

Well, it was better than nothing. He aimed the laser gun and fired, holding his finger over the trigger for continuous stream of laser light. The crystals in the mountain served to reflect the laser, lighting up the entire crevice.

And then it blew.

For the second time that day, his body flew through the air.

His back hit a tree trunk and he dropped to the ground, unable to move.

The entire mountain shook, explosions and tremors running through the earth, shaking the trees, the rocks, the dirt.

He attempted to move again, but couldn't draw a breath, couldn't make his body respond.

The two humans crouched beside him, speaking words he couldn't hear, tugging at his arms, trying to get him to move.

The land slid beneath them, sending them skiing down the slope as parts of the ground simply fell away, crashing in on the mine.

"This way," Cambry yelled, angling them down and away from the site of the explosion. At least he heard her this time. "Move, Paal, before we're buried!"

As if he wasn't trying. His limbs wouldn't respond.

"Paal, if you want to see your female and meet your baby, you need to move!"

Leti. And his young. It was his young, he knew it had to be.

The females hauled him up. His feet obeyed this time and he ran. He ran for Leti. Because not seeing her again wasn't an option.

———

Leti helped run Zandian crystals from the Crystal Bath to the exhausted pilots who had docked on the palatial pod for refueling.

Their plan had worked. The pilots heard them and were cycling in to refuel and recharge briefly before going back out.

"Did you see the battleships that departed from this pod?" she couldn't stop herself from asking. "Paal and Cambry and Lily's?"

The human pilot beside her whipped his head so fast she startled backward. "Cambry was on one of those ships?" His face turned pale. Now that she inspected his haggard face, she saw a resemblance. He must be Cambry's brother.

"Wh-what is it?" she barely forced out a whisper.

A haunted look came into his eyes. "Those ships went down on the west side of the planet."

Her breath whooshed out of her, leaving her empty lungs quivering for several interminable moments.

No. It couldn't be. Paal couldn't be dead. He *wasn't* dead.

Cambry's brother's expression held the same level of terror mixed with denial and a dose of irrational hope.

"They're not dead," she declared stubbornly when she finally regained the ability to speak.

"They can't be," the pilot concurred.

Behind them, Lamira breathed, "It's done."

Every being on the dock stopped speaking to listen to her prediction.

A broad smile split her face. "Fluut is dead. Without his leadership, Zandia will soon be won."

Leti joined the others in a great cheer. If Fluut was dead, that meant Paal had been successful. Which surely meant he was still alive, right?

The pilots who'd been resting surged to their feet. "Let's get back out there and take our planet," one of them said, running for his battleship.

"Oh! It's nearly ready," cried the servant refueling it.

Other warriors ran for their ships, waving off the servants hustling to finish. Within a few moments, they'd all departed and the energy on the deck was decidedly different.

A vibration buzzed through every being. The stale taste of fear and desperation faded, brightened by the cheerier notes of hope.

Winning Zandia was still possible.

All might not be lost.

———

Bringing the mine down around Fluut was one thing. Considering the way the entire mountain imploded, Paal was fairly confident of their success.

But now getting back to civilization posed a problem.

He, Cambry and Lily had hiked the remainder of the planet rotation, but without mapping equipment, he wasn't certain he was leading them in the right direction. Basically, he'd kept his sights on the battleships in the sky and figured they must be over the capital. But he hadn't seen one for a long stretch.

Which could mean the battle was over.

But who had won?

"Look!" Lily cried, pointing toward the sky. "It's the palatial pod!"

Sure enough, the pod appeared to be landing.

He flicked on his comms unit, which had received nothing but a crackle all day. "Commander Paal to flight deck, come in flight deck."

"Ronan, here." The young man's voice was exuberant. "You did it, Commander. Zandia is ours!"

The females beside him screamed, throwing their arms around each other and then him.

"I have your location, and we're sending a ship to extract you now."

His legs turned weak with relief and joy. "Thank the one true Zandian star," he breathed.

Ronan chuckled and ended the communication.

He tried to stay in the moment, but his mind wouldn't stop running over his biggest problem. Now that they had a place to live, would he have a female to share it with?

Could he convince Leti to give him another chance?

The battleship zoomed into view and landed and the hatch opened. Paal expected to see a warrior come out, but instead, his little female burst from the entrance, running for him.

His knees hit the spongy earth, too weak with gratitude and relief to hold him. Or maybe it was to beg her forgiveness—he wasn't sure.

"Paal!" She barrelled toward him, throwing her arms around his neck and nearly knocking him over.

Two more battleships skidded to a stop around them, and Rok and Lundric tumbled out and raced for their mates.

"Leti, beautiful female. Can you forgive me?" He'd rehearsed his apology so many times on the trip, it tumbled out now, even though she didn't seem to be listening. "I had my head wedged when I accused you of trying to trap me. I don't care if that young is mine or not." She laid dozens of kisses on his cheeks and forehead, still strangling him in a tight embrace. "I'm claiming you, and I claim that young. You're mine. It doesn't matter if you want me or not."

"Your apology needs work." Leti laughed and only then did he notice the wetness on her face.

He wiped her tears. "Oh stars, please don't cry."

"No, these are happy tears." She gave him a tremulous smile. "So it doesn't matter if I want you or not? You're forcing me into this?" There was a tease in her voice, but he ran a frustrated hand over his closely shorn head.

"That's not what I meant. I'm trying to say I know you're not trying to trick me into mating you. Or if you are, then I accept. I want to be trapped by you. Because you're mine as much as I'm yours, lovely."

Veck, he'd botched this speech royally.

Leti didn't seem to care. She kissed his neck. "It's your baby," she murmured in his ear.

"It is? Are you sure?" He gave his head a shake. "I don't care either way, sweet girl. *You're* mine, and that means the babe is too."

"No, it's yours. I only said that to push you away."

He ran his hands up and down her sides. "But you've changed your mind about that?" His voice sounded choked, even to his own ears. He brought one hand to rest on her ass and squeezed.

Her husky laugh turned his dick crystal-hard. "Yes, I changed my mind. I want you for my mate. Only you. This baby and I need you."

In a flash he had her on her back on the ground, claiming her mouth as he thrust the hard bulge of his cock into the notch between her legs.

"Oh hey there, Paal. I think you should wait until you're back in your chamber for that!" Rok called out, laughing.

He didn't want to pull back, wanted to keep kissing his mate until the sun rose, but he forced himself off and lifted her to her feet.

A beautiful blush colored her neck and then he had to kiss her again.

"Mine," he growled when they broke apart.

Her smile lit up the entire galaxy. "Yes, yours."

CHAPTER ELEVEN

"Paal, we're going to be late for the gathering."

All right, maybe she didn't care. Not when her mate had her bent over the dresser, fucking her like he was about to go back out to battle. It was the tenth time he'd claimed her since they returned to his chamber in the palatial pod the night before, which was now resting in the capital of Zandia, right where it belonged.

"I just. Can't. Get enough," Paal growled through clenched teeth. "...going to *veck* you all planet rotation." His fingers dug into her hips, holding her in place as he drove deep.

"Yes, Master," she murmured, knowing what it did to him to be called *master*.

He roared, pivoting their bodies and throwing her over the edge of the sleepdisk instead. His purpose for the change immediately became clear. He thrust into her now with his full weight, slapping his loins against her ass, which had already been reddened by his palm.

"More, Master," she whimpered, though it seemed impossible for him to give her more.

Oh, but he did.

He drew farther back and slammed deeper with each stroke until she babbled incoherent pleading words about letting her come.

A roar and he slammed deep. Another bellow as he came.

Her body catapulted her into orgasm, every muscle trembling and shaking as her channel squeezed the last drop of cum out of him.

He collapsed over her. "Now I might let you wash up," he panted.

She smiled.

"But I'll probably *veck* you in the washtube, too."

"Paal, Prince Zander will be honoring you at the meeting. We can't be late."

He groaned and lifted his weight from her, then helped her to stand. He turned her around and picked her up, straddling his waist, to carry her to the washtube.

She sighed and tucked her face against his neck. Being cared for by this male was such pleasure.

How much more tender would he be when they had their child? She couldn't wait to see how it changed him. Them. Sweet mother earth, she was having a baby! They would be a family.

It seemed life couldn't get any sweeter.

———

Paal stood in his crisp white Zandian dress robes with Leti tucked up against his side. His mother wiggled her fingers in a dainty wave from across the plaza. Seeing her with her new beau—hell, seeing her at all—didn't bother him a bit this planet rotation.

Leti had helped him heal that wound.

They stood in a semi-circle on the ruined marble expanse. The servants had cleared the majority of the rubble to make space for the gathering. All Zandians gathered, along with the humans and a few other species who had come from the training pod.

Many were wounded, bandaged or in hoverseats.

Prince Zander stood on a makeshift dais—a stack of broken marble— and activated an amplifier in his collar. "Welcome, my loyal subjects and honored guests. Welcome to your home—our giving planet, Zandia.

"Let me first offer my deepest gratitude at the sacrifice so many of you have made to get us here.

"We honor each and every lost life." Zander bowed his head for a moment of silence.

"We honor our wounded.

"We honor those who cared for our wounded.

"We honor those who showed great courage and risk to get us here today. In particular, I wish to recognize Paal, son of Paal; Cambry, mate of Lundric; and Lily, mate of Rok for changing the tide of the battle by taking out our enemy king. Please come forward to receive your crystal of recognition."

Leti beamed at him as he stepped forward and Master Seke placed a ribbon with a large Zandian crystal around each of their necks.

Paal looked over and was shocked to see his mother wiping tears. Again she waved. He smiled and bowed in her direction.

Zander waited until they'd returned to their places before he spoke again. "We honor our non-Zandian comrades who joined this fight with us. You were promised a home here on Zandia, and it will be yours. We must determine how best to accomplish a co-existence, but I am confident we can. As you know, my mate is human. My young is a half-breed." Zander stretched a hand out toward Lamira, who stood to his right. She bowed her head over the babe in her arms.

"Rebuilding our planet is important, but repopulation is an even more pressing concern. As such, we will be developing a rehabitation plan to encourage both resettlement and mating.

"The Zandians require brides.

"I will work with my team this week on developing a policy and structure, but I will tell you this—those standing before me now will have first priority in obtaining homesteads. *So long as you are mated.* As we are dangerously short on females, mating in multiples seems to be the best solution.

"If you wish to receive a land and homestead grant, I suggest you form a group, find a female, and ready yourselves to petition. That's all I'll say for now." He bowed.

For the hundredth time that planet rotation, Paal pulled his female up against his body and claimed her mouth. "Good thing I already have my bride." He gently thumbed her nipple, where his piercing ring hung. "Freshly pierced." He gazed down at her, basking in the glow of her warm smile. "I'm just trying to figure out where I'll hang this on you." He palmed the heavy crystal around his neck as if weighing it.

To his delight, his female blushed.

"I'm sure we'll find some use for it." He grinned and nibbled at her lips again. "Is it time for your next *vecking?*"

She wound her arms around his neck. "I think it must be." The huskiness in her voice had him lifting her up to straddle his waist as he marched back to the palatial pod.

He had serious business to take care of—pleasuring his female.

The prince and his rehabitation plans could wait.

Please enjoy this preview of
Night of the Zandians: A Reverse Harem Romance
(Zandian Brides Book 1)

Night of the Zandians - Chapter One

Riya

The Zandians require brides.

Prince Zander—no, *King* Zander now that he's taken back his planet—stands in front of all of us, human and Zandians alike, and makes his intentions for repopulation clear.

I gaze around at the throng gathered in front of what used to be the palace. Everything seems so vast and empty under a bright sky, devoid of any cloud cover. The Zandian sun reflects off the white marble stone that makes up the rubble, nearly blinding me.

How can such a small group possibly ever rebuild this planet, dedicated as they—we— are?

The devastation in Zandia's capital is so absolute that it makes me sick to my stomach. The crumbled ruins of once-majestic buildings, now heaps of marble rubble and twisted metal, look as gruesome as any bloody wound I tended during the battle.

I shouldn't care—it's not my planet. My planet was raped and ruined a thousand years ago by the Ocretions, but Zandia's been dangled in front of us humans like Shangri-la. A place we'll be able to be free.

Supposedly.

But what Zander's saying now puts ice cold fear into me.

A shiver runs down my spine and I can't stop my gaze from flicking to the giant Zandian warrior across the plaza.

Tarren.

The one whose firm thigh I straddled when I sewed up the gash splitting the side of his face. He's standing with two other Zandians and—sweet mother Earth—they're all looking at me!

A lock of my thick black hair blows into my face on a hot, dry wind that smells of nothing except ash, and I brush it back with impatience, then wipe more dust from my strong thighs, bare beneath my—short tunic. I haven't had a chance to wash or change since the battle—I've been tending the wounded non-stop. The warrior beside Tarren lets his gaze slide to my bare legs and heat crawls up my neck. I should've found a pair of leggings before this meeting.

"If you wish to receive a land and homestead grant, I suggest you form a group, find a female, and ready yourselves to petition," King Zander declares.

My stomach knots. *Find a female.*

I'm not an idiot. I know what that means for me. For the other human females of breeding age. We've just become breeders. We're probably no better off than any breeding slave in the galaxy.

My mouth goes dry and I have to will myself not to look across the plaza at the warrior again. Will he and his friends come for me? Claim me? How will it work? Do I have to be willing, or can they just come carry me off?

King Zander has said we're no longer slaves, yet there's nowhere else we can go in the galaxy where our freedom will be recognized. In other words, we have no choice but to accept whatever the Zandians offer.

And it sounds to me like my only option is to become a Zandian bride.

I scrunch up my hands at my sides, not because I'm making fists to defend myself, but to stop my fingers from shaking.

I don't want to be claimed by one alien warrior, much less two or three. Or —stars forbid—more!

I barely hear the rest of the announcement, but when the gathering breaks up, I seek out Lily. She's a human mated to a Zandian and sister to the Queen. She might know more about what I can expect.

Already the air in the plaza crackles with sexual tension, as if the king's proclamation has every warrior ready to fight to claim a female.

There are no more Zandian females—at least none who are unmated—so the females Zander referred to are human. Former slaves, like me.

Oh hell. I tug my tunic down as if I can make it grow to cover my bare thighs.

Several Zandian warriors eye me from across the cracked plaza. I really should have changed my clothes before I came out. I suddenly realize how provocative my boots must look below bare legs.

On the training pod we females were protected by warriors like Lundric, who has a human mate. I was able to dress for pure comfort and ignore any interest my bare skin garnered. After what I've endured at the hands of the Ocretians, I preferred to keep myself apart.

I find Lily, but she's talking with her mate. I sense warriors closing in on me from all sides.

Fuck.

Like a coward, I run.

I head straight for the makeshift med bay where I've been working all night. It's a stupid place to go, but I haven't been assigned a room yet, and I don't know where else to hide.

As soon as I'm there, though, the memory of treating Tarren's wounds comes rushing back.

The way my core heated standing so close to him. The way he gripped my buttocks when I stabbed his cheek with the needle.

I lean against the metal wall of the crashed ship which became my headquarters to steady my breath.

I'm not interested in the male. I'm not interested in any male.

Of course, it may not matter what I'm interested in.

King Zander wants the planet repopulated.

As soon as possible.

The Zandians have taken back their planet.
Now they need brides.

All human females have been assigned to mates. Yes, *mates,* multiple.

I've been given to three handsome males--cousins. Huge, purple and horned, they act like they want to eat me for breakfast.

After what I've been through with previous slave masters, I don't know how I'll survive this. But I have to. It's adapt or be sent off-planet, which would mean my death, considering I'm wanted for murder.

My mates cannot find out I'm not able to reproduce. I need to keep my secret, figure out a way to survive, stay focused. But when the Zandian warriors claim me, they make me forget my past and scream with pleasure.

I can't let myself fall for them.

If they learn my secret, I'll lose more than my life.

I'll lose my heart.

Night of the Zandians: A Reverse Harem Romance
Zandian Brides, Book One
By Renee Rose and Rebel West

Get Ready...
for the next Zandian series - Zandian Brides!

The Zandians have taken back their planet.
Now they need brides.

All human females have been assigned to mates. Yes, *mates,* multiple.

I've been given to three handsome males—cousins. Huge, purple and horned, they act like they want to eat me for breakfast.

After what I've been through with previous slave masters, I don't know how I'll survive this. But I have to. It's adapt or be sent off-planet, which would mean my death, considering I'm wanted for murder.

My mates cannot find out I'm not able to reproduce. I need to keep my secret, figure out a way to survive, stay focused. But when the Zandian warriors claim me, they make me forget my past and scream with pleasure.

I can't let myself fall for them.

If they learn my secret, I'll lose more than my life.

I'll lose my heart.

Night of the Zandians: A Reverse Harem Romance
Zandian Brides, Book One
By Renee Rose and Rebel West

OTHER TITLES BY RENEE ROSE

Paranormal

Wolf Ridge High Series

Alpha Bully

Alpha Knight

Step Alpha

Alpha King

Alpha Varsity

Bad Boy Alphas Series

Alpha's Temptation

Alpha's Danger

Alpha's Prize

Alpha's Challenge

Alpha's Obsession

Alpha's Desire

Alpha's War

Alpha's Mission

Alpha's Bane

Alpha's Secret

Alpha's Prey

Alpha's Sun

Shifter Ops

Alpha's Moon

Alpha's Vow

Alpha's Revenge

Alpha's Fire

Alpha's Rescue

Alpha's Command

Werewolves of Wall Street

Big Bad Boss: Midnight

Big Bad Boss: Moon Mad

Big Bad Boss: Marked

Big Bad Boss: Mated

Two Marks Series

Untamed

Tempted

Desired

Enticed

Wolf Ranch Series

Rough

Wild

Feral

Savage

Fierce

Ruthless

Primal

Alpha Doms Series

Dominion (Full Series Collection)

The Alpha's Hunger

The Alpha's Promise

The Alpha's Punishment

The Alpha's Protection

Contemporary
Yacht Kings

Revenge

Chicago Bratva

"Prelude" in Black Light: Roulette War

The Director

The Fixer

"Owned" in Black Light: Roulette Rematch

The Enforcer

The Soldier

The Hacker

The Bookie

The Cleaner

The Player

The Gatekeeper

Vegas Underground Mafia Romance

King of Diamonds

Mafia Daddy

Jack of Spades

Ace of Hearts

Joker's Wild

His Queen of Clubs

Dead Man's Hand

Wild Card

Master Me Series

Her Royal Master

Yes, Doctor

Her Russian Master

Her Marine Master

Her Fire Master

Her Hollywood Master

Her Stepbrother Master

Made Men Series

Don't Tease Me

Don't Tempt Me

Don't Make Me

Alpha Mountain

Hero

Rebel

Warrior

Chicago Sin

Den of Sins

Rooted in Sin

Double Doms Series

Theirs to Punish

Theirs to Protect

Holiday Feel-Good

Scoring with Santa

Saved

Other Contemporary

Black Light: Valentine Roulette

Black Light: Roulette Redux

Black Light: Celebrity Roulette

Black Light: Roulette War

Black Light: Roulette Rematch

Punishing Portia (written as Darling Adams)

The Professor's Girl

Safe in his Arms

Sci-Fi

Zandian Masters Series

His Human Slave

His Human Prisoner

Training His Human

His Human Rebel

His Human Vessel

His Mate and Master

Zandian Pet

Their Zandian Mate

His Human Possession

Zandian Brides

Night of the Zandians

Bought by the Zandians

Mastered by the Zandians

Zandian Lights

Kept by the Zandian
Claimed by the Zandian
Stolen by the Zandian
Rescued by the Zandian

Other Sci-Fi
The Hand of Vengeance
Her Alien Masters

9 781637 204740